CIRQUE DU FREAK:
THE VAMPIRE'S ASSISTANT

Other titles by
DARREN SHAN

THE SAGA OF DARREN SHAN

THE DEMONATA

*Also available on CD

DARREN SHAN

CIRQUE DU FREAK:
THE VAMPIRE'S ASSISTANT

CIRQUE DU FREAK

THE VAMPIRE'S ASSISTANT

TUNNELS OF BLOOD

HarperCollins *Children's Books*

For all things freaky, check out the official
Darren Shan website at www.darrenshan.com

Cirque Du Freak, *The Vampire's Assistant* and *Tunnels of Blood* were first published
individually in Great Britain by HarperCollins *Children's Books* in 2000
First published in the three-in-one edition *Vampire Blood Trilogy* by
HarperCollins *Children's Books* in 2003
This edition published in 2009

HarperCollins *Children's Books* is a division of HarperCollins *Publishers* Ltd
77-85 Fulham Palace Road, Hammersmith, London, W6 8JB

www.harpercollins.co.uk

2

ISBN-13: 978 0 00 730650 3

Darren Shan asserts the moral right to be identified as the author of the work.

Printed and bound in Great Britain by
Clays Ltd, St Ives plc

DARREN SHAN

CIRQUE DU FREAK

THE SAGA OF DARREN SHAN
BOOK 1

This freakish show could never have gone public but for
the efforts of my hard-working laboratory assistants:

Biddy & Liam – 'The Gruesome Twosome'
'Diabolical' Domenica de Rosa
'Growling' Gillie Russell
Emma 'The Exterminator' Schlesinger
and
'Lord of the Crimson Night' – Christopher Little

Thanks are also due to my feasting companions:
the Horrible Creatures of HarperCollins. And the ghoulish
pupils of Askeaton Primary School (and others) who served as
willing guinea pigs and braved nightmares to make this book
as tight, dark and chilling as possible.

INTRODUCTION

I'VE ALWAYS been fascinated by spiders. I used to collect them when I was younger. I'd spend hours rooting through the dusty old shed at the bottom of our garden, hunting the cobwebs for lurking eight-legged predators. When I found one, I'd bring it in and let it loose in my bedroom.

It used to drive my mum mad!

Usually, the spider would slip away after no more than a day or two, never to be seen again, but sometimes they hung around longer. I had one who made a cobweb above my bed and stood sentry for almost a month. Going to sleep, I used to imagine the spider creeping down, crawling into my mouth, sliding down my throat and laying loads of eggs in my belly. The baby spiders would hatch after a while and eat me alive, from the inside out.

I loved being scared when I was little.

When I was nine, my mum and dad gave me a small tarantula. It wasn't poisonous or very big, but it was the greatest gift I'd ever received. I played with that spider almost every waking hour of the day. Gave it all sorts of treats: flies and cockroaches and tiny worms. Spoilt it rotten.

Then, one day, I did something stupid. I'd been watching

a cartoon in which one of the characters was sucked up by a vacuum cleaner. No harm came to him. He squeezed out of the bag, dusty and dirty and mad as hell. It was very funny.

So funny, I tried it myself. With the tarantula.

Needless to say, things didn't happen quite like they did in the cartoon. The spider was ripped to pieces. I cried a lot, but it was too late for tears. My pet was dead, it was my fault, and there was nothing I could do about it.

My parents nearly hollered the roof down when they found out what I'd done — the tarantula had cost quite a bit of money. They said I was an irresponsible fool, and from that day on they never again let me have a pet, not even an ordinary garden spider.

I started with that tale from the past for two reasons. One will become obvious as this book unfolds. The other reason is:

This is a true story.

I don't expect you to believe me — I wouldn't believe it myself if I hadn't lived it — but it is. Everything I describe in this book happened, just as I tell it.

The thing about real life is, when you do something stupid, it normally costs you. In books, the heroes can make as many mistakes as they like. It doesn't matter what they do, because everything comes good at the end. They'll beat the bad guys and put things right and everything ends up hunky-dory.

In real life, vacuum cleaners kill spiders. If you cross a busy road without looking, you get whacked by a car. If you fall out of a tree, you break some bones.

Real life's nasty. It's cruel. It doesn't care about heroes and happy endings and the way things should be. In real life, bad things happen. People die. Fights are lost. Evil often wins.

I just wanted to make that clear before I began.

One more thing: my name isn't really Darren Shan. Everything's true in this book, *except* for names. I've had to change them because... well, by the time you get to the end, you'll understand.

I haven't used *any* real names, not mine, my sister's, my friends or teachers. Nobody's. I'm not even going to tell you the name of my town or country. I daren't.

Anyway, that's enough of an introduction. If you're ready, let's begin. If this was a made-up story, it would begin at night, with a storm blowing and owls hooting and rattling noises under the bed. But this is a real story, so I have to begin where it really started.

It started in a toilet.

CHAPTER ONE

I WAS in the toilet at school, sitting down, humming a song. I had my trousers on. I'd come in near the end of English class, feeling sick. My teacher, Mr Dalton, is great about things like that. He's smart and knows when you're faking and when you're being serious. He took one look at me when I raised my hand and said I was ill, then nodded his head and told me to make for the toilet.

"Throw up whatever's bugging you, Darren," he said, "then get your behind back in here."

I wish every teacher was as understanding as Mr Dalton.

In the end, I didn't get sick, but still felt queasy, so I stayed on the toilet. I heard the bell ring for the end of class and everybody came rushing out on their lunch break. I wanted to join them but knew Mr Dalton would give out if he saw me in the yard so soon. He doesn't get mad if you trick him but he goes quiet and won't speak to you for ages, and that's almost worse than being shouted at.

So, there I was, humming, watching my watch, waiting. Then I heard someone calling my name.

"Darren! Hey, Darren! Have you fallen in or what?"

I grinned. It was Steve Leopard, my best friend. Steve's real surname was Leonard, but everyone called him Steve Leopard. And not just because the names sound alike. Steve used to be what my mum calls "a wild child". He raised hell wherever he went, got into fights, stole in shops. One day – he was still in a pushchair – he found a sharp stick and prodded passing women with it (no prizes for guessing where he stuck it!).

He was feared and despised everywhere he went. But not by me. I've been his best friend since Montessori, when we first met. My mum says I was drawn to his wildness, but I just thought he was a great guy to be with. He had a fierce temper, and threw scary tantrums when he lost it, but I simply ran away when that happened and came back again once he'd calmed down.

Steve's reputation had softened over the years – his mum took him to see a lot of good counsellors who taught him how to control himself – but he was still a minor legend in the schoolyard and not someone you messed with, even if you were bigger and older than him.

"Hey, Steve," I called back. "I'm in here." I hit the door so he'd know which one I was behind.

He hurried over and I opened the door. He smiled when he saw me sitting down with my trousers on. "Did you puke?" he asked.

"No," I said.

"Do you think you're gonna?"

"Maybe," I said. Then I leaned forward all of a sudden and made a sick noise. Bluurgh! But Steve Leopard knew me too well to be fooled.

"Give my boots a polish while you're down there," he said, and laughed when I pretended to spit on his shoes and rub them with a sheet of toilet paper.

"Did I miss anything in class?" I asked, sitting up.

"Nah," he said. "The usual crap."

"Did you do your history homework?" I asked.

"It doesn't have to be done until tomorrow, does it?" he asked, getting worried. Steve's always forgetting about homework.

"The day after tomorrow," I told him.

"Oh," he said, relaxing. "Even better. I thought… " He stopped and frowned. "Hold on," he said. "Today's Thursday. The day after tomorrow would be… "

"Got you!" I yelled, punching him on the shoulder.

"Ow!" he shouted. "That hurt." He rubbed his arm but I could tell he wasn't really hurt. "Are you coming out?" he asked then.

"I thought I'd stay in here and admire the view," I said, leaning back on the toilet seat.

"Quit messing," he said. "We were five-one down when I came in. We're probably six or seven down now. We need you." He was talking about football. We play a game every lunchtime. My team normally wins but we'd lost a lot of our best players. Dave Morgan broke his leg. Sam White transferred to another school when his family moved. And Danny Curtain had stopped playing football in order to spend lunch hanging out with Sheila Leigh, the girl he fancies. Idiot!

I'm our best full-forward. There are better defenders and midfielders, and Tommy Jones is the best goalkeeper in the whole school. But I'm the only one who can stand up front and score four or five times a day without fail.

"OK," I said, standing. "I'll save you. I've scored a hat trick every day this week. It would be a pity to stop now."

We passed the older guys – smoking around the sinks as usual – and hurried to my locker so I could change into my trainers. I used to have a great pair, which I won in a writing competition. But the laces snapped a few months ago and the rubber along the sides started to fall off. And then my feet grew! The pair I have now are OK but they're not the same.

We were eight-three down when I got on the pitch. It wasn't a real pitch, just a long stretch of yard with painted goal posts at either end. Whoever painted them was a right idiot. He put the crossbar too high at one end and too low at the other!

"Never fear, Hotshot Shan is here!" I shouted as I ran onto the pitch. A lot of players laughed or groaned, but I could see my team mates picking up and our opponents growing worried.

I made a great start and scored two goals inside a minute. It looked like we might come back to draw or win. But time ran out. If I'd arrived earlier we'd have been OK but the bell rang just as I was hitting my stride, so we lost nine-seven.

As we were leaving the pitch, Alan Morris ran into the yard, panting and red-faced. They're my three best friends: Steve Leopard, Tommy Jones and Alan Morris. We must be the oddest four people in the whole world, because only one of us – Steve – has a nickname.

"Look what I found!" Alan yelled, waving a soggy piece of paper around under our noses.

"What is it?" Tommy asked, trying to grab it.

"It's— " Alan began, but stopped when Mr Dalton shouted at us.

"You four! Inside!" he roared.

"We're coming, Mr Dalton!" Steve roared back. Steve is Mr Dalton's favourite and gets away with stuff that the rest of us couldn't do. Like when he uses swear words sometimes in his stories. If I put in some of the words Steve has, I'd have been kicked out long ago.

But Mr Dalton has a soft spot for Steve, because he's special. Sometimes he's brilliant in class and gets everything right, while other times he can't even spell his own name. Mr Dalton says he's a bit of an *idiot savant*, which mean he's a stupid genius!

Anyway, even though he's Mr Dalton's pet, not even Steve can get away with turning up late for class. So whatever Alan had, it would have to wait. We trudged back to class, sweaty and tired after the game, and began our next lesson.

Little did I know that Alan's mysterious piece of paper was to change my life forever. For the worse!

CHAPTER TWO

WE HAD Mr Dalton again after lunch, for history. We were studying World War II. I wasn't too keen on it, but Steve thought it was great. He loved anything to do with killing and war. He often said he wanted to be a mercenary soldier – one who fights for money – when he grew up. And he meant it!

We had maths after history, and – incredibly – Mr Dalton for a third time! Our usual maths teacher was off sick, so others had been filling in for him as best they could all day.

Steve was in seventh heaven. His favourite teacher, three classes in a row! It was the first time we'd had Mr Dalton for maths, so Steve started showing off, telling him where we were in the book, explaining some of the trickier problems as though speaking to a child. Mr Dalton didn't mind. He was used to Steve and knew exactly how to handle him.

Normally Mr Dalton runs a tight ship – his classes are fun but we always come out of them having learned something – but he wasn't very good at maths. He tried hard but we could tell he was in over his head, and while he was busy trying to come to grips with things – his head buried in the maths book, Steve by his side making "helpful" suggestions – the rest of us began to fidget and talk softly to each other and pass notes around.

I sent a note to Alan, asking to see the mysterious piece of paper he'd brought in. He refused at first to pass it around, but I kept sending notes and finally he gave in. Tommy sits just two seats over from him, so he got it first. He opened it up and began studying it. His face lit up while he was reading and his jaw slowly dropped. When he passed it on to me — having read it three times — I soon saw why.

It was a flyer, an advertising pamphlet for some sort of travelling circus. There was a picture of a wolf's head at the top. The wolf had its mouth open and saliva was dripping from its teeth. At the bottom were pictures of a spider and a snake, and they looked vicious too.

Just beneath the wolf, in big red capital letters, were the words:

CIRQUE DU FREAK

Underneath that, in smaller writing:

FOR ONE WEEK ONLY – CIRQUE DU FREAK!!
SEE:
SIVE AND SEERSA – THE TWISTING TWINS!
THE SNAKE-BOY! THE WOLF MAN! GERTHA TEETH!
LARTEN CREPSLEY AND HIS PERFORMING SPIDER – MADAM OCTA!
ALEXANDER RIBS! THE BEARDED LADY! HANS HANDS!
RHAMUS TWOBELLIES – WORLD'S FATTEST MAN!

Beneath all that was an address where you could buy tickets and find out where the show was playing. And right at the bottom, just above the pictures of the snake and spider:

NOT FOR THE FAINT-HEARTED!
CERTAIN RESERVATIONS APPLY!

"Cirque Du Freak?" I muttered softly to myself. Cirque was French for circus... Circus of Freaks! Was this a *freak show*?! It looked like it.

I began reading the flyer again, immersed in the drawings and descriptions of the performers. In fact, I was so immersed, I forgot about Mr Dalton. I only remembered him when I realised the room was silent. I looked up, and saw Steve standing alone at the head of the class. He stuck out his tongue at me and grinned. Feeling the hairs on the back of my neck prickle, I stared over my shoulder and there was Mr Dalton, standing behind me, reading the flyer, lips tight.

"What is this?" he snapped, snatching the paper from my hands.

"It's an advert, sir," I answered.

"Where'd you get it?" he asked. He looked really angry. I'd never seen him this worked up. "Where'd you get it?" he asked again.

I licked my lips nervously. I didn't know how to answer. I wasn't going to drop Alan in the soup — and I knew he wouldn't own up by himself: even Alan's best friends know he's not the bravest in the world — but my mind was stuck in low gear and I couldn't think of a reasonable lie. Luckily, Steve stepped in.

"Sir, it's mine," he said.

"Yours?" Mr Dalton blinked slowly.

"I found it near the bus stop, sir," Steve said. "Some old guy threw it away. I thought it looked interesting, so I picked it up. I was going to ask you about it later, at the end of class."

"Oh." Mr Dalton tried not to look flattered but I could tell he was. "That's different. Nothing wrong with an inquisitive mind. Sit down, Steve." Steve sat. Mr Dalton stuck a bit of Blu-Tack on the flyer and pinned it to the blackboard.

"Long ago," he said, tapping the flyer, "there used to be real freak shows. Greedy con men crammed malformed people in cages and— "

"Sir, what's *malformed* mean?" somebody asked.

"Someone who doesn't look ordinary," Mr Dalton said. "A person with three arms or two noses; somebody with no legs; somebody very short or very tall. The con men put these poor people – who were no different to you or me, except in looks – on display and called them freaks. They charged the public to stare at them, and invited them to laugh and tease. They treated the so-called "freaks" like animals. Paid them little, beat them, dressed them in rags, never allowed them to wash."

"That's cruel, sir," Delaina Price – a girl near the front – said.

"Yes," he agreed. "Freak shows were cruel, monstrous creations. That's why I got angry when I saw this." He tore down the flyer. "They were banned years ago, but every so often you'll hear a rumour that they're still going strong."

"Do you think the Cirque Du Freak is a real freak show?" I asked.

Mr Dalton studied the flyer again, then shook his head. "I doubt it," he said. "Probably just a cruel hoax. Still," he added, "if it *was* real, I hope nobody here would dream of going."

"Oh, no, sir," we all said quickly.

"Because freak shows were terrible," he said. "They pretended to be like proper circuses but they were cesspits of evil. Anybody who went to one would be just as bad as the people running it."

"You'd have to be really twisted to want to go to one of those, sir," Steve agreed. And then he looked at me, winked, and mouthed the words: "We're going!"

CHAPTER THREE

STEVE PERSUADED Mr Dalton to let him keep the flyer. He said he wanted it for his bedroom wall. Mr Dalton wasn't going to give it to him but then changed his mind. He cut off the address at the bottom before handing it over.

After school, the four of us — me, Steve, Alan Morris and Tommy Jones — gathered in the yard and studied the glossy flyer.

"It's got to be a fake," I said.

"Why?" Alan asked.

"They don't allow freak shows any more," I told him. "Wolf-men and snake-boys were outlawed years ago. Mr Dalton said so."

"It's not a fake!" Alan insisted.

"Where'd you get it?" Tommy asked.

"I stole it," Alan said softly. "It belongs to my big brother." Alan's big brother was Tony Morris, who used to be the school's biggest bully until he got thrown out. He's huge and mean and ugly.

"You *stole* from *Tony*?!?" I gasped. "Have you got a death wish?"

"He won't know it was me," Alan said. "He had it in a pair of trousers that Mum threw in the washing machine. I stuck a blank piece of paper in when I took this out. He'll think the ink got washed off."

"Smart," Steve nodded.

"Where did Tony get it?" I asked.

"There was a guy passing them out in an alley," Alan said. "One of the circus performers, a Mr Crepsley."

"The one with the spider?" Tommy asked.

"Yeah," Alan answered, "only he didn't have the spider with him. It was night and Tony was on his way back from the pub." Tony's not old enough to get served in a pub, but hangs around with older guys who buy drinks for him. "Mr Crepsley handed the paper to Tony and told him they're a travelling freak show who put on secret performances in towns and cities across the world. He said you had to have a flyer to buy tickets and they only give them to people they trust. You're not supposed to tell anyone else about the show. I only found out because Tony was in high spirits – the way he gets when he drinks – and couldn't keep his mouth shut."

"How much are the tickets?" Steve asked.

"Fifteen pounds each," Alan said.

"Fifteen pounds!" we all shouted.

"Nobody's going to pay fifteen pounds to see a bunch of freaks!" Steve snorted.

"I would," I said.

"Me too," Tommy agreed.

"And me," Alan added.

"Sure," Steve said, "but *we* don't have fifteen pounds to throw away. So it's academic, isn't it?"

"What does *academic* mean?" Alan asked.

"It means we can't afford the tickets, so it doesn't matter if we would buy them or not," Steve explained. "It's easy to say you *would* buy something if you know you *can't*."

"How much *do* we have?" Alan asked.

"Tuppence ha'penny," I laughed. It was something my dad often said.

"I'd love to go," Tommy said sadly. "It sounds great." He studied the picture again.

"Mr Dalton didn't think too much of it," Alan said.

"That's what I mean," Tommy said. "If Sir doesn't like it, it must be super. Anything that adults hate is normally brilliant."

"Are we sure we don't have enough?" I asked. "Maybe they have discounts for children."

"I don't think children are allowed in," Alan said, but he told me how much he had anyway. "Five pounds seventy."

"I've got twelve pounds exactly," Steve said.

"I have six pounds eighty-five pence," Tommy said.

"And I have eight pounds twenty-five," I told them. "That's more than thirty pounds in all," I said, adding it up in my head. "We get our pocket money tomorrow. If we pool our— "

"But the tickets are nearly sold out," Alan interrupted. "The first show was yesterday. It finishes Tuesday. If we go, it'll have to be tomorrow night or Saturday, because our parents won't let us out any other night. The guy who gave Tony the flyer said the tickets for both those nights were almost gone. We'd have to buy them tonight."

"Well, so much for that," I said, putting on a brave face.

"Maybe not," Steve said. "My mum keeps a wad of money in a jar at home. I could borrow some and put it back when we get our pocket money."

"You mean steal?" I asked.

"I mean *borrow*," he snapped. "It's only stealing if you don't put it back. What do you say?"

"How would we get the tickets?" Tommy asked. "It's a school night. We wouldn't be let out."

"I can sneak out," Steve said. "I'll buy them."

"But Mr Dalton snipped off the address," I reminded him. "How will you know where to go?"

"I memorised it," he grinned. "Now, are we gonna stand here all night making up excuses, or are we gonna go for it?"

We looked at each other, then — one by one — nodded silently.

"Right," Steve said. "We hurry home, grab our money, and meet back here. Tell your parents you forgot a book or something. We'll lump the money together and I'll add the rest from the pot at home."

"What if you can't steal — I mean, borrow the money?" I asked.

He shrugged. "Then the deal's off. But we won't know unless we try. Now: hurry!"

With that, he sprinted away. Moments later, making up our minds, Tommy, Alan and me ran too.

CHAPTER FOUR

THE FREAK show was all I could think about that night. I tried forgetting it but couldn't, not even when I was watching my favourite TV shows. It sounded so weird: a snake-boy, a Wolf Man, a performing spider. I was especially excited by the spider.

Mum and Dad didn't notice anything was up, but Annie did. Annie is my younger sister. She can be a bit annoying but most of the time she's cool. She doesn't run to Mum telling tales if I misbehave, and she knows how to keep a secret.

"What's wrong with you?" she asked after dinner. We were alone in the kitchen, washing up.

"Nothing's wrong," I said.

"Yes there is," she said. "You've been behaving funny all night."

I knew she'd keep asking until she got the truth, so I told her about the freak show.

"It sounds great," she agreed, "but there's no way you'd get in."

"Why not?" I asked.

"I bet they don't let children in. It sounds like a grown-up sort of show."

"They probably wouldn't let a brat like *you* in," I said nastily, "but me and the others would be OK." That upset her, so

I apologised. "I'm sorry," I said. "I didn't mean that. I'm just annoyed because you're probably right. Annie, I'd give anything to go!"

"I've got a make-up kit I could lend you," she said. "You can draw on wrinkles and stuff. It'd make you look older."

I smiled and gave her a big hug, which is something I don't do very often. "Thanks, sis," I said, "but it's OK. If we get in, we get in. If we don't, we don't."

We didn't say much after that. We finished drying and hurried into the TV room. Dad got back home a few minutes later. He works on building sites all over the place, so he's often late. He's grumpy sometimes but was in a good mood that night and swung Annie round in a circle.

"Anything exciting happen today?" he asked, after he'd said hello to Mum and given her a kiss.

"I scored another hat trick at lunch," I told him.

"Really?" he said. "That's great. Well done."

We turned the TV down while Dad was eating. He likes peace and quiet when he eats, and often asks us questions or tells us about his day at work.

Later, Mum went to her room to work on her stamp albums. She's a serious stamp collector. I used to collect too, when I was younger and more easily amused.

I popped up to see if she had any new stamps with exotic animals or spiders on them. She hadn't. While I was there, I sounded her out about freak shows.

"Mum," I said, "have you ever been to a freak show?"

"A what?" she asked, concentrating on the stamps.

"A freak show," I repeated. "With bearded ladies and wolf-men and snake-boys."

She looked up at me and blinked. "A snake-boy?" she asked. "What on Earth is a snake-boy?"

"It's a…" I stopped when I realised I didn't know. "Well, that doesn't matter," I said. "Have you ever been to one?"

She shook her head. "No. They're illegal."

"If they weren't," I said, "and one came to town, would you go?"

"No," she said, shivering. "Those sorts of things frighten me. Besides, I don't think it would be fair on the people in the show."

"What do you mean?" I asked.

"How would *you* like it," she said, "if you were stuck in a cage for people to look at?"

"I'm not a freak!" I said huffily.

"I know," she laughed, and kissed the top of my head. "You're my little angel."

"Mum, don't!" I grumbled, wiping my forehead with my hand.

"Silly," she smiled. "But imagine you had two heads or four arms, and somebody stuck you on show for people to make fun of. You wouldn't like that, would you?"

"No," I said, shuffling my feet.

"Anyway, what's all this about a freak show?" she asked. "Have you been staying up late, watching horror films?"

"No," I said.

"Because you know your Dad doesn't like you watching— "

"I wasn't staying up late, OK?" I shouted. It's really annoying when parents don't listen.

"OK, Mister Grumpy," she said. "No need to shout. If you don't like my company, go downstairs and help your father weed the garden."

I didn't want to go, but Mum was upset that I'd shouted at her, so I left and went down to the kitchen. Dad was coming in from the back and spotted me.

"So this is where you've been hiding," he chuckled. "Too busy to help the old man tonight?"

"I was on my way," I told him.

"Too late," he said, taking off his wellies. "I'm finished."

I watched him putting on his slippers. He has huge feet. He takes size 12 shoes! When I was younger, he used to stand me on his feet and walk me around. It was like being on two long skateboards.

"What are you doing now?" I asked.

"Writing," he said. My dad has pen pals all over the world, in America, Australia, Russia and China. He says he likes to keep in touch with his global neighbours, though I think it's just an excuse to go into his study for a nap!

Annie was playing with dolls and stuff. I asked if she wanted to come to my room for a game of bed-tennis using a sock for a ball, and shoes for rackets, but she was too busy arranging her dolls for a pretend picnic.

I went to my room and dragged down my comics. I have loads of cool comics, *Superman*, *Batman*, *Spiderman* and *Spawn*. *Spawn*'s my favourite. He's a superhero who used to be a demon in Hell. Some of the *Spawn* comics are quite scary but that's why I love them.

I spent the rest of the night reading comics and putting them in order. I used to swap with Tommy, who has a huge collection, but he kept spilling drinks on the covers and crumbs between the pages, so I stopped.

Most nights I go to bed by ten, but Mum and Dad forgot about me, and I stayed up until nearly half-past ten. Then Dad saw the light in my room and came up. He pretended to be cross but he wasn't really. Dad doesn't mind too much if I stay up late. Mum's the one who nags me about that.

"Bed," he said, "or I'll never be able to wake you in the morning."

"Just a minute, Dad," I told him, "while I put my comics away and brush my teeth."

"OK," he said, "but make it quick."

I stuck the comics into their box and stuffed it back up on the shelf over my bed.

I put on my pyjamas and went to brush my teeth. I took my time, brushed slowly, and it was almost eleven when I got into bed. I lay back, smiling. I felt very tired and knew I'd fall asleep in a couple of seconds. The last thing I thought about was the Cirque Du Freak. I wondered what a snake-boy looked like, and how long the bearded lady's beard was, and what Hans Hands and Gertha Teeth did. Most of all, I dreamed about the spider.

CHAPTER FIVE

THE NEXT morning, Tommy, Alan and me waited outside the gates for Steve, but there was no sign of him by the time the bell rang for class, so we had to go in.

"I bet he's dossing," Tommy said. "He couldn't get the tickets and now he doesn't want to face us."

"Steve's not like that," I said.

"I hope he brings the flyer back," Alan said. "Even if we can't go, I'd like to have the flyer. I'd stick it up over my bed and— "

"You couldn't stick it up, stupid!" Tommy laughed.

"Why not?" Alan asked.

"Because Tony would see it," I told him.

"Oh yeah," Alan said glumly.

I was miserable in class. We had geography first, and every time Mrs Quinn asked me a question, I got it wrong. Normally geography's my best subject, because I know so much about it from when I used to collect stamps.

"Had a late night, Darren?" she asked when I got my fifth question wrong.

"No, Mrs Quinn," I lied.

"I think you did," she smiled. "There are more bags under

your eyes than in the local supermarket!" Everybody laughed at that – Mrs Quinn didn't crack jokes very often – and I did too, even though I was the butt of the joke.

The morning dragged, the way it does when you feel let down or disappointed. I spent the time imagining the freak show. I made-believe I was one of the freaks, and the owner of the circus was a nasty guy who whipped everybody, even when they got stuff right. All the freaks hated him, but he was so big and mean, nobody said anything. Until one day, he whipped me once too often, and I turned into a wolf and bit his head off! Everybody cheered and I was made the new owner.

It was a pretty good daydream.

Then, a few minutes before break, the door opened and guess who walked in? Steve! His mother was behind him and she said something to Mrs Quinn, who nodded and smiled. Then Mrs Leonard left and Steve strolled over to his seat and sat down.

"Where were you?" I asked in a furious whisper.

"At the dentist's," he said. "I forgot to tell you I was going."

"What about— "

"That's enough, Darren," Mrs Quinn said. I shut up instantly.

At break, Tommy, Alan and me almost smothered Steve. We were shouting and pulling at him at the same time.

"Did you get the tickets?" I asked.

"Were you really at the dentist's?" Tommy wanted to know.

"Where's my flyer?" Alan asked.

"Patience, boys, patience," Steve said, pushing us away and laughing. "All good things to those who wait."

"Come on, Steve, don't mess us around," I told him. "Did you get them or not?"

"Yes and no," he said.

"What does *that* mean?" Tommy snorted.

"It means I have some good news, some bad news, and some

crazy news," he said. "Which do you want to hear first?"

"*Crazy* news?" I asked, puzzled.

Steve pulled us off to one side of the yard, checked to make sure no one was about, then began speaking in a whisper.

"I got the money," he said, "and sneaked out at seven o'clock, when Mum was on the phone. I hurried across town to the ticket booth, but do you know who was there when I arrived?"

"Who?" we asked.

"Mr Dalton!" he   said. "He was there with a couple of policemen. They were dragging a small guy out of the booth – it was only a small shed, really – when suddenly there was this huge bang and a great cloud of smoke covered them all. When it cleared, the small guy had disappeared."

"What did Mr Dalton and the police do?" Alan asked.

"Examined the shed, looked around a bit, then left."

"They didn't see you?" Tommy asked.

"No," Steve said. "I was well hidden."

"So you didn't get the tickets," I said sadly.

"I didn't say that," he contradicted me.

"You *got* them?" I gasped.

"I turned to leave," he said, "and found the small guy behind me. He was tiny, and dressed in a long cloak which covered him from head to toe. He spotted the flyer in my hand, took it, and held out the tickets. I handed over the money and— "

"You got them!" we roared delightedly.

"Yes," he beamed. Then his face fell. "But there was a catch. I told you there was bad news, remember?"

"What is it?" I asked, thinking he'd lost them.

"He only sold me two," Steve said. "I had the money for four, but he wouldn't take it. He didn't say anything, just tapped the bit on the flyer about "certain reservations", then handed me a card which said the Cirque Du Freak only sold two tickets per flyer.

I offered him extra money — I had nearly seventy pounds in total — but he wouldn't accept it."

"He only sold you *two* tickets?" Tommy asked, dismayed.

"But that means … " Alan began.

"… only two of us can go," Steve finished. He looked around at us grimly. "Two of us will have to stay at home."

CHAPTER SIX

IT WAS Friday evening, the end of the school week, the start of the weekend, and everybody was laughing and running home as quick as they could, delighted to be free. *Except* a certain miserable foursome who hung around the schoolyard, looking like the end of the world had arrived. Their names? Steve Leonard, Tommy Jones, Alan Morris and me, Darren Shan.

"It's not fair," Alan moaned. "Who ever heard of a circus only letting you buy two tickets? It's stupid!"

We all agreed with him, but there was nothing we could do about it apart from stand around, stubbing the ground with our feet, looking sour.

Finally, Alan asked the question which was on everybody's mind.

"So, who gets the tickets?"

We looked at each other and shook our heads uncertainly.

"Well, Steve *has* to get one," I said. "He put in more money than the rest of us, and he went to buy them, so he has to get one, agreed?"

"Agreed," Tommy said.

"Agreed," Alan said. I think he would have argued about it,

except he knew he wouldn't win.

Steve smiled and took one of the tickets. "Who goes with me?" he asked.

"I brought in the flyer," Alan said quickly.

"Nuts to that!" I told him. "Steve should get to choose."

"Not on your life!" Tommy laughed. "You're his best friend. If we let him pick, he'll pick you. I say we fight for it. I have boxing gloves at home."

"No way!" Alan squeaked. He's small and never gets into fights.

"I don't want to fight either," I said. I'm no coward but I knew I wouldn't stand a chance against Tommy. His dad teaches him how to box properly and they have their own punching bag. He would have floored me in the first round.

"Let's pick straws for it," I said, but Tommy didn't want to. He has terrible luck and never wins anything like that.

We argued about it a bit more, until Steve came up with an idea. "I know what to do," he said, opening his school bag. He tore the two middle sheets of paper out of an exercise book and, using his ruler, carefully cut them into small pieces, each one roughly the same size as the ticket. Then he got his empty lunch box and dumped the paper inside.

"Here's how it works," he said, holding up the second ticket. "I put this in, put the top on and shake it about, OK?" We nodded. "You stand side by side and I'll throw the bits of paper over your heads. Whoever gets the ticket wins. Me and the winner will give the other two their money back when we can afford it. Is that fair enough, or does somebody have a better idea?"

"Sounds good to me," I said.

"I don't know," Alan grumbled. "I'm the youngest. I'm not able to jump as high as— "

"Quit yapping," Tommy said. "*I'm* the smallest, and I don't mind. Besides, the ticket might come out on the bottom of the pile, float down low and be in just the right place for the shortest person."

"All right," Alan said. "But no shoving."

"Agreed," I said. "No rough stuff."

"Agreed," Tommy nodded.

Steve put the top on the box and gave it a good long shake. "Get ready," he told us.

We stood back from Steve and lined up in a row. Tommy and Alan were side by side, but I kept out of the way so I'd have room to swing both arms.

"OK," Steve said. "I'll throw everything in the air on the count of three. All set?" We nodded. "One," Steve said, and I saw Alan wiping sweat from around his eyes. "Two," Steve said, and Tommy's fingers twitched. "Three!" Steve yelled, jerked off the lid and tossed the paper high up into the air.

A breeze came along and blew the bits of paper straight at us. Tommy and Alan started yelling and grabbing wildly. It was impossible to see the ticket in among the scraps of paper.

I was about to start grabbing, when all of a sudden I got an urge to do something strange. It sounded crazy, but I've always believed in following an urge or a hunch.

So what I did was, I shut my eyes, stuck out my hands like a blind man, and waited for something magical to happen.

As I'm sure you know, usually when you try something you've seen in a movie, it doesn't work. Like if you try doing a wheelie with your bike, or making your skateboard jump up in the air. But every once in a while, when you least expect it, something clicks.

For a second I felt paper blowing by my hands. I was going to grab at them but something told me it wasn't time. Then, a second later, a voice inside me yelled, "NOW!"

I shut my hands really fast.

The wind died down and the pieces of paper drifted to the

ground. I opened my eyes and saw Alan and Tommy down on their knees, searching for the ticket.

"It's not here!" Tommy said.

"I can't find it anywhere!" Alan shouted.

They stopped searching and looked up at me. I hadn't moved. I was standing still, my hands shut tight.

"What's in your hands, Darren?" Steve asked softly.

I stared at him, unable to answer. It was like I was in a dream, where I couldn't move or speak.

"He doesn't have it," Tommy said. "He can't have. He had his eyes shut."

"Maybe so," Steve said, "but there's *something* in those fists of his."

"Open them," Alan said, giving me a shove. "Let's see what you're hiding."

I looked at Alan, then Tommy, then Steve. And then, very slowly, I opened my right-hand fist.

There was nothing there.

My heart and stomach dropped. Alan smiled and Tommy started looking down at the ground again, trying to find the missing ticket.

"What about the other hand?" Steve asked.

I gazed down at my left-hand fist. I'd almost forgotten about that one! Slowly, even slower than first time, I opened it.

There was a piece of green paper smack-dab in the middle of my hand, but it was lying face down, and since there was nothing on its back, I had to turn it over, just to be sure. And there it was, in red and blue letters, the magical name:

CIRQUE DU FREAK.

I had it. The ticket was mine. I was going to the freak show with Steve. "YEEEEEEESSSSSSSSSSSSSSS!!!!" I screamed, and punched the air with my fist. I'd won!

CHAPTER SEVEN

THE TICKETS were for the Saturday show, which was just as well, since it gave me a chance to talk to my parents and ask if I could stay over at Steve's Saturday night.

I didn't tell them about the freak show, because I knew they would say no if they knew about it. I felt bad about not telling the whole truth, but at the same time, I hadn't really told a lie: all I'd done was keep my mouth shut.

Saturday couldn't go quickly enough for me. I tried keeping busy, because that's how you make time pass without noticing, but I kept thinking about the Cirque Du Freak and wishing it was time to go. I was quite grumpy, which was odd for me on a Saturday, and Mum was glad to see the back of me when it was time to go to Steve's.

Annie knew I was going to the freak show and asked me to bring her back something, a photo if possible, but I told her cameras weren't allowed (it said so on the ticket) and I didn't have enough money for a T-shirt. I told her I'd buy her a badge if they had them, or a poster, but she'd have to keep it hidden and not tell Mum and Dad where she'd got it if they found it.

Dad dropped me off at Steve's at six o'clock. He asked what

time I wanted to be collected in the morning. I told him midday if that was OK.

"Don't watch horror movies, OK?" he said before he left. "I don't want you coming home with nightmares."

"Oh, Dad!" I groaned. "Everyone in my class watches horror movies."

"Listen," he said, "I don't mind an old Vincent Price film, or one of the less scary Dracula movies, but none of these nasty new ones, OK?"

"OK," I promised.

"Good man," he said, and drove off.

I hurried up to the house and rang the bell four times, which was my secret signal to Steve. He must have been standing right inside, because he opened the door straightaway and dragged me in.

"About time," he growled, then pointed to the stairs. "See that hill?" he asked, speaking like a soldier in a war film.

"Yes, sir," I said, snapping my heels together.

"We have to take it by dawn."

"Are we using rifles or machine guns, sir?" I asked.

"Are you mad?" he barked. "We'd never be able to carry a machine gun through all that mud." He nodded at the carpet.

"Rifles it is, sir," I agreed.

"And if we're taken," he warned me, "save the last bullet for yourself."

We started up the stairs like a couple of soldiers, firing imaginary guns at imaginary foes. It was childish, but great fun. Steve 'lost' a leg on the way and I had to help him to the top. "You may have taken my leg," he shouted from the landing, "and you may take my life, but you'll never take my country!"

It was a stirring speech. At least, it stirred Mrs Leonard, who came through from the downstairs living room to see what the racket was. She smiled when she saw me and asked if I wanted anything to eat or drink. I didn't. Steve said he'd like some caviar and champagne, but it wasn't funny the way he said it, and I didn't laugh.

Steve doesn't get on with his mum. He lives alone with her — his dad left when Steve was very young — and they're always arguing and shouting. I don't know why. I've never asked him. There are certain things you don't discuss with your friends if you're boys. Girls can talk about stuff like that, but if you're a boy you have to talk about computers, football, war and so on. Parents aren't cool.

"How will we sneak out tonight?" I asked in a whisper as Steve's mum went back into the living room.

"It's OK," Steve said. "She's going out." He often called her *she* instead of *Mum*. "She'll think we're in bed when she gets back."

"What if she checks?"

Steve laughed nastily. "Enter my room without being asked? She wouldn't dare."

I didn't like Steve when he talked like that, but I said nothing in case he went into one of his moods. I didn't want to do anything that might spoil the show.

Steve dragged out some of his horror comics and we read them aloud. Steve has great comics, which are only meant for adults. My mum and dad would hit the roof if they knew about them!

Steve also has loads of old magazines and books about monsters and vampires and werewolves and ghosts.

"Does a stake have to be made out of wood?" I asked when I'd finished reading a Dracula comic.

"No," he said. "It can be metal or ivory, even plastic, as long as it's hard enough to go right through the heart."

"And that will kill a vampire?" I asked.

"Every time," he said.

I frowned. "But you told me you have to cut off their heads and stuff them with garlic and toss them in a river."

"Some books say you have to," he agreed. "But that's to make sure you kill the vampire's spirit as well as its body, so it can't come back as a ghost."

"Can a vampire come back as a ghost?" I asked, eyes wide.

"Probably not," Steve said. "But if you had the time, and wanted to make sure, cutting off the head and getting rid of it would be worth doing. You don't want to take any chances with vampires, do you?"

"No," I said, shivering. "What about werewolves? Do you need silver bullets to kill them?"

"I don't think so," Steve said. "I think normal bullets can do the job. You might have to use lots of them, but they should work."

Steve knows everything there is to know about horror facts. He's read every sort of horror book there is. He says every story has at least some bit of truth in it, even if most are made up.

"Do you think the Wolf Man at the Cirque Du Freak is a werewolf?" I asked.

Steve shook his head. "From what I've read," he said, "the wolf-men in freak shows are normally just very hairy guys. Some of them are more like animals than people, and eat live chickens and stuff, but they're not werewolves. A werewolf would be no good in a show, because it can only turn into a wolf when there's a full moon. Every other night, it would be a normal guy."

"Oh," I said. "What about the snake-boy? Do you— "

"Hey," he laughed, "save the questions for later. The shows long ago were terrible. The owners used to starve the freaks and keep them locked up in cages and treat them like dirt. But I don't know what this one will be like. They might not even be real freaks: they might only be people in costumes."

The freak show was being held at a place near the other side of town. We had to leave not long after nine o'clock, to make sure we got there in time. We could have got a cab, except we'd used most of our pocket money to replace the cash Steve took from his mum. Besides, it was more fun walking. It was spookier!

We told ghost stories as we walked. Steve did most of the talking, because he knows way more than me. He was on top form. Sometimes he forgets the ends of stories, or gets names mixed up, but not tonight. It was better than being with Stephen King!

It was a long walk, longer than we thought, and we almost didn't make it on time. We had to run the last half-kilometre. We were panting like dogs when we got there.

The venue was an old theatre which used to show movies. I'd passed it once or twice in the past. Steve told me once that it was shut down because a boy fell off the balcony and got killed. He said it was haunted. I asked my dad about it, and he said it was a load of lies. It's hard sometimes to know whether you should believe the stories your dad tells you or the ones your best friend tells you.

There was no name outside the door, and no cars parked nearby, and no queue. We stopped out front and bent over until we got our breath back. Then we stood and looked at the building. It was tall and dark and covered in jagged grey stones. Lots of the windows were broken, and the door looked like a giant's open mouth.

"Are you sure this is the place?" I asked, trying not to sound scared.

"This is what it says on the tickets," Steve said and checked again, just to be sure. "Yep, this is it."

"Maybe the police found out and the freaks had to move on," I said. "Maybe there isn't any show tonight."

"Maybe," Steve said.

I looked at him and licked my lips nervously. "What do you think we should do?" I asked.

He stared back at me and hesitated before replying. "I think we should go in," he finally said. "We've come this far. It'd be silly to turn back now, without knowing for sure."

"I agree," I said, nodding. Then I gazed up at the scary building and gulped. It looked like the sort of place you saw in a horror movie, where lots of people go in but don't come out. "Are you scared?" I asked Steve.

"No," he said, but I could hear his teeth chattering and knew he was lying. "Are *you*?" he asked.

"Course not," I said. We looked at each other and grinned. We knew we were both terrified, but at least we were together. It's not so bad being scared if you're not alone.

"Shall we enter?" Steve asked, trying to sound cheerful.

"Might as well," I said.

We took a deep breath, crossed our fingers, then started up the steps (there were nine stone steps leading up to the door, each one cracked and covered with moss) and went in.

CHAPTER EIGHT

WE FOUND ourselves standing in a long, dark, cold corridor. I had my jacket on, but shivered all the same. It was freezing!

"Why is it so cold?" I asked Steve. "It was warm outside."

"Old houses are like that," he told me.

We started to walk. There was a light down by the other end, so the further in we got, the brighter it became. I was glad of that. I don't think I could have made it otherwise: it would have been too scary!

The walls were scratched and scribbled-on, and bits of the ceiling were flaky. It was a creepy place. It would have been bad enough in the middle of the day, but this was ten o'clock, only two hours away from midnight!

"There's a door here," Steve said and stopped. He pushed it ajar and it creaked loudly. I almost turned and ran. It sounded like the lid of a coffin being tugged open!

Steve showed no fear and stuck his head in. He said nothing for a few seconds, while his eyes got used to the dark, then pulled back. "It's the stairs up to the balcony," he said.

"Where the kid fell from?" I asked.

"Yes."

"Do you think we should go up?" I asked.

He shook his head. "I don't think so. It's dark up there, no sign of any sort of light. We'll try it if we can't find another way in, but I think— "

"Can I help you boys?" somebody said behind us, and we nearly jumped out of our skins!

We turned around quickly and the tallest man in the world was standing there, glaring down on us as if we were a couple of rats. He was so tall, his head almost touched the ceiling. He had huge bony hands and eyes that were so dark, they looked like two black coals stuck in the middle of his face.

"Isn't it rather late for two little boys like yourselves to be out and about?" he asked. His voice was as deep and croaky as a frog's, but his lips hardly seemed to move. He would have made a great ventriloquist.

"We… " Steve began, but had to stop and lick his lips before he could continue. "We're here to see the Cirque Du Freak," he said.

"*Are* you?" The man nodded slowly. "Do you have tickets?"

"Yes," Steve said, and showed his.

"Very good," the man muttered. Then he turned to me and said: "How about you, Darren? Do you have a ticket?"

"Yes," I said, reaching into my pocket. Then I stopped dead in my tracks. *He knew my name!* I glanced at Steve and he was shaking in his boots.

The tall man smiled. He had black teeth and some were missing, and his tongue was a dirty shade of yellow. "My name is Mr Tall," he said. "I own the Cirque Du Freak."

"How did you know my friend's name?" Steve asked bravely.

Mr Tall laughed and bent down, so he was eyeball-to-eyeball with Steve. "I know lots of things," he said softly. "I know your names. I know where you live. I know you don't like your mummy or your daddy." He turned to face me and I took a step back. His breath stank to the high heavens. "I know you didn't tell your parents you were coming here. And I know how you won your ticket."

"*How?*" I asked. My teeth were shaking so much, I wasn't sure if he heard me or not. If he did, he decided not to answer, because next he stood up and turned away from us.

"We must hurry," he said, beginning to walk. I thought he would take giant steps, but he didn't, he took short ones. "The show is about to begin. Everyone else is present and seated. You are late, boys. You're lucky we didn't start without you."

He turned a corner at the end of the corridor. He was only two or three steps in front of us, but when we turned the corner, he was sitting behind a long table covered with a black cloth which reached down to the floor. He was wearing a tall red hat now, and a pair of gloves.

"Tickets, please," he said, reached out, took them, opened his mouth and put the tickets in, then chewed them to pieces and swallowed!

"Very well," he said. "You may go in now. We normally don't welcome children, but I can see you are two fine, courageous young men. We will make an exception."

There were two blue curtains in front of us, drawn across the end of the hall. Steve and me looked at each other and gulped.

"Do we walk straight on?" Steve asked.

"Of course," Mr Tall said.

"Isn't there a lady with a torch?" I asked.

He laughed. "If you want someone to hold your hand," he said, "you should have brought a baby-sitter!"

That made me mad and I forgot for a moment how afraid I was. "All right," I snapped, stepping forward, surprising Steve. "If that's the way it is... " I walked forward quickly and pushed past the curtains.

I don't know what those curtains were made of, but they felt like spider webs. I stopped once past. I was in a short corridor and another pair of curtains were draped across the walls a few metres in front. There was a sound behind and then Steve was by my side. We could hear noises on the other side of the curtains.

"Do you think it's safe?" I asked.

"I think it's safer to go forward than backwards," he answered. "I don't think Mr Tall would like it if we turned back."

"How do you think he knew all that stuff about us?" I asked.

"He must be able to read minds," Steve replied.

"Oh," I said, and thought about that for a few seconds. "He nearly scared the life out of me," I admitted.

"Me too," Steve said.

Then we stepped forward.

It was a huge room. The chairs had been ripped out of the theatre long ago, but deck chairs had been set up in their place. We looked for spare seats. The entire theatre was packed, but we were the only children there. I could feel people watching us and whispering.

The only spaces were in the fourth row from the front. We had to step over lots of legs to get there and people were grumbling. When we sat down, we realised they were good seats, because we were right in the middle and nobody tall was in front of us. We had a perfect view of the stage and could see everything.

"Do you think they sell popcorn?" I asked.

"At a freak show?" Steve snorted. "Get real! They might sell snake eggs and lizard eyes, but I'll bet anything you like they don't sell popcorn!"

The people in the theatre were a mixed bunch. Some were dressed stylishly, others in tracksuits. Some were as old as the hills, others just a few years older than Steve and me. Some chatted confidently to their companions and behaved as though at a football match, others sat quietly in their chairs and gazed around nervously.

What everyone shared was a look of excitement. I could see it in their eyes, the same light that was shining in Steve's and mine. We all somehow knew that we were in for something special, the like of which we'd never seen before.

Then a load of trumpets blew and the whole place went quiet. The trumpets blew for ages and ages, getting louder and louder, and every light went out until the theatre was pitch black. I began to get scared again, but it was too late to leave.

All of a sudden, the trumpets stopped and there was silence. My ears were ringing and for a few seconds I felt dizzy. Then I recovered and sat up straight in my seat.

Somewhere high up in the theatre, someone switched on a green light and the stage lit up. It looked eerie! For about a minute nothing else happened. Then two men came on, pulling a cage. It was on wheels and covered with what looked like a huge bearskin rug. When they got to the middle of the stage they stopped, dropped the ropes and ran back into the wings.

For a few seconds more — silence. Then the trumpets blew again, three short blasts. The rug came flying off the cage and the first freak was revealed.

That was when the screaming began.

CHAPTER NINE

THERE WAS no need for the screaming. The freak was quite shocking, but he was chained up inside the cage. I think the people who screamed did it for fun, the way people scream on a roller coaster, not because they were actually afraid.

It was the Wolf Man. He was very ugly, hair all over his body. He only wore a piece of cloth around his middle, like Tarzan, so we could see his hairy legs and belly and back and arms. He had a long bushy beard which covered most of his face. His eyes were yellow and his teeth were red.

He shook the bars of the cage and roared. It was pretty frightening. Lots more people screamed when he roared. I nearly screamed myself, except I didn't want to look like a baby.

The Wolf Man went on shaking the bars and jumping about, before calming down. When he was sitting on his backside, the way dogs do, Mr Tall walked on and spoke.

"Ladies and gentlemen," he said, and even though his voice was low and croaky, everybody could hear what he was saying, "welcome to the Cirque Du Freak, home of the world's most remarkable human beings.

"We are an ancient circus," he went on. "We have toured for

five hundred years, bringing the grotesque to generation after generation. Our line-up has changed many times, but never our aim, which is to astound and terrify you! We present acts both frightening and bizarre, acts you can find nowhere else in the world.

"Those who are easily scared should leave now," he warned. "I'm sure there are people who came tonight thinking this was a joke. Maybe they thought our freaks would be people in masks, or harmless misfits. *This is not so!* Every act you see tonight is real. Each performer is unique. And none are harmless."

That was the end of his speech and he walked offstage. Two pretty women in shiny suits came on next and unlocked the door of the Wolf Man's cage. A few people looked scared but nobody left.

The Wolf Man was yapping and howling when he first came out of the cage, until one of the ladies hypnotised him with her fingers. The other lady spoke to the crowd.

"You must be very quiet," she said in a foreign accent. "The Wolf Man will not be able to hurt you as long as we control him but a loud sound could wake him up, and then he would be deadly!"

When they were ready, they stepped down from the stage and walked the hypnotised Wolf Man through the theatre. His hair was a dirty grey colour and he walked with a stoop, fingers hanging down around his knees.

The ladies stayed by his side and warned people to be quiet. They let you stroke him if you wanted, but you had to do it gently. Steve rubbed him when he went by but I was afraid he might wake up and bite me, so I didn't.

"What did it feel like?" I asked, as quietly as I could.

"It was spiky," Steve replied, "like a hedgehog." He lifted his fingers to his nose and sniffed. "It smells strange too, like burning rubber."

The Wolf Man and ladies were about halfway down the rows of seats when there was a big BANG! I don't know what made the noise, but suddenly the Wolf Man began roaring and he shoved the ladies away from him.

People screamed and those nearest him leapt from their seats and ran. One woman wasn't quick enough, and the Wolf Man leapt on her and dragged her to the ground. She was screaming fit to burst, but nobody tried to help her. He rolled her over on to her back and bared his teeth. She stuck a hand up to push him away, but he got his teeth on it and *bit it off*!

A couple of people fainted when they saw that and loads more began yelling and running. Then, out of nowhere, Mr Tall appeared behind the Wolf Man and wrapped his arms around him. The Wolf Man struggled for a few seconds, but Mr Tall whispered something in his ear and he relaxed. While Mr Tall led him back to the stage, the women in the suits calmed down the crowd and told them to return to their seats.

While the crowd hesitated, the woman with the bitten-off hand went on screaming. Blood was pumping out of the end of her wrist, covering the ground and other people. Steve and me were staring at her, our mouths wide open, wondering if she was going to die.

Mr Tall returned from the stage, picked up the severed hand and gave a loud whistle. Two people in blue robes with hoods over their heads ran forward. They were short, not much bigger than me or Steve, but with thick arms and legs, and lots of muscles. Mr Tall sat the woman up and whispered something in her ear. She stopped screaming and sat still.

Mr Tall took hold of the wrist, then reached into his pocket and took out a small brown leather pouch. He opened it with his free hand and sprinkled a sparkly pink powder on to the bleeding wrist. Then he stuck the hand against it and nodded to the two people in the blue suits. They produced a pair of needles and loads of orange string. And then, to the amazement of everybody in the theatre, they started to stitch the hand back on to the wrist!

The people in blue robes stitched for five or six minutes. The woman didn't feel any pain, even though their needles were going in and out of her flesh, all the way around the wrist. When finished, they put their needles and unused thread away and returned to wherever they'd come from. Their hoods never slipped from their faces, so I couldn't tell if they were men or women. When they'd gone, Mr Tall let go of the woman's hand and stepped back.

"Move your fingers," he said. The woman stared at him blankly. "Move your fingers!" he said again, and this time she gave them a wiggle.

They moved!

Everybody gasped. The woman stared at the fingers as though she didn't believe they were real. She gave them another wiggle. Then she stood and lifted the hand above her head. She shook it as hard as she could, and it was good as new! You could see the stitches but there was no more blood and the fingers seemed to be working fine.

"You will be OK," Mr Tall told her. "The stitches will fall out after a couple of days. It will be fine after that."

"Maybe that's not good enough!" someone shouted, and a big red-faced man stepped forward. "I'm her husband," he said, "and I say we should go to a doctor and then the police! You can't let a wild animal like that out into a crowd! What if he'd bitten her head off?"

"Then she would be dead," Mr Tall said calmly.

"Listen, buster," the husband began, but Mr Tall interrupted.

"Tell me, sir," Mr Tall said, "where were *you* when the Wolf Man was attacking?"

"*Me?*" the man asked.

"Yes," Mr Tall said. "You are her husband. You were sitting beside her when the beast escaped. Why did you not leap to her rescue?"

"Well, I… There was no time… I couldn't… I wasn't… "

No matter what he said, the husband couldn't win, because there was only one true answer: he had been running away, looking after himself.

"Listen to me," Mr Tall said. "I gave fair warning. I said this show could be dangerous. This is not a nice, safe circus where nothing goes wrong. Mistakes can and do happen, and sometimes people end up a lot worse off than your wife. That's why this show is banned. That's why we must play in old theatres in the middle of the night. Most of the time, things go smoothly and nobody gets hurt. But we cannot guarantee your safety."

Mr Tall turned around in a circle and seemed to look everybody in the eye while turning. "We cannot guarantee *anybody's* safety," he roared. "Another accident like this is unlikely, but it *could* happen. Once again I say, if you are afraid, leave. Leave now, before it is too late!"

A few people did leave. But most stayed to see the rest of the show, even the woman who nearly lost her hand.

"Do you want to go?" I asked Steve, half-hoping he'd say yes. I was excited but scared as well.

"Are you crazy?" he said. "This is great! *You* don't want to go, do you?"

"No way," I lied, and slapped on a shaky little smile.

If only I hadn't been so scared of looking like a coward! I could have left and everything would have been fine. But no, I had to act like a big man and sit it out to the end. If you only knew how many times I've wished since then that I'd fled with all the speed in my body and never looked back…

CHAPTER TEN

As soon as Mr Tall had left the stage and we'd settled back into our seats, the second freak, Alexander Ribs, came on. He was more of a comedy act than a scary one, which was just what we needed to calm us down after the terrifying start. I happened to look over my shoulder while he was on, and noticed two of the blue-hooded people down on their knees, cleaning blood from the floor.

Alexander Ribs was the skinniest man I'd ever seen. He looked like a skeleton! There seemed to be no flesh on him. He would have been frightening, except he had a wide friendly smile.

Funny music played and he danced around the stage. He was dressed in ballet clothes and looked so ridiculous that soon everyone was laughing. After a while, he stopped dancing and began stretching. He said he was a contortionist (somebody with bones like rubber, who can bend every which-way).

First, he tilted his head back so far, it looked like it had been cut off. He turned round so we could see his upside-down face, then went on leaning backwards until his head was touching the floor! Then he put his hands round the backs of his legs and pulled his head through until it was sticking up in front of him.

It looked like it was growing out of his stomach!

He got a huge round of clapping for that, after which he straightened up and began twisting his body around like a curly-wurly straw! He kept twisting and twisting, five times around, until his bones began to creak from the strain. He stood like that for a minute, then began to unwind really, really fast.

Next, he got two drumsticks with furry ends. He took the first drumstick and hit one of his bony ribs with it. He opened his mouth and a musical note sprang out! It sounded like the noise pianos make. Then he closed his mouth and struck a rib on the other side of his body. This time it was a louder, higher note.

After a few more practice goes, he kept his mouth open and began playing songs! He played "London Bridge Is Falling Down", some songs by The Beatles, and the theme tunes from a few well-known TV shows.

The skinny man left the stage to shouts for more. But none of the freaks ever came back to do an encore.

After Alexander Ribs came Rhamus Twobellies, and he was as fat as Alexander was thin. He was eNORmous! The floorboards creaked as he walked out onto the stage.

He walked close to the edge and kept pretending he was about to topple forward. I could see people in the front rows getting worried, and some jumped back out of the way when he got close. I don't blame them: he would have squashed them flat as a pancake if he fell!

He stopped in the middle of the stage. "Hello," he said. He had a nice voice, low and squeaky. "My name is Rhamus Twobellies, and I really have two bellies! I was born with them, the same way certain animals are. The doctors were stunned and said I was a freak. That's why I joined this show and am here tonight."

The ladies who had hypnotised the Wolf Man came out with two trolleys full of food: cakes, chips, hamburgers, packets of sweets and heads of cabbage. There was stuff there that I hadn't even seen before, never mind tasted!

"Yum-yum," Rhamus said. He pointed to a huge clock being lowered by ropes from above. It stopped about three metres above his head. "How long do you think it will take me to eat all this?" he asked, pointing to the food. "There will be a prize for the person who guesses closest."

"An hour!" somebody yelled.

"Forty-five minutes!" somebody else roared.

"Two hours, ten minutes and thirty-three seconds," another person shouted. Soon everybody was calling out. I said an hour and three minutes. Steve said twenty-nine minutes. The lowest guess was seventeen minutes.

When we were finished guessing, the clock started to tick and Rhamus started to eat. He ate like the wind. His arms moved so fast, you could hardly see them. His mouth didn't seem to close at all. He shovelled food in, swallowed and moved on.

Everybody was amazed. I felt sick as I watched. Some people actually *were* sick!

Finally, Rhamus scoffed the last bun and the clock above his head stopped ticking.

Four minutes and fifty-six seconds! He'd eaten all that food in less than five minutes! I could hardly believe it. It didn't seem possible, even for a man with two bellies.

"That was nice," Rhamus said, "but I could have done with more dessert."

While we clapped and laughed, the ladies in shiny suits rolled the trolleys away and brought on a new one, packed with glass statues and forks and spoons and bits of metal junk.

"Before I begin," Rhamus said, "I must warn you not to try this at home! I can eat things which would choke and kill normal people. Do not try to copy me! If you do, you may die."

He began eating. He started with a couple of nuts and bolts, which he sucked down without blinking. After a few handfuls he gave his big round belly a shake and we could hear the noise of the metal inside.

His belly heaved and he spat the nuts and bolts back out! If there had only been one or two, I might have thought he was keeping them under his tongue or at the sides of his cheeks, but not even Rhamus Twobellies' mouth was big enough to hold that load!

Next, he ate the glass statues. He crunched the glass up into small pieces before swallowing it with a drink of water. Then he ate the spoons and forks. He twisted them up into circles with his hands, popped them into his mouth and let them slide down. He said his teeth weren't strong enough to tear through metal.

After that, he swallowed a long metal chain, then paused to catch his breath. His belly began rumbling and shaking. I didn't know what was going on, until he gave a heave and I saw the top of the chain come out of his mouth.

As the chain came out, I saw that the spoons and forks were wrapped around it! He had managed to poke the chain through the hoops inside his belly. It was unbelievable.

When Rhamus left the stage, I thought nobody could top such an act.

I was wrong!

CHAPTER ELEVEN

A COUPLE of people in the blue-hooded robes came around after Rhamus Twobellies, selling gifts. There was some really cool stuff, like chocolate models of the nuts and bolts that Rhamus ate, and rubber dolls of Alexander Ribs which you could bend and stretch. And there were clippings of the Wolf Man's hair. I bought a bit of that: it was tough and wiry, sharp as a knife.

"There will be more novelties later," Mr Tall announced from the stage, "so don't spend all your money right away."

"How much is the glass statue?" Steve asked. It was the same sort that Rhamus Twobellies had eaten. The person in the blue hood didn't say anything, but stuck out a sign with the price on. "I can't read," Steve said. "Will you tell me how much it costs?"

I stared at Steve and wondered why he was lying. The person in the hood still didn't speak. This time he (or she) shook his head quickly and moved on before Steve could ask anything else.

"What was that about?" I asked.

Steve shrugged. "I wanted to hear it speak," he said, "to see if it was human or not."

"Of course it's human," I said. "What else could it be?"

"I don't know," he said. "That's why I was asking. Don't you think it's strange that they keep their faces covered all the time?"

"Maybe they're shy," I said.

"Maybe," he said, but I could tell he didn't believe that.

When the people selling the gifts were finished, the next freak came on. It was the bearded lady, and at first I thought it was meant to be a joke, because she didn't have a beard!

Mr Tall stood behind her and said, "Ladies and gentlemen, this is a very special act. Truska here is new to our family. She is one of the most incredible performers I have ever seen, with a truly unique talent."

Mr Tall walked off. Truska was very beautiful, dressed in flowing red robes which had many slashes and gaps. Lots of the men in the theatre began to cough and shift around in their seats.

Truska stepped closer to the edge of the stage, so we could see her better, then said something that sounded like a seal barking. She put her hands on her face, one at either side, and stroked the skin gently. Then she held her nose shut with two fingers and tickled her chin with her other hand.

An extraordinary thing happened: she began to grow a beard! Hairs crept out, first on her chin, then her upper lip, then the sides of her face, finally all over. It was long and blonde and straight.

It grew about ten or eleven centimetres, then stopped. She took her fingers away from her nose and stepped down into the crowd, where she walked around and let people pull on the beard and stroke it.

The beard continued growing as she walked, until finally it reached down to her feet! When she arrived at the rear of the theatre, she turned and walked back to the stage. Even though there was no breeze in here, her hair blew about wildly, tickling people's faces as she passed.

When she was back on the stage, Mr Tall asked if anybody had a pair of scissors. Lots of women did. Mr Tall invited a few up.

"The Cirque Du Freak will give one solid bar of gold to anyone who can slice off Truska's beard," he said, and held up a small yellow ingot to show he wasn't joking.

That got a lot of people excited and for ten minutes nearly everybody in the theatre tried cutting off her beard. But they couldn't! Nothing could cut through the bearded lady's hair, not even a pair of garden shears which Mr Tall handed out. The funny thing was, it still felt soft, just like ordinary hair!

When everyone had admitted defeat, Mr Tall emptied the stage and Truska stood in the middle again. She stroked her cheeks as before and held her nose, but this time the beard grew back in! It took about two minutes for the hairs to disappear back inside, and then she looked exactly as she had when she first came out. She left to huge applause and the next act came on almost directly after.

His name was Hans Hands. He began by telling us about his father, who'd been born without legs. Hans' father learned to get around on his hands just as well as other people could on their feet, and had taught his children his secrets.

Hans then sat down, pulled up his legs and wrapped his feet around his neck. He stood on his hands, walked up and down the stage, then hopped off and challenged four men – picked at random – to a race. They could race on their feet; he'd race on his hands. He promised a bar of gold to anyone who could beat him.

They used the aisles of the theatre as a race track, and despite his disadvantage, Hans beat the four men easily. He claimed he could sprint a hundred metres in eight seconds on his hands, and nobody in the theatre doubted him. Afterwards he performed some impressive gymnastic feats, proving that a person could manage just as well without legs as with them. His act wasn't especially exciting but it was enjoyable.

There was a short pause after Hans had left, then Mr Tall came on. "Ladies and gentlemen," he said, "our next act is another unique and perplexing one. It can also be quite dangerous, so I ask that you make no noise and do not clap until you are told it is safe."

The whole place went quiet. After what had happened with the Wolf Man earlier, nobody needed telling twice!

When it was quiet enough, Mr Tall walked off the stage. He shouted out the name of the next freak as he went, but it was a soft shout: "Mr Crepsley and Madam Octa!"

The lights went down low and a creepy-looking man walked onto the stage. He was tall and thin, with very white skin and only a small crop of orange hair on the top of his head. He had a large scar running down his left cheek. It reached to his lips and made it look like his mouth was stretching up the side of his face.

He was dressed in dark-red clothes and carried a small wooden cage, which he put on a table. When he was set, he turned and faced us. He bowed and smiled. He looked even scarier when he smiled, like a crazy clown in a horror movie I once saw! Then he started to explain about the act.

I missed the first part of his speech because I wasn't looking at the stage. I was watching Steve. You see, when Mr Crepsley walked out, there had been total silence, except for one person who had gasped loudly.

Steve.

I stared curiously at my friend. He was almost as white as Mr Crepsley and was shaking all over. He'd even dropped the rubber model of Alexander Ribs that he'd bought.

His eyes were fixed on Mr Crepsley, as though glued to him, and as I watched him watch the freak, the thought which crossed my mind was: "He looks like he's seen a ghost!"

CHAPTER TWELVE

"IT IS not true that all tarantulas are poisonous," Mr Crepsley said. He had a deep voice. I managed to tear my eyes away from Steve and trained them on the stage. "Most are as harmless as the spiders you find anywhere in the world. And those which *are* poisonous normally only have enough poison in them to kill very small creatures.

"But some are deadly!" he went on. "Some can kill a man with one bite. They are rare, and only found in extremely remote areas, but they do exist.

"I have one such spider," he said and opened the door of the cage. For a few seconds nothing happened, but then the largest spider I had ever seen crawled out. It was green and purple and red, with long hairy legs and a big fat body. I wasn't afraid of spiders, but this one looked terrifying.

The spider walked forward slowly. Then its legs bent and it lowered its body, as though waiting for a fly.

"Madam Octa has been with me for several years," Mr Crepsley said. "She lives far longer than ordinary spiders. The monk who sold her to me said some of her kind live to be twenty or thirty years old. She is an incredible creature, both poisonous and intelligent."

While he was speaking, one of the blue-hooded people led a goat onto the stage. It was making a frightened bleating noise and kept trying to run. The hooded person tied it to the table and left.

The spider began moving when it saw and heard the goat. It crept to the edge of the table, where it stopped, as if awaiting an order. Mr Crepsley produced a shiny tin whistle – he called it a flute – from his trouser pocket and blew a few short notes. Madam Octa immediately leaped through the air and landed on the goat's neck.

The goat gave a leap when the spider landed, and began bleating loudly. Madam Octa took no notice, hung on and moved a few centimetres closer to the head. When she was ready, she bared her fangs and sunk them deep into the goat's neck!

The goat froze and its eyes went wide. It stopped bleating and, a few seconds later, toppled over. I thought it was dead, but then realised it was still breathing.

"This flute is how I control Madam Octa," Mr Crepsley said, and I looked away from the fallen goat. He waved the flute slowly above his head. "Though we have been together such a long time, she is not a pet, and would surely kill me if I ever lost it.

"The goat is paralysed," he said. "I have trained Madam Octa not to kill outright with her first bite. The goat would die in the end, if we left it – there is no cure for Madam Octa's bite – but we shall finish it quickly." He blew on the flute and Madam Octa moved up the goat's neck until she was standing on its ear. She bared her fangs again and bit. The goat shivered, then went totally still.

It was dead.

Madam Octa dropped from the goat and crawled towards the front of the stage. The people in the front rows became very alarmed and some jumped to their feet. But they froze at a short command from Mr Crepsley.

"Do not move!" he hissed. "Remember your earlier warning: a sudden noise could mean death!"

Madam Octa stopped at the edge of the stage, then stood on her two back legs, the same as a dog! Mr Crepsley blew softly on his flute and she began walking backwards, still on two feet. When she reached the nearest leg of the table, she turned and climbed up.

"You will be safe now," Mr Crepsley said, and the people in the front rows sat down again, as slowly and quietly as they could. "But please," he added, "do not make any loud noises, because if you do, she might come after *me*."

I don't know if Mr Crepsley was really scared, or if it was part of the act, but he looked frightened. He wiped the sleeve of his right arm over his forehead, then placed the flute back in his mouth and whistled a strange little tune.

Madam Octa cocked her head, then appeared to nod. She crawled across the table until she was in front of Mr Crepsley. He lowered his right hand, and she crept up his arm. The thought of those long hairy legs creeping along his flesh made me sweat all over. And I *liked* spiders! People who were afraid of them must have been nervously chewing the insides of their cheeks to pieces.

When she got to the top of his arm, she scuttled along his shoulder, up his neck, over his ear, and didn't stop until she reached the top of his head, where she lowered her body. She looked like a funny sort of a hat.

After a while, Mr Crepsley began playing the flute again. Madam Octa slid down the other side of his face, along the scar, and walked around until she was standing upside-down on his chin. Then she spun a string of web and dropped down on it.

She was hanging about ten centimetres below his chin now, and slowly began rocking from side to side. Soon she was swinging about level with his ears. Her legs were tucked in, and from where I was sitting she looked like a ball of wool.

Then, as she made an upward swing, Mr Crepsley threw his head back and she went flying straight up into the air. The thread snapped and she tumbled around and around. I watched her go up, then come down. I thought she'd land on the floor or the table, but she didn't. Instead, she landed in Mr Crepsley's mouth!

I nearly got sick when I thought of Madam Octa sliding down his throat and into his belly. I was sure she'd bite him and kill him. But the spider was a lot smarter than I knew. As she was falling, she'd stuck her legs out and they had caught on his lips.

He brought his head forward, so we could see his face. His mouth was wide open and Madam Octa was hanging between his lips. Her body throbbed in and out of his mouth and she looked like a balloon which he was blowing up and letting the air out of.

I wondered where the flute was and how he was going to control the spider now. Then Mr Tall appeared with another flute. He couldn't play as well as Mr Crepsley, but he was good enough to make Madam Octa take notice. She listened, then moved from one side of Mr Crepsley's mouth to the other.

I didn't know what she was doing at first, so I craned my neck to see. When I saw the bits of white on Mr Crepsley's lips I understood: she was spinning a web!

When she was finished, she lowered herself from his chin, like she had before. There was a large web spun across Mr Crepsley's mouth. He began chewing and licking the web! He ate the whole of it, then rubbed his belly (being careful not to hit Madam Octa) and said, "Delicious. Nothing tastier than fresh spider webs. They are a treat where I come from."

He made Madam Octa push a ball across the table, then got her to balance on top of it. He set up small pieces of gym gear, tiny weights and ropes and rings, and put her through her paces.

She was able to do all the things a human could, like lift weights above her head and climb ropes and pull herself up on the rings.

Then he brought out a tiny dinner set. There were mini plates and knives and forks and teeny-weeny glasses. The plates were filled with dead flies and other small insects. I don't know what was in the glasses.

Madam Octa ate that dinner as neatly as you please. She was able to pick up the knives and forks, four at a time, and feed herself. There was even a fake saltcellar which she sprinkled over one of the dishes!

It was round about the time she was drinking from the glass that I decided Madam Octa was the world's most amazing pet. I would have given everything I owned for her. I knew it could never be – Mum and Dad wouldn't let me keep her even if I could buy her – but that didn't stop me from wishing.

When the act was over, Mr Crepsley put the spider back in her cage and bowed low while everybody clapped. I heard a lot of people saying it wasn't fair to have killed the poor goat, but it had been thrilling.

I turned to Steve to tell him how great I thought the spider was, but he was watching Mr Crepsley. He didn't look scared any more, but he didn't look normal either.

"Steve, what's wrong?" I asked.

He didn't answer.

"Steve?"

"Ssshhh!" he snapped, and wouldn't say another word until Mr Crepsley had left. He watched the odd-looking man walk back to the wings. Then he turned to me and gasped: "This is amazing!"

"The spider?" I asked. "It *was* great. How do you think—"

"I'm not talking about the spider!" he snapped. "Who cares about a silly old arachnid? I'm talking about Mr... Crepsley."

He paused before saying the man's name, as though he'd been about to call him something different.

"Mr Crepsley?" I asked, confused. "What was so great about him? All he did was play the flute."

"You don't understand," Steve said angrily. "You don't know who he really is."

"And *you* do?" I asked.

"Yes," he said, "as a matter of fact I do." He rubbed his chin and started looking worried again. "I just hope he doesn't know I know. If he does, we might never make it out of here alive… "

CHAPTER THIRTEEN

THERE WAS another break after Mr Crepsley and Madam Octa's act. I tried getting Steve to tell me more about who the man was, but his lips were sealed. All he said was: "I have to think about this." Then he closed his eyes, lowered his head and thought hard.

They were selling more cool stuff during the break: beards like the bearded lady's, models of Hans Hands and, best of all, rubber spiders which looked like Madam Octa. I bought two, one for me and one for Annie. They weren't as good as the real thing but they'd have to do.

They were also selling candy webs. I bought six of those, using up the last of my money, and ate two while waiting for the next freak to come out. They tasted like candy floss. I stuck the second one over my lips and licked at it, the same way Mr Crepsley had.

The lights went down and everybody settled back into their seats. Gertha Teeth was next up. She was a big woman with thick legs, thick arms, a thick neck and a thick head.

"Ladies and gentlemen, I am Gertha Teeth!" she said. She sounded strict. "I have the strongest teeth in the world! When I was a baby, my father put his fingers in my mouth, playing with me, and I bit two of them off!"

A few people laughed, but she stopped them with a furious look. "I am not a comedian!" she snapped. "If you laugh at me again, I will come down and bite your nose off!" That sounded quite funny, but nobody dared chuckle.

She spoke very loudly. Every sentence was a shout and ended in an exclamation mark (!).

"Dentists all over the world have been astounded by my teeth!" she said. "I have been examined in every major dental centre, but nobody has been able to work out why they are so tough! I have been offered huge amounts of money to become a guinea pig, but I like travelling and so I have refused!"

She picked up four steel bars, each about thirty centimetres long, but different widths. She asked for volunteers and four men went up on stage. She gave each of them a bar and said to try bending them. They did their best, but weren't able. When they had failed, she took the thinnest bar, put it in her mouth, and bit clean through it!

She handed the two halves back to one of the men. He stared at them in shock, then put one end in his own mouth and bit on it, to check that it was real steel. His howls when he almost cracked his teeth proved that it was.

Gertha did the same to the second and third bars, each of which was thicker than the first. When it came to the fourth, the thickest of the lot, she chewed it to pieces like a chocolate bar.

Next, two of the blue-hooded assistants brought out a large radiator and she bit holes in it! Then they gave her a bike and she gnashed it up into a little ball, tyres and all! I don't think there was anything in the world Gertha Teeth couldn't chew her way through if she set her mind to it.

She called more volunteers up on stage. She gave one a sledgehammer and a large chisel, one a hammer and smaller chisel, and the other an electric saw. She lay flat on her back and put the large chisel in her mouth. She nodded at the first volunteer to swing the sledgehammer at the chisel.

The man raised the sledgehammer high above his head and brought it down. I thought he was going to smash her face open and so did lots of others, judging by the gasps and people covering their hands with their eyes.

But Gertha was no fool. She swung out of the way and the sledgehammer slammed into the floor. She sat up and spat the chisel out of her mouth. "Hah!" she snorted. "How crazy do you think I am?"

One of the blue-hoods came out and took the sledgehammer from the man. "I only called you up to show the sledgehammer is real!" she told him. "Now," she said to those of us in the audience, "watch!"

She lay back again and stuck the chisel in her mouth. The blue-hood waited a moment, then raised the sledgehammer high and swung it down, faster and harder than the man had. It struck the top of the chisel and there was a fierce noise.

Gertha sat up. I expected to see teeth falling out of her mouth, but when she opened it and removed the chisel, there wasn't as much as a crack to be seen! She laughed and said: "Hah! You thought I had bitten off more than I could chew!"

She let the second volunteer go to work, the one with the smaller hammer and chisel. She warned him to be careful of her gums, then let him position the chisel on her teeth and whack away at them. He nearly hammered his arm off, but he wasn't able to harm them.

The third volunteer tried sawing them off with the electric saw. He ran the saw from one side of her mouth to the other, and sparks were flying everywhere, but when he put it down and the dust cleared, Gertha's teeth were as white, gleaming and solid as ever.

The Twisting twins, Sive and Seersa, came on after her. They were identical twins and they were contortionists like Alexander Ribs. Their act involved twisting their bodies around each other so they looked like one person with two fronts instead of a back, or two upper bodies and no legs. They were skilful and it was pretty interesting, but dull compared to the rest of the performers.

When Sive and Seersa were finished, Mr Tall came out and thanked us for coming. I thought the freaks would come out again and line up in a row, but they didn't. Instead, Mr Tall said we could buy more stuff at the back of the hall on our way out. He asked us to mention the show to our friends. Then he thanked us again for coming and said that the show was over.

I was a bit disappointed that it had ended so weakly, but it was late and I suppose the freaks were tired. I got to my feet, picked up the stuff I'd bought, and turned to say something to Steve.

He was looking behind me, up at the balcony, his eyes wide. I turned to see what he was looking at, and as I did, people behind us began to scream. When I looked up, I saw why.

There was a huge snake up on the balcony, one of the longest I had ever seen, and it was sliding down one of the poles towards the people at the bottom!

CHAPTER FOURTEEN

THE SNAKE'S tongue flicked in and out of its mouth and it seemed mighty hungry. It wasn't very colourful – dark green, with a few flecks of brighter colours here and there – but it looked deadly.

The people beneath the balcony ran back towards their seats. They were screaming and dropping stuff as they ran. A few people fainted and some fell and were crushed. Steve and me were lucky to be near the front: we were the smallest people in the theatre and would have been trampled to dust if we'd been caught in the rush.

The snake was about to slither onto the floor when a strong light fixed itself to the snake's face. The reptile froze and stared into the light without blinking. People stopped running and the panic died down. Those who had fallen pulled themselves back to their feet, and fortunately nobody appeared to be badly hurt.

There was a sound behind us. I turned to look back at the stage. A boy was up there. He was about fourteen or fifteen, very thin, with long yellowy-green hair. His eyes were oddly shaped, narrow like the snake's. He was dressed in a long white robe.

The boy made a hissing noise and raised his arms above his

head. The robe fell away and everybody who was watching him let out a loud gasp of surprise. His body was covered in scales!

From head to toe he sparkled, green and gold and yellow and blue. He was wearing a pair of shorts but nothing else. He turned around so we could see his back, and that was the same as the front, except a few shades darker.

When he faced us again, he lay down on his belly and slid off the stage, just like a snake. It was then that I remembered the snake-boy on the flyer and put two and two together.

He stood when he reached the floor and walked towards the back of the theatre. I saw, as he passed, that he had strange hands and feet: his fingers and toes were joined to each other by thin sheets of skin. He looked a bit like that monster I saw in an old horror film, the one who lived in the black lagoon.

He stopped a few metres away from the pillar and crouched down. The light which had been blinding the snake snapped off and it began to move again, sliding down the last stretch of pole. The boy made another hissing noise and the snake paused. I recalled reading somewhere once that snakes can't hear, but can feel sounds.

The snake-boy shuffled a short bit to his left, then his right. The snake's head followed him but didn't lunge. The boy crept closer to the snake, until he was within its range. I expected it to strike and kill him, and I wanted to scream at him to run.

But the snake-boy knew what he was doing. When he was close enough he reached out and tickled the snake beneath its chin with his odd webbed fingers. Then he bent forward and kissed it on the nose!

The snake wrapped itself around the boy's neck. It coiled about him a couple of times, leaving its tail draped over his shoulder and down his back like a scarf.

The boy stroked the snake and smiled. I thought he was going to walk through the crowd, letting the rest of us rub it, but he didn't. Instead he walked over to the side of the theatre, away from the path to the door. He unwrapped the snake and put it down on the floor, then tickled it under its chin once more.

The mouth opened wide this time, and I saw its fangs. The snake-boy lay down on his back a short bit away from the snake, then began wriggling towards it!

"No," I said softly to myself. "Surely he's not going to…"

But yes, he stuck his head in the snake's wide-open mouth!

The snake-boy stayed inside the mouth for a few more seconds, then slowly eased out. He wrapped the snake about him once more, then rolled around and around until the snake covered him completely, except for his face. He managed to hop to his feet and grin. He looked like a rolled-up carpet!

"And that, ladies and gentlemen," said Mr Tall from the stage behind us, "really is the end." He smiled and leapt from the stage, vanishing in midair in a puff of smoke. When it cleared, I saw him by the back of the theatre, holding the exit curtains open.

The pretty ladies and mysterious blue-hooded people were standing to his left and right, their arms loaded with trays full of goodies. I was sorry I hadn't saved some of my money.

Steve said nothing while we were waiting. I could tell from the serious look on his face that he was still thinking, and from past experience I knew there was no point trying to talk to him. When Steve went into one of his moods, nothing could jolt him out of it.

When the rows behind us had cleared out, we made our way to the back of the theatre. I brought the stuff I'd bought with me. I also lugged Steve's gifts, because he was so wrapped up in his thoughts, he would have dropped them or left them behind.

Mr Tall was standing at the back, holding the curtains open, smiling at everyone. The smile widened when we approached.

"Well, boys," he said, "did you enjoy the show?"

"It was fabulous!" I said.

"You weren't scared?" he asked.

"A little," I admitted, "but no more than anybody else."

He laughed. "You're a tough pair," he said.

There were people behind us, so we hurried on, not wanting to hold them up. Steve looked about when we entered the short corridor between the two sets of curtains, then leaned over and whispered in my ear: "Go back by yourself."

"What?" I asked, stopping. The people who had been behind us were chatting with Mr Tall, so there was no rush.

"You heard," he said.

"Why should I?" I asked.

"Because I'm not coming," he said. "I'm staying. I don't know how things will turn out, but I have to stay. I'll follow you home later, after I've… " His voice trailed off and he pulled me forward.

We pushed past the second set of curtains and entered the corridor with the table, the one covered by the long black cloth. The people ahead of us had their backs to us. Steve looked over his shoulder, to make sure nobody could see, then dived underneath the table and hid behind the cloth!

"Steve!" I hissed, worried he was going to get us into trouble.

"Go on!" he hissed back.

"But you can't— " I began.

"Do what I say!" he snapped. "Go, quick, before we're caught."

I didn't like it but what else could I do? Steve sounded like he'd go ape if I didn't obey him. I'd seen Steve get into fierce rages before and he wasn't someone you wanted to mess with when he was angry.

I started walking, turned the corner and began down the long corridor leading to the front door. I was walking slowly, thinking, and the people in front got further ahead. I glanced over my shoulder and saw there was still nobody behind me.

And then I spotted the door.

It was the one we'd stopped by on our way in, the one leading up to the balcony. I paused when I reached it and checked behind one last time. Nobody there.

"OK," I said to myself, "I'm staying! I don't know what Steve's up to, but he's my best friend. If he gets into trouble, I want to be there to help him out."

Before I could change my mind, I opened the door, slipped through, shut it quickly behind me and stood in the dark, my heart beating as fast as a mouse's.

I stood there for ages, listening while the last of the audience filed out. I could hear their murmurs as they discussed the show in hushed, frightened, but excited tones. Then they were gone and the place was quiet. I thought I'd be able to hear noises from inside the theatre, people cleaning up and fixing the chairs back in place, but the whole building was silent as a graveyard.

I climbed the stairs. My eyes had got used to the dark and I could see pretty well. The stairs were old and creaky and I was half-afraid they would snap under my feet and send me hurtling to my death, but they held.

When I reached the top I discovered I was standing in the middle of the balcony. It was very dusty and dirty up here, and cold too. I shivered as I crept down towards the front.

I had a great view of the stage. The lights were still on and I could see everything in perfect detail. Nobody was about, not the freaks, not the pretty ladies, not the blue-hoods – not Steve. I sat back and waited.

About five minutes later, I spotted a shadow creeping slowly towards the stage. It pulled itself up, then stood and walked to the centre, where it stopped and turned around.

It was Steve.

He started towards the left wing, then stopped and set off

towards the right. He stopped again. I could see him chewing on his nails, trying to decide which way to go.

Then a voice came from high above his head. "Are you looking for *me*?" it asked. A figure swooped down onto the stage, its arms out to its sides, a long red cloak floating behind it like a pair of wings.

Steve nearly jumped out of his skin when the figure hit the stage and rolled into a ball. I toppled backwards, terrified. When I rose to my knees again, the figure was standing and I was able to make out its red clothes, orange hair, pale skin and huge scar.

Mr Crepsley!

Steve tried speaking, but his teeth were shaking too much.

"I saw you watching me," Mr Crepsley said. "You gasped aloud when you first saw me. Why?"

"B-b-b-because I kn-kn-know who you a-are," Steve stuttered, finding his voice.

"I am Larten Crepsley," the creepy-looking man said.

"No," Steve replied. "I know who you *really* are."

"Oh?" Mr Crepsley smiled, but there was no humour in it. "Tell me, little boy," he sneered, "who am I, *really*?"

"Your real name is Vur Horston," Steve said, and Mr Crepsley's jaw dropped in astonishment. And then Steve said something else, and my jaw dropped too.

"*You're a vampire*," he said, and the silence which followed was as long as it was terrifying.

CHAPTER FIFTEEN

MR CREPSLEY (or Vur Horston, if that was his real name) smiled. "So," he said, "I have been discovered. I should not be surprised. It had to happen eventually. Tell me, boy, who sent you?"

"Nobody," Steve said.

Mr Crepsley frowned. "Come, boy," he growled, "do not play games. Who are you working for? Who put you onto me and what do they want?"

"I'm not working for anybody," Steve insisted. "I've lots of books and magazines at home about vampires and monsters. There was a picture of you in one of them."

"A *picture*?" Mr Crepsley asked suspiciously.

"A painting," Steve replied. "It was done in 1903, in Paris. You were with a rich woman. The story said the two of you almost married, but she found out you were a vampire and dumped you."

Mr Crepsley smiled. "As good a reason as any. Her friends thought she was inventing a fantastic story to make herself look better."

"But it wasn't a story, was it?" Steve asked.

"No," Mr Crepsley agreed. "It was not." He sighed and fixed Steve with a fierce gaze. "Though it might have been better for *you* if it had been!" he boomed.

If I'd been in Steve's place, I would have fled as soon as he said that. But Steve didn't even blink.

"You won't hurt me," he said.

"Why not?" Mr Crepsley asked.

"Because of my friend," Steve said. "I told him all about you and if anything happens to me, he'll tell the police."

"They will not believe him," Mr Crepsley snorted.

"Probably not," Steve agreed. "But if I turn up dead or go missing, they'll have to investigate. You wouldn't like that. Lots of police asking questions, coming here in the *daytime...*"

Mr Crepsley shook his head with disgust. "Children!" he snarled. "I hate children. What is it you want? Money? Jewels? The rights to publish my story?"

"I want to join you," Steve said.

I nearly fell off the balcony when I heard that. *Join him?*

"What do you mean?" Mr Crepsley asked, as stunned as I was.

"I want to become a vampire," Steve said. "I want you to make me a vampire and teach me your ways."

"You are crazy!" Mr Crepsley roared.

"No," Steve said, "I'm not."

"I cannot turn a child into a vampire," Mr Crepsley said. "I would be murdered by the Vampire Generals if I did."

"What are Vampire Generals?" Steve asked.

"Never you mind," Mr Crepsley said. "All you need to know is, it cannot be done. We do not blood children. It creates too many problems."

"So don't change me straightaway," Steve said. "That's OK. I don't mind waiting. I can be an apprentice. I know vampires often have assistants who are half-human, half-vampire. Let me be one. I'll work hard and prove myself, and when I'm old enough… "

Mr Crepsley stared at Steve and thought it over. He clicked his fingers while he was thinking and a chair flew up onto the stage from the front row! He sat down on it and crossed his legs.

"Why do you want to be a vampire?" he asked. "It is not much fun. We can only come out at night. Humans despise us. We have to sleep in dirty old places like this. We can never marry or have children or settle down. It is a horrible life."

"I don't care," Steve said stubbornly.

"Is it because you want to live forever?" Mr Crepsley asked. "If so, I must tell you — we do not. We live far longer than humans, but we die all the same, sooner or later."

"I don't care," Steve said again. "I want to come with you. I want to learn. I want to become a vampire."

"What about your friends?" Mr Crepsley asked. "You would not be able to see them again. You would have to leave school and home and never return. What about your parents? Would you not miss them?"

Steve shook his head miserably and looked down at the floor. "My dad doesn't live with us," he said softly. "I hardly ever see him. And my mum doesn't love me. She doesn't care what I do. She probably won't even notice I'm gone."

"That is why you want to run away? Because your mother does not love you?"

"Partly," Steve said.

"If you wait a few years, you will be old enough to leave by yourself," Mr Crepsley said.

"I don't want to wait," Steve replied.

"And your friends?" Mr Crepsley asked again. He looked quite kind at the moment, though still a bit scary. "Would you miss the boy you came with tonight?"

"Darren?" Steve asked, then nodded. "Yes, I'll miss my friends, Darren especially. But it doesn't matter. I want to be a vampire more than I care about them. And if you don't accept me, I'll tell the police and become a vampire hunter when I grow up!"

Mr Crepsley didn't laugh. Instead he nodded seriously. "You have thought this through?" he asked.

"Yes," Steve said.

"You are certain it is what you want?"

"Yes," came the answer.

Mr Crepsley took a deep breath. "Come here," he said. "I will have to test you first."

Steve stood beside Mr Crepsley. His body blocked my view of the vampire, so I couldn't see what happened next. All I know is, they spoke to each other very softly, then there was a noise like a cat lapping up milk.

I saw Steve's back shaking and I thought he was going to fall over but somehow he managed to stay upright. I can't even begin to tell you how frightened I was, watching this. I wanted to leap to my feet and cry out, "No, Steve, stop!"

But I was too scared to move, terrified that, if Mr Crepsley knew I was here, there would be nothing to stop him from killing and eating both me and Steve.

All of a sudden, the vampire began coughing. He pushed Steve away from him and stumbled to his feet. To my horror, I saw his mouth was red, covered in blood, which he quickly spat out.

"What's wrong?" Steve asked, rubbing his arm where he had fallen.

"You have bad blood!" Mr Crepsley screamed.

"What do you mean?" Steve asked. His voice was trembling.

"You are evil!" Mr Crepsley shouted. "I can taste the menace in your blood. You are savage."

"That's a lie!" Steve yelled. "You take that back!"

Steve ran at Mr Crepsley and tried to punch him, but the vampire knocked him to the floor with one hand. "It is no good," he growled. "Your blood is bad. You can never be a vampire!"

"Why not?" Steve asked. He had started to cry.

"Because vampires are not the evil monsters of lore," Mr Crepsley said. "We respect life. You have a killer's instincts, but we are not killers.

"I will not make you a vampire," Mr Crepsley insisted. "You must forget about it. Go home and get on with your life."

"No!" Steve screamed. "I won't forget!" He stumbled to his feet and pointed a shaking finger at the tall, ugly vampire. "I'll get you for this," he promised. "I don't care how long it takes. One day, Vur Horston, I'll track you down and kill you for rejecting me!"

Steve jumped from the stage and ran towards the exit. "One day!" he called back over his shoulder, and I could hear him laughing as he ran, a crazy kind of laugh.

Then he was gone and I was alone with the vampire.

Mr Crepsley sat where he was for a long time, his head between his hands, spitting bits of blood out onto the stage. He wiped his teeth with his fingers, then with a large handkerchief.

"Children!" he snorted aloud, then stood, still wiping his teeth, glanced one last time out over the chairs at the theatre (I ducked down low for fear he might spot me), then turned and walked back to the wings. I could see drops of blood dripping from his lips as he went.

I stayed where I was for a long, long time. It was tough. I'd never been as scared as I was up there on the balcony. I wanted to rush out of the theatre as fast as my feet would carry me.

But I stayed. I made myself wait until I was sure none of the freaks or helpers were about, then slowly crept back up the balcony, down the stairs, into the corridor, and finally out into the night.

I stood outside the theatre for a few seconds, staring up at the moon, studying the trees until I was sure there were no vampires lurking on any of the branches. Then, as quietly as I could, I raced for home. *My* home, not Steve's. I didn't want to be near Steve right then. I was almost as scared of Steve as I was of Mr Crepsley. I mean, he *wanted* to be a vampire! What sort of lunatic actually *wants* to be a vampire?

CHAPTER SIXTEEN

I DIDN'T ring Steve that Sunday. I told Mum and Dad we'd had a bit of an argument and that was why I'd come home early. They weren't happy about it, especially my having walked home so late at night by myself. Dad said he was going to dock my pocket money and was grounding me for a month. I didn't argue. The way I saw it, I was getting off lightly. Imagine what they'd have done to me if they knew about the Cirque Du Freak!

Annie loved her presents. She gobbled the candy down quick and played with the spider for hours. She made me tell her all about the show. She wanted to know what every freak looked like and what they'd done. Her eyes went wide when I told her about the Wolf Man and how he bit off a woman's arm.

"You're joking," she said. "That can't be true."

"It is," I vowed.

"Cross your heart?" she asked.

"Cross my heart."

"Swear on your eyes?"

"I swear on my eyes," I promised. "May rats gnaw them out if I'm telling a lie."

"Wow!" she gasped. "I wish I'd been there. If you ever go again, will you take me?"

"Sure," I said, "but I don't think the freak show comes here that often. They move about a lot."

I didn't tell Annie about Mr Crepsley being a vampire or Steve wanting to become one, but I thought about the two of them all day long. I wanted to ring Steve but didn't know what to say. He would be bound to ask why I didn't go back to his place, and I didn't want to tell him that I'd stayed in the theatre and spied on him.

Imagine: a real-life vampire! I used to believe they were real but then my parents and teachers convinced me they weren't. So much for the wisdom of grown-ups!

I wondered what vampires were really like, whether they could do everything the books and films said they could. I had seen Mr Crepsley make a chair fly, and I'd seen him swoop down from the roof of the theatre, and I'd seen him drink some of Steve's blood. What else could he do? Could he turn into a bat, into smoke, into a rat? Could you see him in a mirror? Would sunlight kill him?

As much as I thought about Mr Crepsley, I thought just as much about Madam Octa. I wished once again that I could buy one like her, one I could control. I could join a freak show if I had a spider like that, and travel the world, having marvellous adventures.

Sunday came and went. I watched TV, helped Dad in the garden and Mum in the kitchen (part of my punishment for coming home late by myself), went for a long walk in the afternoon, and daydreamed about vampires and spiders.

Then it was Monday and time for school. I was nervous going in, not sure what I was going to say to Steve, or what he might say to me. Also, I hadn't slept much over the weekend (it's hard to sleep when you've seen a real vampire), so I was tired and groggy.

Steve was in the yard when I arrived, which was unusual. I normally got to school before him. He was standing apart from the rest of the kids, waiting for me. I took a deep breath, then walked over and leaned against the wall beside him.

"Morning," I said.

"Morning," he replied. There were dark circles under his eyes and I bet he'd slept even less than me the last couple of nights. "Where did you get to after the show?" he asked.

"I went home," I told him.

"Why?" he asked, watching me carefully.

"It was dark outside and I wasn't looking where I was going. I took a few wrong turns and got lost. By the time I found myself somewhere familiar, I was closer to home than to your house."

I made the lie sound as convincing as possible, and I could see him trying to figure out if it was the truth or not.

"You must have got into a lot of trouble," he said.

"Tell me about it!" I groaned. "No pocket money, grounded for a month, and Dad said I'm going to have to do loads of chores. Still," I said with a grin, "it was worth it, right? I mean, was the Cirque Du Freak superb or what!"

Steve studied me for one more moment, then decided I was telling the truth. "Yeah," he said, returning my smile. "It was great."

Tommy and Alan arrived and we had to tell them everything. We were pretty good actors, Steve and me. You'd never have guessed that he had spoken to a vampire on Friday, or that I had seen him.

I could tell, as the day wore on, that things would never be quite the same between me and Steve. Even though he believed what I'd told him, part of him still doubted me. I caught him looking at me oddly from time to time, as though I was someone who had hurt him.

For my part, I didn't want to get too close to him any longer. It scared me, what he'd said to Mr Crepsley, and what the vampire had said to him. Steve was evil, according to Mr Crepsley. It worried me. After all, Steve was prepared to become a vampire and kill people for their blood. How could I go on being friends with someone like that?

We got chatting about Madam Octa later that afternoon. Steve and me hadn't said much about Mr Crepsley and his spider. We were afraid to talk about him, in case we let something slip. But Tommy and Alan kept pestering us and eventually we filled them in on the act.

"How do you think he controlled the spider?" Tommy asked.

"Maybe it was a fake spider," Alan said.

"It wasn't a fake," I snorted. "None of the freaks were fake. That was why it was so brilliant. You could tell everything was real."

"So how did he control it?" Tommy asked again.

"Maybe the flute is magic," I said, "or else Mr Crepsley knows how to charm spiders, the way Indians can charm snakes."

"But you said Mr Tall controlled the spider as well," Alan said, "when Mr Crepsley had Madam Octa in his mouth."

"Oh. Yes. I forgot," I said. "Well, I guess that means they must have used magic flutes."

"They didn't use magic flutes," Steve said. He had been quiet most of the day, saying less than me about the show, but Steve never could resist hammering someone with facts.

"So what *did* they use?" I asked.

"Telepathy," Steve answered.

"Is that something to do with telephones?" Alan asked.

Steve smiled, and Tommy and me laughed (although I wasn't entirely sure what "telepathy" meant, and I bet Tommy wasn't either). "Moron!" Tommy chuckled, and punched Alan playfully.

"Go on, Steve," I said, "tell him what it means."

"Telepathy is when you can read somebody else's mind," Steve explained, "or send them thoughts without speaking. That's how they controlled the spider, with their minds."

"So what's with the flutes?" I asked.

"Either they're just for show," Steve said, "or, more likely, you need them to attract her attention."

"You mean anyone could control her?" Tommy asked.

"Anyone with a brain, yes," Steve said. "Which counts you out, Alan," he added, but smiled to show he didn't mean it.

"You wouldn't need magic flutes or special training or anything?" Tommy asked.

"I wouldn't think so," Steve answered.

The talk moved on to something else after that – football, I think – but I wasn't listening. Because all of a sudden there was a new thought running through my mind, setting my brain on fire with ideas. I forgot about Steve and vampires and everything.

"You mean anyone could control her?"

"Anyone with a brain, yes."

"You wouldn't need magic flutes or special training or anything?"

"I wouldn't imagine so."

Tommy's and Steve's words kept bouncing through my mind, over and over, like a stuck CD.

Anyone could control her. That anyone could be *me*. If I could get my hands on Madam Octa and communicate with her, she could be my pet and I could control her and…

No. It was foolish. Maybe I could control her, but I would never own her. She was Mr Crepsley's and there was no way in the world that he would part with her, not for money or jewels or…

The answer hit me in a flash. A way to get her off him. A way to make her mine. *Blackmail!* If I threatened the vampire –

I could say I'd set the police onto him – he'd have to let me keep her.

But the thought of going face to face with Mr Crepsley terrified me. I knew I couldn't do it. That left just one other option: I'd have to *steal* her!

CHAPTER SEVENTEEN

EARLY MORNING would be the best time to steal the spider. Having performed so late into the night, most members of the Cirque Du Freak would probably sleep in until eight or nine. I'd sneak into camp, find Madam Octa, grab her and run. If that wasn't possible — if the camp was active — I'd simply return home and forget about it.

The difficult part was picking a day. Wednesday was ideal: the last show would have played the night before, so the circus would in all likelihood have pulled out before midday and moved on to its next venue before the vampire could awake and discover the theft. But what if they left town directly after the show, in the middle of the night? Then I'd miss my big chance.

It had to be tomorrow — Tuesday. That meant Mr Crepsley would have the whole of Tuesday night to search for his spider — for *me* — but that was a risk I'd just have to take.

I went to bed a bit earlier than usual. I was tired and ready to fall asleep, but was so excited, I thought I wouldn't be able to. I kissed Mum goodnight and shook Dad's hand. They thought I was trying to win my pocket money back, but it was in case something happened to me at the theatre and I never saw them again.

I have a radio which is also an alarm clock, and I set the alarm to five o'clock in the morning, then stuck my headphones on and plugged them into the radio. That way, I could wake up nice and early without waking anyone else.

I fell asleep quicker than I expected and slept straight through till morning. If I had any dreams, I can't remember them.

Next thing I knew, the alarm was sounding. I groaned, turned over, then sat up in bed, rubbing my eyes. I wasn't sure where I was for a few seconds, or why I was awake so early. Then I remembered the spider and the plan, and grinned happily.

The grin didn't last long, because I realised the alarm wasn't coming through my headphones. I must have rolled over in my sleep and pulled the cord out! I leapt across my bed and slammed the alarm off, then sat in the early morning darkness, heart pounding, listening for noises.

When I was sure my parents were still asleep, I slid out of bed and got dressed as quietly as I could. I went to the toilet and was about to flush when I thought of the noise it would make. I yanked my hand away from the lever and wiped the sweat from my brow. They would surely have heard that! A narrow escape. I'd have to be more careful when I got to the theatre.

I slipped downstairs and let myself out. The sun was on its way up and it looked like it would be a bright day.

I walked quickly and sang songs to pep me up. I was a bundle of nerves and almost turned back a dozen times. Once I actually *did* turn and start walking home, but then I remembered the way the spider had hung from Mr Crepsley's jaws, and the tricks she had performed, and swung around again.

I can't explain why Madam Octa meant so much to me, or why I was placing my life in such peril to have her. Looking back, I'm no longer sure what drove me on. It was simply a dreadful need I couldn't ignore.

The crumbling old building looked even creepier by day. I could see cracks running down the front, holes nibbled by rats and mice, spider webs in the windows. I shivered and hurried round to the rear. It was deserted. Empty old houses, junk yards, scrap heaps. There would be people moving about later in the day, but right then it looked like a ghost town. I didn't even see a cat or a dog.

As I'd thought, there were plenty of ways to get into the theatre. There were two doors and loads of windows to choose from.

Several cars and vans were parked outside the building. I didn't spot any signs or pictures on them, but I was sure they belonged to the Cirque Du Freak. It suddenly struck me that the freaks most probably slept in the vans. If Mr Crepsley had a home in one of them, my plan was sunk.

I snuck into the theatre, which felt even colder than it had been on Saturday night, and tiptoed down a long corridor, then another, then another! It was like a maze back here and I started worrying about finding my way out. Maybe I should go back and bring a ball of string, so I could mark my way and—

No! It was too late for that. If I left, I'd never have the guts to return. I'd just have to remember my steps as best I could and say a little prayer when it came time to leave.

I saw no sign of any freaks, and began to think I was on a fool's errand, that they were all in the vans or in nearby hotels. I'd been searching for twenty minutes and my legs felt heavy after so much walking. Maybe I should quit and forget the crazy plan.

I was about to give up when I found a set of stairs leading down to a cellar. I paused at the top for ages, biting my lips, wondering if I should go down. I'd seen enough horror films to know this was the most likely spot for a vampire, but I'd also seen loads where the hero walked down to a similar cellar, only to be attacked, murdered and chopped up into little pieces!

Finally I took a deep breath and started down. My shoes were making too much noise, so I eased them off and padded along in just my socks. I picked up loads of splinters, but was so nervous, I didn't feel the pain.

There was a huge cage near the bottom of the stairs. I edged over to it and looked through the bars. The Wolf Man was inside, lying on his back, asleep and snoring. He twitched and moaned as I watched. I jumped back from the cage. If he woke, his howls would bring the whole freak show down on me in seconds flat!

As I was stumbling backwards, my foot hit something soft and slimy. I turned my head slowly and saw I was standing over the snake-boy! He was stretched out on the floor, his snake wrapped around him, and his eyes were wide open!

I don't know how I managed not to scream or faint, but somehow I kept quiet and stayed on my feet, and that saved me. Because, even though the snake-boy's eyes were open, he was fast asleep. I knew by the way he was breathing: deeply, heavily, in and out.

I tried not to think about what would have happened if I'd fallen on him and the snake and woken them up.

Enough was enough. I gave one last look around the dark cellar, promising myself I'd leave if I didn't spot the vampire. For a few seconds I saw nothing and got ready to scram, but then I noticed what might have been a large box near one of the walls.

It *might* have been a large box. But it wasn't. I knew all too well what it really was. It was a coffin!

I gulped, then walked carefully over to the coffin. It was about two metres long and eighty centimetres wide. The wood was dark and stained. Moss was growing in patches, and I could see a family of cockroaches in one of the corners.

I'd love to say I was brave enough to lift the lid and peek inside, but of course I wasn't and didn't. Even the thought of *touching* the coffin gave me the shivers!

I searched for Madam Octa's cage. I felt sure she wouldn't be far from her master, and right enough, there was the cage, on the floor by the head of the coffin, covered by a big red cloth.

I glanced inside, to make sure, and there she was, her belly pulsing, her eight legs twitching. She looked horrible and terrifying this close up, and for a second I thought about leaving her. All of a sudden it seemed like a stupid idea, and the thought of touching her hairy legs or letting her anywhere near my face filled me with dread.

But only a true coward would turn back now. So I picked up the cage and laid it in the middle of the cellar. The key was hanging from the lock and one of the flutes was tied to the bars at the side.

I took out the note I had written back home the night before. It was simple, but had taken me ages to write. I read it as I stuck it to the top of the coffin with a piece of gum.

> Mr Crepsley,
>   I know who and what you are. I have taken Madam Octa and am keeping her. Do not come looking for her. Do not come back to this town. If you do, I will tell everyone that you are a vampire and you will be hunted down and killed. I am not Steve. Steve knows nothing about this. I will take good care of the spider.

Of course, I didn't sign it!

Mentioning Steve probably wasn't a good idea, but I was sure the vampire would think of him anyway, so it was just as well to clear his name.

With the note pinned in place, it was time to go. I picked up the cage and hurried up the stairs as fast as I could (being as silent as possible). I slipped my shoes back on and found my way out. It was easier than I'd imagined: the halls looked brighter after the dark of the cellar. When I got outside I walked slowly round to the front of the theatre, then ran for home, stopping for nothing, leaving the theatre and the vampire and my fear far behind. Leaving everything behind – except for Madam Octa!

CHAPTER EIGHTEEN

I MADE it back about twenty minutes before Mum and Dad got up. I hid the spider cage at the back of my wardrobe, under a pile of clothes, leaving enough holes so Madam Octa could breathe. She should be safe there: Mum left the tidying of the room to me, and hardly ever came in rooting around.

I slipped into bed and pretended to be asleep. Dad called me at a quarter to eight. I put on my school clothes and walked downstairs, yawning and stretching as though I'd only just woken. I ate breakfast quickly and hurried back upstairs to check on Madam Octa. She hadn't moved since I'd stolen her. I gave the cage a small shake but she didn't budge.

I would have liked to stay home and keep an eye on her but that was impossible. Mum always knows when I fake being sick. She's too smart to be fooled.

That day felt like a week. The seconds seemed to drag like hours, and even break and lunch-time went slowly! I tried playing football but my heart wasn't in it. I couldn't concentrate in class and kept giving stupid answers, even to simple questions.

Finally it ended and I was able to rush home and up to my room.

Madam Octa was in the same spot as earlier. I was half-afraid she was dead, but I could see her breathing. Then it struck me: she was waiting to be fed! I'd seen spiders this way before. They could sit still for hours at a time, waiting for their next meal to come along.

I wasn't sure what I should feed her, but I guessed it wasn't too different to what ordinary spiders ate. I hurried out into the garden, pausing only to snatch an empty jam jar from the kitchen.

It didn't take long to collect a couple of dead flies, a few bugs and a long wriggly worm, then back inside I raced, hiding the jam jar inside my T-shirt, so Mum couldn't see it and start asking questions.

I closed my bedroom door and stuck a chair against it so nobody could come in, then placed Madam Octa's cage on my bed and removed the cloth.

The spider squinted and crouched down lower at the sudden surge of light. I was about to open the door and throw the food in when I remembered I was dealing with a poisonous spider who could kill me with a couple of bites.

I lifted the jar over the cage, picked out one of the live insects and dropped it. It landed on its back. Its feet twitched in the air and then it managed to roll over onto its belly. It began crawling towards freedom but didn't get far.

As soon as it moved, Madam Octa pounced. One second she was standing still as a cocoon in the middle of the cage, the next she was over the insect, baring her fangs.

She swallowed the bug down quick. It would have fed a normal spider for a day or two, but to Madam Octa it was no more than a light snack. She made her way back to her original spot and looked at me as if to say, "OK, that was nice. Now where's the main course?"

I fed her the entire contents of the jar. The worm put up

a good fight, twisting and turning madly, but she got her fangs into it and ripped it in half, then into quarters. She seemed to enjoy the worm the most.

I had an idea and fetched my diary from underneath my mattress. My diary is my most prized possession, and it's because I wrote everything down in it that I'm able to write this book. I remember most of the story anyway, but whenever I get stuck, all I have to do is open the diary and check the facts.

I folded the diary open to the back page, then wrote down all that I knew about Madam Octa: what Mr Crepsley had said about her in the show, the tricks she knew, the food she liked. I put one tick beside food she liked a lot, and two ticks beside food she loved (so far, only the worm). This way I'd be able to work out the best way to feed her, and what to give her as a treat when I wanted her to do a trick.

I brought up some grub from the fridge next: cheese, ham, lettuce and corned beef. She ate just about everything I gave her. It looked like I was going to be kept busy trying to feed this ugly lady!

Tuesday night was horrible. I wondered what Mr Crepsley would think when he woke and found his spider missing and a note in its place. Would he leave like I told him, or would he come looking for his pet? Maybe, since the two of them could speak with each other telepathically, he would be able to trace her *here*!

I spent hours sitting up in bed, holding a cross to my chest. I wasn't sure if the cross would work or not. I know they work in the movies but I remembered talking to Steve once and he said a cross was no good by itself. He said they only worked if the person using them was good.

I finally fell asleep about two in the morning. If Mr Crepsley had come, I would have been completely defenceless, but luckily, when I woke in the morning, there was no sign of his having been, and Madam Octa was still resting in the wardrobe.

I felt a lot better that Wednesday, especially when I popped by the old theatre after school and saw the Cirque Du Freak had left. The cars and vans were gone. No trace of the freak show remained.

I'd done it! Madam Octa was mine!

I celebrated by buying a pizza. Ham and pepperoni. Mum and Dad wanted to know what the special occasion was. I said I just felt like something different, offered them – and Annie – a slice, and they left it at that.

I fed the scraps to Madam Octa and she loved them. She ran around the cage licking up every last crumb. I made a note in my diary: "For a special treat, a piece of pizza!"

I spent the next couple of days getting her used to her new home. I didn't let her out of the cage, but I carried it around the room so she could see every corner and get to know the place. I didn't want her to be nervous when I finally freed her.

I talked to her all the time, telling her about my life and family and home. I told her how much I admired her and the sort of food I was going to get her and the type of tricks we were going to do. She might not have understood everything I said, but she seemed to.

I went to the library after school on Thursday and Friday and read as much about spiders as I could find. There was all sorts of stuff I hadn't known. Like they can have up to eight eyes, and the threads of their webs are gluey fluids which harden when they're let out into the air. But none of the books mentioned performing spiders, or ones with telepathic powers. And I couldn't find any pictures of spiders like Madam Octa. It looked like none of the people who wrote these books had seen a spider like her. She was unique!

When Saturday came, I decided it was time to let her out of her cage and try a few tricks. I had practised with the flute and could play a few very simple tunes quite well. The hard part was sending thoughts to Madam Octa while playing. It was going to be tricky, but I felt I was up to it.

I closed my door and shut my windows. It was Saturday afternoon. Dad was working and Mum had gone to the shops with Annie. I was all alone, so if anything went wrong, it would be entirely my fault, and I would be the only one to suffer.

I placed the cage in the middle of the floor. I hadn't fed Madam Octa since last night. I figured she might not want to perform if she was full of food. Animals can be lazy, just like humans.

I removed the cloth, put the flute in my mouth, turned the key and opened the tiny door to the cage. I stepped back and squatted down low, so she could see me.

Madam Octa did nothing for a while. Then she crept to the door, paused and sniffed the air. She looked too fat to squeeze through the gap, and I began to think I must have overfed her. But somehow she managed to suck her sides in and ease out.

She sat on the carpet in front of the cage, her big round belly throbbing. I thought she might walk around the cage, to check the room out, but she didn't show the faintest sign of having any interest in the room.

Her eyes were glued to *me!*

I gulped loudly and tried not to let her sense my fear. It was difficult but I managed not to shake or cry. The flute had slipped a couple of centimetres from my lips while I was watching her but I was still holding it. It was time to start playing, so I pressed it back between my lips and prepared to blow.

That was when she made her move. In one giant leap, she sprang across the room. She flew forward, up into the air, jaws open, fangs ready, hairy legs twitching — *straight at my unprotected face!*

CHAPTER NINETEEN

IF SHE had connected, she would have sunk her fangs into me and I would have died. But luck was on my side, and instead of landing on flesh, she slammed against the end of the flute and went flying off to the side.

She landed in a ball and was dazed for a couple of seconds. Reacting rapidly, aware that my life depended on speed, I stuck the flute between my lips and played like a madman. My mouth was dry but I blew regardless, not daring to lick my lips.

Madam Octa cocked her head when she heard the music. She struggled to her legs and swayed from side to side, as though drunk. I sneaked a quick breath, then started playing a slower tune, which wouldn't tire my fingers or lungs.

"Hello, Madam Octa," I said inside my head, shutting my eyes and concentrating. "My name's Darren Shan. I've told you that before but I don't know if you heard. I'm not even sure if you can hear it now.

"I'm your new owner. I'm going to treat you real good and feed you loads of insects and meat. But only if *you* are good and do everything I tell you and don't attack me again."

She had stopped swaying and was staring at me. I wasn't sure if she was listening to my thoughts or planning her next leap.

"I want you to stand on your back legs now," I told her. "I want you to stand on your two back legs and take a little bow."

For a few seconds she didn't respond. I went on playing and thinking, asking her to stand, then commanding her, then begging her. Finally, when I was almost out of breath, she raised herself and stood on her two legs, the way I wanted. Then she took a little bow and relaxed, awaiting my next order.

She was obeying me!

The next order I gave was for her to crawl back into her cage. She did as I bid, and this time I only had to think it once. As soon as she was inside, I closed the door and fell back on my bum, letting the flute fall from my mouth.

The shock I'd got when she jumped at me! My heart was beating so fast, I was afraid it was going to run up my neck and leap out of my mouth! I lay on the floor for ages, staring at the spider, thinking about how close to death I had come.

That should have been warning enough. Any sensible person would have left the door shut and forgot about playing with such a deadly pet. It was too dangerous. What if she hadn't hit the flute? What if Mum had come home and found me dead on the floor? What if the spider then attacked her or Dad or Annie? Only the world's dumbest person would run a risk like that again.

Step forward – Darren Shan!

It was crazy, but I couldn't stop myself. Besides, the way I saw it, there was no point having stolen her if I was going to keep her locked up in a silly old cage.

I was a bit cleverer this time. I unlocked the door but didn't open it. Instead I played the flute and told *her* to push it open. She did, and when she came out she seemed as harmless as a kitten and did everything I'd communicated.

I made her do lots of tricks. Made her hop about the room

like a kangaroo. Then had her hang from the ceiling and draw pictures with her webs. Next I got her lifting weights (a pen, a box of matches, a marble). After that I told her to sit in one of my remote control cars. I turned it on and it looked like she was driving! I crashed it into a pile of books, but made her jump off at the last moment, so she wasn't hurt.

I played with her for about an hour and would have happily continued all afternoon, but I heard Mum arriving home and knew she would think it odd if I stayed up in my room all day. The last thing I wanted was her or Dad prying into my private affairs.

So I stuck Madam Octa back in the wardrobe and trotted downstairs, trying to look as natural as possible.

"Were you playing a CD up there?" Mum asked. She had four bags full of clothes and hats, which she and Annie were unpacking on the kitchen table.

"No," I said.

"I thought I heard music," she said.

"I was playing a flute," I told her, trying to sound casual.

She stopped unpacking. "*You?*" she asked. "Playing a *flute?*"

"I do know how to play one," I said. "You taught me when I was five years old, remember?"

"I remember," she laughed. "I also remember when you were six and told me flutes were for girls. You swore you were never going to look at one again!"

I shrugged as though it was no big thing. "I changed my mind," I said. "I found a flute on the way home from school yesterday and got to wondering if I could still play."

"Where did you find it?" she asked.

"On the road."

"I hope you washed it out before you put it in your mouth. There's no telling where it might have been."

"I washed it," I lied.

"This is a lovely surprise," she smiled, then ruffled my hair and gave my cheek a big wet kiss.

"Hey! Quit it!" I yelled.

"We'll make a Mozart out of you yet," she said. "I can see it now: you playing a piano in a huge concert hall, dressed in a beautiful white suit, your father and I in the front row…"

"Get real, Mum," I chuckled. "It's only a flute."

"From small acorns, oak trees grow," she said.

"He's as thick as an oak tree," Annie giggled.

I stuck my tongue out at her in response.

The next few days were great. I played with Madam Octa whenever I could, feeding her every afternoon (she only needed one meal a day, as long as it was a large one). And I didn't have to worry about locking my bedroom door because Mum and Dad agreed not to enter when they heard me practising the flute.

I considered telling Annie about Madam Octa but decided to wait a while longer. I was getting on well with the spider but could tell she was still uneasy around me. I wouldn't bring Annie in until I was sure it was completely safe.

My schoolwork improved during the next week, and so did my goal-scoring. I scored twenty-eight goals between Monday and Friday. Even Mr Dalton was impressed.

"With your good marks in class and your prowess on the field," he said, "you could turn into the world's first professional footballer-cum-university professor! A cross between Pele and Einstein!"

I knew he was only pulling my leg but it was nice of him to say it all the same.

It took ages to work up the nerve to let Madam Octa climb up my body and over my face, but I finally tried it on Friday afternoon. I played my best song and didn't let her start until I'd told her several times what I wanted her to do. When I thought we were ready, I gave her the nod and she began creeping up the leg of my trousers.

It was fine until she reached my neck. The feel of those long thin hairy legs almost caused me to drop the flute. I would have been a dead duck if I had, because she was in the perfect place to sink her fangs. Luckily, my nerve held and I went on playing.

She crawled over my left ear and up to the top of my head, where she lay down for a rest. My scalp itched beneath her but I had sense enough not to try scratching it. I studied myself in the mirror and grinned. She looked like one of those French hats, a beret.

I made her slide down my face and dangle from my nose on one of her web-strings. I didn't let her into my mouth, but I got her to swing from side to side like she'd done with Mr Crepsley, and had her tickle my chin with her legs.

I didn't let her tickle me too much, in case I started laughing and dropped the flute!

When I put her back in her cage that Friday night, I felt like a king, like nothing could ever go wrong, that my whole life was going to be perfect. I was doing well in school and at football, and had the sort of pet any boy would trade all his worldly goods for. I couldn't have been happier if I'd won the lottery or a chocolate factory.

That, of course, was when everything went wrong and the whole world crashed down around my ears.

CHAPTER TWENTY

STEVE POPPED over for a visit late Saturday afternoon. We hadn't said much to each other all week and he was the last person I was expecting. Mum let him in and called me downstairs. I saw him when I was halfway down, paused, then shouted for him to come up.

He gazed about my room as though he hadn't been here for months. "I'd almost forgotten what this place looks like," he said.

"Don't be silly," I said. "You were here a couple of weeks ago."

"It seems longer." He sat on the bed and turned his eyes on me. His face was serious and lonely. "Why have you been avoiding me?" he asked softly.

"What do you mean?" I pretended I didn't know what he was talking about.

"You've been steering clear of me these past two weeks," he said. "It wasn't obvious at first, but each day you've been spending less time with me. You didn't even pick me when we were playing basketball in P.E. last Thursday."

"You're not very good at basketball," I said. It was a lame excuse, but I couldn't think of a better one.

"I was confused at first," Steve said, "but then I figured it out. You didn't get lost the night of the freak show, did you? You stuck around, up in the balcony probably, and saw what happened between me and Vur Horston."

"I saw nothing of the sort," I snapped.

"No?" he asked.

"No," I lied.

"You didn't see anything?"

"No."

"You didn't see me talking to Vur Horston?"

"No!"

"You didn't— "

"Look, Steve," I interrupted, "whatever happened between you and Mr Crepsley is your business. I wasn't there, didn't see it, don't know what you're talking about. Now if— "

"Don't lie to me, Darren," he said.

"I'm not lying!" I lied.

"Then how did you know I was talking about Mr Crepsley?" he asked.

"Because… " I bit my tongue.

"I said I was talking to *Vur Horston*," Steve smiled. "Unless you were there, how would you know that Vur Horston and Larten Crepsley are one and the same?"

My shoulders sagged. I sat on the bed beside Steve. "OK," I said, "I admit it. I was in the balcony."

"How much did you see and hear?" Steve asked.

"Everything. I couldn't see what he was doing when he was sucking out your blood, or hear what he was saying. But apart from that… "

"…everything," Steve finished with a sigh. "That's why you've been avoiding me: because he said I was evil."

"Partly," I said. "But mostly because of what *you* said. Steve, you asked him to turn you into a vampire! What if he *had* turned you into one and you'd come after me? Most vampires go after people they know first, don't they?"

"In books and films, yes," Steve said. "This is different. This is real life. I wouldn't have hurt you, Darren."

"Maybe," I said. "Maybe not. The point is, I don't want to find out. I don't want to be friends with you any more. You could be dangerous. What if you met another vampire and this one granted your wish? Or what if Mr Crepsley was right and you're really evil and— "

"I'm not evil!" Steve shouted, and shoved me back on the bed. He leapt on my chest and stuck his fingers in my face. "Take that back!" he roared. "Take that back, or so help me, I'll jerk your head off and— "

"I take it back! I take it back!" I shrieked. Steve was heavy on my chest, his face flushed and furious. I would have said anything to get him off.

He sat perched on my chest a few seconds longer, then grunted and rolled off. I sat up, gasping, rubbing my face where he had poked it.

"Sorry," Steve mumbled. "That was over the top. But I'm upset. It hurt, what Mr Crepsley said, and you ignoring me at school. You're my best friend, Darren, the only person I can really talk to. If you break up our friendship, I don't know what I'll do."

He started to cry. I watched him for a few seconds, torn between fear and sympathy. Then my nobler self got the better of me and I put an arm around his shoulder. "It's OK," I said. "I'll still be your friend. C'mon, Steve, quit crying, OK?"

He tried but it took a while for the tears to stop. "I must look a right fool," he finally sniffed.

"Nonsense," I said. "*I'm* the fool. I should have stood by you. I was a coward. I never stopped to imagine what you must be going through. I was only thinking of myself and Madam— " I pulled a face and stopped talking.

Steve stared at me curiously. "What were you going to say?" he asked.

"Nothing," I said. "It was a slip of the tongue."

He grunted. "You're a bad liar, Shan. Always were. Tell me what it was you were about to let slip."

I studied his face, wondering if I should tell him. I knew I shouldn't, that it could only mean trouble, but I felt sorry for him. Besides, I needed to tell someone. I wanted to show off my wonderful pet and the great tricks we could do.

"Can you keep a secret?" I asked.

"Of course," he snorted.

"This is a big one. You can't tell anyone, OK? If I tell you, it has to stay between the two of us. If you ever talk... "

"... *you'll* talk about me and Mr Crepsley," Steve said, grinning. "You have me over a barrel. No matter what you tell me, you know I can't grass, even if I wanted to. What's the big secret?"

"Wait a minute," I said. I got off the bed and opened the door to the room. "Mum?" I shouted.

"Yes?" came her muffled reply.

"I'm showing Steve my flute," I yelled. "I'm going to teach him how to play it, but only if we're not disturbed, OK?"

"OK," she called back.

I closed the door and smiled at Steve. He looked puzzled. "A flute?" he asked. "Your big secret is a flute?"

"That's part of it," I said. "Listen, do you remember Madam Octa? Mr Crepsley's spider?"

"Of course," he said. "I wasn't paying much attention to her when she was on but I don't think anyone could ever forget a creature like that. Those hairy legs: brrrr!"

I opened the door to the wardrobe while he was speaking and got out the cage. His eyes squinted when he saw it, then widened. "That's not what I think it is, is it?" he asked.

"That depends," I said, whipping off the cloth. "If you think it's a deadly performing spider – you're right!"

"Hell's bells!" he gasped, almost falling off the bed in shock. "That's a… she's a… where did… Wow!"

I was delighted with his reaction. I stood over the cage, smiling like a proud father. Madam Octa lay on the floor, quiet as ever, paying no attention to me or Steve.

"She's awesome!" Steve said, crawling closer for a better look. "She looks just the same as the one in the circus. I can't believe you found one that looks so similar. Where'd you get her? A pet shop? From a zoo?"

My smile slipped. "I got her from the Cirque Du Freak, of course," I said uneasily.

"From the freak show?" he asked, face crinkling. "They were selling live spiders? I didn't see any. How much did she cost?"

I shook my head and said: "I didn't buy her, Steve. I… Can't you guess? Don't you understand?"

"Understand what?" he asked.

"That's not a *similar* spider," I said. "That's the *same one*. It's Madam Octa."

He stared at me, as though he hadn't heard what I'd said. I was about to repeat, it but he spoke up before I could. "The… same … one?" he asked in a slow, trembling voice.

"Yes," I said.

"You mean… that's… Madam Octa? *The* Madam Octa?"

"Yes," I said again, laughing at his shock.

"That's… Mr Crepsley's spider?"

"Steve, what's wrong? How many times do I have to say it for you to— "

"Wait a minute," he snapped, shaking his head. "If this is really Madam Octa, how did you get your hands on her? Did you find her outside? Did they sell her off?"

"Nobody would sell a great spider like this," I said.

"That's what I thought," Steve agreed. "So how did… " He left the question hanging in the air.

"I stole her," I said, puffing up proudly. "I went back to the theatre that Tuesday morning, crept in, found where she was and snuck out with her. I left a note telling Mr Crepsley not to come looking for her or I'd report his being a vampire to the police."

"You… you… " Steve was gasping. His face had turned white and he looked like he was about to collapse.

"Are you all right?" I asked.

"You… imbecile!" he roared. "You lunatic! You moron!"

"Hey!" I shouted, upset.

"Idiot! Dumbo! Cretin!" he yelled. "Do you realise what you've done? Have you any idea what sort of trouble you're in?"

"Huh?" I asked, bewildered.

"You stole a vampire's spider!" Steve shouted. "You stole from a member of the undead! What do you think he's going to do when he catches up with you, Darren? Spank your bottom and give you fifty lines? Tell your parents and make them ground you? We're talking about a *vampire*! He'll rip out your throat and feed you to the spider! He'll tear you to pieces and— "

"No, he won't," I said calmly.

"Of course he will," Steve replied.

"No," I said, "he *won't*. Because he won't find me. I stole the spider the Tuesday before last, so he's had nearly two whole weeks to track me down, but there hasn't been a sign of him. He left with the circus and won't ever come back, not if he knows what's good for him."

"I dunno," Steve said. "Vampires have long memories. He might return when you're grown up and with kids of your own."

"I'll worry about that when and if it happens," I said. "I've got away with it for the time being. I wasn't sure I would –

I thought he'd track me down and kill me — but I did. So quit with the names, all right?"

"You're something else," he laughed, shaking his head. "I thought *I* was daring, but stealing a vampire's pet! I never would have thought you had it in you. What made you do it?"

"I had to have her," I told him. "I saw her on stage and knew I'd do anything to get her. Then I discovered Mr Crepsley was a vampire and realised I could blackmail him. It's wrong, I know, but he's a vampire, so it's not *too* bad, is it? Stealing from someone bad: in a way it's a good thing, right?"

Steve laughed. "I don't know if it's good or bad," he said. "All I know is, if he ever comes looking for her, I wouldn't want to be in your shoes."

He studied the spider again. He stuck his face up close to the cage (but not close enough for her to strike him) and watched her belly bulging in and out.

"Have you let her out of the cage yet?" he asked.

"Every day," I said. I picked up the flute and gave a toot. Madam Octa jumped forward a couple of centimetres. Steve yelped and fell back on his bum. I howled with laughter.

"You can control her?" he gasped.

"I can make her do everything Mr Crepsley did," I said, trying not to sound boastful. "It's quite easy. She's perfectly safe as long as you concentrate. But if you let your thoughts wander for even a second… " I drew a finger across my throat and made a choking noise.

"Have you let her make a web over your lips?" Steve asked. His eyes were shining brightly.

"Not yet," I said. "I'm worried about letting her in my mouth: the thought of her slipping down my throat terrifies me. Besides, I'd need a partner to control her while she spun the web, and so far I've been alone."

"So far," Steve grinned, "but not any more." He got up and clapped his hands. "Let's do it. Teach me how to use that fancy tin whistle and let me at her. I'm not afraid to let her in my mouth. C'mon, let's go, let's go, let's go go go go GO!"

I couldn't ignore excitement like that. I knew it was unwise to involve Steve with the spider on such short notice – I should have made sure he got to know her better – but I ignored common sense and gave in to his wishes.

I told him he couldn't play the flute, not until he'd practised, but he could play with Madam Octa while I was controlling her. I ran him through the tricks we were going to do and made sure he understood everything.

"Being quiet is vital," I said. "Don't say anything. Don't even whistle loudly. Because if you disturb my attention and I lose control of her…"

"Yeah, yeah," Steve sighed. "I know. Don't worry. I can be quiet as a mouse when I want."

When he was ready, I unlocked Madam Octa's cage and began playing. She advanced at my order. I could hear Steve drawing in his breath, a little scared now that she was out in the open, but he gave no sign that he wanted to stop, so I went on blowing and started her off on her routine.

I let her do a lot of stuff by herself before allowing her near Steve. We'd developed a great understanding over the last week or so. The spider had grown used to my mind and the way it thought, and had learned to obey my commands almost before I finished sending them. I'd learned that she could work from the shortest of instructions: I only had to use a few words to prompt her into action.

Steve watched the show in total silence. He nearly clapped a few times but caught himself before his hands could meet and produce a noise. Instead of clapping, he gave me the thumbs-up sign and mouthed the words "Great", "Super", "Brilliant" and so on.

When the time came for Steve to take part in the act, I gave him the nod that we had agreed upon. He gulped, took a deep breath, then nodded back. He rose to his feet and stepped forward, keeping to the side so I wouldn't lose sight of Madam Octa. Then he sank to his knees and waited.

I played a new tune and sent a new set of orders. Madam Octa sat still, listening. When she knew what I wanted, she started creeping towards Steve. I saw him shivering and licking his lips. I was going to cancel the act and send the spider back to her cage, but then he stopped shaking and became calmer, so I continued.

He gave a small shudder when she started crawling up the leg of his trousers, but that was a natural response. I still got the shakes sometimes when I felt her hairy legs brushing against my skin.

I made Madam Octa crawl up the back of his neck and tickle his ears with her legs. He giggled softly and the last traces of his fear vanished. I felt more confident now that he was calmer, and so moved the spider round to the front of his face, where she built small cobwebs over his eyes and slid down his nose and bounced off his lips.

Steve was enjoying it and so was I. There were lots of new things I was able to do now that I had a partner.

She was on his right shoulder, preparing to slide down his arm, when the door opened and Annie walked in.

Normally Annie never enters my room before knocking. She's a great kid, not like other brats her age, and nearly always knocks politely and waits for a reply. But that evening, by sheer bad luck, she happened to barge in.

"Hey, Darren, where's my— " she started to say, then stopped.

She saw Steve and the monstrous spider on his shoulder, its fangs glinting as though getting ready to bite, and she did the natural thing.

She screamed.

The sound alarmed me. My head turned, the flute slid from my lips, and my concentration snapped. My link to Madam Octa disintegrated. She shook her head, took a couple of quick steps closer to Steve's throat, then bared her fangs and appeared to grin.

Steve roared with fear and surged to his feet. He swiped at the spider, but she ducked and his hand missed. Before he could try again, Madam Octa lowered her head, quick as a snake, and *sank her poison-tipped fangs deep into his neck!*

CHAPTER TWENTY-ONE

STEVE STIFFENED as soon as the spider bit him. His yells stopped dead in his throat, his lips turned blue, his eyes snapped wide open. For what seemed an eternity (though it couldn't have been more than three or four seconds), he tottered on his feet. Then he crumpled to the floor like a scarecrow.

The fall saved him. As with the goat at the Cirque Du Freak show, Madam Octa's first bite knocked Steve out, but didn't kill him straight off. I saw her moving along his neck before he fell, searching for the right spot, preparing for the second, killer bite.

The fall disturbed her. She slipped from Steve's neck and it took her a few seconds to climb back up.

Those seconds were all I needed.

I was in a state of shock, but the sight of her emerging over his shoulder like some terrible arachnid sunrise spurred me into life. I stooped for the flute, jammed it almost through the back of my throat, and blew the loudest note of my entire life.

"STOP!" I screamed inside my head, and Madam Octa leapt about half a metre into the air.

"Back inside the cage!" I commanded, and she hopped down from Steve's body and sped across the floor. As soon as she passed the bars of the door, I lunged forward and slammed it shut.

With Madam Octa taken care of, my attention turned to Steve. Annie was still screaming but I couldn't worry about her until I'd seen to my poisoned friend.

"Steve?" I asked, crawling close to his ear, praying for an answer. "Are you OK? Steve?" There was no reply. He was breathing, so I knew he was alive, but that was all. There was nothing else he could do. He couldn't talk or move his arms. He wasn't even able to blink.

I became aware of Annie standing behind me. She'd stopped screaming but I could feel her shaking.

"Is... is he... dead?" she asked in a tiny voice.

"Of course not!" I snapped. "You can see him breathing, can't you? Look at his belly and chest."

"But... why can't he move?" she asked.

"He's paralysed," I told her. "The spider injected him with poison which stops his limbs working. It's like putting him to sleep, except his brain's still active and he can see and hear everything."

I didn't know if this was true. I hoped it was. If the poison had left the heart and lungs alone, it might also have skipped his brain. But if it had got into his skull...

The thought was too terrible to consider.

"Steve, I'm going to help you up," I said. "I think if we move you around, the poison will wear off."

I stuck my arms around Steve's waist and hauled him to his feet. He was heavy but I took no notice of the weight. I dragged him around the room, shaking his arms and legs, talking to him as I went, telling him he was going to be all right, there wasn't enough poison in one bite to kill him, he would recover.

After ten minutes of this, there was no change and I was too tired to carry him any longer. I dropped him on the bed, then carefully arranged his body so he would be comfortable. His eyelids were open. They looked weird and were scaring me, so I closed them, but then he looked like a corpse, so I opened them again.

"Will he be all right?" Annie asked.

"Of course he will," I said, trying to sound positive. "The poison will wear off after a while and he'll be right as rain. It's only a matter of time."

I don't think she believed me but she said nothing, only sat on the edge of the bed and watched Steve's face like a hawk. I began wondering why Mum hadn't been up to investigate. I crept over to the open door and listened at the top of the stairs. I could hear the washing machine rumbling in the kitchen below. That explained it: our washing machine is old and clunky. You can't hear anything over the noise it makes if you're in the kitchen and it's turned on.

Annie was no longer on the bed when I returned. She was down on the floor, studying Madam Octa.

"It's the spider from the freak show, isn't it?" she asked.

"Yes," I admitted.

"The poisonous one?"

"Yes."

"How did you get it?" she asked.

"That's not important," I said, blushing.

"How did she get loose?" Annie asked.

"I let her out," I said.

"You *what*?!"

"It wasn't the first time," I told her. "I've had her for nearly two weeks. I've played with her lots of times. It's perfectly safe as long as there are no noises. If you hadn't come barging in when you did, she would have been— "

119

"No you don't," she growled. "You aren't laying the blame on me. Why didn't you tell me about her? If I'd known, I wouldn't have come busting in."

"I was going to," I said. "I was waiting until I was sure it was safe. Then Steve came and… " I couldn't continue.

I stuck the cage back in the wardrobe, where I wouldn't have to look at Madam Octa. I joined Annie by the bed and studied Steve's motionless form. We sat silently for almost an hour, just watching.

"I don't think he's going to recover," she finally said.

"Give it more time," I pleaded.

"I don't think time will help," she insisted. "If he was going to recover, he should be moving a bit by now."

"What do *you* know about it?" I asked roughly. "You're a child. You know nothing!"

"That's right," she agreed calmly. "But *you* don't know any more about it than me, do you?" I shook my head unhappily. "So stop pretending you do," she said.

She laid a hand on my arm and smiled bravely to show she wasn't trying to make me feel bad. "We have to tell Mum," she said. "We have to get her up here. She might know what to do."

"And if she doesn't?" I asked.

"Then we have to take him to a hospital," Annie said.

I knew she was right. I'd known it all along. I just didn't want to admit it.

"Let's give it another quarter of an hour," I said. "If he hasn't moved by then, we call her."

"A quarter of an hour?" she asked uncertainly.

"Not a minute more," I promised.

"OK," she agreed.

We sat in silence again and watched our friend. I thought about Madam Octa and how I was going to explain this to Mum.

To the doctors. To the *police*! Would they believe me when I told them Mr Crepsley was a vampire? I doubted it. They'd think I was lying. They might throw me in jail. They might say, since the spider was mine, I was to blame. They might charge me with murder and lock me away!

I checked my watch. Three minutes to go. No change in Steve.

"Annie, I need to ask a favour," I said.

She looked at me suspiciously. "What?"

"I don't want you to mention Madam Octa," I said.

"Are you crazy?" she shouted. "How else are you going to explain what's happened?"

"I don't know," I admitted. "I'll tell them I was out of the room. The bite marks are tiny. They look like small bee stings and are going down all the time. The doctors might not even notice them."

"We can't do that," Annie said. "They might need to examine the spider. They might— "

"Annie, if Steve dies, I'll be blamed," I said softly. "There are parts to this I can't tell you, that I can't tell anybody. All I can say is, if the worst happens, I'll be left carrying the can. Do you know what they do to murderers?"

"You're too young to be tried for murder," she said, but sounded uncertain.

"No, I'm not," I told her. "I'm too young to go to a real prison but they have special places for children. They'd hold me in one of those until I turned eighteen and then... Please, Annie." I started to cry. "I don't want to go to jail."

She started crying too. We held onto each other and sobbed like a couple of babies. "I don't want them to take you away," she wept. "I don't want to lose you."

"Then do you promise not to tell?" I asked. "Will you go back to your bedroom and pretend you saw and heard none of this?"

She nodded sadly. "But not if I think the truth can save him," she added. "If the doctors say they can't save him unless they find what bit him, I'm telling. OK?"

"OK," I agreed.

She got to her feet and headed for the door. She stopped in the middle of the room, turned, came back and kissed me on the forehead. "I love you, Darren," she said, "but you were a fool to bring that spider into this house, and if Steve dies, I think you *are* the one who should be blamed."

Then she ran from the room, sobbing.

I waited a few minutes, holding Steve's hand, begging him to recover, to show some sign of life. When my prayers weren't answered, I got to my feet, opened the window (to explain how the mystery attacker got in), took a deep breath, then ran downstairs, screaming for my mother.

CHAPTER TWENTY-TWO

THE AMBULANCE nurses asked my mother if Steve was diabetic or epileptic. She wasn't sure but didn't think so. They also asked about allergies and the like, but she explained that she wasn't his mother and didn't know.

I thought they'd take us with them in the ambulance, but they said there wasn't room. They got the number of Steve's phone and the name of his mum, but she wasn't home. One of the nurses asked my mother if she'd drive after them to hospital, to fill in as many of the forms as she could, so they could make a start. She agreed and bundled me and Annie into the car. Dad still wasn't home, so she rang him on his mobile to explain where we'd be. He said he'd come straight over.

That was a miserable ride. I sat in the back, trying not to meet Annie's eye, knowing I should tell the truth, but too afraid to. What made it even worse was, I knew if *I* was the one lying in a coma, Steve would own up immediately.

"What happened in there?" Mum asked over her shoulder. She was driving as fast as she could without breaking the speed limit, so wasn't able to look back at me. I was glad: I don't think I could have lied straight to her face.

"I'm not sure," I said. "We were chatting. Then I had to go to the toilet. When I got back..."

"You didn't see anything?" she asked.

"No," I lied, feeling my ears reddening with shame.

"I can't understand it," she muttered. "He felt so stiff and his skin was turning blue. I thought he was dead."

"I think he was bitten," Annie said. I nearly gave her a dig in the ribs, but at the last second remembered I was depending on her to keep my secret.

"Bitten?" Mum asked.

"There were a couple of marks on his neck," Annie said.

"I saw them," Mum said. "But I don't think that's it, dear."

"Why not?" Annie asked. "If a snake or a... *spider* got in and bit him..." She glanced over at me and blushed a little, recalling her promise.

"A spider?" Mum shook her head. "No, dear, spiders don't go around biting people and sending them into shock, not around here."

"So what was it?" Annie asked.

"I'm not sure," Mum replied. "Maybe he ate something that didn't agree with him, or had a heart attack."

"Children don't have heart attacks," Annie snorted.

"They do," Mum said. "It's rare, but it can happen. Still, the doctors will sort all that out. They know more about these things than we do."

I wasn't used to hospitals, so I spent some time looking around while Mum was filling in the forms. It was the whitest place I'd ever seen: white walls, white floors, white uniforms. It wasn't very busy but there was a buzz to the place, a sound of bed springs and coughing, machines humming, knives slicing, doctors speaking softly.

We didn't say much while sitting there. Mum said Steve had

been admitted and was being examined but it might be a while before they discovered what was wrong. "They sounded optimistic," she said.

Annie was thirsty, so Mum sent me with her to get drinks from the machine round the corner. Annie glanced around while I was putting in the coins, to make sure nobody could overhear.

"How long are you going to wait?" she asked.

"Until I hear what they have to say," I told her. "We'll let them examine him. Hopefully they'll know what sort of poison it is and be able to cure him by themselves."

"And if they can't?" she asked.

"Then I tell them," I promised.

"What if he dies before that?" she asked softly.

"He won't," I said.

"But what if— "

"He won't!" I snapped. "Don't talk like that. Don't even *think* like that. We have to hope for the best. We must believe he will pull through. Mum and Dad have always told us good thoughts help make sick people better, haven't they? He needs us to believe in him."

"He needs the truth more," she grumbled, but let the matter drop. We took the drinks back to the bench and drank in silence.

Dad arrived not long after, still in his work clothes. He kissed Mum and Annie and squeezed my shoulder manfully. His dirty hands left grease marks on my T-shirt, but that didn't bother me.

"Any news?" he asked.

"None yet," Mum said. "They're examining him. It could be hours before we hear anything."

"What happened to him, Angela?" Dad asked.

"We don't know yet," Mum said. "We'll have to wait and see."

"I hate waiting," Dad grumbled, but since he had no other choice, he had to, the same as the rest of us.

Nothing further happened for a couple of hours, until Steve's mum arrived. Her face was white like Steve's, and her lips were pinched together. She made straight for me, grabbed me by the shoulders and shook me hard. "What have you done to him?" she screeched. "Have you hurt my boy? Have you killed my Steve?"

"Here! Stop that!" Dad gasped.

Steve's mum ignored him. "What have you done?" she screamed again, and shook me even harder. I tried to say "Nothing" but my teeth were clattering. "What have you done? What have you done?" she repeated, then suddenly stopped shaking me, let go and collapsed to the floor, where she bawled like a baby.

Mum got off the bench and crouched beside Mrs Leonard. She stroked the back of her head and whispered kind words to her, then helped her up and sat down with her. Mrs Leonard was still crying, and was now moaning about what a bad mother she'd been and how much Steve hated her.

"You two go and play somewhere else," Mum said to Annie and me. We started away. "Darren," Mum called me back. "Don't take any notice of what she was saying. She doesn't blame you. She's just afraid."

I nodded miserably. What would Mum say if she knew Mrs Leonard was right and I *was* to blame?

Annie and me found a couple of arcade games which kept us busy. I didn't think I'd be able to play but after a few minutes I forgot about Steve and the hospital and got caught up in the games. It was nice to slip away from the worries of the real world for a while, and if I hadn't run out of coins, I might have stayed there all night.

When we returned to our chairs, Mrs Leonard had calmed down and was off with Mum, filling out forms. Annie and me sat and the waiting began all over again.

Annie began yawning about ten o'clock and that set me off too. Mum took one look at us and ordered us home. I started to argue but she cut me short.

"You can't do any good here," she said. "I'll ring as soon as I hear anything, even if it's the middle of the night, OK?"

I hesitated. This would be my final chance to mention the spider. I came very close to spilling the beans, but I was tired and couldn't find the words. "OK," I said glumly, then left.

Dad drove us home. I wondered what he'd do if I told him about the spider, Mr Crepsley and the rest. He would have punished me, I'm sure, but that's not why I didn't tell him: I kept quiet because I knew he'd be ashamed of the way I'd lied and put my own well-being before Steve's. I was afraid he'd hate me.

Annie was asleep by the time we got home. Dad lifted her in from the back seat and took her to bed. I walked slowly up to my room and got undressed. I kept cursing myself under my breath.

Dad looked in as I was putting my clothes away. "Will you be OK?" he asked. I nodded. "Steve will recover," he said. "I'm sure of it. The doctors know their stuff. They'll bring him round."

I nodded again, not trusting myself to answer. Dad stood in the doorway a moment longer, then sighed, left, and stomped downstairs to his study.

I was hanging my trousers up in the wardrobe when I noticed Madam Octa's cage. Slowly, I pulled it out. She was lying in the middle, breathing easily, calm as ever.

I studied the colourful spider and wasn't impressed by what I saw. She was bright, yes, but ugly and hairy and nasty. I began to hate her. She was the real villain, the one who bit Steve for no good reason. I had fed her and cared for her and played with her. This was how she repaid me.

"You bloody monster!" I snarled, shaking the cage. "You ungrateful creep!"

I gave the cage another shake. Her legs gripped the bars tightly. This made me madder and I yanked the cage roughly from side to side, trying to make her lose her grip, hoping to hurt her.

I spun about in a circle, whirling the cage around by the handle. I was cursing, calling her every name under the sun, wishing she was dead, wishing I'd never set eyes on her, wishing I had the guts to take her out of the cage and squeeze her to death.

Finally, as my rage reached bursting point, I hurled the cage as far away from me as possible. I wasn't looking where I was throwing, and got a shock when I saw it sail through the open window and out into the night.

I watched it flying away, then hurried after it. I was scared it would hit the ground and break open, because I knew if the doctors weren't able to save Steve by themselves, they might be able to with the help of Madam Octa: if they studied her, they might find out how to cure him. But if she escaped...

I rushed to the window. I was too late to grab for the cage but at least I could see where it landed. I watched as it floated out and down, praying it wouldn't break. It seemed to take ages to fall.

Just before it hit the ground, a hand darted out from the shadows of the night and snatched it from the air.

A hand?!?

I leaned forward quickly for a better view. It was a dark night and at first I couldn't see who was down there. But then the person stepped forward and all was revealed.

First, I saw his wrinkly hands holding the cage. Then his long red clothes. Then his cropped orange hair. Then his long ugly scar. And, finally, his sharp toothy grin.

It was *Mr Crepsley*. The *vampire*.

And he was smiling up at me!

CHAPTER TWENTY-THREE

I STOOD by the window, expecting him to turn into a bat and come flying up, but he did nothing apart from shake the cage gently to make sure Madam Octa was all right.

Then, still smiling, he turned and walked away. Within a matter of seconds he had been swallowed from sight by the night.

I shut the window and fled to the safety of my bed, where my mind turned inside-out with questions. How long had he been down there? If he knew where Madam Octa was, why hadn't he taken her before this? I thought he'd be furious, but he seemed amused. Why hadn't he ripped out my throat like Steve said he would?

Sleep was impossible. I was more terrified now than I had been the night after stealing the spider. Back then I could tell myself that he didn't know who I was and so couldn't find me.

I thought about telling Dad. After all, a vampire knew where we lived and had reason to bear a grudge against us. Dad should know. He should be warned and given a chance to prepare a defence. But...

He wouldn't believe me. Especially not now that Madam

Octa was gone. I imagined trying to convince him that vampires were real, that one had been to our house and might come back. He'd think I was a nutter.

I was able to snooze a bit when dawn rolled round, because I knew the vampire couldn't launch an attack until sunset. It wasn't much of a sleep, but even a small bit of rest did me good and I was able to think clearly when I woke. I realised, as I thought it over, that I had no reason to be afraid. If the vampire had wanted to kill me, he could have done it last night when I was unprepared. For some reason, he didn't want me dead, at least not yet.

With that worry off my mind, I could focus on Steve and my real problem: whether to reveal the truth or not. Mum had stayed at the hospital all night, taking care of Mrs Leonard, ringing round to let friends and neighbours know of Steve's illness. If she had been home, I might have told her, but the thought of telling Dad filled me with dread.

Ours was a very quiet house that Sunday. Dad cooked eggs and sausages for breakfast, and burned them as he normally does when he cooks, but we didn't complain. I hardly even tasted the food as I gulped it down. I wasn't hungry. The only reason I ate was to pretend it was any other average Sunday.

Mum rang as we were finishing. She had a long talk with Dad. He didn't say much, only nodded and grunted. Annie and I sat still, trying to hear what was being said. He came in and sat down when he was finished talking.

"How is he?" I asked.

"Not good," Dad said. "The doctors don't know what to make of it. It seems Annie was right: it is poison. But not like any they know. They've sent samples to experts in other hospitals, and hopefully one of them will know more about it. But… " He shook his head.

"Will he die?" Annie asked quietly.

"Maybe," Dad said, being honest. I was glad of that. All too often adults lie to kids about serious matters. I'd rather know the truth about death than be lied to.

Annie started to cry. Dad picked her up and perched her on his lap. "Hey, now, there's no need to cry," he said. "It's not over yet. He's still alive. He's breathing and his brain doesn't seem to have been affected. If they can figure out a way to fight the poison in his body, he should be fine."

"How long does he have?" I asked.

Dad shrugged. "The way he is, they could keep him alive for ages with machines."

"You mean like someone in a coma?" I asked.

"Exactly."

"How long before they have to start using machines?" I asked.

"A few days, they think," Dad answered. "They can't say for sure, seeing as how they don't know what they're dealing with, but they think it will be a couple of days before his respiratory and coronary systems begin to shut down."

"His what?" Annie asked between sobs.

"His lungs and heart," Dad explained. "As long as those are working, he's alive. They have to use a drip to feed him but otherwise he's OK. It's when – *if* – he stops breathing by himself that the trouble really begins."

A couple of days. It wasn't much. The day before, he'd had a whole lifetime to look forward to. Now he had a couple of days.

"Can I go see him?" I asked.

"This afternoon, if you feel up to it," Dad said.

"I'll feel up to it," I vowed.

The hospital was busier this time, packed with visitors. I'd never seen so many boxes of chocolates and flowers. Everybody seemed to be carrying one or the other. I wanted to buy something for Steve at the hospital shop but had no money.

I expected Steve to be on the children's ward but he was in a room by himself, because the doctors wanted to study him, and also because they weren't sure if what he had was catching. We had to wear masks and gloves and long green gowns when we entered.

Mrs Leonard was asleep in a chair. Mum made a sign for us to be quiet. She gave us a hug, one by one, then spoke to Dad.

"A couple of results have come in from other hospitals," she told him, her voice muffled by the mask. "All negative."

"Surely *someone* knows what this is," Dad said. "How many different types of poison can there be?"

"Thousands," she said. "They've sent specimens to foreign hospitals. Hopefully one of them will have a record of it, but it's going to be some time before they get back to us."

I studied Steve while they were talking. He was tucked neatly into the bed. A drip was attached to one arm, and wires and stuff to his chest. There were needle marks where doctors had taken samples of his blood. His face was white and stiff. He looked terrible!

I started crying and couldn't stop. Mum put her arms around me and hugged me tight, but that only made it worse. I tried telling her about the spider but I was crying too much for my words to be heard. Mum kept hugging and kissing and shushing me, and eventually I quit trying.

New visitors arrived, relatives of Steve's, and Mum decided to leave them alone with him and his mother. She led us out, removed my mask and wiped the tears from my face with a tissue.

"There," she said. "That's better." She smiled and tickled me until I grinned back. "He'll be OK," she promised. "I know he looks bad, but the doctors are doing all they can. We have to trust them and hope for the best, OK?"

"OK," I sighed.

"I thought he looked quite good," Annie said, squeezing my hand. I smiled thankfully at her.

"Are you coming home now?" Dad asked Mum.

"I'm not sure," she said. "I think I should stick around a little longer in case— "

"Angela, you've done enough for the time being," Dad said firmly. "I bet you didn't get any sleep last night, did you?"

"Not much," Mum admitted.

"And if you stay on now, you won't get any today either. Come on, Angie, let's go." Dad calls Mum "Angie" when he's trying to sweet-talk her into something. "There are other people who can look after Steve and his mum. Nobody expects you to do everything."

"All right," she agreed. "But I'm coming back tonight to see if they need me."

"Fair enough," he said, and led the way out to the car. It hadn't been much of a visit but I didn't complain. I was glad to get away.

I thought about Steve as we drove home, how he looked and *why* he looked that way. I thought about the poison in his veins and felt pretty sure the doctors would fail to cure it. I bet no doctor in the world had ever come across poison from a spider like Madam Octa before.

However bad Steve had looked today, I knew he'd look a lot worse after another couple. I imagined him hooked up to a breathing machine, his face covered with a mask, tubes sticking into him. It was a horrible thought.

There was only one way to save Steve. Only one person who might know about the poison and how to beat it.

Mr Crepsley.

As we pulled into the drive back home and got out of the car, I made up my mind: I was going to track him down and make him do what he could to help Steve. As soon as it got dark, I'd sneak out and find the vampire, wherever he might be. And if I couldn't force it out of him and come back with a cure...

...I wouldn't come back at all.

CHAPTER TWENTY-FOUR

I HAD to wait until nearly eleven o'clock. I would have gone earlier, while Mum was at the hospital, but a couple of Dad's pals came round with kids of their own and I had to play host.

Mum returned home about ten. She was tired, so Dad quickly cleared the house of visitors. They had a cup of tea and a chat in the kitchen, then went up to bed. I let them drift off to sleep, then snuck downstairs and let myself out the back door.

I sped through the dark like a comet. Nobody saw or heard me, I moved so fast. I had a cross in one pocket, which I'd found in Mum's jewellery box, and a bottle of holy water in the other, which one of Dad's pen friends had sent to us years ago. I wasn't able to find a stake. I'd thought about bringing a sharp knife instead, but probably would only have cut myself. I'm clumsy with knives.

The old theatre was pitch black and deserted. I used the front door this time.

I didn't know what I'd do if the vampire wasn't here, but somehow I sensed he would be. It was like the day Steve threw the scraps of paper up in the air with the winning ticket hidden amongst them, and I shut my eyes and reached out blindly. It was *destiny*.

It took a while to find the cellar. I'd brought a torch but the battery was almost dead and it flickered out after a couple of minutes, leaving me to grope through the dark like a mole. When I did find the steps, I started straight down, not giving fear time to catch up.

The further down I went, the brighter it got, until I reached the bottom and saw five tall flickering candles. I was surprised – weren't vampires supposed to be afraid of fire? – but glad.

Mr Crepsley was waiting for me at the other end of the cellar. He was sitting at a small table, playing a game of cards with himself.

"Good morning, Master Shan," he said, without looking up.

I cleared my throat before replying. "It's not morning," I said. "It's the middle of the night."

"To me, that is morning," he said, then looked up and grinned. His teeth were long and sharp. This was the closest to him I'd been and I expected to spot all sorts of details – red teeth, long ears, narrow eyes – but he looked like a normal human, albeit a tremendously ugly one.

"You've been waiting for me, haven't you?" I asked.

"Yes," he nodded.

"How long have you known where Madam Octa was?"

"I found her the night you stole her," he said.

"Why didn't you take her then?"

He shrugged. "I was going to, but I got to thinking about the sort of boy who would dare steal from a vampire, and I decided you might be worth further study."

"Why?" I asked, trying to stop my knees from knocking together.

"Why indeed?" he replied mockingly. He clicked his fingers and the cards on the table jumped together and slid back into the packet by themselves. He put it away and cracked his knuckles.

"Tell me, Darren Shan, why have you come? Is it to steal from me again? Do you still desire Madam Octa?"

I shook my head. "I never want to see that monster again!" I snarled.

He laughed. "She will be so sad to hear that."

"Don't make fun of me," I warned him. "I don't like being teased."

"No?" he asked. "And what will you do if I continue?"

I pulled out the cross and bottle of holy water and held them up. "I'll strike you with these!" I roared, expecting him to fall back, frozen with fear. But he didn't. Instead he smiled, clicked his fingers again, and suddenly the cross and plastic bottle were no longer in my hands. They were in *his*.

He studied the cross, chuckled and squeezed it into a little ball, as though it was made of tinfoil. Next he uncorked the holy water and drank it.

"You know what I love?" he asked. "I love people who watch lots of horror movies and read horror books. Because they believe what they read and hear, and come packing silly things like crosses and holy water, instead of weapons which could do real damage, like guns and hand grenades."

"You mean... crosses don't... hurt you?" I stammered.

"Why should they?" he asked.

"Because you're... evil," I said.

"Am I?" he asked.

"Yes," I said. "You must be. You're a vampire. Vampires are evil."

"You should not believe everything you are told," he said. "It is true that our appetites are rather exotic. But just because we drink blood does not mean that we are evil. Are vampire bats evil when they drink the blood of cows and horses?"

"No," I said. "But that's different. They're animals."

"Humans are animals too," he told me. "If a vampire kills

a human, then yes, he is evil. But one who just takes a little blood to fill his rumbling belly… Where is the harm in that?"

I couldn't answer. I was numb and no longer knew what to believe. I was at his mercy, alone and defenceless.

"I see you are not in the mood for a debate," he said. "Very well. I will save the speeches for another time. So tell me, Darren Shan: what is it you want if not my spider?"

"She bit Steve Leonard," I told him.

"The one known as Steve Leopard," he said, nodding. "A nasty business. Still, little boys who play with things they do not understand can hardly complain if— "

"I want you to make him better!" I yelled, interrupting.

"*I?*" he asked, acting surprised. "But I am not a doctor. I am not a specialist. I am just a circus performer. A freak. Remember?"

"No," I said. "You're more. I know you can save him. I know you have the power."

"Maybe," he said. "Madam Octa's bite is deadly, but for every poison there exists an antidote. Maybe I do have the cure. Maybe I have a bottle of serum which will restore your friend's natural physical functions."

"Yes!" I shouted gleefully. "I knew it! I knew it! I— "

"But maybe," Mr Crepsley said, raising a long bony finger to silence me, "it is a small bottle. Maybe there is only a tiny amount of serum. Maybe it is very precious. Maybe I want to save it for a real emergency, in case Madam Octa ever bites *me*. Maybe I do not want to waste it on an evil little brat."

"No," I said softly. "You have to give it to me. You have to use it on Steve. He's dying. You can't let him die."

"I most certainly can," Mr Crepsley laughed. "What is your friend to me? You heard him the night he was here: he said he would become a vampire hunter when he grew up!"

"He didn't mean it," I gasped. "He only said that because he was angry."

"Perhaps," Mr Crepsley mused, tugging at his chin and stroking his scar. "But again, I ask: why should I save Steve Leopard? The serum was expensive and cannot be replaced."

"I can pay for it," I cried, and that was what he had been waiting for. I saw it in his eyes, the way they narrowed, the way he hunched forward, smiling. This was why he hadn't taken Madam Octa that first night. This was why he hadn't left town.

"Pay for it?" he asked slyly. "But you are only a boy. You cannot possibly have enough money to buy the cure."

"I'll pay in bits," I promised. "Every week for fifty years, or as long as you want. I'll get a job when I grow up and give you all my money. I swear."

He shook his head. "No," he said softly. "Your money does not interest me."

"What *does* interest you?" I asked in a low voice. "I'm sure you have a price. That's why you waited for me, isn't it?"

"You are a clever young man," he said. "I knew that when I woke up to find my spider gone and your note in her place. I said to myself, 'Larten, there goes a most remarkable child, a true prodigy. There goes a boy who is going places'."

"Quit with the bull and tell me what you want," I snarled.

He laughed nastily, then grew serious. "You remember what Steve Leopard and I talked about?" he asked.

"Of course," I replied. "He wanted to become a vampire. You said he was too young, so he said he'd become your assistant. That was all right by you, but then you found out he was evil, so you said no."

"That about sums it up," he agreed. "Except, if you recall, I was not too keen on the idea of an assistant. They can be useful but also a burden."

"Where's all this leading?" I asked.

"I have had a rethink since then," he said. "I decided it might not be such a bad thing after all, especially now that I have been separated from the Cirque Du Freak and will have to fend for myself. An assistant could be just what the witch doctor ordered." He smiled at his little joke.

I frowned. "You mean you'll let Steve become your assistant now?"

"Heavens, no!" he yelped. "That monster? There is no telling what he will do as he matures. No, Darren Shan, I do not want Steve Leopard to be my assistant." He pointed at me with his long bony finger again, and I knew what he was going to say seconds before he said it.

"You want *me!*" I sighed, beating him to the punch, and his dark, sinister smile told me I was right.

CHAPTER TWENTY-FIVE

"YOU'RE CRAZY!" I yelled, stumbling backwards. "There's no way I'd become your assistant! You must be mad to even think such a thing!"

Mr Crepsley shrugged. "Then Steve Leopard dies," he said simply.

I stopped retreating. "Please," I begged, "there must be another way."

"The issue is not open to debate," he said. "If you wish to save your friend, you must join me. If you refuse, we have nothing further to discuss."

"What if I— "

"Do not waste my time!" he snapped, pounding on the table. "I have lived in this dirty hole for two weeks, putting up with fleas and cockroaches and lice. If you are not interested in my offer, say so and I will leave. But do not waste my time with other options, because there are none."

I nodded slowly and took a few steps forward. "Tell me more about being a vampire's assistant," I said.

He smiled. "You will be my travelling companion," he explained. "You will travel with me across the world. You will be my eyes and hands during the day. You will guard me while I sleep. You will find food for me if it is scarce. You will take my clothes to the laundry. You will polish my shoes. You will look after Madam Octa. In short, you will see to my every need. In return, I will teach you the ways of the vampires."

"Do I *have* to become a vampire?" I asked.

"Eventually," he said. "At first you will only have some vampire powers. I will make you a half-vampire. That means you will be able to move about during the day. You will not need much blood to keep you ticking over. You will have certain powers but not all. And you will only age at a fifth the regular rate, instead of the full vampire's tenth."

"What does that mean?" I asked, confused.

"Vampires do not live forever," he explained, "but we do live far longer than humans. We age about one-tenth the regular rate. Which means, for every ten years that pass, we age one. As a half-vampire, you will age one year for every five."

"You mean, for every five years that pass, I'll only be one year older?" I asked.

"That is right."

"I dunno," I muttered. "It sounds dodgy to me."

"It is your choice," he said. "I cannot force you to become my assistant. If you decide it is not to your liking, you are free to leave."

"But Steve will die if I do that!" I cried.

"Yes," he agreed. "It is your assistance or his life."

"That's not much of a choice," I grumbled.

"No," he admitted, "it is not. But it is the only one on offer. Do you accept?"

I thought it over. I wanted to say no, run away and never return. But if I did, Steve would die. Was he worth such a deal? Did I feel guilty enough to offer my life for his? The answer was:

Yes.

"OK," I sighed. "I don't like it, but my hands are tied. I just want you to know this: if I ever get the chance to betray you, I will. If the opportunity arises to pay you back, I'll take it. You'll never be able to trust me."

"Fair enough," he said.

"I mean it," I warned him.

"I know you do," he said. "That is why I want you. A vampire's assistant must have spirit. Your fighting quality is exactly what drew me to you. You will be a dangerous lad to have around, I am sure, but in a fight, when the chips are down, I am just as sure you will be a worthy ally."

I took a deep breath. "How do we do it?" I asked.

He stood and pushed the table aside. Stepped forward until he was about half a metre away. He seemed tall as a building. There was a foul smell to him that I hadn't noticed before, the smell of *blood*.

He raised his right hand and showed me the back of it. His nails weren't especially long but they looked sharp. He raised his left hand and pressed the nails of the right into the fleshy tips of his left-hand fingers. Then he used his other set of nails to mark the right-hand fingers in the same way. He winced as he did it.

"Lift your hands," he grunted. I was watching the blood drip from his fingers and didn't obey the command. "Now!" he yelled, grabbing my hands and jerking them up.

He dug his nails into the soft tips of my fingers, all ten of them at once. I cried out with pain and fell back, tucking my hands in at my sides, rubbing them against my jacket.

"Do not be such a baby," he jeered, tugging my hands free.

"It hurts!" I howled.

"Of course it does," he laughed. "It hurt me too. Did you think becoming a vampire was easy? Get used to the pain. Much of it lies ahead."

He put a couple of my fingers in his mouth and sucked some blood out. I watched as he rolled it around his mouth, testing it. Finally he nodded and swallowed. "It is good blood," he said. "We can proceed."

He pressed his fingers against mine, wound to wound. For a few seconds there was a numb feeling at the ends of my arms. Then I felt a gushing sensation and realised my blood was moving from my body to his through my left hand, while his blood was entering mine through my right.

It was a strange, tingling feeling. I felt his blood travel up my right arm, then down the side of my body and over to the left. When it reached my heart there was a stabbing pain and I nearly collapsed. The same thing was happening to Mr Crepsley and I could see him grinding his teeth and sweating.

The pain lasted until Mr Crepsley's blood crept down my left arm and started flowing back into his body. We remained joined a couple more seconds, until he broke free with a shout. I fell backwards to the floor. I was dizzy and felt sick.

"Give me your fingers," Mr Crepsley said. I looked across and saw him licking his. "My spit will heal the wounds. You will lose all your blood and die otherwise."

I glanced down at my hands and saw blood leaking out. Stretching them forth, I let the vampire put them in his mouth and run his rough tongue over the tips.

When he released them, the flow had stopped. I wiped the leftover blood off on a rag. I studied my fingers and noted they now had ten tiny scars running across them.

"That is how you recognise a vampire," Mr Crepsley told me. "There are other ways to change a human but the fingers are the simplest and least painful method."

"Is that it?" I asked. "Am I a half-vampire now?"

"Yes," he said.

"I don't feel any different," I told him.

"It will take a few days for the effects to become apparent," he said. "There is always a period of adjustment. The shock would be too great otherwise."

"How do you become a full vampire?" I asked.

"The same way," he said, "only you stay joined longer, so more of the vampire's blood enters your body."

"What will I be able to do with my new powers?" I asked. "Will I be able to change into a bat?"

His laughter rocked the room. "A bat!" he shrieked. "You do not believe those silly stories, do you? How on Earth could somebody the size of you or I turn into a tiny flying rat? Use your brain, boy. We can no more turn into bats, rats or fog than we can turn into ships, planes or monkeys!"

"So what can we do?" I asked.

He scratched his chin. "There is too much to explain right now," he said. "We must tend to your friend. If he does not get the antidote before tomorrow morning, the serum will not work. Besides, we have plenty of time to discuss secret powers." He grinned. "You could say we have all the time in the world."

CHAPTER TWENTY-SIX

MR CREPSLEY led the way up the stairs and out of the building. He walked confidently through the darkness. I thought I could see a bit better than I could when coming in, but that might just have been because my eyes were used to the dark, not because of the vampire blood in my veins.

Once outside, he told me to hop up on his back. "Keep your arms wrapped around my neck," he said. "Do not let go or make any sudden movements."

As I was getting up, I looked down and saw he was wearing slippers. I thought it was strange but didn't say anything.

When I was on his back, he started running. I didn't notice anything odd at first, but soon began to realise how fast buildings were zipping by. Mr Crepsley's legs didn't seem to be moving that quickly. Instead, it was as if the world was moving faster and we were slipping past it!

We reached the hospital in a couple of minutes. Normally it would have taken twenty minutes, and that was if you sprinted all the way.

"How did you do that?" I asked, sliding down.

"Speed is relative," he said, tugging his red cloak tight around his shoulders, pulling back into the shadows so we could not be seen, and that was all the answer he gave.

"Which room is your friend in?" he asked.

I told him Steve's room number. He looked up, counting windows, then nodded and told me to hop back up on his back. When I was in position, he walked over to the wall, took off his slippers and laid his fingers and toes against the wall. Then he shoved his nails forward, into the brick!

"Hmmm," he muttered. "It is crumbly but it will hold us. Do not panic if we slip. I know how to land on my feet. It takes a very long fall to kill a vampire."

He climbed up the wall, digging his nails in, moving a hand forward, then a foot, then the other hand and foot, one after the other. He moved quickly and within moments we were at Steve's window, crouching on the ledge, gazing in.

I wasn't sure of the time, but it was very late. Nobody was in the room apart from Steve. Mr Crepsley tried the window. It was locked. He laid the fingers of one hand beside the glass covering the latch, then clicked the fingers of his other hand.

The latch sprang open! He shoved the window up and stepped inside. I got down from his back. While he checked the door, I examined Steve. His breathing was more ragged than it had been and there were new tubes all over his body, hooked up to menacing-looking machines.

"The poison has worked rapidly," Mr Crepsley said, gazing down at him over my shoulder. "We might be too late to save him." I felt my insides turn to ice at his words.

Mr Crepsley bent over and rolled up one of Steve's eyelids. For a few long seconds he stared at the eyeball and held Steve's right-hand wrist. Finally he grunted.

"We are in time," he said, and I felt my heart lifting. "But it is a good job you did not wait any longer. A few more hours and he would have been a goner."

"Just get on with it and cure him," I snapped, not wanting to know how close to death my best friend had come.

Mr Crepsley reached into one of his many pockets and produced a small glass vial. He turned on the bedside lamp and held the bottle up to the light to examine the serum. "I must be careful," he told me. "This antidote is almost as lethal as the poison. A couple of drops too many and... " He didn't need to finish.

He tilted Steve's head to one side and told me to hold it that way. He leaned one of his nails against the flesh of Steve's neck and made a small cut. Blood oozed out. He stuck his finger over it, then removed the cork of the bottle with his other hand.

He lifted the vial to his mouth and prepared to drink. "What are you doing?" I asked.

"It must be passed on by mouth," he said. "A doctor could inject it but I do not know about needles and the like."

"Is that safe?" I asked. "Won't you pass on germs?"

Mr Crepsley grinned. "If you want to call a doctor, feel free," he said. "Otherwise, have some faith in a man who was doing this long before your grandfather was born."

He poured the serum into his mouth, then rolled it from side to side. He leaned forward and covered the cut with his lips. His cheeks bulged out, then in, as he blew the serum into Steve.

He sat back when he was finished and wiped around his mouth. He spat the last of the fluid onto the floor. "I am always afraid of swallowing that stuff by accident," he said. "One of these nights, I am going to take a course and learn how to do this the easy way."

I was about to reply, but then Steve moved. His neck flexed, then his head, then his shoulders. His arms twitched and his legs started to jerk. His face creased up and he began to moan.

"What's happening?" I asked, afraid that something had gone wrong.

"It is all right," Mr Crepsley said, putting away the bottle. "He was on the brink of death. The journey back is never a pleasant one. He will be in pain for some time, but he will live."

"Will there be any side effects?" I asked. "He won't be paralysed from the waist down or anything?"

"No," Mr Crepsley said. "He will be fine. He will feel a bit stiff and will catch colds very easily, but otherwise he will be the same as he was before."

Steve's eyes shot open suddenly and focused on me and Mr Crepsley. A puzzled look swept across his face and he tried speaking. But his mouth wouldn't work, and then his eyes went blank and closed again.

"Steve?" I called, shaking him. "Steve?"

"That is going to happen a lot," Mr Crepsley said. "He will be slipping in and out of consciousness all night. By morning he should be awake and by afternoon he will be sitting up and asking for dinner.

"Come," he said. "Let us go."

"I want to stick around a while longer, to make sure he recovers," I replied.

"You mean you want to make sure I have not tricked you," Mr Crepsley laughed. "We will come back tomorrow and you will see that he is fine. We really must go now. If we stay any— "

All of a sudden, the door opened and a nurse walked in!

"What's going on here?" she shouted, stunned to see us. "Who the hell are— "

Mr Crepsley reacted quickly, grabbed Steve's bed covers and threw them over the nurse. She fell down as she tried to remove the sheets, getting her hands stuck in their folds.

"Come," Mr Crepsley hissed, rushing to the window. "We have to leave immediately."

I stared at the hand he was holding out, then at Steve, then at the nurse, then at the open door.

Mr Crepsley lowered his hand. "I see," he said in a bleak voice. "You are going to go back on our deal." I hesitated, opened my mouth to say something, then — acting without thinking — turned and made a dash for the door!

I thought he would stop me, but he did nothing, only howled after me as I ran: "Very well. Run, Darren Shan! It will do you no good. You are a creature of the night now. You are one of us! You will be back. You will come crawling on your knees, begging for help. Run, fool, run!"

And he began to laugh.

His laughter followed me through the corridor, down the stairs and out the front door. I kept glancing over my shoulder as I ran, expecting him to swoop down on me, but there was no sign of him on the way home, not a glimpse or a smell or a sound.

All that remained of him was his laughter, which echoed through my brain like a witch's cackling curse.

CHAPTER TWENTY-SEVEN

I ACTED surprised when Mum got off the phone that Monday morning and told me Steve had recovered. She was excited and did a little dance with me and Annie in the kitchen.

"He snapped out of it by himself?" Dad asked.

"Yes," she said. "The doctors can't understand it, but nobody's complaining."

"Incredible," Dad muttered.

"Maybe it's a miracle," Annie said and I had to turn my head aside to hide my smile. Some miracle!

While Mum set off to see Mrs Leonard, I started out for school. I was half-afraid the sunlight would burn me when I left the house, but of course it didn't. Mr Crepsley had told me I would be able to move about during the day.

I wondered, from time to time, if it had been a bad dream. It seemed crazy, looking back. Deep down I knew it was real, but I tried believing otherwise, and sometimes almost did.

The part I hated most was the thought of being stuck in this body for so long. How would I explain it to Mum and Dad and everybody else? I'd look silly after a couple of years, especially at school, stuck in a class with people who looked older than me.

I went to visit Steve on Tuesday. He was sitting up, watching TV, eating a box of chocolates. He was delighted to see me and told me about his stay in hospital, the food, the games nurses brought him to play with, the presents that were piling up.

"I'll have to get bitten by poisonous spiders more often," he joked.

"I wouldn't make a habit of it if I were you," I told him. "You might not get well next time."

He studied me thoughtfully. "You know, the doctors are baffled," he said. "They don't know what made me sick and they don't know how I recovered."

"You didn't tell them about Madam Octa?" I asked.

"No," he said. "There didn't seem much point. It would have meant trouble for you."

"Thanks."

"What happened to her?" he asked. "What did you do with her after she bit me?"

"I killed her," I lied. "I got mad and stomped her to death."

"Really?" he asked.

"Really."

He nodded slowly, never taking his eyes off me. "When I first woke up," he said, "I thought I saw *you*. I must have been mistaken, because it was the middle of the night. But it was a life-like dream. I even thought I saw someone with you, tall and ugly, dressed in red, with orange hair and a long scar down the left side of his face."

I didn't say anything. I couldn't. I looked down at the floor and squeezed my hands together.

"Another funny thing," he said. "The nurse who discovered me awake swore there were two people in the room, a man and a boy. The doctors think it was her mind playing tricks and have said it doesn't matter. Strange, though, isn't it?"

"Very strange," I agreed, unable to look him in the eye.

I began noticing changes in myself over the next couple of days. I found it hard getting to sleep when I went to bed, and kept waking in the middle of the night. My hearing improved and I was able to hear people talking from far away. In school, I could listen to voices from the next two rooms, almost as if there were no walls between my class and theirs.

I began to get fitter. I was able to run about the yard during break and lunch without working up a sweat. Nobody could keep up with me. I was also more aware of my body and was able to control it. I could make a football do pretty much what I wanted, dribbling around opponents at will. I scored sixteen goals on Thursday.

I grew stronger, too. I was able to do push-ups and pull-ups now, as many as I liked. I didn't have new muscles — none that I could see — but there was a strength flowing through me which hadn't been there before. I had yet to test it properly but I believed it might be immense.

I tried hiding my new talents but it was difficult. I explained away the running and soccer skills by saying I was exercising and practising a lot more, but other things were trickier.

Like when the bell rang on Thursday at the end of lunch. The ball had just been kicked into the air by the goalie who I'd put sixteen goals past. It was coming towards me, so I stuck up my right hand to catch it. I did, but as I squeezed, my nails sunk in and burst it!

And when I was eating dinner at home that night, I wasn't concentrating. I could hear our next-door neighbours having a fight and I was listening to their argument. I was eating chips and sausages, and after a while I noticed the food was tougher than it should be. I glanced down and realised I'd bitten the head off the fork and was chewing it to pieces! Luckily, no one saw, and I was able to slip it into the dustbin as I was washing up.

Steve rang that Thursday night. He'd been let out of hospital. He was supposed to take things easy for a few days and not come in to school until after the weekend, but he said he was going crazy with boredom and had persuaded his mum to let him come tomorrow.

"You mean you *want* to come to school?" I asked, shocked.

"Sounds weird, doesn't it?" he laughed. "Normally I'm looking for an excuse to stay home. Yet now, when I have one, I want to go! But you don't know how dull it is being stuck indoors alone all the time. It was fun for a couple of days, but a whole week of it... Brrr!"

I thought of telling Steve the truth but wasn't sure how he'd take it. He had *wanted* to become a vampire. I didn't think he'd like knowing Mr Crepsley had picked me instead of him.

And telling Annie was out of the question. She hadn't mentioned Madam Octa since Steve recovered but I often found her watching me. I don't know what was going through her head, but my guess is it was something like: "Steve got better, but it wasn't because of *you*. You had the chance to save him and you didn't. You told a lie and risked his life, just so you wouldn't get into trouble. Would you have done the same if it had been *me*?"

Steve was the centre of attention that Friday. The whole class crowded round and begged for his story. They wanted to know what had poisoned him, how he'd survived, what the hospital had been like, if they'd operated on him, if he had any scars, and so on.

"I don't know what bit me," he said. "I was at Darren's house. I was sitting by the window. I heard a noise but before I could look to see what it was, I got bitten and passed out." This was the story we had agreed upon when I went to visit him at the hospital.

I felt stranger than ever that Friday. I spent the morning gazing round the classroom, feeling out of place. It seemed so pointless. "I shouldn't be here," I kept thinking. "I'm not a normal kid any more. I should be out earning my living as a vampire's assistant. What good will English, history and geography do me now? This isn't my scene."

Tommy and Alan told Steve about my skill on the football field. "He's running like the wind these days," Alan said.

"And playing like Pele," Tommy added.

"Really?" Steve asked, looking at me oddly. "What's brought on the big change, Darren?"

"There isn't any change," I lied. "I'm just on a roll. I'm lucky."

"Listen to Mr Modest!" Tommy laughed. "Mr Dalton has said he might put him forward for the under-seventeen football team. Imagine one of us playing for the under-seventeens! Nobody our age has ever made that team."

"No," Steve mused. "They haven't."

"Aw, it's just Sir talking," I said, trying to brush it aside.

"Maybe," Steve said. "*Maybe.*"

I played badly that lunch-time, on purpose. I could tell Steve was suspicious. I don't think he knew what was going on, but he sensed something was different about me. I ran slowly and missed chances I normally would have put away even without the special powers.

My ploy worked. By the end of the game he'd stopped studying my every move and was beginning to joke with me again. But then something happened which ruined everything.

Alan and me were running for the same ball. He shouldn't have been going for it, because I was closest. But Alan was a bit younger than the rest of us and sometimes acted stupidly. I thought about pulling back but I was sick of playing badly. Lunch was nearly over and I wanted to score at least one goal.

So I decided, the hell with Alan Morris. That's my ball and if he gets in my way, tough!

We clashed with each other just before reaching the ball. Alan gave a yell and went flying. I laughed, trapped the ball under my foot and turned towards goal.

The sight of blood stopped me in my tracks.

Alan had landed awkwardly and cut his left knee. It was a bad gash and blood was welling up. He had started to cry and was making no move to cover it with a tissue or scrap of cloth.

Somebody kicked the ball away from beneath my foot and set off with it. I took no notice. My eyes were focused on Alan. More specifically, on Alan's knee. More specifically still, on Alan's *blood*.

I took a step towards him. Then another. I was standing over him now, blocking the light. He gazed up and must have seen something odd in my face, because he stopped crying and stared at me uneasily.

I dropped to my knees and, before I knew what I was doing, I had covered the cut on his leg with my mouth and was sucking out his blood and gulping it down!

This went on for a few seconds. My eyes were closed and the blood filled my mouth. It tasted lovely. I'm not sure how much I would have drunk or how much harm I would have done to Alan. Luckily, I didn't get the chance to find out.

I became aware of people around me and opened my eyes. Nearly everyone had stopped playing and was staring at me in horror. I removed my lips from Alan's knee and looked around at my friends, wondering how to explain this.

Then the solution hit me and I jumped up and spread my arms. "I am the vampire lord!" I yelled. "I am the king of the undead! I will suck the blood from all of you!"

They stared at me in shock, then laughed. They thought it

was a joke! They thought I was only pretending to be a vampire.

"You're a nutter, Shan," somebody said.

"That's gross!" a girl squealed as fresh blood dripped down my chin. "You should be locked away!"

The bell rang and it was time to return to class. I was feeling pleased with myself. I thought I'd fooled everybody. But then I noticed someone near the back of the crowd and my joy faded. It was Steve, and his dark face told me he knew exactly what had happened. He hadn't been fooled at all.

He *knew*.

CHAPTER TWENTY-EIGHT

I AVOIDED Steve that evening and rushed straight home. I was confused. Why had I attacked Alan? I didn't want to drink anybody's blood. I hadn't been looking for a victim. So how come I'd jumped on him like a wild animal? And what if it happened again? And what if next time there was nobody around to stop me and I went on sucking until...

No, that was a crazy thought. The sight of blood had taken me by surprise, that was all. I hadn't been expecting it. I would learn from this experience and next time I'd be able to hold myself back.

The taste of blood was still in my mouth, so I went to the bathroom and washed it out with several glasses of water, then brushed my teeth.

I studied myself in the mirror. My face looked the same as ever. My teeth weren't any longer or sharper. My eyes and ears were the same. I had the same old body. No extra muscles, no added height, no fresh patches of hair. The only visible difference was in my nails, which had hardened and darkened.

So why was I acting so strangely?

I drew one of my nails along the glass of the mirror and

it made a long deep scratch. "I'll have to be careful of those," I thought to myself.

My attack on Alan aside, I didn't appear to be too badly off. In fact, the more I thought about it, the less dreadful it seemed. OK, it would take a long time to grow up, and I'd have to be careful if I saw fresh blood. Those were downers.

But apart from that, life should be fine. I was stronger than anybody else my age, faster and fitter. I could become an athlete or a boxer or a footballer. My age would work against me but if I was talented enough, that wouldn't matter.

Imagine: a vampire footballer! I'd make millions. I'd be on TV chat shows, people would write books about me, a film would be made of my life, and I might be asked to make a song with a famous band. Maybe I could get work in the movie business as a stuntman for other kids. Or...

My thoughts were interrupted by a knock on the door. "Who is it?" I asked.

"Annie," came the reply. "Are you finished yet? I've been waiting for ages to use the bath."

"Come in," I told her. "I'm done."

She entered. "Admiring yourself in the mirror again?" she asked.

"Of course," I grinned. "Why shouldn't I?"

"If I had a face like yours, I'd stay away from mirrors," she giggled. She had a towel wrapped around her. She turned on the bath taps and ran a hand under the water to make sure it wasn't too hot. Then she sat on the edge of the tub and studied me.

"You look strange," she said.

"I don't," I said. Then, looking in the mirror, I asked: "Do I?"

"Yeah," she said. "I don't know what it is, but there's something different about you."

"You're just imagining things," I told her. "I'm the same as I always was."

"No," she said, shaking her head. "You're definitely… " The tub began filling up, so she stopped speaking and turned aside to turn off the taps. As she was bending over, my eyes focused on the curve of her neck, and suddenly my mouth went dry.

"As I was saying, you look— " she began, turning back around.

She stopped when she saw my eyes.

"Darren?" she asked nervously. "Darren, what are— "

I raised my right hand and she went quiet. Her eyes widened and she stared silently at my fingers as I waved them slowly from side to side, then around in small circles. I wasn't sure how I was doing it, but I was hypnotising her!

"Come here," I growled, voice deeper than normal. Annie rose and obeyed. She moved as if sleepwalking, eyes blank, arms and legs stiff.

When she stopped before me, I traced the outline of her neck with my fingers. I was breathing heavily and seeing her as though through a misty cloud. My tongue slowly licked around my lips and my belly rumbled. The bathroom felt as hot as a furnace, and I could see beads of sweat rolling down Annie's face.

I walked around the back of her, my hands never leaving her flesh. I could feel the veins throbbing as I stroked them, and when I pressed down on one near the bottom of her neck, I could see it standing out, blue and beautiful, begging to be ripped open and sucked dry.

I bared my teeth and leaned forward, jaws wide open.

At the last moment, as my lips touched her neck, I caught sight of my reflection in the mirror, and thankfully that was enough to make me pause.

The face in the mirror was a twisted, unfamiliar mask, full of red eyes, sharp wrinkles and a vicious grin. I lifted my head for a closer look. It was me but at the same time it wasn't. It was like there were two people sharing one body, a normal human boy and a savage animal of the night.

As I stared, the ugly face faded and the urge to drink blood passed. I gazed at Annie, horrified. I'd been about to *bite* her! I would have *fed* on my own sister!

I fell away from her with a cry and covered my face with my hands, afraid of the mirror and what I might see. Annie staggered backwards, then looked around the bathroom in a dazed kind of way.

"What's going on?" she asked. "I feel odd. I came in for a bath, didn't I? Is it ready?"

"Yes," I said softly. "It's ready."

I was ready too. Ready to become a vampire!

"I'll leave you to get on with it," I said, and let myself out.

I fell against the wall in the hall, where I spent a couple of minutes taking deep breaths and trying to calm down.

It couldn't be controlled. The thirst for blood was something I wouldn't be able to beat. I didn't even have to see spilt blood now. Just thinking of it had been enough to bring out the monster in me.

I stumbled to my room and collapsed upon my bed. I cried as I lay there, because I knew my life as a human had come to an end. I could no longer live as plain old Darren Shan. The vampire in me could not be controlled. Sooner or later it would make me do something terrible and I would end up killing Mum or Dad or Annie.

I couldn't let that happen. I *wouldn't*. My life was no longer important, but those of my friends and family were. For their sakes, I would have to travel far away, to a place where I could do no harm.

I waited for dark to fall, then let myself out. No hanging around this time until my parents fell asleep. I didn't dare, because I knew one of them would come to my room before going to bed. I could picture it, Mum bending over to kiss me goodnight, getting the shock of her life as I bit into her neck.

I didn't leave a note or take anything with me. I wasn't able to think about such things. All I knew was, I had to get out, the sooner the better. Anything that delayed my exit was bad.

I walked quickly and was soon at the theatre. It no longer looked scary. I was used to it. Besides, vampires have nothing to fear from dark, haunted buildings.

Mr Crepsley was waiting for me inside the front door.

"I heard you coming," he said. "You lasted longer in the world of humans than I thought."

"I sucked blood from one of my best friends," I told him. "And I almost bit my younger sister."

"You escaped lightly," he said. "Many vampires kill someone close to them before realising they are doomed."

"There's no way back, is there?" I asked sadly. "No magic potion to make me human again or keep me from attacking people?"

"The only thing that can stop you now," he said, "is the good old stake through the heart."

"Very well," I sighed. "I don't like it, but I guess I've no other choice. I'm yours. I won't run away again. Do with me as you wish."

He nodded slowly. "You probably will not believe this," he said, "but I know what you are going through and I feel sorry for you." He shook his head. "But that is neither here nor there. We have work to do and cannot afford to waste time. Come, Darren Shan," he said, taking my hand. "We have much to do before you can assume your rightful place as my assistant."

"Like what?" I asked, confused.

"First of all," he said, with a sly smile, "we have to *kill you!*"

CHAPTER TWENTY-NINE

I SPENT my last weekend saying silent goodbyes. I visited every one of my favourite spots: library, swimming pool, cinema, parks, football stadium. I went to some of the places with Mum or Dad, some with Alan Morris or Tommy Jones. I would have liked to spend time with Steve but couldn't bear to face him.

I got the feeling, every so often, that I was being followed, and the hairs on the back of my neck stood on end. But whenever I turned to look, nobody was there. Eventually I put it down to nerves and ignored it.

I treated every minute with my family and friends as if it was special. I paid close attention to their faces and voices, so I would never forget. I knew I'd never see these people again and that tore me apart inside, but it was the way it had to be. There was no going back.

They could do nothing wrong that weekend. Mum's kisses didn't embarrass me, Dad's orders didn't bother me, Alan's stupid jokes didn't annoy me.

I spent more time with Annie than with anybody else. I was going to miss her the most. I gave her piggyback rides and swung her round by the arms and took her to the football stadium with me and Tommy. I even played with her dolls!

Sometimes I felt like crying. I'd look at Mum or Dad or Annie and realise how much I loved them, how empty my life would be without them. I had to turn aside at moments like that and take long, deep breaths. A couple of times that didn't work and I rushed away to cry in private.

I think they guessed something was wrong. Mum came into my room that Saturday night and stayed for ages, tucking me into bed, telling me stories, listening to me talk. It had been years since we'd spent time together like that. I felt sorry, after she'd gone, that we hadn't had more nights like this.

In the morning, Dad asked if there was anything I wanted to discuss with him. He said I was a growing lad and would be going through lots of changes, and he'd understand if I had mood swings or wanted to go off by myself. But he would always be there for me to talk to.

"*You'll* be there, but *I* won't be!" I felt like crying, but I kept quiet, nodded my head and thanked him.

I behaved as perfectly as possible. I wanted to leave a fine final impression, so they would remember me as a good son, a good brother, a good friend. I didn't want anybody thinking badly of me when I was gone.

Dad was going to take us out to a restaurant for dinner that Sunday, but I asked if we could stay home to eat. This would be my last meal with them and I wanted it to be special. When I was looking back on it in later years, I wanted to be able to remember us together, at home, a happy family.

Mum cooked my favourite food: chicken, roast potatoes, corn-on-the-cob. Annie and me had freshly squeezed orange juice to drink. Mum and Dad shared a bottle of wine. We had strawberry cheesecake for dessert. Everybody was in good form. We sang songs. Dad cracked terrible jokes. Mum played a tune with a pair of spoons. Annie recited a few poems. Everybody joined in for a game of charades.

It was a day I wished would never end. But, of course, all days must, and finally, as it always does, the sun dropped and the darkness of night crept across the sky.

Dad looked up after a while, then at his watch. "Time for bed," he said. "You two have school in the morning."

"No," I thought, "I don't. I don't have school ever again." That should have cheered me up — but all I could think was: "No school means no Mr Dalton, no friends, no football, no school trips."

I delayed going to bed as long as I could. I spent ages taking off my clothes and putting on my pyjamas; longer still washing my hands and face and teeth. Then, when it could be avoided no longer, I went downstairs to the living room, where Mum and Dad were talking. They looked up, surprised to see me.

"Are you all right, Darren?" Mum asked.

"I'm fine," I said.

"You're not feeling sick?"

"I'm fine," I assured her. "I just wanted to say goodnight." I put my arms around Dad, then kissed him on the cheek. Next I did the same with Mum. "Goodnight," I said to each.

"This is one for the books," Dad laughed, rubbing his cheek where I had kissed him. "How long since he kissed the two of us goodnight, Angie?"

"Too long," Mum smiled, patting my head.

"I love you," I told them. "I know I haven't said it very often, but I do. I love the both of you and always will."

"We love you too," Mum said. "Don't we, Dermot?"

"Of course we do," Dad said.

"Well, *tell* him," she insisted.

Dad sighed. "I love you, Darren," he said, rolling his eyes in a way he knew would make me laugh. Then he gave me a hug. "Really I do," he said, serious this time.

I left them then. I stood outside the door a while, listening to them talk, reluctant to depart.

"What do you think brought that on?" Mum asked.

"Kids," Dad snorted. "Who knows how their minds work?"

"There's something up," Mum said. "He's been acting oddly for some time now."

"Maybe he's got a girlfriend," Dad suggested.

"Maybe," Mum said, but didn't sound convinced.

I'd lingered long enough. I was afraid, if I waited any longer, I might rush into the room and tell them what was really the matter. If I did, they'd stop me from going ahead with Mr Crepsley's plan. They'd say that vampires weren't real and fight to keep me with them, in spite of the danger.

I thought of Annie and how close I'd come to biting her, and knew I must not let them stop me.

I trudged upstairs to my room. It was a warm night and the window was open. That was important.

Mr Crepsley was waiting in the wardrobe. He emerged when he heard me closing the door. "It is stuffy in there," he complained. "I feel sorry for Madam Octa, having had to spend so much time in— "

"Shut up," I told him.

"No need to be rude," he sniffed. "I was merely passing a comment."

"Well, don't," I said. "You might not think much of this place but I do. This has been my home, my room, my wardrobe, ever since I can remember. And I'm never going to see it again after tonight. This is my last little while here. So don't badmouth it, all right?"

"I am sorry," he said.

I took one long last look around the room, then sighed unhappily. I pulled a bag out from underneath the bed and handed it to Mr Crepsley. "What is this?" he asked suspiciously.

"Some personal stuff," I told him. "My diary. A picture of my family. A couple of other bits and pieces. Nothing that will be missed. Will you mind it for me?"

"Yes," he said.

"But only if you promise not to look through it," I said.

"Vampires have no secrets from each other," he said. But, when he saw my face, he tutted lightly and shrugged. "I will not open it," he promised.

"All right," I said, taking a deep breath. "Do you have the potion?" He nodded and handed over a small dark bottle. I looked inside. The liquid was dark and thick and foul-smelling.

Mr Crepsley moved behind me and laid his hands on my neck.

"You're sure this will work?" I asked nervously.

"Trust me," he said.

"I always thought a broken neck meant people couldn't walk or move," I said.

"No," he replied. "The bones of the neck do not matter. Paralysis only happens if the spinal cord – a long muscle running down the middle of the neck – breaks. I will be careful not to damage it."

"Won't the doctors think it's odd?" I asked.

"They will not check," he said. "The potion will slow your heart down so much, they will be sure you are dead. They will find the broken neck and put two and two together. If you were older, they might go ahead with an autopsy. But no doctor likes cutting a child open.

"Now, are you totally clear on what is going to happen and how you must act?" he asked.

"Yes," I said.

"There must be no mistakes," he warned. "If you make just one slip our plans will fall apart."

"I'm not a fool! I know what to do!" I snapped.

"Then do it," he said.

So I did.

With one angry gesture, I swallowed the contents of the bottle. I grimaced at the taste, then shuddered as my body started to stiffen. There wasn't much pain but an icy feeling spread through my bones and veins. My teeth began to chatter.

It took about ten minutes for the poison to work its deadly charms. At the end of that time I couldn't move any of my limbs, my lungs weren't working (well, they were, but very, very slowly) and my heart had stopped (again, not fully, but enough for its beat to be undetectable).

"I am going to snap the neck now," Mr Crepsley said, and I heard a quick clicking sound as he jerked my head to one side. I couldn't feel anything: my senses were dead. "There," he said. "That should do it. Now I am going to toss you out of the window."

He carried me over and stood there a moment with me, breathing in the night air.

"I have to toss you hard enough to make it look genuine," he said. "You might break some bones in the fall. They will start hurting when the potion wears off after a few days but I will fix them up later on.

"Here we go!"

He picked me up, paused a moment, then hurled me out and down.

I fell quickly, the house whizzing past in a blur, and landed heavily on my back. My eyes were open and I found myself staring at a drain at the foot of the house.

For a while my body went undetected, so I lay there, listening to the sounds of the night. In the end, a passing neighbour spotted me and investigated. I couldn't see his face but I heard his gasp when he turned me over and saw my lifeless body.

He rushed straight around to the front of the house and pounded on the door. I could hear his voice as he shouted for my mother and father. Then their voices as he led them round back. They thought he was pulling their leg or had been mistaken. My father was marching angrily and muttering to himself.

The footsteps stopped when they rounded the bend and saw me. For a long, terrible moment there was complete silence. Then Dad and Mum rushed forward and picked me up.

"Darren!" Mum screamed, clutching me to her chest.

"Let go, Angie," Dad shouted, prying me free and laying me down on the grass.

"What's wrong with him, Dermot?" Mum wailed.

"I don't know. He must have fallen." Dad stood and gazed up at my open bedroom window. I could see his hands flexing into fists.

"He's not moving," Mum said calmly, then grabbed me and shook me fiercely. "He's not moving!" she screamed. "He's not moving. He's— "

Dad once again eased her hands away. He beckoned our neighbour over and handed Mum to him. "Take her inside," he said softly. "Ring for an ambulance. I'll stay here and look after Darren."

"Is he... dead?" our neighbour asked. Mum moaned loudly when he said it and buried her face in her hands.

Dad shook his head softly. "No," he said, giving Mum's shoulder a light squeeze. "He's just paralysed, like his friend was."

Mum lowered her hands. "Like Steve?" she asked half-hopefully.

"Yes," Dad smiled. "And he'll snap out of it like Steve. Now go ring for help, OK?"

Mum nodded, then hurried away with our neighbour. Dad held his smile until she was out of sight, then bent over me, checked my eyes and felt my wrist for a pulse. When he found no sign of life, he laid me back down, brushed a lock of hair out of my eyes, then did something I'd never expected to see.

He started to cry.

And that was how I came to enter a new, miserable phase of my life, namely – *death*.

CHAPTER THIRTY

IT DIDN'T take the doctors long to pronounce their verdict. They couldn't find any breath or pulse or movement. It was an open-and-shut case as far as they were concerned.

The worst thing was knowing what was going on around me. I wished that I'd asked Mr Crepsley to give me another potion, which could have put me to sleep. It was terrible, hearing Mum and Dad crying, Annie screaming for me to come back.

Friends of the family began arriving after a couple of hours, the cue for more sobbing and moans.

I'd have loved to avoid this. I would have rather run away with Mr Crepsley in the middle of the night, but he'd told me that wasn't possible.

"If you run away," he'd said, "they would follow. There would be posters up everywhere, pictures in the papers and with the police. We would know no peace."

Faking my death was the only way. If they thought I was dead, I'd be free. Nobody comes searching for a dead person.

Now, as I heard the sadness, I cursed both Mr Crepsley and myself. I shouldn't have done it. I shouldn't have put them through this.

Still, looking on the bright side, at least this would be the end of it. They were sad, and would be for some time, but they would get over it eventually (I hoped). If I'd run away, the misery could have lasted forever: they might have lived the rest of their lives hoping I'd come back, searching, believing I would one day return.

The undertaker arrived and cleared the room of visitors. He and a nurse undressed me and examined my body. Some of my senses were returning and I could feel his cold hands prodding and poking me.

"He's in excellent condition," he said softly to the nurse. "Firm, fresh and unmarked. I'll have very little to do with this one. Just some rouge to make him look a little redder round the cheeks."

He rolled up my eyelids. He was a chubby, happy-looking man. I was afraid he'd spot life in my eyes but he didn't. All he did was roll my head gently from side to side, which made the broken bones in my neck creak.

"So fragile a creature is man," he sighed, then went ahead with the rest of the examination.

They took me back home that night and laid me in the living room on a long table with a large cloth spread across it, so people could come and say goodbye.

It was weird, hearing all those people discussing me as though I wasn't there, talking about my life and what I'd been like as a baby and how fine a boy I was and what a good man I would have grown up to be if I'd lived.

What a shock they'd have got if I leaped up and shouted: "*Boo!*"

Time dragged. I don't think I can explain how boring it was to lie still for hours on end, unable to move or laugh or scratch my nose. I couldn't even stare at the ceiling because my eyes were shut!

I had to be careful as feelings returned to my body. Mr Crepsley had told me this would happen, that tingles and itches would start, long before I fully recovered. I couldn't move, but if I'd made a real effort, I could have twitched a little, which might have given the game away.

The itches nearly drove me mad. I tried ignoring them but it was impossible. They were everywhere, scampering up and down my body like tiny spiders. They were worst around my head and neck, where the bones had snapped.

People finally began leaving. It must have been late, because soon the room was empty and totally silent. I lay there by myself for a time, enjoying the quiet.

And then I heard a noise.

The door to the room was opening, very slowly and very quietly.

Footsteps crossed the room and stopped by the table. My insides went cold, and it wasn't because of the potion. Who was here? For a moment I thought it might be Mr Crepsley but he had no reason to come creeping into the house. We were set to meet at a later date.

Whoever it was, he – or she – was keeping very quiet. For a couple of minutes there was no sound at all.

Then I felt hands on my face.

He raised my eyelids and shone a small torch onto my pupils. The room was too dark for me to see who he was. He grunted, lowered the lids, then pried open my mouth and laid something on my tongue: it felt like a piece of thin paper but it had a strange, bitter taste.

After removing the object from my mouth, he picked up my hands and examined the fingertips. Next there was the sound of a camera taking photos.

Finally he stuck a sharp object – it felt like a needle – into me. He was careful not to prick me in places where I would bleed, and stayed away from my vital organs. My senses had partially returned, but not fully, so the needle didn't cause much pain.

After that, he left. I heard his footsteps crossing the room, as quietly as before, then the door opening and closing, and that was that. The visitor, whoever it had been, was gone, leaving me puzzled and a little bit scared.

Early the next morning, Dad came in and sat with me. He spoke for a long time, telling me all the things he'd had planned for me, the college I would have gone to, the job he'd wanted for me. He cried a lot.

Towards the end, Mum came in and sat with him. They cried on each other's shoulders and tried to comfort themselves. They said they still had Annie and could maybe have another child or adopt one. At least it had been quick and I hadn't been in pain. And they would always have their memories.

I hated being the cause of so much hurt. I would have given anything in the world to spare them this.

There was a lot of activity later that day. A coffin was brought in and I was laid inside. A priest came and sat with the family and their friends. People streamed in and out of the room.

I heard Annie crying, begging me to stop fooling and sit up. It would have been much easier if they'd taken her away, but I guess they didn't want her to grow up feeling they'd robbed her of her chance to say goodbye to her brother.

Finally, the lid was placed on the coffin and screwed into place. I was lifted off the table and led out to the hearse. We drove slowly to church, where I couldn't hear much of what was being said. Then, with Mass out of the way, they carried me to the graveyard, where I could hear every word of the priest's speech and the sobs and moans of the mourners.

And then they buried me.

CHAPTER THIRTY-ONE

ALL SOUNDS faded away as they lowered me down the dark, dank hole. There was a jolt when the coffin hit bottom, then the rain-like sound of the first handfuls of soil being tossed upon the lid.

There was a long silence after that, until the grave diggers began shovelling the earth back into the grave.

The first few clods fell like bricks. The heavy dull thuds shook the coffin. As the grave filled and earth piled up between me and the topside world, the sounds of the living grew softer, until finally they were only faraway muffles.

At the end there were faint pounding noises, as they patted the mound of earth flat.

And then complete silence.

I lay in the quiet darkness, listening to the earth settle, imagining the sound of worms crawling towards me through the dirt. I'd thought it would be scary but it was actually quite peaceful. I felt safe down here, protected from the world.

I spent the time thinking about the last few weeks, the flyer for the freak show, the strange force that had made me close my eyes and reach blindly for the ticket, my first glimpse of the dark theatre, the cool balcony where I had watched Steve talking with Mr Crepsley.

There were so many vital moments. If I'd missed the ticket, I wouldn't be here. If I hadn't gone to the show, I wouldn't be here. If I hadn't stuck around to see what Steve was up to, I wouldn't be here. If I hadn't stolen Madam Octa, I wouldn't be here. If I'd said no to Mr Crepsley's offer, I wouldn't be here.

A world of "ifs", but it made no difference. What was done was done. If I could go back in time...

But I couldn't. The past was behind me. The best thing now would be to stop looking over my shoulder. It was time to forget the past and look to the present and future.

As the hours passed, movement returned. It came to my fingers first, which curled into fists, then slipped from my chest, where they had been crossed by the undertaker. I flexed them several times, slowly, working the itches out of my palms.

My eyes opened next but that wasn't much good. Open or closed, it was all the same down here: perfect darkness.

The feelings brought pain. My back ached from where I'd fallen out of the window. My lungs, and heart – having been out of the habit of beating – hurt. My legs were cramped, my neck was stiff. The only part of me which escaped the pain was my big right toe!

It was when I started breathing that I began to worry about the air in the coffin. Mr Crepsley had said I could survive for up to a week in my coma-like state. I didn't need to eat or use the toilet or breathe. But now that my breath was back, I became aware of the small amount of air and how quickly I was using it up.

I didn't panic. Panic would make me gasp and use more air. I remained calm and breathed softly. Lay as still as I could: movement makes you breathe more.

I had no way of knowing the time. I tried counting inside my head but kept losing track of the numbers and having to go back and start over.

I sang silent songs to myself and told stories beneath my

breath. I wished they'd buried me with a TV or a radio, but I guess there's not much call for such items among the dead.

Finally, after what seemed like several centuries stacked one on top of the other, the sounds of digging reached my ears.

He dug quicker than any human, so fast it seemed he wasn't digging at all, but rather sucking the soil out. He reached me in what must have been record time, less than a quarter of an hour. As far as I was concerned, it wasn't a moment too soon.

He knocked three times on the coffin lid, then started unscrewing it. It took a couple of minutes, then he threw the lid wide open and I found myself staring up at the most beautiful night sky I had ever seen.

I took a deep breath and sat up, coughing. It was a fairly dark night but after spending so much time underground it seemed bright as day to me.

"Are you all right?" Mr Crepsley asked.

"I feel dead tired," I grinned weakly.

He smiled at the joke. "Stand up so I can examine you," he said. I winced as I stood: I had pins and needles all over. He ran his fingers lightly up my back, then over my front. "You were lucky," he said. "No broken bones. Just a bit of bruising which will die down after a couple of days."

He pulled himself up out of the grave, then reached down and gave me a hand up. I was still pretty stiff and sore.

"I feel like a pincushion that's been squashed," I complained.

"It will take a few days for the after-effects to pass," he said. "But do not worry: you are in good shape. We are lucky they buried you today. If they had waited another day to put you under, you would be feeling much worse."

He hopped back into the grave and closed the coffin lid. When he emerged, he picked up his shovel and began tossing the earth back in.

"Do you want me to help?" I asked.

"No," he said. "You would slow me down. Go for a stroll and walk some of the stiffness out of your bones. I will call when I am ready to move on."

"Did you bring my bag?" I asked.

He nodded at a nearby headstone, from which the bag was hanging.

I got the bag and checked to see if he'd searched it. There was no sign of his having invaded my privacy, but I couldn't tell for sure. I'd just have to take him at his word. Anyway, it didn't matter much: there was nothing in my diary he didn't already know.

I went for a walk among the graves, testing my limbs, shaking my legs and arms, enjoying it. Any feeling, even pins and needles, was better than none at all.

My eyes were stronger than ever before. I was able to read names and dates on headstones from several metres away. It was the vampire blood in me. After all, didn't vampires spend their whole lives in the dark? I knew I was only a half-vampire, but all the—

Suddenly, as I was thinking about my new powers, a hand reached out from behind one of the graves, wrapped itself around my mouth, then dragged me down to the ground and out of sight of Mr Crepsley!

I shook my head and opened my mouth to scream, but then saw something that stopped me dead in my tracks. My attacker, whoever he was, had a hammer and a large wooden stake, the tip of which was pointing *directly at my heart*!

CHAPTER THIRTY-TWO

"IF YOU move even a fraction," my attacker warned, "I'll drive this right through you without blinking!"

The chilling words didn't have half as much impact on me as the familiar voice which uttered them.

"*Steve?!?*" I gasped, glancing up from the tip of the stake to find his face. It was him, sure enough, trying to look brave, but really quite terrified. "Steve, what the— " I began but he cut me short with a poke of the stake.

"Not a word!" he hissed, crouching down behind the stone pillar. "I don't want your *friend* overhearing."

"My...? Oh, you mean Mr Crepsley," I said.

"Larten Crepsley, Vur Horston," Steve sneered. "I don't care what you call him. He's a vampire. That's all that bothers me."

"What are you doing here?" I whispered.

"Vampire hunting," he growled, prodding me again with the stake. "And lookee here: seems like I found me a pair!"

"Listen," I said, more annoyed than worried (if he was going to kill me, he would have done it immediately, not sit around talking first, like they do in the movies), "if you're going to stick that thing in me, do it. If you want to talk, put it away. I'm sore enough as it is without you making new holes in me."

He stared, then pulled the stake back a few centimetres.

"Why are you here?" I asked. "How did you know to come?"

"I was following you," he said. "I followed you all weekend after seeing what you did to Alan. I saw Crepsley going into your house. I saw him toss you out the window."

"You're the one who sneaked into the living room!" I gasped, remembering the mysterious late-night visitor.

"Yes," he nodded. "The doctors were very quick to sign your death certificate. I wanted to check for myself, to see if you were still ticking."

"The piece of paper in my mouth?" I asked.

"Litmus paper," he said. "It changes colour when you stick it on a damp surface. When you stick it on a *living* body. That and the marks on the fingers tipped me off."

"You know about the marks on the fingers?" I asked, amazed.

"I read about it in a very old book," he said. "The same one, in fact, that I found Vur Horston's portrait in. There was no mention of it anywhere else, so I thought it was just another vampire myth. But then I studied your fingers and— "

He stopped and cocked his head. I realised I could no longer hear digging sounds. For a moment there was silence. Then Mr Crepsley's voice hissed across the graveyard.

"Darren, where are you?" he called. "Darren?"

Steve's face collapsed with fear. I could hear his heart beating and see the beads of sweat rolling down his cheeks. He didn't know what to do. He hadn't thought this through.

"I'm fine," I shouted, causing Steve to jump.

"Where are you?" Mr Crepsley asked.

"Over here," I replied, standing, ignoring Steve's stake. "My legs were weak, so I lay down for a minute."

"Are you all right?" he asked.

"I'm fine," I said. "I'll rest a bit more, then try them again. Give me a shout when you're ready."

I squatted back down so I was face to face with Steve. He didn't look so brave any longer. The tip of the stake was pointing down at the ground, a threat no more, and his whole body sagged miserably. I felt sorry for him.

"Why did you come here, Steve?" I asked.

"To kill you," he said.

"To *kill* me? For heaven's sake, why?" I asked.

"You're a vampire," he said. "What other reason do I need?"

"But you've nothing against vampires," I reminded him. "*You* wanted to become one."

"Yes," he snarled. "*I* wanted to, but *you're* the one who did. You planned this all along, didn't you? You told him I was evil. You made him reject me so that you could— "

"You're talking nonsense," I sighed. "I never wanted to become a vampire. I only agreed to join him in order to save your life. You would have died if I hadn't become his assistant."

"A likely story," he snorted. "To think I used to believe you were my friend. Hah!"

"I am your friend!" I cried. "Steve, you don't understand. I would never do anything to harm you. I hate what's happened to me. I only did it to— "

"Spare me the sob story," he sniffed. "How long were you planning this? You must have gone to him that night of the freak show. That's how you got Madam Octa, wasn't it? He gave her to you in return for your becoming his assistant."

"No, Steve, that's not true. You mustn't believe that." But he did believe it. I could see it in his eyes. Nothing I said was going to change his opinion. As far as he was concerned, I'd betrayed him. I had stolen the life he felt should have been his. He would never forgive me.

"I'm going now," he said, starting to crawl away. "I thought I'd be able to kill you tonight, but I was wrong. I'm too young. I'm not strong enough or brave enough.

"But heed this, Darren Shan," he said. "I'll grow. I'll get older and stronger and braver. I'm going to devote my entire life to developing my body and my mind, and when the day comes... when I'm ready... when I'm fully equipped and properly prepared...

"I'm going to hunt you down and kill you," he vowed. "I'm going to become the world's best vampire hunter and there won't be a single hole you can find that I won't be able to find too. Not a hole nor a rock nor a cellar.

"I'll track you to the ends of the Earth if I have to," he said, face glowing madly. "You and your mentor. And when I find you, I'll drive steel-tipped stakes through your hearts, then chop off your heads and fill them with garlic. Then I'll burn you to ashes and scatter you across running water. I won't take any chances. I'll make sure you never come back from the grave again!"

He paused, produced a knife, and cut a small cross into the flesh of his left palm. He held it up so I could see the blood dripping from the wound.

"On this blood, I so swear it!" he declared, then turned and ran, disappearing in seconds into the shadows of the night.

I could have run after him, following the trail of blood. If I'd called Mr Crepsley, we could have tracked him down and put an end to both Steve Leopard and his threats. It would have been the wise thing to do.

But I didn't. I couldn't. He was my friend...

CHAPTER THIRTY-THREE

MR CREPSLEY was smoothing over the mound of earth when I returned. I watched him work. The shovel was large and heavy but he handled it as if it was made out of paper. I wondered how strong he was and how strong I would one day be.

I considered telling him about Steve but was afraid he'd go after him. Steve had suffered enough. Besides, his threat was an idle one. He'd forget about me and Mr Crepsley in a few weeks, when something new grabbed his attention.

I hoped.

Mr Crepsley looked up and frowned. "Are you sure you are all right?" he asked. "You seem very uptight."

"So would you if you'd spent the day in a coffin," I replied.

He laughed out loud. "Master Shan, I have spent more time in coffins than many of the truly dead!" He gave the grave one last hard whack, then broke the shovel into little pieces and tossed them away. "Is the stiffness wearing off?" he asked.

"It's better than it was," I said, twisting my arms and waist. "I wouldn't like to fake my death too often though."

"No," he mused. "Well, hopefully it will not be necessary again. It is a dangerous stunt. Many things can go wrong."

I stared at him. "You told me I'd be safe as houses," I said.

"I lied. The potion sometimes drives its patients too far towards death and they never recover. And I could not be sure they would not perform an autopsy on you. And... Do you want to hear all this?" he asked.

"No," I said sickly. "I don't." I took an angry swing at him. He ducked out of the way easily, laughing as he did.

"You told me it was safe!" I shouted. "You lied!"

"I had to," he said. "There was no other way."

"What if I'd died?" I snapped.

He shrugged. "I would be down one assistant. No great loss. I am sure I could have found another."

"You... you... Oh!" I kicked the ground angrily. There were lots of things I could have called him but I didn't like using bad language in the presence of the dead. I'd tell him what I thought about his trickery later.

"Are you ready to go?" he asked.

"Give me a minute," I said. I jumped up on one of the taller headstones and gazed around at the town. I couldn't see much from here but this would be my last glimpse of the place where I had been born and lived, so I took my time and treated every dark alley as a posh cul-de-sac, every crumbling bungalow as a sheikh's palace, every two-storey building as a skyscraper.

"You will grow used to leaving after a time," Mr Crepsley said. He was standing on the stone behind me, perched on little more than thin air. His face was gloomy. "Vampires are always saying goodbye. We never stop anywhere very long. We are forever picking up our roots and moving on to pastures new. It is our way."

"Is the first time the hardest?" I asked.

"Yes," he said, nodding. "But it never gets easy."

"How long before I get used to it?" I wanted to know.

"Maybe a few decades," he said. "Maybe longer."

Decades. He said it as though he was talking of months.

"Can we never make friends?" I asked. "Can we never have homes or wives or families?"

"No," he sighed. "Never."

"Does it get lonely?" I asked.

"Terribly so," he admitted.

I nodded sadly. At least he was being truthful. As I've said before, I'd always rather the truth — however unpleasant it might be — than a lie. You know where you stand with the truth.

"OK," I said, hopping down. "I'm ready." I picked up my bag and dusted some graveyard dirt from it.

"You may ride on my back if you wish," Mr Crepsley offered.

"No, thank you," I replied politely. "Maybe later, but I'd rather walk the stiffness out of my legs first."

"Very well," he said.

I rubbed my belly and listened to it growl. "I haven't eaten since Sunday," I told him. "I'm hungry."

"Me too," he said. Then he took my hand in his and grinned bloodthirstily. "Let us go *eat*."

I took a deep breath and tried not to think about what would be on the menu. I nodded nervously and squeezed his hand. We turned and faced away from the graves. Then, side by side, the vampire and his assistant, we began walking...

...into the night.

DARREN SHAN

THE VAMPIRE'S ASSISTANT

THE SAGA OF DARREN SHAN

BOOK 2

For:

Granny and Grandad – tough old fogeys

OBEs (Order of the Bloody Entrails) to:
Caroline 'tracker' Paul
Paul 'the pillager' Litherland

Heads off to:
Biddy 'Jekyll' and Liam 'Hyde'
Gillie 'grave robber' Russell
The hideously creepy HarperCollins gang
and
Emma and Chris (from 'Ghouls Are Us')

INTRODUCTION

My NAME'S Darren Shan. I'm a half-vampire.

I wasn't born that way. I used to be ordinary. I lived at home with my parents and younger sister, Annie. I enjoyed school and had lots of friends.

I liked reading horror stories and watching scary movies. When a freak show came to town, my best mate, Steve Leopard, got tickets and we went. It was great, really spooky and weird. A super night out.

But the weirdest part came after the show. Steve recognized one of the characters from the show ... he'd seen a drawing of him in an old book and knew he was— a *vampire*. He stuck around after the show and asked the vampire to turn *him* into one, too! Mr Crepsley — the vampire — would have, but he found out Steve's blood was evil, and that was the end of that.

Or it *would* have been the end, except *I* stuck around, too, to see what Steve was up to.

I wanted nothing to do with vampires, but I'd always loved spiders — I used to keep them as pets — and Mr Crepsley had a poisonous performing spider, Madam Octa, which could do all sorts of great tricks. I stole her and left a note for the vampire, saying I'd tell people about him if he came after me.

To cut a long story short, Madam Octa bit Steve and he ended up in hospital. He would have died, so I went to Mr Crepsley and asked him to save Steve. He agreed, but in return *I had to become a half-vampire and travel with him as his assistant!*

I ran away after he'd turned me into a half-vampire (by pumping part of his own horrible blood into me) and saved Steve, but then I realized I was hungry for blood, and was afraid I'd do something terrible (like bite my sister) if I stayed at home.

So Mr Crepsley helped me fake my death. I was buried alive and then, in the dead of night, with no one around, he dug me up and we set off together. My days as a human were over. My nights as a vampire's assistant had begun.

CHAPTER ONE

IT WAS a dry, warm night, and Stanley Collins had decided to walk home after the Scouts' meeting. It wasn't a long walk – less than two kilometres – and though the night was dark, he knew every step of the way as surely as he knew how to tie a reef knot.

Stanley was a Scout Master. He loved the Scouts. He'd been one when he was a boy, and kept in contact when he grew up. He'd turned his three sons into first-rate Scouts and, now that they'd grown up and left home, he was helping the local kids.

Stanley walked quickly to keep warm. He was only wearing shorts and a T-shirt, and even though it was a nice night, his arms and legs were soon covered in goosebumps. He didn't mind. His wife would have a lovely cup of hot chocolate and currant buns waiting for him when he got home. He'd enjoy them all the more after a good, brisk walk.

Trees grew along both sides of the road home, making it very dark and dangerous for anyone who wasn't used to it. But Stanley had no fears. On the contrary, he loved the night. He enjoyed listening to the sound of his feet crunching through the long grass and briars.

Crunch. Crunch. Crunch.

He smiled. When his sons were young, he'd pretend there were monsters lying in wait up in the trees as they walked home. He'd make scary noises and shake the leaves of low-hanging branches when the boys weren't looking. Sometimes they'd burst into screams and run for home at top speed, and Stanley would follow after them, laughing.

Crunch. Crunch. Crunch.

If he was having trouble getting to sleep at night, he would imagine the sounds of his feet as they made their way home, and that always helped him drift off into a happy dream.

It was the nicest sound in the world, as far as Stanley was concerned, better than all the music of Mozart and Beethoven.

Crunch. Crunch. Crunch.

Snap.

Stanley stopped and frowned. That had sounded like a stick breaking, but how could it have been? He would have felt it if he'd stepped on a twig. And there were no cows or sheep in the nearby fields.

He stood still for about half a minute, listening curiously. When there were no more sounds, he shook his head and smiled. It had been his imagination playing tricks. He'd tell the wife about it when he got home and they'd have a good laugh.

He started walking again.

Crunch. Crunch. Crunch.

There. Back to the familiar sounds. There was nobody else about. He would have heard more than a single branch snapping if there was. Nobody could creep up on Stanley J. Collins. He was a trained Scout Master. His ears were as sharp as a fox's.

Crunch. Crunch. Crunch. Crunch. Cru—

Snap.

He stopped again, the fingers of fear tightening around his beating heart.

That hadn't been his imagination. He'd heard it, clear as a bell. A twig snapping, somewhere overhead. And before it snapped: had there been the slightest rustling sound, as if something was moving?

Stanley gazed up at the trees but it was too dark to see. There could have been a monster the size of a car up there and he wouldn't have been able to spot it. Ten monsters. A hundred! A thou—

Oh, that was silly. There were no monsters in the trees. Monsters didn't exist. Monsters weren't real. It was a squirrel or an owl, something ordinary like that.

Stanley raised a foot and began to bring it down.

Snap.

His foot hung in the air and his heart pounded quickly. That was no squirrel! The sound was too sharp. Something *big* was up there. Something that *shouldn't* be up there. Something that had never been there before. Something that—

Snap!

The sound was closer this time, lower down, and all of a sudden Stanley could stand it no longer. He ran.

Stanley was a large man, but fairly fit for his age. Still, it had been a long time since he'd run this fast, and after a hundred metres he was out of breath and had a stitch in his side.

He slowed to a halt and bent over, gasping for air.

Crunch.

His head shot up.

Crunch. Crunch. Crunch.

There were footsteps coming towards him! Slow, heavy footsteps. He listened, terrified, as they came closer and closer. Had the monster leapt ahead of him through the trees? Had it climbed down? Was it coming to finish him off? Was ...

Crunch. Crunch.

The footsteps stopped and Stanley was able to make out a figure. It was smaller than he'd expected, no bigger than a boy. He straightened up, gathered his courage about him like a cloak, and stepped forward for a better look.

It *was* a boy! A small, frightened-looking boy, dressed in a dirty suit.

Stanley smiled and shook his head. What a fool he'd been! The wife would have a field day when he told her about this.

"Are you OK, lad?" Stanley asked.

The boy didn't answer.

Stanley didn't recognize the youngster, but a lot of new families had moved into the area recently. He no longer knew every child in the neighbourhood.

"Can I help you?" he asked. "Are you lost?"

The boy shook his head slowly. There was something strange about him, something that made Stanley feel uneasy. It might have been the effect of the darkness and shadows, but the boy looked very pale, very thin, very ... *hungry.*

"Are you all right?" Stanley asked, stepping closer. "Can I—"

SNAP!

The sound came from directly overhead, loud and menacing.

The boy leapt back quickly, out of the way.

Stanley just had time to glance up and spot a huge red shape which might have been a bat, slashing its way down through the branches of the trees.

And then the red monster was on him. Stanley opened his mouth to scream, but before he could, the monster's hands — *claws?* — clamped over his mouth. There was a brief struggle, then Stanley was sliding to the floor, unconscious, unseeing, unknowing.

Above him, the two creatures of the night moved in for the feed.

CHAPTER TWO

"IMAGINE A man his age wearing a Scout's uniform," Mr Crepsley snorted as he turned our victim over.

"Were you ever in the Scouts?" I asked.

"They did not have them in my day," he replied.

He patted the man's meaty legs and grunted. "Plenty of blood in this one," he said.

I watched as Mr Crepsley searched the leg for a vein, then cut it open — a small slice — using one of his fingernails. As soon as blood oozed out, he clamped his mouth around the cut and sucked. He didn't believe in wasting any of the "precious red mercury", as he sometimes called it.

I stood uncertainly by his side as he drank. This was the third time I'd taken part in an attack, but I still wasn't used to the sight of the vampire sucking blood from a helpless human being.

It had been almost two months since my "death", but I was having a tough time adjusting to the change. It was hard to believe my old way of life was finished, that I was a half-vampire and could never go back. I knew I had to eventually leave my human side behind. But it was easier said than done.

Mr Crepsley lifted his head and licked his lips.

"A good vintage," he joked, shuffling back from the body. "Your turn," he said.

I took a step forward, then stopped and shook my head.

"I *can't*," I said.

"Do not be stupid," he growled. "You have shied away twice already. It is time you drank."

"I can't!" I cried.

"You have drunk animal blood," he said.

"That's different. This is a human."

"So what?" Mr Crepsley snapped. "*We* are not. You have to start treating humans the same as animals, Darren. Vampires cannot live on animal blood alone. If you do not start drinking human blood, you will grow weak. If you continue to avoid it, you will die."

"I know," I said miserably. "You've explained it to me. And I know we don't hurt those we drink from, not unless we drink too much. But ..." I shrugged unhappily.

He sighed. "Very well. It is hard, especially when you are only a half-vampire and the hunger is not so great. I will let you abstain this time. But you must feed soon. For your own sake."

He returned to the cut and cleaned away the blood – which had been leaking out while we were talking – from around the man's leg. Then he worked up a mouthful of spit and slowly let it dribble over the cut. He rubbed it in with a finger, then sat back and watched.

The wound closed and healed. Within a minute there was nothing left apart from a small scar that the man probably wouldn't notice when he awoke.

That's how vampires protect themselves. Unlike in the movies, they don't kill people when they drink, not unless they are starving, or get carried away and go too far. They drink in small doses, a bit here, a bit there. Sometimes they attack people out in the open, as we had just done. Other times, they creep into bedrooms late at night, or into hospital wards, or police cells.

The people they drink from hardly ever know they've been fed on by a vampire. When this man woke, he would remember only a falling red shape. He wouldn't be able to explain why he'd passed out or what had happened to him while he was unconscious. If he found the scar, he'd be more likely to think it was the mark of aliens than a vampire.

Hah. *Aliens!* Not many people know that vampires started the UFO stories. It was the perfect cover. People all over the world were waking up to find strange scars on their body, and were blaming it on imaginary aliens.

Mr Crepsley had knocked the Scout Master out with his breath. Vampires can breathe out a special kind of gas, which makes people faint. When Mr Crepsley wanted to send someone to sleep, he breathed into a cupped fist, then held his hand over the person's nose and mouth. Seconds later, they were out for the count, and wouldn't wake for at least twenty or thirty minutes.

Mr Crepsley examined the scar and made sure it had healed correctly. He took good care of his victims. He seemed to be a nice man, from what I'd seen of him – apart from the fact that he was a vampire!

"Come," he said, standing. "The night is young. We will go find a rabbit or a fox for you."

"You don't mind me not drinking from him?" I asked.

Mr Crepsley shook his head. "You will drink eventually," he said. "When you are hungry enough."

"*No,*" I said silently behind him, as he turned to walk away. "I won't. Not from a human. I'll never drink from a human. *Never!*"

CHAPTER THREE

I AWOKE early in the afternoon, as usual. I'd gone to bed shortly before dawn, the same time as Mr Crepsley. But while he had to stay asleep until night fell again, I was free to rise and move about in the daylight world. It was one of the advantages of being only a half-vampire.

I fixed a late breakfast of marmalade on toast — even vampires have to eat normal food; blood alone won't keep us going — and settled down in front of the hotel television. Mr Crepsley didn't like hotels. He usually slept out in the open, in an old barn or a ruined building or a large crypt, but I was having none of that. I told him straight-up after a week of sleeping rough that I'd had enough of it. He grumbled a bit, but gave way in the end.

The last two months had passed very quickly, because I'd been so busy learning about being a vampire's assistant. Mr Crepsley wasn't a good teacher, and didn't like repeating himself, so I had to pay attention and learn fast.

I was very strong now. I could lift enormous weights and crush marbles to pieces with my fingers. If I shook hands with a human I had to take care not to break the bones in their fingers. I could do chin-ups all night long, and could throw a metal ball further than any grown-up. (I measured my throw one day, then checked in a book and discovered I'd set a new world record! I was excited at first, but then realized I couldn't tell anybody about it. Still, it was nice to know I was a world champion.)

My fingernails were really thick, and the only way I could shorten them was with my teeth: clippers and scissors were no good on my new, tough nails. They were a nuisance: I kept ripping my clothes when I was putting them on or taking them off, and digging holes in my pockets when I stuck my hands in.

We'd covered a lot of distance since that night in the cemetery. First we'd fled at top vampire speed, me on Mr Crepsley's back, invisible to human eyes, gliding across the land like a couple of high-speed ghosts. That's called *flitting*. But flitting is tiring work, so after a couple of nights we began taking trains and buses.

I don't know where Mr Crepsley got the money for our travel and hotels and food. He had no wallet that I could see and no bank cards, but every time he had to pay for something, out came the cash.

I hadn't grown fangs. I'd been expecting them to sprout, and had been checking my teeth in the mirror every night for three weeks before Mr Crepsley caught me.

"What are you doing?" he asked.

"Looking for fangs," I told him.

He stared at me for a few seconds, then burst out laughing. "We do not grow fangs, you ass!" he roared.

"But ... how do we bite people?" I asked, confused.

"We do not," he told me, still laughing. "We cut them with our nails and suck the blood out. We only use our teeth in emergencies."

"So I won't grow fangs?"

"No. Your teeth will be harder than any human's, and you will

201

be able to bite through skin and bone if you wish, but it is messy. Only stupid vampires use their teeth. And stupid vampires tend not to last very long. They get hunted down and killed."

I was a bit disappointed to hear that. It was one of the things I liked most about those old vampire movies: the vampires had looked so cool when they'd bared their fangs.

But, after some thought, I decided I was better off without the fangs. The fingernails making holes in my clothes were bad enough. I would have been in real trouble if my teeth had grown and I'd started cutting chunks out of my cheeks as well!

Most of the old vampire stories were untrue. We couldn't change shape or fly. Crosses and holy water didn't hurt us. All garlic did was give us bad breath. Our reflections could be seen in mirrors, and we cast shadows.

Some of the myths were true though. A vampire couldn't be photographed or filmed with a video camera. There's something odd about vampire atoms, which means all that comes out on film is a dark blur. I could still be photographed, but you wouldn't get a clear photo of me, no matter how good the light.

Vampires were friendly with rats and bats. We couldn't turn into them, as some books and films claimed, but they liked us – they knew from the smell of our blood that we were different to humans – and often cuddled up to us while we were sleeping or came around looking for scraps of food.

Dogs and cats, for some reason, hated us.

Sunlight *would* kill a vampire, but not quickly. A vampire could walk about during the day, if he wrapped up in lots of clothes. He'd tan quickly, and start to go red within a quarter of an hour. Four or five hours of sunlight would kill him.

A stake through the heart would kill us, of course, but so would a bullet or a knife or electricity. We could drown or be crushed to death or catch certain diseases. We were tougher to kill than normal people, but we weren't indestructible.

There was more I had to learn. Loads more. Mr Crepsley said it would be years before I knew everything and was able to get along by myself. He said a half-vampire who didn't know what he was doing would be dead within a couple of months, so I had to stick to him like glue, even if I didn't want to.

When the toast and marmalade were finished, I sat and bit my nails for a few hours. There wasn't anything good on TV, but I didn't want to go outside, not without Mr Crepsley. We were in a small town, and people made me nervous. I kept expecting them to see through me, to know what I was and to come after me with stakes.

When night fell, Mr Crepsley emerged and rubbed his belly. "I am starving," he said. "I know it is early, but let us head out now. I should have taken more of that silly Scout-man's blood. I think I will track down another human." He looked at me with one raised eyebrow. "Maybe you will join me this time."

"Maybe," I said, though I knew I wouldn't. It was the one thing I'd sworn I would never do. I might have to drink the blood of animals to stay alive, but I would never feast on one of my own kind, no matter what Mr Crepsley said, or how much my belly rumbled. I was a half-vampire, yes, but I was also half-human, and the thought of attacking a living person filled me with horror and disgust.

CHAPTER FOUR

BLOOD ...

MR Crepsley spent much of his time teaching me about blood. It's vital to vampires. Without it we grow weak and old and die. Blood keeps us young. Vampires age at a tenth the human rate (for every ten years that pass vampires only age one), but without human blood, we age even quicker than humans, maybe twenty or thirty years in the space of a year or two. As a half-vampire, who aged at a fifth the human rate, I didn't have to drink as much human blood as Mr Crepsley – but I would have to drink some to live.

The blood of animals – dogs, cows, sheep – keeps vampires ticking over, but there are some animals they – we – can't drink from: cats, for instance. If a vampire drinks a cat's blood, he might as well pour poison down his throat. We also can't drink from monkeys, frogs, most fish and snakes.

Mr Crepsley hadn't told me the names of all the dangerous animals. There were loads, and it would take time to learn which were safe and which weren't. His advice was to always ask before I tried something new.

Vampires had to feed on humans once a month or so. Most

feasted once a week. That way, they didn't have to take much blood. If you only fed once a month, you had to drink a lot of blood in one go.

Mr Crepsley said it was dangerous to go too long without drinking. He said the thirst could make you drink more than you meant to, and you were likely to end up killing the person you drank from.

"A vampire who sups frequently can control himself," he said. "One who drinks only when he must will end up sucking wildly. The hunger inside us must be fed to be controlled."

Fresh blood was best. If you drank from a living human, the blood was full of goodness and you didn't need to take very much. But blood began to go sour when a person died. If you drank from a dead body, you had to drink a lot more.

"The general rule is, never drink from a person who has been dead more than a day," Mr Crepsley explained.

"How will I know how long a person's been dead?" I asked.

"The taste of the blood," he said. "You will learn to tell good blood from bad. Bad blood is like sour milk, only worse."

"Is drinking bad blood dangerous?" I asked.

"Yes. It will sicken you, maybe turn you mad or even kill you." Brrrr!

We could bottle fresh blood and keep it for as long as we liked, for use in emergencies. Mr Crepsley had several bottles of blood stored in his cloak. He sometimes had one with a meal, as if it was a small bottle of wine.

"Could you survive on bottled blood alone?" I asked one night.

"For a while," he said. "But not in the long run."

"How do you bottle it?" I asked curiously, examining one of the glass bottles. It was like a test-tube, only the glass was slightly darker and thicker.

"It is tricky," he said. "I will show you how it is done, the next time I am filling up."

Blood ...

It was what I needed most, but also what I feared most. If I drank a human's blood, there was no going back. I'd be a vampire for life. If I avoided it, I might become a human again. Perhaps the vampire blood in my veins would wear out. Maybe I wouldn't die. Maybe only the vampire in me would die, and then I could return home to my family and friends.

It wasn't much of a hope – Mr Crepsley had said it was impossible to become human again, and I believed him – but it was the only dream I had to cling to.

CHAPTER FIVE

Days and nights passed, and we moved on. We wandered from towns to villages to cities. I wasn't getting on very well with Mr Crepsley. Nice as he was, I couldn't forget that he was the one who'd pumped vampire blood into my veins and made it impossible for me to stay with my family.

I hated him. Sometimes, during the day, I'd think about driving a stake through his heart while he was sleeping, and hitting off on my own. I might have, too, except I knew I couldn't survive without him. For the moment I needed Larten Crepsley. But when the day came that I could look after myself ...

I was in charge of Madam Octa. I had to find food for her and exercise her and clean out her cage. I didn't want to – I hated the spider almost as much as I hated the vampire – but Mr Crepsley said I was the one who'd stolen her, so I could look after her.

I practised a few tricks with her every now and then, but my heart wasn't in it. She didn't interest me any more and as the weeks passed I played with her less and less.

The one good thing about being on the road was being able to visit loads of places I hadn't been before, seeing all sorts of sights. I loved travelling. But, since we travelled at night, I didn't get to see much of our surroundings!

One day, while Mr Crepsley was sleeping, I got tired of being indoors. I left a note on the TV, in case I wasn't back when he woke, then set off. I had very little money, and no idea where I would go, but that didn't matter. Just getting out of the hotel and spending some time by myself was wonderful.

It was a large town but fairly quiet. I checked out a few toy stores and played some free computer games in them. I'd never been very good on computers before, but with my new reflexes and skills, I was able to do pretty much anything I wanted.

I raced through levels of speed games, knocked out every opponent in martial arts tournaments, and zapped all the aliens from the skies in sci-fi adventures.

After that I toured the town. There were plenty of fountains and statues and parks and museums, all of which I examined with interest. But going around the museums reminded me of Mum — she loved taking me to museums — and that upset me: I always felt lonely and miserable when I thought of Mum, Dad or Annie.

I spotted a group of boys my age playing hockey on a tarmac quad. There were eight players on each side. Most had plastic sticks, though a few had wooden ones. They were using an old white tennis ball as a puck.

I stopped to watch and, after a few minutes, one of the boys came to size me up.

"Where are you from?" he asked.

"Out of town," I said. "I'm staying at a hotel with my father." I hated calling Mr Crepsley that but it was the safest thing to say.

"He's from out of town," the boy called back to his mates, who had stopped playing.

"Is he part of the Addams Family?" one of them shouted back, and they all laughed.

"What's that supposed to mean?" I asked, offended.

"Have you looked at yourself in a mirror lately?" the boy said.

I glanced down at my dusty suit and knew why they were laughing: I looked like something out of *Oliver Twist*.

"I lost the bag with my normal clothes," I lied. "These are all I have. I'm getting new stuff soon."

"You'd want to," the boy smiled, then asked if I could play hockey. When I said I could, he invited me to play with them.

"You can be on my team," he said, handing me a spare stick. "We're six-two down. My name's Michael."

"Darren," I said in reply, testing the stick.

I rolled up the legs of my trousers and checked my laces were tied properly. While I was doing that, the opposition scored another goal. Michael cursed loudly and dragged the ball back to the centre.

"You want to help touch-off?" he asked me.

"Sure."

"Come on, then," he said, tapped the ball to me and moved ahead, waiting for me to pass back.

It had been a long time since I'd played hockey – at school, in PE, we'd usually have to choose between hockey and football, and I never passed up a chance for a game of footie – but with the stick in my hands and the ball at my feet, it seemed like only yesterday.

I knocked the ball from left to right a few times, making sure I hadn't forgotten how to control it, then looked up and focused on the goal.

There were seven players between me and the goalkeeper. None of them rushed to tackle me. I guess they felt there was no need, being five goals up.

I set off. A big kid – the other team's captain – tried blocking me, but I slipped around him easily. I was past another two before they could react, then dribbled round a fourth. The fifth player slid in with his stick at knee level, but I jumped over him with ease, dummied the sixth and shot before the seventh and final defender could get in the way.

Even though I hit the ball quite softly, it went much harder than the goalie was expecting and flew into the top right-hand corner of the goal. It bounced off the wall and I caught it in the air.

I turned, smiling, and looked back at my team-mates. They were still in their own half, staring at me in shock. I carried the ball back to the halfway line and set it down without saying a word. Then I turned to Michael and said, "Seven-three."

He blinked slowly, then smiled. "Oh yes!" he chortled softly, then winked at his team-mates. "I think we're going to enjoy this!"

I had a great time for a while, controlling the course of play, rushing back to defend, picking players out with pin-point passes. I scored a couple of goals and set up four more. We were leading nine-seven, and coasting. The other team hated it, and had made us give them two of our best players, but it made no difference. I could have given them everybody except our goalkeeper and still knocked the stuffing out of them.

Then things got nasty. The captain of the other team — Danny — had been trying to foul me for ages, but I was too quick for him and danced around his raised stick and stuck-out legs. But then he began to punch my ribs and stand on my toes and slam his elbows into my arms. None of it hurt me, but it annoyed me. I hate sore losers.

The crunch came when Danny pinched me in a *very* painful place! Even vampires have their limits. I gave a roar and crouched down, wincing from the pain.

Danny laughed and sped away with the ball.

I rose after a few seconds, mad as hell. Danny was halfway down the pitch. I set off after him. I brushed the players between us aside — it didn't matter if they were on his team or mine — then slid in behind him and swiped at his legs with my stick. It would have been a dangerous tackle if it had come from a human. Coming from a half-vampire ...

There was a sharp snapping sound. Danny screamed and went down. Play stopped immediately. Everybody in the quad knew the difference between a yell of pain and a scream of real agony.

I got to my feet, already sorry for what I'd done, wishing I could take it back. I looked at my stick, hoping to find it broken in two, hoping that had been what made the snapping noise. But it wasn't.

I'd broken both of Danny's shin-bones.

His lower legs were bent awkwardly and the skin around the shins was torn. I could see the white of bone in amongst the red.

Michael bent to examine Danny's legs. When he rose, there was a horrified look in his eyes.

"You've cracked his legs wide open!" he gasped.

"I didn't mean to," I cried. "He squeezed my ..." I pointed to the spot beneath my waist.

"You broke his legs!" Michael shouted, then backed away from me. Those around him backed away as well.

They were *afraid* of me.

Sighing, I dropped my stick and left, knowing I'd make matters worse if I stayed and waited for grown-ups to arrive. None of the boys tried to stop me. They were too scared. They were terrified of me ... Darren Shan ... a *monster*.

CHAPTER SIX

IT WAS dark when I got back. Mr Crepsley was up. I told him we should skip town straight away, but didn't tell him why. He took one look at my face, nodded and started gathering our belongings.

We said little that night. I was thinking how rotten it was to be a half-vampire. Mr Crepsley sensed there was something wrong with me, but didn't bother me with questions. It wasn't the first time I'd been sulky. He was getting used to my mood-swings.

We found an abandoned church to sleep in. Mr Crepsley lay out on a long pew, while I made a bed for myself on a pile of moss and weeds on the floor.

I woke early and spent the day exploring the church and the small cemetery outside. The headstones were old and many were cracked or covered with weeds. I spent several hours cleaning a patch of them, pulling weeds away and washing the stones with water I fetched from a nearby stream. It kept my mind off the hockey game.

A family of rabbits lived in a nearby burrow. As the day went by, they crept closer, to see what I was up to. They were curious little fellows, especially the young ones. At one point, I pretended to be asleep and a couple edged closer and closer, until they were only half a metre away.

When they were as close as they were likely to get, I leapt up and shouted "Boo!" and they went running away like wildfire. One fell head over heels and rolled away down the mouth of its burrow.

That cheered me up greatly.

I found a shop in the afternoon and bought some meat and veg. I set a fire when I returned to the church, then fetched the pots and pans bag from beneath Mr Crepsley's pew. I searched among the contents until I found what I was looking for. It was a small tin-shaped pot. I carefully laid it upside-down on the floor, then pressed the metal bulge on the top.

The tin mushroomed out in size, as folded-in panels opened up. Within five seconds it had become a full-sized pot, which I filled with water and stuck on the fire.

All the pots and pans in the bag were like this. Mr Crepsley got them from a woman called Evanna, long ago. They weighed the same as ordinary cookware, but because they could fold up small, they were easier to carry around.

I made a stew, as Mr Crepsley had taught me. He believed everybody should know how to cook.

I took leftover bits of the carrots and cabbage outside and dropped them by the rabbit burrow.

Mr Crepsley was surprised to find dinner – well, it was breakfast from his point of view – waiting for him when he awoke. He sniffed the fumes from the bubbling pot and licked his lips.

"I could get used to this," he smiled, then yawned, stretched and ran a hand through the short crop of orange hair on his head. Then he scratched the long scar running down the left side of his face. It was a familiar routine of his.

I'd often wanted to ask how he got his scar, but I never had. One night, when I was feeling brave, I would.

There were no tables, so we ate off our laps. I got two of the folded-up plates out of the bag, popped them open and fetched the knives and forks. I served up the food and we tucked in.

Towards the end, Mr Crepsley wiped around his mouth with a silk napkin and coughed awkwardly.

"It is very nice," he complimented me.

"Thank you," I replied.

"I ... um ... that is ..." He sighed. "I never was very good at being subtle," he said, "so I will come right out and say it: what went wrong yesterday? Why were you so upset?"

I stared at my almost empty plate, not sure if I wanted to answer or not. Then, all of a sudden, I blurted out the whole story. I hardly took a breath between the start and finish.

Mr Crepsley listened carefully. When I was done, he thought about it for a minute or two before speaking.

"It is something you must get used to," he said. "It is a fact of life that we are stronger than humans, faster and tougher. If you play with them, they will be hurt."

"I didn't mean to hurt him," I said. "It was an accident."

Mr Crepsley shrugged. "Listen, Darren, there is no way you can stop this happening again, not if you mix with humans. No matter how hard you try to be normal, you are not. There will always be accidents waiting to happen."

"What you're saying is, I can't have friends any more, right?" I nodded sadly. "I'd figured that out by myself. That's why I was so sad. I'd been getting used to the idea of never being able to go back home to see my old friends, but it was only yesterday that I realized I'd never be able to make new ones either. I'm stuck with *you*. I can't have any other friends, can I?"

He rubbed his scar and pursed his lips. "That is not true," he said. "You can have friends. You just have to be careful. You—"

"That's not good enough!" I cried. "You said it yourself; there will always be an accident waiting to happen. Even shaking hands is dangerous. I could cut their wrists open with my nails!"

I shook my head slowly. "No," I said firmly. "I won't put people's lives in danger. I'm too dangerous to have friends any more. Besides, it's not like I can make a true friend."

"Why not?" he asked.

"True friends don't keep secrets from one another. I could never tell a human that I was a vampire. I'd always have to lie and pretend to be someone I'm not. I'd always be afraid he'd find out what I was and hate me."

"It is a problem every vampire shares," Mr Crepsley said.

"But every vampire isn't a child!" I shouted. "What age were you when you were changed? Were you a man?" He nodded. "Friends aren't that important to adults. My dad told me that grown-ups get used to not having loads of friends. They've work and hobbies and other stuff to keep them busy. But my friends were the most important thing in my life, apart from my family. Well, you took my family away when you pumped your stinking blood into me. Now you've ruined the chances of my ever having a proper friend again.

"Thanks a lot," I said angrily. "Thanks for making a monster out of me and wrecking my life."

I was close to tears, but didn't want to cry, not in front of him. So I stabbed at the last piece of meat on my plate with my fork and rammed it into my mouth, where I chewed upon it fiercely.

Mr Crepsley was quiet after my outburst. I couldn't tell if he was angry or sorry. For a while, I thought I'd said too much. What if he turned around and said, "If that is the way you feel, I will leave you"? What would I do then?

I was thinking of apologizing when he spoke in a soft voice and surprised me.

"I am sorry," he said. "I should not have blooded you. It was a poor call. You were too young. It has been so long since I was a boy, I had forgotten what it was like. I never thought of your friends and how much you would miss them. It was wrong of me to blood you. Terribly wrong. I ..."

He trailed off into silence. He looked so miserable, I almost felt sorry for him. Then I remembered what he'd done to me and I hated him again. Then I saw wet drops at the corners of his eyes, which might have been tears, and felt sorry for him once more.

I was very confused.

"Well, there's no use moaning about it," I finally said. "We can't go back. What's done is done, right?"

"Yes," he sighed. "If I could, I would take back my terrible gift. But that is not possible. Vampirism is for ever. Once somebody has been changed, there is no changing back.

"Still," he said, mulling it over, "it is not as bad as you think. Perhaps ..." His eyes narrowed thoughtfully.

"Perhaps what?" I asked.

"We *can* find friends for you," he said. "You do not have to be stuck with me all the time."

"I don't understand." I frowned. "Didn't we just agree it wasn't safe for me to be around humans?"

"I am not talking about humans," he said, starting to smile. "I am talking about people with special powers. People like us. People you can tell your secrets to ..."

He leant across and took my hands in his.

"Darren," he said, "what do you think about going back and becoming a member of the Cirque Du Freak?"

CHAPTER SEVEN

THE MORE we discussed the idea, the more I liked it. Mr Crepsley said the Cirque performers would know what I was and would accept me as one of their own. The line-up of the show often changed, and there was nearly always someone who would be around my own age. I'd be able to hang out with them.

"What if I don't like it there?" I asked.

"Then we leave," he said. "I enjoyed travelling with the Cirque, but I am not crazy about it. If you like it, we stay. If you do not, we hit the road again."

"They won't mind me tagging along?" I asked.

"You will have to pull your weight," he replied. "Mr Tall insists on everybody doing something. You will have to help set up chairs and lights, sell souvenirs, clean up afterwards, or do the cooking. You will be kept busy, but they will not over-work you. We will have plenty of time for our lessons."

We decided to give it a go. At least it would mean a proper bed every night. My back was stiff from sleeping on floors.

Mr Crepsley had to find out where the show was before we could set off. I asked him how he was going to do that. He told me he was able to home in on Mr Tall's thoughts.

"You mean he's telepathic?" I asked, remembering what Steve had called people who could talk to each other using only their brains.

"Sort of," Mr Crepsley said. "We cannot speak to each other with our thoughts but I can pick up his … *aura*, you could call it. Once I locate that, tracking him down will be no problem."

"Could I locate his aura?" I wanted to know.

"No," Mr Crepsley said. "Most vampires – along with a few gifted humans – can, but half-vampires cannot."

He sat down in the middle of the church and closed his eyes. He was quiet for about a minute. Then his eyelids opened and he stood.

"Got him," he said.

"So soon?" I asked. "I thought it would take longer."

"I have searched for his aura many times," Mr Crepsley explained. "I know what to look for. Finding him is as easy as finding a needle in a haystack."

"That's supposed to be hard, isn't it?"

"Not for a vampire," he grunted.

While we were packing to leave, I found myself gazing around the church. Something had been bothering me, but I wasn't sure whether I should mention it to Mr Crepsley or not.

"Go on," he said, startling me. "Ask whatever it is that is on your mind."

"How did you know I wanted to ask something?" I gawped.

He laughed. "It does not take a vampire to know when a child is curious. You have been bursting with a question for ages. What is it?"

I took a deep breath. "Do you believe in God?" I asked.

Mr Crepsley looked at me oddly, then nodded slowly. "I believe in the gods of the vampires."

I frowned. "Are there vampire gods?"

"Of course," he said. "Every race has gods: Egyptian gods, Indian gods, Chinese gods. Vampires are no different."

"What about heaven?" I asked.

"We believe in Paradise. It lies beyond the stars. When we die, if we have lived good lives, our spirits float free of the earth, to traverse the stars and galaxies, and come at last to a wonderful world at the other side of the universe – Paradise."

"And if they don't live good lives?"

"They stay here," he said. "They remain bound to earth as ghosts, doomed to wander the face of this planet for ever."

I thought about that. "What's a *good life* for a vampire?" I asked. "How do they make it to Paradise?"

"Live cleanly," he said. "Do not kill unless necessary. Do not hurt people. Do not spoil the world."

"Drinking blood isn't evil?" I asked.

"Not unless you kill the person you drink from," Mr Crepsley said. "And even then, sometimes, it can be a good thing."

"Killing someone can be *good*?" I gasped.

Mr Crepsley nodded seriously. "People have souls, Darren. When they die, those souls go to heaven or Paradise. But it is possible to keep a part of them here. When we drink small amounts of blood, we do not take any of a person's essence. But if we drink lots, we keep part of them alive within us."

"How?" I asked, frowning.

"By draining a person's blood, we absorb some of that person's memories and feelings," he said. "They become part of us and we can see the world the way they saw it, and remember things which might otherwise have been forgotten."

"Like what?"

He thought a moment. "One of my dearest friends is called Paris Skyle," he said. "He is very old. Many centuries ago, he was friends with William Shakespeare."

"*The* William Shakespeare – the guy who wrote the plays?"

Mr Crepsley nodded. "Plays and poems. But not all of Shakespeare's poetry was recorded; some of his most famous verses were lost. When Shakespeare was dying, Paris drank from him – Shakespeare asked him to – and was able to tap into those lost poems and have them written down. The world would have been a poorer place without them."

"But ..." I stopped. "Do you only do that with people who ask, and who are dying?"

"Yes," he said. "It would be evil to kill a healthy person. But to drink from friends who are close to death, and keep their memories and experiences alive ..." He smiled. "That is very good indeed.

"Come," he said then. "Brood about it on the way. We must be off."

I hopped on Mr Crepsley's back when we were ready to leave, and off we flitted. He still hadn't explained how he could move so fast. It wasn't that he ran quickly; it was more like the world slipped by as he ran. He said all full vampires could flit.

It was nice, watching the countryside drift away behind us. We ran up hills and across vast plains, faster than the wind. There was complete silence while we were flitting and nobody ever noticed us. It was as if we were surrounded by a magic bubble.

While we flitted I thought about what Mr Crepsley had said, about keeping people's memories alive by drinking from them. I wasn't sure how that would work, and made up my mind to ask him more about it at a later date.

Flitting was hard work; the vampire was sweating and I could see him starting to struggle. To help, I took out a bottle of human blood, uncorked it and held it to his lips so he could drink.

He nodded his silent thanks, wiped the sweat from his brow, and continued.

Finally, as the sky was beginning to lighten, he slowed to a halt. I hopped down off his back and looked around. We were in the middle of a country road, fields and trees all around us, not a house to be seen.

"Where's the Cirque Du Freak?" I asked.

"A few kilometres further ahead," he said, pointing. He was kneeling down, panting for breath.

"Did you run out of steam?" I asked, unable to keep the giggles out of my voice.

"No," he glared. "I could have made it, but did not want to arrive looking flushed."

"You'd better not rest too long," I warned him. "Morning's on its way."

"I know precisely what time it is!" he snapped. "I know more about mornings and dawns than any living human. We have plenty of time on our side. A whole forty-three minutes yet."

"If you say so."

"I *do*." He stood, annoyed, and began to walk. I waited until he was a bit in front, then ran ahead of him.

"Hurry up, old man," I jeered. "You're getting left behind."

"Keep it up," he growled. "See what it gets you. A clip around the ear and a boot up the pants."

He started trotting after a couple of minutes, and the two of us jogged along, side by side. I was in good spirits, happier than I'd been for months. It was nice having something to look forward to.

We passed a ragged bunch of campers on our way. They were starting to wake up and move around. A couple waved to us. They were funny looking people: long hair, strange clothes, weighed down with fancy earrings and bracelets.

There were banners and flags all over the camp. I tried reading them, but it was hard to focus while I was jogging, and I didn't want to stop. From what I could gather, the campers had something to do with a protest against a new bypass.

The road was very curvy. After the fifth bend, we finally spotted the Cirque Du Freak, nestled in a clearing by the banks of a river. It was quiet – everyone was sleeping, I imagined – and, if we'd been in a car and not looking for the vans and tents, it would have been easy to miss.

It was an odd place for the circus to be. There was no hall or big tent for the freaks to perform in. I figured this must be a resting point between two towns.

Mr Crepsley weaved between the vans and cars with confidence. He knew exactly where he was going. I followed, less sure of myself, remembering the night I crept past the freaks and stole Madam Octa.

Mr Crepsley stopped at a long silver van and knocked on the door. It opened almost immediately and the towering figure of Mr Tall was revealed. His eyes looked darker than ever in the dim light. If I hadn't known better, I would have sworn he had no eyeballs, only two black, empty spaces.

"Oh, it's you," he said, voice low, lips hardly moving. "I thought I felt you searching for me." He craned over Mr Crepsley and looked down to where I was shaking. "I see you've brought the boy."

"May we come in?" Mr Crepsley asked.

"Of course. What is it one is supposed to say to you vampires?" He smiled. "Enter of your own free will?"

"Something like that," Mr Crepsley replied, and from the smile on his face, I knew it was an old joke between them.

We entered the van and sat. It was pretty bare inside, just a few shelves with posters and leaflets for the Cirque, the tall red hat and gloves I'd seen him wear before, a couple of knick-knacks and a foldaway bed.

"I didn't expect you back so soon, Larten," Mr Tall said. Even when he was sitting down he looked enormous.

"A swift return had not been on the agenda, Hibernius." *Hibernius?* That was a strange name. Still, it suited him somehow. Hibernius Tall. It had an odd ring to it.

"Did you run into trouble?" Mr Tall asked.

"No," Mr Crepsley said. "Darren was not happy. I decided he would be better off here, among those of his own kind."

"I see." Mr Tall studied me curiously. "You have come a long way since I saw you last, Darren Shan," he said.

"I preferred it where I was," I grumbled.

"Then why did you leave?" he asked.

I glared at him. "You know why," I said coldly.

He nodded slowly.

"Is it OK if we stay?" Mr Crepsley asked.

"Of course," Mr Tall replied immediately. "Delighted to have you back, actually. We're a bit under-staffed at the moment. Alexander Ribs, Sive and Seersa, and Gertha Teeth are off on holidays or business. Cormac Limbs is on his way to join us, but is late getting here. Larten Crepsley and his amazing performing spider will be an invaluable addition to the line-up."

"Thank you," Mr Crepsley said.

"What about me?" I asked boldly.

Mr Tall smiled. "You are less valuable," he said, "but welcome all the same."

I snorted, but said nothing.

"Where shall we be playing?" Mr Crepsley asked next.

"Right here," Mr Tall told him.

"*Here?*" I piped up in surprise.

"That puzzles you?" Mr Tall enquired.

"It's in the middle of nowhere," I said. "I thought you only played in towns and cities, where you'd get big audiences."

"We *always* get a big audience," Mr Tall said. "No matter where we play, people will come. Usually we stick to more populated areas, but this is a slow time of the year for us. As I've said, several of our best performers are absent, as are ... certain other members of our company."

A strange, secretive look passed between Mr Tall and Mr Crepsley, and I felt I was being left out of something.

"So we are resting for a while," Mr Tall went on. "We shall not be putting on any shows for a few days. We're relaxing."

"We passed a road-camp on our way," Mr Crepsley said. "Are they causing any problems?"

"The foot-soldiers of NOP?" Mr Tall laughed. "They're too busy defending trees and rocks to interfere with us."

"What's NOP?" I asked.

"Nature's Opposing Protectors," Mr Tall explained. "They're Eco Warriors. They run around the country, trying to stop new roads and bridges being built. They've been here a couple of months, but are due to move on soon."

"Are they real warriors?" I asked. "Do they have guns and grenades and tanks?"

The two adults almost laughed their heads off.

"He can be quite silly sometimes," Mr Crepsley said between fits of laughter, "but he is not as dumb as he seems."

I felt my face reddening, but held my tongue. I knew from experience that it's no use getting mad at grown-ups when they laugh at you; it only makes them laugh even harder.

"They call themselves warriors," Mr Tall said, "but they're not really. They chain themselves to trees and pour sand into the engines of JCBs and toss nails in the path of cars. That sort of thing."

"Why—" I started, but Mr Crepsley interrupted.

"We do not have time for questions," he said. "A few more minutes and the sun will be up." He rose and shook Mr Tall's hand. "Thank you for having us back, Hibernius."

"My pleasure," Mr Tall replied.

"I trust you took good care of my coffin?"

"Of course."

Mr Crepsley smiled happily and rubbed his hands together. "That is what I miss most when I am away. It will be nice to bed down in it once more."

"What about the boy?" Mr Tall asked. "Do you want us to knock together a coffin for him?"

"Don't even think about it!" I shouted. "You won't get me in one of those again!" I remembered what it felt like to be in a coffin, when I was buried alive, and shivered.

Mr Crepsley smiled. "Put Darren in with one of the other performers," he said. "Somebody his own age, if possible."

Mr Tall thought a moment. "How about Evra?"

Mr Crepsley's smile spread. "Yes. I think putting him in with Evra is a marvellous idea."

"Who's Evra?" I asked nervously.

"You will find out," Mr Crepsley promised, opening the door to the van. "I will leave you to Mr Tall. He will take care of you. I have to be away."

And then he was gone, off to find his beloved coffin.

I glanced over my shoulder and found Mr Tall standing directly behind me. I don't know how he crossed the room so quickly. I didn't even hear him moving to stand up.

"Shall we go?" he said.

I gulped and nodded.

He led the way through the camp-site. The morning was breaking and I saw a couple of lights coming on in a few of the caravans and tents. Mr Tall led me to an old grey tent, big enough for five or six people.

"Here are some blankets," he said, handing over a bunch of woolly sheets. "And a pillow." I don't know where he got them from — he hadn't had them when we left the van — but was too tired to ask. "You may sleep as late as you wish. I will come for you when you are awake and explain your duties. Evra will take care of you until then."

I lifted the flap of the tent and looked inside. It was too dark to see anything. "Who's Evra?" I asked, turning back to Mr Tall. But he was gone, having disappeared with his usual rapid, silent speed.

I sighed and entered, clutching the blankets to my chest. I let the flap fall back into place, then stood quietly inside, waiting for my eyes to adjust. I could hear someone breathing softly, and could make out a vague shape in a hammock in the darkness beyond the middle of the tent. I looked for somewhere to make my bed. I didn't want my tent-mate tripping over me when he was getting up.

I walked forward a few blind steps. Suddenly, something slithered towards me through the darkness. I stopped and stared ahead, wishing desperately that I could see (without the light of the stars or moon, even a vampire struggles to make things out).

"Hello?" I called softly. "Are you Evra? I'm Darren Shan. I'm your new—"

I stopped. The slithering noise had reached my feet. As I stood, rooted to the spot, something fleshy and slimy wrapped itself around my legs. I instantly knew what it was, but didn't dare look down until it had climbed more than halfway up my body. Finally, as its coils curled around my chest, I worked up the courage to lower my eyes and lock gazes with that of a long, thick, hissing ... *snake!*

CHAPTER EIGHT

I STOOD frozen with fear for more than an hour, staring into the snake's deathly cold eyes, waiting for it to strike.

Finally, with the light of the strong morning sun shining through the canvas of the tent, the sleeping shape in the hammock shifted, yawned, sat up and looked around.

It was the snake-boy and he got a shock when he saw me. He rocked back in the hammock and raised the covers, as though to protect himself. Then he saw the snake wrapped around me and breathed easily.

"Who are you?" he asked sharply. "What are you doing here?"

I shook my head slowly. I didn't dare speak in case the movement of my lungs caused the snake to strike.

"You'd better answer," he warned, "or I'll tell her to take your eyes out."

"I ... I ... I'm Duh–Darren Sh–Sh–Shan," I stuttered. "Mr Tuh–Tall told me to cuh–come in. He said I wuh–wuh–was to be your new ruhruh–ruh–roommate."

"Darren Shan?" The snake-boy frowned, then pointed knowingly. "You're Mr Crepsley's assistant, aren't you?"

"Yes," I said quietly.

The snake-boy grinned. "Did he know Mr Tall was putting you in with me?" I nodded and he laughed. "I've never yet met a vampire without a nasty sense of humour."

He swung down out of the hammock, crossed the tent, took hold of the snake's head and began unwrapping it. "You're OK," he assured me. "In fact, you were never in danger. The snake's been asleep the whole time. You could have tugged her off and she wouldn't have stirred. She's a deep sleeper."

"She's *asleep*?" I squeaked. "But ... how come she wrapped herself around me?"

He smiled. "She sleep-crawls."

"*Sleep-crawls!*" I stared at him, then at the snake, which hadn't moved while he was unwinding her. The last of her coils came free and I was able to step away to one side. My legs were stiff and full of pins and needles.

"A sleep-crawling snake." I laughed uneasily. "Good job she's not a sleep-*eating* snake!"

The snake-boy tucked his pet away in a corner and stroked her head lovingly. "She wouldn't have eaten you even if she had woken up," he informed me. "She ate a goat yesterday. Snakes her size don't have to eat very often."

Leaving his snake, he threw back the tent-flap and stepped out. I followed quickly, not wanting to be left alone with the reptile.

I studied him closely outside. He was exactly as I remembered: a few years older than me, very thin with long yellow-green hair, narrow eyes, strangely webbed fingers and toes; his body was covered in scales of green, gold, yellow and blue. He was wearing a pair of shorts and nothing else.

"By the way," he said, "my name's Evra Von." He held out a hand and we shook. His palm felt slippery, but dry. A few of the scales came off and stuck to my hand when I pulled it away. They were like scraps of coloured dead skin.

"Evra Von what?" I asked.

"Just plain Von," he said, rubbing his stomach. "You hungry?"

"Yes," I said, and went with Evra to get something to eat.

The camp was alive with activity. Since there had been no show the night before, most of the freaks and their helpers had gone to bed early, and so were up and about earlier than usual.

I was fascinated by the hustle and bustle. I hadn't realized there were so many people working for the Cirque. I'd thought it would just be the performers and assistants I'd seen the night I went to the show with Steve, but as I looked around I saw that those were just the tip of the iceberg. There were at least two dozen people walking or talking, washing or cooking, none of whom I'd seen before.

"Who are all these?" I asked.

"The backbone of the Cirque Du Freak," Evra replied. "They do the driving, set up the tents, the laundry, the cooking, mend our costumes, clear up after shows. It's a big operation."

"Are they normal humans?" I asked.

"Most of them," he said.

"How did they come to work here?"

"Some are related to the performers. Some are friends of Mr Tall. Some just wandered in, liked what they saw and stayed."

"People can do that?" I asked.

"If Mr Tall likes the look of them," Evra said. "There are always vacancies at the Cirque Du Freak."

Evra stopped at a large camp-fire and I stopped beside him. Hans Hands (a man who could walk on his hands and run faster on them than the world's fastest sprinter) was resting on a log, while Truska (the Bearded Lady, who grew her beard whenever she wanted) cooked sausages on a wooden stick. Several humans were sitting or lying about.

"Morning greetings, Evra Von," Hans Hands said.

"How do, Hans," Evra replied.

"Who's your young friend?" Hans asked, eyeing me suspiciously.

"This is Darren Shan," Evra said.

"*The* Darren Shan?" Hans asked, eyebrows raising.

"None other," Evra grinned.

"What do you mean ... '*The* Darren Shan'?" I asked.

"You're famous round these parts," Hans said.

"Why? Because I'm a —" I lowered my voice "— half-vampire?"

Hans laughed pleasantly. "Half-vampires are nothing new. If I had a gold coin for every half-vampire I'd seen, I'd have ..." He scrunched up his face and thought. "Twenty-nine gold coins. But *young* half-vampires are a different matter. I never saw or heard of a boy your age living it up amongst the ranks of the walking dead. Tell me: have the Vampire Generals been round to inspect you yet?"

"Who are the Vampire Generals?" I asked.

"They're—"

"Hans!" a lady washing clothes barked. He stopped speaking and looked around guiltily. "Do you think Larten would enjoy hearing you spreading tales?" she snapped.

Hans pulled a face. "Sorry," he said. "It's the fresh morning air. I'm not used to it. Makes me say things I shouldn't."

I wanted him to explain about the Vampire Generals, but it would have been impolite to ask.

Truska checked the sausages, pulled a couple off the stick and handed them out. She smiled when she came to me and said something in a strange, foreign language.

Evra laughed. "She wants to know if you like sausages or if you're a vegetarian."

"That's a good one!" Hans chuckled. "A vampire vegetarian!"

"You speak her language?" I asked Evra.

"Yes," he said proudly. "I'm still learning – it's the hardest language I've ever tried to learn – but I'm the only one in the camp who knows what she's saying. I'm excellent at languages," he boasted.

"What language is it?" I asked.

"I don't know," he said, frowning. "She won't tell me."

That sounded odd, but I didn't want to say anything to offend him. Instead, I took one of the sausages and smiled my thanks. I bit into it and had to let go straight away; it was roasting hot! Evra laughed and handed me a mug of water. I drank until my mouth was back to normal, then blew on the sausage to cool it down.

We sat with Hans and Truska and the others for a while, chatting and eating and soaking up the morning sun. The grass was damp with dew, but none of us minded. Evra introduced me to everyone in the group. There were too many names for me to memorize in one go, so I just smiled, shook hands and filed the faces away.

Mr Tall appeared before long. One moment he wasn't there, the next he was standing behind Evra, warming his hands over the fire.

"You're up early, Master Shan," Mr Tall remarked.

"I couldn't sleep," I told him. "I was too –" I looked over at Evra and smiled "– wound-up."

"I hope it will not affect your ability to work," Mr Tall said.

"I'll be fine," I said. "I'm ready and able."

"You're sure?"

"I'm sure."

"That's what I like to hear." He produced a large notebook and flipped through the pages. "Let's see what we can find for you to do today," he mused. "Tell me: are you a good cook?"

"I can cook a stew. Mr Crepsley taught me."

"Have you ever cooked for a company of thirty or forty?"

"No."

"Too bad. Maybe you'll learn." He flicked through another couple of pages. "Can you sew and stitch?"

"No."

"Have you washed clothes before?"

"By hand?"

"Yes."

"No."

"Hurm." He flicked on some more, then snapped the book shut. "OK," he said, "until we find a more permanent position for you, stick with Evra and help him with his chores. Does that sound fair?"

"I'd like that," I said.

"You don't mind, Evra?" he asked the snake-boy.

"Not at all," Evra replied.

"Very well. It's settled. Evra will be in charge of you until further notice. Do what he says. When your colleague-in-blood arises —" he meant Mr Crepsley "— you're free to spend the night with him if he so desires. We'll see how you get on, then make a decision on how best to utilize your talents."

"Thank you," I said.

"My pleasure," he replied.

I expected him to vanish in the blink of an eye then, but instead he turned and walked away slowly, whistling, enjoying the sunshine.

"Well, Darren," Evra said, sticking a scaly arm around my shoulders, "looks like you and me are partners now. How do you feel about that?"

"I feel good ... partner."

"Excellent!" He clapped my shoulder and gulped down the

last of his sausage. "Then let's get busy."

"What do we do first?" I asked.

"What we'll be doing first every morning," Evra said, setting off. "Milking the poison from the fangs of my snake."

"Oh," I said, coming to a halt. "Is it dangerous?"

"Only if she bites before we finish," Evra said, then laughed at my expression and pushed me ahead of him to the tent.

CHAPTER NINE

EVRA DID the milking himself — to my great relief — then we dragged the snake outside and laid her on the grass. We fetched buckets of water and scrubbed her down with very soft sponges.

After that, we had to feed the Wolf Man. His cage was near the back of the camp-site. He roared when he saw us coming. He looked as angry and dangerous as he had that night I visited the Cirque with Steve. He shook the bars and swiped at us if we got too close — which we didn't!

"Why is he so vicious?" I asked, tossing him a large chunk of raw meat, which he grabbed in mid-air and bit into.

"Because he's a real Wolf Man," Evra said. "He's not just somebody very hairy. He's half-human, half-wolf."

"Isn't it cruel to keep him chained up?" I asked, throwing him another slice of meat.

"If we didn't, he'd run riot and kill people. The mix of human and wolf blood has driven him mad. He wouldn't just kill when he was hungry; if he was free, he'd murder all the time."

"Isn't there a cure?" I asked, feeling sorry for him.

"There isn't a cure because it isn't a disease," Evra explained.

"This isn't something he caught, it's how he was born. This is what he is."

"How did it happen?" I asked.

Evra looked at me seriously. "Do you really want to know?"

I stared at the hairy beast in the cage, ripping up the meat as if it was candy-floss, then gulped and said, "No, I suppose I don't."

We handled a variety of jobs after that. We peeled potatoes for that night's dinner, helped repair a tyre on one of the cars, spent an hour painting the roof of a van and walked a dog. Evra said most days were like this, just wandering through the camp, seeing what needed doing, helping out as and when required.

In the evening we took a load of cans and broken bits of glass to the tent of Rhamus Twobellies, a huge man who could eat anything. I wanted to stay and watch him eat, but Evra hurried me out. Rhamus didn't like people watching him eat in private.

We had a lot of time to ourselves, and during our quieter moments we told each other about our lives, where we'd come from and how we'd grown up.

Evra had been born to ordinary parents. They'd been horrified when they saw him. They abandoned him at an orphanage, where he stayed until a nasty circus owner bought him at the age of four.

"Those were bad days," he said quietly. "He used to beat me and treat me like a real snake. He kept me locked up in a glass cage and let people pay to look and laugh at me."

He'd been with the circus for seven long, miserable years, touring small towns, being made to feel ugly and freakish and useless.

Finally, Mr Tall came to the rescue.

"He turned up one night," Evra said. "He appeared suddenly, out of the darkness, and stood by my cage for a long time, watching me. He didn't say a word. Neither did I.

"The circus owner came. He didn't know who Mr Tall was, but thought he might be a rich man, interested in buying me. He stated his price and stood back, waiting for an answer.

"Mr Tall didn't say anything for a few minutes. Then his left hand grabbed the circus owner by the neck. He squeezed once and that was the end of him. He fell to the floor, dead. Mr Tall opened the door to my cage and said, "Let's go, Evra." I think Mr Tall's able to read minds, which is how he knew my name."

Evra was quiet after that. He had a faraway look in his eyes.

"Do you want to see something amazing?" he said eventually, snapping out of his thoughtful mood.

"Sure," I said.

He turned to face me, then stuck out his tongue and pushed it up over his lip and *right up his nose!*

"Ewww! Gross!" I yelled delightedly.

He pulled the tongue back and grinned. "I've got the longest tongue in the world," he said. "If my nose was big enough, I could poke my tongue all the way to the top, down my throat and back out my mouth again."

"You couldn't!" I laughed.

"Probably not," he giggled. "But it's still pretty impressive." He ran the tongue out again and this time licked around his nostrils, one after the other. It was revolting but hilarious.

"That's the most disgusting thing I've ever seen," I laughed.

"I bet you wish you could do it," Evra said.

"I wouldn't, even if I could," I lied. "Don't you get snot all over your tongue?"

"I don't have any snot," Evra said.

"What? No snot?"

"It's true," he said. "My nose is different to yours. There's no snot or dirt or hairs. My nostrils are the cleanest part of my whole body."

"What does it taste like?" I asked.

"Lick my snake's belly and you'll find out," he replied. "It's the same taste as that."

I laughed and said I wasn't *that* interested!

Later, when Mr Crepsley asked me what I'd done all day, I replied simply: "I made a friend."

CHAPTER TEN

WE'D BEEN with the Cirque two days and nights. I spent my days with Evra, helping him, and my nights with Mr Crepsley, learning about vampires. I was going to bed earlier than I had been, though I rarely hit the sack before one or two in the morning.

I'd struck up a strong friendship with Evra. He was older than me, but he was shy – probably because of his troubled past – so we were pretty well suited.

As the third day rolled by, I found myself gazing around the small groups of vans and cars and tents, feeling like I'd been part of the scene for years.

I was starting to suffer from the effects of going so long without drinking human blood. I wasn't as strong as I had been, and couldn't move as quickly as I could before. My eyesight had dulled, as had my hearing and sense of smell. I was much stronger and quicker than I'd been as a human, but I could feel my powers slipping, a bit more every day.

I didn't mind. I'd rather lose some strength than drink from a human.

I was relaxing with Evra on the edge of the camp-site that

afternoon when we spotted a figure in the bushes.

"Who's that?" I asked.

"A kid from a nearby village," Evra said. "I've seen him hanging around before."

I watched the boy in the bushes. He was trying hard not to be seen, but to a person with my powers – fading though they were – he was as obvious as an elephant. I was curious to know what he was doing, so I turned to Evra and said, "Let's have fun."

"What are you planning?" he asked.

"Lean in and I'll tell you."

I whispered my plan in his ear. He grinned and nodded, then stood and pretended to yawn.

"I'll be off, Darren," he said. "See you later."

"See you, Evra," I replied loudly. I waited until he was gone, then stood and walked back to the camp myself.

When I was out of sight of the boy in the bushes, I doubled back, using the caravans and tents to mask my movements. I walked about a hundred metres to the left, then crept forward until I was level with the boy, and sneaked towards him.

I stopped ten metres away. I was a little bit behind him, so he couldn't see me. His eyes were still glued to the camp. I looked over his head and saw Evra, who was even closer than I was. He made an "OK" sign with his thumb and index finger.

I crouched down low and moaned.

"Ohhhh," I groaned. "Wwwooohhhh."

The boy stiffened and looked over his shoulder nervously. He wasn't able to see me.

"Who's there?" he asked.

"Wraaarghhhh," Evra grunted on the other side of him.

The boy's head spun around in the other direction.

"Who's there?" he shouted.

"Ohh-ohh-ohh," I snorted, in the manner of a gorilla.

"I'm not afraid," the boy said, edging backwards. "You're just somebody playing a nasty trick."

"Eee-ee-ee-ee-ee," Evra screeched.

I shook a branch, Evra rattled a bush, then I tossed a stone into the area just ahead of the boy. His head was spinning round like a puppet's, darting all over the place. He didn't know whether it would be safer to run or stay.

"Look, I don't know who you are," he began, "but I'm—"

Evra had sneaked up behind him and now, as the boy spoke, stuck out his extra-long tongue and ran it over the boy's neck, making a hissing snake noise.

That was enough for the boy. He screamed and ran for his life.

Evra and me ran after him, laughing our socks off, making noises all the time. He fled through thorn bushes and nettles as though they weren't there, screaming for help.

We grew tired of the game after a few minutes, and might have let him get away, but then he tripped and went sprawling into a patch of very high grass.

We stood, trying to spot him amongst the grass, but there was no sign of him.

"Where is he?" I asked.

"I can't see him," Evra said.

"Do you think he's all right?"

"I don't know." Evra looked worried. "He might have fallen down a big hole or something."

"Kid?" I shouted. "Are you OK?" No answer. "There's no need to be afraid. We won't hurt you. We were only fooling. We didn't—"

There was a rushing noise behind us, then I felt a hand on my back, shoving me forward into the grass. Evra fell with me and, when we sat up, spluttering with shock, we heard somebody laughing behind us.

We turned slowly, and there was the kid, bent over double with laughter.

"Fooled you! Fooled you!" he sang, dancing about. "I saw you coming from the beginning. I was only pretending to be frightened. I ambushed you. Ha-ha. Ohh-ohh-ohh. Eee-ee-ee."

He was making fun of us and, though we felt pretty foolish, when we stood and looked at each other we burst out laughing. He'd led us into a patch of grass filled with sticky green seeds and we were covered in them from head to foot.

"You look like a walking plant," I joked.

"*You* look like the Jolly Green Giant," Evra replied.

"Both of you look stupid," the boy said. We stared at him and his smile faded a bit. "Well, you *do*," he grumbled.

"I suppose you think this is funny," I snarled. He nodded silently. "Well, I've got news for you, kid," I said, stepping closer, putting on the meanest face I could. I paused menacingly, then burst into a smile. "It is!"

He laughed happily, relieved that we could see the sunny side of things, then stuck out his hands, one to either of us. "Hi," he said as we shook. "My name's Sam Grest. Pleased to meetcha."

"Hi, Sam Grest," I said, and as I shook his hand, I thought to myself, "Looks like this is friend number two."

And he did become my friend. But by the time the Cirque Du Freak moved on, I was wishing with all my heart that I'd never even heard his name.

CHAPTER ELEVEN

SAM LIVED about a kilometre away, with his mum and dad, two younger brothers and a baby sister, three dogs, five cats, two budgies, a turtle, and a tank full of tropical fish.

"It's like living in Noah's Ark," he laughed. "I try and stay out of the house as much as possible. Mum and Dad don't mind. They think children should be free to express their individuality. As long as I turn up for bed at night, they're happy. They don't even care if I miss school every once in a while. They think school's a despotic system of indoctrination, designed to crush the spirit and stamp out creativity."

Sam talked like that all the time. He was younger than me, but you wouldn't have known it by listening to him speak.

"So, you two guys are with the show?" he asked, rolling a piece of pickled onion around his mouth – he loved pickled onions and carried a small plastic jar of them with him. We'd returned to the spot at the edge of the clearing. Evra was lying in the grass, I was sitting on a low-hanging branch, Sam was climbing the tree above me.

"What sort of a show is it?" he asked, before we could answer his first question. "There are very few markings on the vans. At first I thought you were travellers. Then, after observing for a while, I decided you must be performers of one sort or another."

"We're masters of the macabre," Evra said. "Agents of mutations. Lords of the surreal." He was speaking like that to show he could match Sam's fancy way with the language. I wish I could have spouted a few grand-sounding sentences, but I'd never been good with words.

"It's a magic show?" Sam asked excitedly.

"It's a freak show," I said.

"A *freak* show?" His jaw dropped open and the bit of pickled onion fell out. I had to move quickly to dodge it. "Two-headed men and anomalies such as that?"

"Sort of," I said, "but our performers are magical, wonderful artists, not just people who look different."

"Cool!" He glanced at Evra. "Of course, I could see from the start that you were dermatologically challenged – " he was talking about Evra's skin (I looked the word up in a dictionary later) "–but I'd no idea there might be other members like you among your company."

He looked over towards the camp, eyes alight with curiosity. "This is most fascinating," he sighed. "What other bizarre examples of the human form do your numbers hoard?"

"If you mean, 'What other sort of performers are there?', the answer is loads," I told him. "We have a bearded lady, of course."

"A Wolf Man," Evra said.

"A man with two bellies," I added.

We went through the entire list, Evra mentioning some I'd never seen. The line-up of the Cirque Du Freak often changed. Performers came and went, depending on where the show was playing.

Sam was greatly impressed and, for the first time since we'd met, had nothing to say. He listened silently, eyes wide, sucking

243

on one of his pickled onions, shaking his head every so often as though he couldn't believe what he was hearing.

"It's incredible," he said softly when we finished. "You must be the luckiest kids on the planet. Living with real circus freaks, travelling the world, privy to solemn and magnificent secrets. What I wouldn't give to trade places with you ..."

I smiled to myself. I don't think he'd have liked to trade places with *me*, not if he knew my full story.

"Hey!" he said, a thought striking him. "I don't suppose you could swing it for me to join? I'm a hard worker, bright as a button, used to responsibility. I'd be an asset. Could I join? As an assistant? Please?"

Evra and me smiled at each other.

"I don't think so, Sam," Evra said. "We don't take on many kids. If you were older, or if your parents wanted to join, that would be different."

"But they wouldn't mind," Sam insisted. "They'd be delighted for me. They're always saying travel broadens the mind. They'd love the idea of me going around the world, having adventures, seeing marvellous, mystical sights."

Evra shook his head. "Sorry. Maybe when you're older."

Sam pouted and kicked some leaves off a nearby branch. They floated down over me and a couple stuck in my hair.

"It's not fair," Sam grumbled. "People always say 'when you're older'. Where would the world be if Alexander the Great had 'waited until he was older'? And how about Joan of Arc? If she'd 'waited until she was older', the English might have conquered and colonized France. Who decides when someone's old enough to make decisions for themselves? It should be down to the individual."

He ranted on for a while longer, complaining about adults and the "corrupt, bloody system" and about the time being ripe for a children's revolution. It was like listening to a crazy politician on television.

"If a child wants to open a chocolate factory, let him open one," Sam stormed. "If he wants to become a jockey, fine. If he wants to be an explorer and set off for strange, cannibal-populated islands, OK! We're the slaves of the modern generation. We're—"

"Sam," Evra interrupted. "Do you want to come see my snake?"

Sam broke out into a smile. "Do I!" he yelled. "I thought you'd never ask. C'mon, let's go." Leaping down out of the tree, he set off for the camp-site at top speed, speeches forgotten. We followed slowly, laughing gently, feeling much older and wiser than we were.

CHAPTER TWELVE

SAM THOUGHT the snake was the coolest thing he'd ever seen. He wasn't a bit scared, and didn't hesitate to wrap her around his neck like a scarf. He asked all sorts of questions: how long was she, what did she eat, how often did she shed her skin, where was she from, what type of snake was she, how fast could she move?

Evra answered all of Sam's questions. He was a snake expert. There wasn't a thing he didn't know about the serpent kingdom. He was even able to tell Sam roughly how many scales the snake had!

We gave Sam a guided tour of the camp-site after that. We took him to see the Wolf Man (Sam was very quiet in the shade of the hairy Wolf Man's van, frightened by the snarling creature within). We introduced him to Hans Hands. Then we chanced upon Rhamus Twobellies practising his act. Evra asked if we could watch and Rhamus let us. Sam's eyes almost popped out of his head when he saw Rhamus chew a cup into tiny pieces, swallow it, piece it back together inside his belly and bring it up his throat and out his mouth.

I was going to fetch Madam Octa and show Sam some of the tricks I could do with her, but I didn't feel too hot. The lack of human blood in my diet was getting to me; my belly often grumbled hungrily, no matter how much food I ate, and I sometimes got sick or had to sit down suddenly. I didn't want to faint or get sick with the spider out of her cage; I knew from experience how deadly she could be if you lost control of her for even a couple of seconds.

Sam would have stayed for ever, but it was getting dark and I knew Mr Crepsley would be waking soon. Evra and me had jobs to do, so we told him it was time he went home.

"Can't I stay a while longer?" he pleaded.

"Your dinner will be ready," Evra said.

"I can eat with you," Sam said.

"There isn't enough food," I lied.

"Well, I'm not very hungry anyway," Sam said. "It's amazing how filling pickled onions can be."

"Maybe he could stay," Evra mused. I stared at him, surprised, but he winked to show he was only pretending.

"Could I?" Sam asked, delighted.

"Sure," Evra said. "But you'll have to help us with our jobs."

"I'll do anything," Sam said. "I don't mind. What is it?"

"The Wolf Man needs feeding and washing and brushing," Evra said.

Sam's smile slipped.

"The wuh—wolf—muh—man?" he asked nervously.

"It's no problem," Evra told him. "He's normally quiet once he's been fed. He hardly ever bites his helpers. If he *does* attack, keep your head clear of his mouth and stick an arm down his throat. It's better to lose an arm than your—"

"You know," Sam said quickly, "I think I *do* have to go home. Mum said something about friends coming over tonight."

"Oh. That's a pity." Evra grinned.

Sam backed away, gazing in the direction of the Wolf Man's

cage. He looked sad to be going, so I called for him to stop.

"What are you doing tomorrow?" I asked.

"Nothing," he said.

"Do you want to come over in the afternoon and hang out with us?"

"You bet!" Sam whooped, then paused. "I won't have to help feed and clean the ...?" He gulped loudly.

"No," Evra said, still smiling.

"Then I'll be here. See you tomorrow, guys."

"See you, Sam," we said together.

He waved, turned and departed.

"Sam's nice, isn't he?" I said to Evra.

"A good kid," Evra agreed. "He could do with not trying to sound so smart all the time, and he's a bit of a scaredy-cat, but otherwise there's nothing wrong with him."

"Do you think he'd fit in if he did join the show?" I asked.

Evra snorted. "Like a mouse in a house full of cats!"

"What do you mean?" I asked.

"This life isn't for everyone. A few weeks away from his family, having to clean out toilets and cook for thirty or forty people ... He'd be running screaming for the hills."

"*We* manage all right," I said.

"We're different," Evra said. "We're not like other people. This is what we're cut out for. Everybody has a place where they belong. This is ours. We're meant to ..."

He stopped and began to frown. He was glancing over my head at something in the distance. I turned to see what was bothering him. For a few seconds I couldn't make out anything, but then, some way off, coming through the trees to the east, I glimpsed the flickering light of a burning torch.

"Who could that be?" I asked.

"I'm not sure," Evra said.

We watched for a few minutes as the torch came closer. I saw figures moving beneath the cover of the trees. I couldn't tell how many there were, but it had to be at least six or seven. Then, as they broke free of the trees, I saw who they were, and goosebumps sprang to life along my neck and arms.

The walkers were the small blue-hooded people that Steve and me had seen the night of the show, the ones who helped sell sweets and toys to the crowd, and assisted with the acts. I'd forgotten about those strange blue-hooded helpers. It had been several months since that night, and I'd had other things on my mind.

They came out of the woods in pairs, one set after the other. I counted twelve in all, though there was a thirteenth member, a taller person walking behind the rest. He was the one shining the torch.

"Where did they come from?" I asked Evra quietly.

"I don't know," he answered. "They left the show a few weeks ago. I've no idea where they went. They keep to themselves mostly."

"Who are they?" I asked.

"They're—" he began to answer, but stopped all of a sudden. His eyes widened with fear.

It was the man bringing up the rear, the thirteenth, taller member of the group – visible now that he was closer – who had scared Evra.

The blue-hooded people passed by silently. As the mysterious thirteenth person approached, I noticed he was dressed differently to the others. He wasn't very tall; he just looked big in comparison to the blue-hoods. He had short white hair, a thick pair of glasses, a sharp yellow suit and long green Wellington boots. He was quite plump and walked with a peculiar little waddle.

He smiled pleasantly at us as he passed. I smiled back but

Evra was rooted to the spot, unable to move the muscles of his mouth.

The blue-hoods and the man with the torch walked further into the camp-site, all the way to the back, where they found a large clear spot. There, the blue-hoods began putting up a tent — they must have been carrying the materials beneath their cloaks — while the larger man headed for Mr Tall's van.

I studied Evra. He was shaking all over and, though his face could never turn white — because of its natural colour — it was paler than it had ever been before.

"What's wrong?" I asked.

He shook his head silently, unable to reply.

"What is it? Why are you so frightened? Who was that man?"

"He ... It ..." Evra cleared his throat and took a deep breath. When he spoke, it was in a low, trembling voice, filled with sheer, blood-chilled terror.

"That was *Mr Tiny*," he said, and I could get no more out of him for ages after that.

CHAPTER THIRTEEN

EVRA'S FEAR faded as evening wore on, but he was very slow to return to normal and was uncommonly edgy the whole night long. I had to take his knife from him and do his share when he was peeling potatoes for the dinner; I was afraid he might slice one of his fingers off.

After we'd eaten and helped wash up, I asked Evra about the mysterious Mr Tiny. We were in the tent and Evra was playing with his snake.

He didn't reply immediately, and for a while I thought he wasn't going to, but in the end he sighed and began to speak.

"Mr Tiny is the leader of the Little People," he said.

"The small guys in the blue-hooded cloaks?" I asked.

"Yes. He calls them Little People. He's their boss. He doesn't come here often – it's been two years since I last saw him – but he gives me the creeps when he does. He's the spookiest man I've ever met."

"He looked all right to me," I said.

"That's what I thought the first time I saw him," Evra agreed. "But wait until you've spoken to him. It's hard to explain, but every time he looks at me, I feel like he's planning to slaughter, skin and roast me."

"He eats people?" I asked, aghast.

"I don't know," Evra said. "Maybe he does, maybe he doesn't. But you get the feeling he *wants* to eat you. And it's not just me being silly; I've discussed it with other members of the Cirque and they feel the same way. Nobody likes him. Even Mr Tall gets fidgety when Mr Tiny's around."

"Well, the Little People must like him, mustn't they?" I asked. "They follow and obey him, don't they?"

"Maybe they're scared of him," Evra said. "Maybe he forces them to obey him. Perhaps they're his slaves."

"Have you ever asked them?"

"They don't talk," Evra said. "I don't know if it's because they can't or they prefer not to, but nobody in the circus has ever been able to get a word out of them. They're very helpful and they'll do whatever you ask but they're as silent as walking dummies."

"Have you ever seen their faces?" I asked.

"Once," Evra said. "Normally they don't let their hoods slip, but one day I was helping a couple of them move a heavy machine. It fell on one of the Little People and crushed him. He didn't make a sound, even though he must have been in a huge amount of pain. His hood fell to the side and I caught a glimpse of his face.

"It was horrible," Evra said quietly, stroking his snake softly. "Full of scars and stitches and crumpled in on itself, as though some giant had squeezed it with his claws. It had no ears or nose, and there was some sort of a mask over its mouth. The skin was grey and dead-looking, and his eyes were like two green bowls near the top of his face. He had no hair."

Evra shivered at the memory. I felt cold myself, thinking about his description.

"What happened to him?" I asked. "Did he die?"

"I don't know," Evra said. "A couple of his brothers – I always think of them as brothers, though they probably aren't – turned up and carted him away."

"You never saw him again?"

"They all look the same," Evra said. "Some are a bit smaller or taller than the rest, but there's no real way of telling them apart. Believe me: I've tried."

Stranger and stranger. I was really interested in Mr Tiny and his Little People. I'd always liked mysteries. Perhaps I could solve this one. Maybe, with my vampire powers, I could find a way to talk with one of the hooded creatures.

"Where do the Little People come from?" I asked.

"Nobody knows," Evra said. "There's usually four or six of them with the Cirque. Sometimes more turn up by themselves. Sometimes Mr Tiny brings new ones in. It was odd that none were here when you arrived."

"You think it had something to do with me and Mr Crepsley coming?" I asked.

"I doubt it," Evra said. "It was probably just coincidence. Or fate." He paused. "Which is another thing: Mr Tiny's first name is Desmond."

"So?"

"He tells people to call him Des."

"So?" I asked again.

"Put it together with his surname," Evra told me.

I did. Mr Des Tiny. Mr Des-Tiny. Mr ...

"*Mr Destiny*," I whispered, and Evra nodded seriously.

I was bursting with curiosity and asked Evra many more questions, but his answers were limited. He knew almost nothing of Mr Tiny, and only slightly more of the Little People. They ate meat. They smelled funny. They moved slowly most of the time. They either didn't feel pain or couldn't show it. And they had no sense of humour.

"How do you know that?" I asked.

"Bradley Stretch," Evra answered darkly. "He used to be with the show. He had rubbery bones and could make his arms and legs stretch.

"He wasn't very nice. He was constantly playing practical jokes on us and he had a nasty way of laughing. He didn't just make you look like a fool: he made you feel like one too.

"We played a show in an Arabian palace. It was a private show for a sheikh. He enjoyed all the acts but especially liked Bradley's. The two got chatting and Bradley told the sheikh he couldn't wear jewellery, because it always slipped off or burst, because of the changing shape of his body.

"The sheikh hurried away and came back with a small gold bracelet. He gave it to Bradley and told him to put it on his wrist. Bradley did. Then the sheikh told him to try shaking it off.

"Well, Bradley made his arm small and big, short and long, but he couldn't shake that bracelet loose. The sheikh said it was magic and could only be removed if the wearer wanted to take it off. It was very valuable, priceless, but he made Bradley a gift of it, to show his appreciation.

"Getting back to the Little People," Evra said. "Bradley loved to tease them. He was always finding new ways to trick them. He fixed traps to hang them up in the air by their feet. He set their cloaks on fire. He squirted washing-up liquid on ropes they were using, to make their hands slip, or glue to make them stick. He put thumb-tacks in their food, he made their tent collapse, he locked them into a van."

"Why was he so mean?" I asked.

"I think because they never reacted," Evra said. "He liked to see people get upset but the Little People never cried or screamed or lashed out. They seemed to take no notice of his pranks. At least, everybody *thought* they took no notice ..."

Evra made a funny noise that was half a laugh, half a moan.

"One morning we woke up and Bradley had disappeared. Nowhere to be found. We searched for him, but when he didn't turn up, we moved on. We weren't worried; performers join and leave the Cirque pretty much as they please. It wasn't the first time one had sneaked away in the middle of the night.

"I thought no more about it until a week or so later. Mr Tiny had been to see us the day before and taken all but two of the Little People with him. Mr Tall told me I had to help the remaining pair with their duties. I tidied around their tent and rolled up their hammocks – they all sleep in hammocks. That's where I got mine from. Did I mention that before?"

He hadn't, but I didn't want to side-track him, so I said nothing.

"After that," he went on, "I gave their pot a wash. It was a big black pot, set on a fire in the middle of the tent. The place must have been full of smoke whenever they cooked, and the pot was covered in grime.

"I took it outside and emptied the remains of their last few meals – scraps of meat and bits of bone – on to the grass. I scrubbed it thoroughly, then took it back inside. Next I decided to gather up the bits of meat in the grass and throw them to the Wolf Man. 'Waste not, want not', as Mr Tall often says.

"As I was gathering up the meat and bone, I noticed something glistening ..."

Evra turned away and rooted through a bag underneath his hammock. When he faced me, he was holding a small gold bracelet. He let my eyes linger on it, then slipped it on over his left hand. He shook his arm as fast as he could but the bracelet never budged.

When he stopped shaking his arm, he slid the bracelet off with the fingers of his right hand and tossed it to me. I caught and examined it, but didn't put it on.

"The bracelet the sheikh gave to Bradley Stretch?" I guessed.

"The same," Evra said.

I handed it back.

"I don't know whether it was because of something especially bad he did," Evra said, fingering the bracelet, "or if they were just tired of the non-stop teasing. What I do know is, ever since, I've gone out of my way to be polite to the small silent people in the dark blue cloaks."

"What did you do with the remains of ... I mean, with the scraps of meat?" I asked. "Did you bury them?"

"Heck, no," Evra said. "I fed them to the Wolf Man, as I'd meant to." Then, in response to my horrified gasp, he said: 'Waste not, want not', remember?"

I stared at him in silence, then began to laugh. Evra chuckled too. In a minute we were rolling about on the floor, hugging our sides.

"We shouldn't laugh," I gasped. "Poor Bradley Stretch. We should be crying."

"I'm laughing too hard to cry," Evra giggled.

"I wonder what he tasted like?"

"I don't know," Evra said. "But I bet he was rubbery."

That made us laugh so much, tears rolled from our eyes and trickled down our cheeks. It was a terrible thing to laugh at, but we couldn't help ourselves.

In the middle of our fit of laughter, the flap to the door of our tent was poked aside by an inquisitive head and Hans Hands entered. "What's the joke?" he asked, but we couldn't tell him. I tried, but every time I started, I began laughing again.

He shook his head and smiled at our foolishness. Then, when we'd quietened down, he told us why he was here.

"I've a message for you two," he said. "Mr Tall wants you to report to his van as soon as possible."

"What's up, Hans?" Evra asked. He was still giggling. "Why does he want us?"

"He doesn't," Hans said. "Mr Tiny is with him. *He's* the one who wants you."

Our laughter stopped instantly. Hans let himself out without any further words.

"Mr Tuh-tuh-tuh-Tiny wants us," Evra gasped.

"I heard," I said. "What do you think he wants?"

"I don't kn–kn–kn–know," Evra stuttered, though I could see what was going through his mind. It was the same thing that was rushing through mine. We were thinking of the Little People, Bradley Stretch, and a big black pot full of scraps of human meat and bone.

CHAPTER FOURTEEN

MR TALL, Mr Crepsley and Mr Tiny were in the van when we entered. Evra was shaking like a leaf but I wasn't especially nervous. Mind you, when I saw the worried looks of Mr Tall and Mr Crepsley, and realized how uneasy they were, it set me on edge a little.

"Come in, boys," Mr Tiny welcomed us as though it was his van and not Mr Tall's. "Sit down, make yourselves at home."

"I'll stand, if it's all the same," Evra said, trying not to let us hear the chatter of his teeth.

"I'll stand too," I said, following Evra's lead.

"As you please," Mr Tiny said. He was the only one sitting.

"I've been hearing a lot about you, young Darren Shan," Mr Tiny said. He was rolling something between his hands: a heart-shaped watch. I could hear it ticking whenever there was a pause in his speech.

"You're quite the lad, by all accounts," Mr Tiny went on. "A most remarkable young man. Sacrificed everything to save a friend. There aren't many would do as much. People are so self-centred these days. It's great to see the world can still produce heroes."

"I'm no hero," I said, blushing at the compliment.

"Of course you are," he insisted. "What is a hero but a person who lays everything on the line for the good of somebody else?"

I smiled proudly. I couldn't understand why Evra was so afraid of this nice, odd man. There was nothing terrible about Mr Tiny. I quite liked him.

"Larten tells me you're reluctant to drink human blood," Mr Tiny said. "I don't blame you. Nasty, repulsive stuff. Can't stand it. Apart from young children, of course. Their blood is scrum-diddlyumptious."

I frowned. "You can't drink blood from them," I said. "They're too small. If you took blood from a young child, you'd kill it."

His eyes widened and so did his smile.

"*So?*" he asked softly.

A chill ran down my spine. If he'd been joking, it would have been in very poor taste, but I could have overlooked it (hadn't I just been laughing about poor Bradley Stretch?). But I could tell from his expression that he was perfectly serious.

All of a sudden, I knew why this man was so feared. *He was evil.* Not just bad or nasty, but pure demonic evil. This was a man I could imagine killing thousands of people, just to hear them scream.

"You know," Mr Tiny said, "your face seems familiar. Have we met before, Darren Shan?"

I shook my head.

"Are you certain?" he asked. "You look *very* familiar."

"I ... would have ... remembered," I gasped.

"You can't always trust memory," Mr Tiny smiled. "It can be a deceptive monster. Still, no matter. Maybe I'm confusing you with somebody else."

By the way his lips twisted into a grin (how had I ever thought that was a nice smile?), I could see he didn't think that. But I was sure he was wrong. There's no way I'd have forgotten meeting a creature like this.

"Down to business," Mr Tiny said. His hands tightened on the heart-shaped watch and for a moment they seemed to glow and melt into its ticking face. I blinked and rubbed my eyes. When I looked again, the illusion — which it must have been — had passed.

"You boys saw me arrive with my Little People," Mr Tiny said. "They're new converts to my cause and are a bit unsure of the ropes. Normally I'd stick around and teach them how to get along, but I have business elsewhere. Still, they're smart and I'm sure they'll learn.

"However, while they're learning, I'd like it if you two fine, decent boys would help ease them into the swing of things. You won't have to do much. Mainly I want you to find food for them. They have such big appetites.

"How about it, boys? I've got the permission of your guardians." He nodded at Mr Tall and Mr Crepsley, who didn't seem happy about the arrangement, but looked resigned. "Will you help poor old Mr Tiny and his Little People?"

I glanced at Evra. I could see he didn't want to agree to the request, but he nodded his head anyway. I did likewise.

"Excellent!" Mr Tiny boomed. "Young Evra Von knows what my darlings like, I'm sure. If you have any problems, report to Hibernius and he'll sort you out."

Mr Tiny waved a hand to let us know we could leave. Evra began edging backwards immediately, but I held my ground.

"Excuse me," I said, summoning all my courage, "but why do you call them Little People?"

Mr Tiny looked around slowly. If he was surprised by my question, he didn't show it, though I could see the mouths of Mr

Tall and Mr Crepsley dropping.

"Because they're little," he explained pleasantly.

"I know that," I said. "But don't they have another name? A proper name? If somebody mentioned 'Little People' to me, I'd think they were talking about Elves or Leprechauns."

Mr Tiny smiled. "They *are* Elves and Leprechauns," he said. "All around the world, you will find legends and stories of small, magical people. Legends have to start somewhere. These legends started with my short, loyal friends."

"Are you telling me those dwarfs in blue cloaks are *Elves*?" I asked disbelievingly.

"No," he said. "Elves don't exist. Those dwarfs — as you so rudely put it — were seen, long ago, by ignorant people, who invented names for them: Elves or Fairies or Sprites. They made up stories about what they were and what they could do."

"What *can* they do?" I asked curiously.

Mr Tiny's smile slipped. "I'd heard you were quite the one for asking questions," he growled, "but nobody told me you were *this* nosy. Remember, Darren Shan: curiosity killed the cat."

"I'm not a cat," I said cheekily.

Mr Tiny leaned forward and his face darkened. "If you ask more questions," he hissed, "you might find yourself turned into one. Nothing in life is for ever, not even the human form."

The watch in his hands glowed again, red like a real heart, and I decided the time had come to take my leave.

"Go to bed now and get a good night's sleep," Mr Crepsley told me before I left. "There will be no lessons tonight."

"And rise early, boys," Mr Tiny added, waving goodbye. "My Little People are always hungry in the mornings. It's not wise to let their hunger go unattended. You never know what they might set their minds — and *teeth* — on if they go unfed for too long."

We hurried out the door and raced back to our tent, where we fell to the floor and listened to our hearts beating loudly.

"Are you crazy?" Evra asked when he could speak. "Talking to Mr Tiny like that, asking him questions, you must be mad!"

"Yes," I said, thinking back on the encounter, wondering where I'd got the nerve from. "I must be."

Evra shook his head in disgust. It was early, but we crawled into bed anyway, where we lay awake for ages, staring at the ceiling of the tent. When I finally dropped off to sleep I dreamt of Mr Tiny and his heart-shaped watch. Only, in my dreams, it wasn't a watch. It was a real human heart. *Mine.* And when he squeezed it ...

Agony.

CHAPTER FIFTEEN

WE ROSE early and went hunting for food for the Little People. We were tired and grumpy and it took time for us to come to life.

After a while I asked Evra what the Little People liked to eat.

"Meat," he replied. "Any kind of animal, they don't care."

"How many animals will we need to catch?" I asked.

"Well, there's twelve of them, but they don't eat a lot. I guess one rabbit or hedgehog between two of them. A larger animal – a fox or a dog – might do three or four."

"Can you eat hedgehogs?" I asked.

"The Little People can," Evra said. "They're not fussy. They'd eat rats and mice too, but we'd have to catch loads to feed so many, so they're not worth bothering with."

We took a sack each and hit off in different directions. Evra told me the meat didn't have to be fresh, so if I found a dead badger or squirrel, I could stick it in the bag and save some time.

I spotted a fox a couple of minutes into the hunt. It had a chicken in its mouth and was on its way home. I tracked it until the moment was right, then pounced on it from behind a bush and dragged it to the ground.

The dead chicken flew from its mouth and it turned, snarling, to bite me. Before it could attack, I moved swiftly, grabbed its neck and twisted sharply to the left. There was a loud crack and that was the end of the fox.

I chucked the chicken into the bag – a welcome bonus – but hung on to the fox for a few minutes. I needed blood, so I found a vein, made a small cut, and started sucking.

Part of me hated this – it seemed inhuman – but I reminded myself that I *wasn't* human any more. I was a half-vampire. This was how my kind acted. I'd felt bad killing foxes and rabbits and pigs and sheep the first few times. But I got used to it. I had to.

Could I get used to drinking human blood? That was the question. I hoped I could avoid feeding on humans, but by the way I was running out of energy, I knew eventually I'd have to ... or die!

I tossed the body of the fox into the bag, then continued hunting. I found a family of rabbits washing their ears in a nearby pond. I crept as close as I could, then struck without warning. They scattered in fear, but not before I'd got my sharp fingernails into three of the little ones.

I added them to the contents of the bag and decided that would do for this trip. The fox, chicken and rabbits should easily feed six or seven of the blue-hoods.

I met Evra back at camp. He'd found a dead dog and badger and was feeling pretty pleased with himself. "The easiest day's hunting I've ever had," he said. "Plus I found a field full of cows. We'll go there tonight and steal one. It'll keep the Little People going for a day or two at least."

"Won't the farmer who owns them notice?" I asked.

"There are dozens of them," Evra said. "By the time he gets round to counting them, we'll be long gone."

"But cows cost money," I said. "I don't mind killing wild

animals, but stealing from a farmer is different."

"We'll leave money for him," Evra sighed.

"Where will we get it?" I asked.

Evra smiled. "The one thing we're never short of at the Cirque Du Freak is money," he assured me.

Later, our chores completed, we teamed up with Sam again. He'd been waiting in the bushes for ages.

"Why didn't you come into the camp?" I asked.

"I didn't like to impose," he said. "Besides, I thought somebody might have let the Wolf Man out. He didn't seem too fond of me when I saw him yesterday."

"He's like that with everyone," Evra told him.

"Maybe," Sam said, "but I figure it's best not to take chances."

Sam was in a questioning mood. He'd obviously been thinking about us a lot since the day before.

"Don't you ever wear shoes?" he asked Evra.

"No," Evra said. "The soles of my feet are extra tough."

"What happens if you step on a thorn or a nail?" Sam asked.

Evra smiled, sat down and gave Sam his foot. "Try scratching it with a sharp twig," he said.

Sam broke off a branch and prodded Evra's sole. I looked on with interest. It was like trying to make a hole in tough leather.

"A sharp piece of glass might slice me," Evra said, "but it doesn't happen very often, and my skin's getting tougher every year."

"I wish I had skin like that," Sam said enviously. Then he turned to me. "How come you wear the same suit all the time?" he asked.

I glanced down at the suit I'd been buried alive in. I'd meant to ask for some new clothes but had forgotten.

"I like it," I said.

"I've never seen a kid wearing a suit like that before," Sam said.

"Not unless at a wedding or a funeral. Are you forced to wear it?"

"No," I said.

"Did you ask your parents if you could join the Cirque?" Evra said then, to distract Sam's attention.

"No," Sam sighed. "I told them about it, of course, but I figured it would be best to take it in stages. I won't tell them until just before I leave, or maybe not until I'm gone."

"You still plan to join?" I asked.

"You bet!" Sam said. "I know you tried putting me off, but I'll get in somehow. You wait. I'll keep coming around, I'll read books and learn everything there is to know about freak shows, then I'll go to your boss and state my case. He won't be able to turn me down."

Evra and I smiled at each other. We knew Sam's dream would never lead to anything, but hadn't the heart to tell him.

We went to see an old deserted railway station later on, about two kilometres away, which Sam had told us about.

"It's great," he said. "They used to work on trains there, repair and paint them and stuff like that. It was a busy station in its day. Then a new firm set up closer to the city and this place went bust. It's a great place to play. There are rusty old railway tracks, empty sheds, a guard house, and a couple of ancient train carriages."

"Is it safe?" Evra asked.

"My mum says it isn't," Sam told us. "It's one of the few places she tells me to stay away from. She says I could fall through the roof of one of the carriages or trip on a rail or something. But I've been there loads of times and nothing's happened."

It was another sunny day and we were strolling along slowly under the cover of the trees, when I smelled something strange. I stopped and sniffed the air. Evra could smell it too.

"What is that?" I asked.

"I don't know," he said, sniffing the air beside me. "Which way is it coming from?"

"I can't tell," I said. It was a thick, heavy, sour smell.

Sam hadn't smelled anything and was walking on ahead of us. He realized we weren't beside him, stopped and turned to see what was keeping us.

"What's wrong?" he asked. "Why aren't you—"

"*Gotcha!*" a voice yelled behind me, and before I could move I felt a firm hand grab my shoulder and spin me around. I glimpsed a large, hairy face, and then I was falling backwards, thrown off-balance by the force of the hand.

CHAPTER SIXTEEN

I LANDED awkwardly and sprained my arm. I gave a shout of pain, then tried twisting away from the hairy figure above me. Before I could, he was crouching by my side, a fierce look on his face.

"Oh, hey, man, I didn't hurt you, did I?" He had a jolly voice and I realized my life wasn't in danger; the look on his face was one of concern, not anger.

"I didn't mean to spook you so much," the man said. "I was just trying to scare you a little, man, for fun."

I sat up and rubbed my elbow. "I'm OK," I said.

"You're sure? It ain't broken, is it? I've got herbs that can help, if it is."

"Herbs can't mend broken bones," Sam said. He'd tracked back and was standing beside Evra.

"They sure can't," the stranger agreed, "but they can elevate you to plains of consciousness where worldly concerns like broken bones are nothing but minor blips on the cosmic map." He paused and stroked his beard. "Of course, they burn out your brain cells too ..."

Sam's blank face showed that even *he* hadn't understood that long sentence.

"I'm OK," I said again. I stood and rotated the arm. "I just twisted it. It'll be fine in a couple of minutes."

"Man, that's good to hear," the stranger sighed. "I'd hate to be the cause of bodily harm. Hurt's a bad trip, man."

I studied him in more detail. He was big, chubby, with a bushy black beard and long scraggly hair. His clothes were dirty and he couldn't have had a bath recently, because he stank to high heaven. That's what the strange smell had been. He was so friendly-looking, it made me feel foolish thinking about how I'd been afraid of him.

"Are you kids locals?" the man asked.

"I am," Sam said. "These two are with the circus."

"Circus?" The man smiled. "There's a circus around here? Oh, man, how did I miss it? Where is it? I love the circus. I never pass up a chance to see clowns in action."

"It's not that sort of circus," Sam told him. "It's a freak-show."

"A freak-show?" The man stared at Sam, then at Evra, whose scales and colour clearly marked him out as one of the performers. "Are you part of a freak-show, man?" he asked.

Evra nodded shyly.

"They don't maltreat you, do they?" the man asked. "They don't whip you or under-feed you or make you do things you don't want?"

"No," Evra smiled.

"You're there of your own free will?"

"Yes," Evra said. "All of us are. It's our home."

"Oh. Well, that's OK," the man said, smiling once more. "You hear rumours about these small travelling shows. You ..." He slapped his forehead. "Oh man, I haven't introduced myself, have I? I'm so dumb sometimes. R.V.'s the name."

"R.V.? That's a funny name," I remarked.

He coughed with embarrassment. "Well," he said, lowering his voice to a whisper, "it's short for Reggie Veggie."

"*Reggie Veggie?*" I laughed.

"Yeah," he grimaced. "Reggie's my real name. Reggie Veggie's what they called me in school, because I'm a vegetarian. Well, I never liked that, so I asked them to call me R.V. instead. Some did, but not many." He looked miserable at the memory. "You can call me Reggie Veggie if you want," he told us.

"R.V. is fine by me," I assured him.

"Me too," Evra said.

"And me," Sam added.

"Cool!" R.V. brightened up. "So, that's my name out in the open. How about you three?"

"Darren Shan," I told him, and we shook hands.

"Sam Grest."

"Evra Von."

"Evra Von what?" R.V. asked, as I had when I first met Evra.

"Just plain Von," Evra said.

"Oh." R.V. smiled. "Cool!"

R.V. was an eco warrior, here to stop a road being built. He was a member of NOP – Nature's Opposing Protectors – and had travelled the length and breadth of the country, saving forests and lakes and animals and famous landmarks.

He offered to show us round his camp and we jumped at the chance. The railway station could wait. This was an opportunity that wouldn't arise every day.

He talked about the environment non-stop as we walked. He told us about all the lousy things being done to Mother Nature, the forests we were destroying, the rivers we were polluting, the air we were poisoning, the animals we were driving to extinction.

"And this is all in our own country!" he said. "I'm not talking about stuff happening somewhere else. This is what we're doing to our own land!"

NOP were fighting to save the earth from greedy, dangerous humans who didn't care what they did to it. They journeyed up and down the country, trying to make other people aware of the dangers. They gave out pamphlets and books about how to protect the environment.

"But raising awareness ain't enough," R.V. told us. "It's a start, but we must do more. We have to stop the pollution and destruction of the countryside. Take this place: they were going to build a road through an old burial mound, a place where druids buried their dead, thousands of years ago. Can you imagine that, man? Destroying a part of history, just to save drivers ten or twenty minutes!"

R.V. shook his head sadly. "These are crazy times, man," he said. "The things we're doing to this planet ... In the future – assuming there is one – people will look back on what we've done and call us idiotic barbarians."

He was very passionate about the environment and, after listening to him for a while, so were Sam, Evra and me. I hadn't thought about it much before, but after a couple of hours with R.V., I realized I should have. As R.V. said, those who don't think and act now can't complain when the world crumbles around their ears later.

His camp-site was an interesting place. The people – twenty or so – slept in hand-made huts which had been built out of branches and leaves and shrubs. Most were as dirty and smelly as R.V., but they were also cheerful and kind and generous.

"How did you stop the road from being built?" Sam asked.

"We dug tunnels beneath the land," R.V. said. "And we sabotaged the machines they sent in. And we alerted the media. Rich cats hate having cameras pointed at them. One TV news crew is as good as twenty active warriors."

Evra asked R.V. if they ever fought hand to hand. R.V. said NOP didn't believe in violent confrontation, but we could see from the look on his face that he wasn't happy about that. "If I had my way," he said quietly, "we'd give as good as we got. We're too nice sometimes. Man, if I was in charge, we'd give those turkeys a taste of what-for!"

R.V. invited us to stay for lunch. It wasn't very nice food – there was no meat, just loads of vegetables and rice and fruit – but we ate plenty, to be polite.

They had lots of mushrooms as well – large and oddly coloured – but R.V. wouldn't let us eat any of those.

"When you're older, man," he chuckled.

We left shortly after lunch. The members of NOP had duties and jobs to be getting on with and we didn't want to be in the way.

R.V. told us we could come back any time, but that they'd probably be moving on in a couple of days.

"We've almost won the fight here," he said. "Another few days and it'll be time to strike out for pastures new. Battles come and go, man, but the war is never ending."

We waved goodbye and hit for home.

"That R.V.'s strange," Sam said after a while. "Imagine giving up everything to go off and fight for animals and the countryside."

"He's doing what he believes in," Evra said.

"I know," Sam said. "And I'm glad he's doing it. We need people like him. It's a pity there aren't more of his kind. Still, it's an odd way to live, isn't it? You'd have to be very dedicated. I don't think I could become an environmental warrior."

"Me neither," I agreed.

"I could," Evra said.

"You could not," I snorted.

"Why not?" he pouted. "I could take my snake and live with them and fight with them."

"You couldn't," I insisted.

"Why not?" he asked.

"Because you're not smelly enough!" I laughed.

Evra pulled a face, then grinned. "They *were* a bit on the pongy side, weren't they?" he admitted.

"They smell worse than my feet when I haven't changed my socks for a week!" Sam guffawed.

"Still," Evra said, "I can think of lots of worse ways to spend my time when I grow up. I'd like to be like R.V. when I'm older."

"Me too," Sam said.

I shrugged. "I guess I could get used to it," I agreed.

We were in high spirits and talked about NOP and R.V. the whole way back to camp. None of us had any idea of the trouble the nice eco warrior would soon create ... or the tragedy he would unwittingly cause.

CHAPTER SEVENTEEN

WE PASSED the next few days in leisurely fashion. Evra and me were kept busy with our chores and with feeding the Little People. I'd tried talking to a couple of the silent blue-hooded creatures, but not one of them so much as looked at me when I spoke.

It was impossible to tell them apart. One stood out because he – or she (or it) – was taller than the others, and one was shorter, and another limped on his left leg. But the rest looked exactly alike.

Sam was helping out more and more around the camp. We didn't take him with us when we went hunting, but let him lend a hand with most of our other jobs. He was a hard worker, determined to impress us and earn himself a full-time position with the Cirque.

I didn't see much of Mr Crepsley. He knew I had to be up early to hunt for the Little People's food, so he left me alone most of the time. I was happy that way; I didn't want him bugging me about drinking human blood.

Then Cormac Limbs arrived, early one morning, which caused great excitement.

"You've got to see this guy," Evra said, dragging me behind him. "He's the most amazing performer who ever lived."

There was already a large crowd around Cormac when we arrived at Mr Tall's van (where he had reported to). People were slapping him on the back and asking what he'd been up to and where he'd been. He smiled at everybody, shook hands and answered their questions. He might have been a star but he wasn't big-headed.

"Evra Von!" he shouted when he saw the snake-boy. He reached over and gave Evra a hug. "How's my favourite two-legged reptile?"

"Fine," Evra said.

"Did you shed your skin lately?" Cormac asked.

"Not recently," Evra said.

"Remember," Cormac said, "I want it when you do. It's valuable. Human snake-skin is worth more than gold in some countries."

"You can have as much of it as you like," Evra assured him. Then he pushed me forward. "Cormac, this is Darren Shan, a friend of mine. He's new at the Cirque and has never seen you before."

"Never seen Cormac Limbs?!?" Cormac shouted, pretending to be upset. "How can this be? I thought everybody in the world had seen the magnificent Cormac Limbs in action."

"I've never even heard of you," I told him.

He clutched his chest as though suffering a heart-attack.

"What is it you do?" I asked.

Cormac looked around at the crowd. "Shall I give a demonstration?"

"Oh yes!" they shouted eagerly.

Cormac looked at Mr Tall, standing at the back of the crowd. Mr Tall sighed and nodded. "You may as well," he said. "They won't leave you alone until you do."

"Very well," Cormac said. "Stand back and give me room."

The crowd moved back immediately. I started to move with them, but Cormac laid a hand on my shoulder and told me to stay.

"Now," he said to the crowd, "I've been travelling for ages and I'm too tired to go through my entire routine, so we'll keep this short and sweet."

He made his right hand into a fist, then stuck out his index finger. "Darren, will you place this finger in your mouth?" he asked.

I glanced at Evra, who signalled for me to do as Cormac asked.

"Now," Cormac said, "bite down on it, please."

I bit softly.

"Harder," Cormac said.

I bit slightly harder.

"Come on, boy," Cormac shouted. "Put some backbone in it. Work those jaws. Are you a shark or a mouse?"

OK. He wanted me to bite hard? Then I would.

I opened my mouth and bit down quickly, meaning to give him a shock. Instead, I was the one who was shocked, because I bit *clean through the finger and snapped it right off!*

I fell back in terror and spat the dead finger from my mouth. My eyes shot up at Cormac Limbs. I expected him to scream, but he only laughed and held up his hand.

There was no blood where I'd bitten the finger off, only a white, jagged stump. As I watched, the most amazing thing happened, *the finger began to grow back!*

I thought I must be imagining it, but as the seconds passed, it continued to grow and soon it was full length again. Cormac held it rigidly in place a few seconds longer, then flexed it in and out to show it was as good as new.

The crowd cheered and I felt my heart settle in my chest.

I looked down at the ground, where I'd spat out the finger, and saw it beginning to rot. Within a minute it was nothing more than a greyish mound of mould.

"Sorry if I frightened you," Cormac said, giving my head a pat.

"That's OK," I told him. "I should have learned by now to expect the unexpected round here. Can I feel the new finger?" He nodded. It felt no different to any of the others. "How do you do it?" I asked, amazed. "Is it an illusion?"

"No illusion," he said. "It's why they call me Cormac *Limbs*. I've been able to grow new limbs – fingers, toes, arms, legs – ever since I was a nipper. My parents discovered my talent when I had an accident with a kitchen knife and cut off part of my nose. I can grow virtually any part of my body anew. Except my head. I haven't tried cutting that off. Best not to tempt fate."

"Doesn't it hurt?" I asked.

"A little," he said, "but not much. When one of my limbs gets cut off, a new one starts to grow almost immediately, so there's only a second or two of pain. It's a bit like—"

"Come, come!" Mr Tall bellowed, cutting him short. "We don't have time for a detailed description. This show has been idle far too long. It's time we entertained the public again, before they forget about us or think we've retired.

"People," he shouted to the crowd and clapped his hands together. "Spread the word. The lull is over. The show goes on tonight!"

CHAPTER EIGHTEEN

THE CAMP was buzzing with activity all afternoon. People were rushing about like ants. A large number were working on putting together the circus tent. I hadn't seen it before. It was an impressive sight when finished, tall and round and red, decorated with pictures of the performers.

Evra and me were kept busy, hammering pegs into the ground to hold the tent in place, arranging seats inside, setting up the stage for the show, preparing props for the performers (we had to find tin cans and nuts and bolts for Rhamus Twobellies to eat, help move the Wolf Man's cage inside the tent, and so on).

It was a huge operation but it moved with incredible speed. Everyone in the camp knew their place and what was expected of them, and there was never any real panic over the course of the day. Everybody worked as part of a team and things came together smoothly.

Sam turned up early in the afternoon. I would have kept him around to help with the work, but Evra said he'd be in the way, so we sent him packing. He was upset and slouched off in a sulk, kicking an empty tin can along in front of him. I felt sorry for him, then realized how I could cheer him up.

"Sam! Wait a minute!" I shouted. "I'll be back in a tick," I told Evra, then rushed off to Mr Tall's van.

I knocked once on the door and it opened instantly. Mr Tall was standing inside and, before I could say a word, he held out two tickets for entry to the Cirque Du Freak.

I stared at the tickets, then at Mr Tall. "How did you know ...?"

"I have my ways," he replied with a smile.

"I haven't any money," I warned him.

"I'll take it out of your wages," he said.

I frowned. "You don't pay me anything."

His smile widened. "Clever old me." He handed over the tickets and closed the door in my face before I could thank him.

I hurried back to Sam and passed on the tickets.

"What are these?" he asked.

"Tickets for tonight's show," I told him. "One for you and one for R.V."

"Oh, wow!" Sam quickly stuck the tickets into his pocket, as if he was afraid they might blow away or vanish. "Thanks, Darren."

"No problem," I said. "The only thing is, it's a late show. We're starting at eleven and it won't be over till nearly one in the morning. Will you be able to make it?"

"Sure," Sam said. "I'll sneak out. Mum and Dad go to bed at half past nine every night. They're early birds."

"If you get caught," I warned him, "don't tell them where you're going."

"My lips are sealed," he promised, then set off at a run to find R.V.

Except for a quick dinner, there was no further break between then and the start of the show. While Evra left to groom his snake, I set up candles inside the circus tent. There were also five huge chandeliers to be hung, four above the crowd, one over the stage, but the Little People handled those.

Mags — a pretty woman who sold toys and sweets during the breaks — asked me to help her get the trays ready, so I spent an hour stacking candy webs and edible "glass" statues and strands of the Wolf Man's hair. There was a new novelty I hadn't seen before: a small model of Cormac Limbs. When you cut a part of it off, a new piece grew in its place. I asked Mags how it worked but she didn't know.

"It's one of Mr Tall's inventions," she said. "He makes a lot of this stuff himself."

I chopped the head off the model and tried peering down the neck, to see what was inside, but a new head grew before I could.

"The models don't last for ever," Mags said. "They rot after a few months."

"Do you tell people that when they're buying them?" I asked.

"Of course," she said. "Mr Tall insists we let the customers know exactly what they're buying. He doesn't approve of conning people."

Mr Crepsley sent for me half an hour before the show began. He was dressing in his stage costume when I entered.

"Polish Madam Octa's cage," he ordered, "then brush your suit down and clean yourself up."

"Why?" I asked.

"You are going on with me," he said.

My eyes lit up. "You mean I'm part of the act?" I gasped.

"A small part," he said. "You can bring the cage on and play the flute when it is Madam Octa's time to spin a web over my mouth."

"Mr Tall normally does that, doesn't he?"

"Normally," Mr Crepsley agreed, "but we are short on performers tonight, so he is going to be performing himself. Besides, you are better suited to assisting than him."

"How so?" I asked.

"You look creepier," he said. "With your pale face and that awful suit, you look like something out of a horror film."

That gave me a bit of a shock. I'd never thought I was creepy looking! I glanced in a mirror and realized I did look a bit of a fright. Because I hadn't drunk human blood, I was much paler than I should have been. The dirty suit made me look even more ghost-like. I made up my mind to find something new to wear in the morning.

The show started promptly at eleven. I hadn't expected much of a crowd — we were in the middle of nowhere and hadn't had much time to notify people about the show — but the tent was packed.

"Where did they all come from?" I whispered to Evra as we watched Mr Tall introduce the Wolf Man.

"Everywhere," he replied quietly. "People always know when one of our shows is on. Besides, though he only told us about it today, Mr Tall probably knew we'd be playing tonight ever since we set up camp."

I watched the show from the wings, enjoying it even more than the first time I'd seen it, because now I knew the people involved and felt like part of the family.

Hans Hands went on after the Wolf Man, followed by Rhamus Twobellies. We had our first break, then Mr Tall took to the stage and darted round the place, never seeming to move, merely vanishing from one spot and appearing somewhere new. Next up was Truska, then it was my turn to go on stage with Mr Crepsley and Madam Octa.

The lights were low but my vampire vision helped me pick out the faces of Sam and R.V. in the crowd. They were stunned to see me, but clapped louder than anybody else. I had to hide my smile of delight: Mr Crepsley had told me to look miserable and glum, to impress the crowd.

I stood to one side as Mr Crepsley made a speech about how deadly Madam Octa was, then opened the door to her cage as an assistant led a goat on to the stage.

There was a loud, angry gasp when Madam Octa killed the goat ... it came from R.V. I knew then that I shouldn't have invited him – I'd forgotten how fond of animals he was – but it was too late to withdraw my invitation.

I was slightly nervous when it was my turn to play the flute and control Madam Octa, feeling every set of eyes in the tent focus on me. I'd never performed to a crowd before and for a few seconds I was afraid my lips wouldn't work or I'd forget the tune. But once I started blowing and sending my thoughts to Madam Octa, I settled into my stride.

As she weaved her web across Mr Crepsley's lips, it struck me that I could get rid of him now if I wanted.

I could make her bite him.

The idea shocked me. I'd thought about killing him before, but never seriously, and not since we'd joined the Cirque. Now here he was, his life in my hands. All it would take was one "slip". I could claim it was an accident. Nobody would be able to prove otherwise.

I watched the spider move back and forth, up and down, her poisonous fangs glinting under the lights of the chandelier. The heat from the candles seemed immense. I was sweating freely. It occurred to me that I could blame the slip of my fingers on the sweat.

Over his mouth she spun her web. His hands were down by his sides. He wouldn't be able to stop her. One wrong toot on the flute was all it needed. One broken note to sever the train of thought between the two of us, and ...

I didn't do it. I played perfectly and safely. I wasn't sure why I'd spared the vampire. Maybe because Mr Tall might know I'd killed him. Maybe because I needed Mr Crepsley to teach me how to survive. Maybe because I didn't want to become a killer.

Or maybe, just maybe, because I was starting to like the vampire. After all, he'd brought me to the Cirque and made me part of his act. I wouldn't have met Evra and Sam if it hadn't been for him. He'd been kind to me, as kind as he could be.

Whatever the reason, I didn't let Madam Octa kill her master, and at the end of the act we took our bows and exited together.

"You thought about killing me," Mr Crepsley said softly once we were backstage.

"What do you mean?" I played dumb.

"You know what I mean," he said. There was a pause. "It would not have worked. I milked most of the poison from her fangs before we went on. Killing the goat took the rest out of her."

"It was a test?" I stared at him, and my hatred grew again. "I thought you were being nice to me!" I cried. "And all the time it was just a rotten old test!"

His face was grave. "I had to know," he said. "I had to know if I could rely on you."

"Well, listen to this," I growled, standing on my toes in order to go eyeball to eyeball with him. "Your test was useless. I didn't kill you this time, but if I ever get the chance again, I'll take it!"

I stormed off in a huff without another word, too upset to stick around to see Cormac Limbs or the end of the show, feeling betrayed, even though deep down I knew what he said made sense.

CHAPTER NINETEEN

I WAS still upset the next morning. Evra kept asking me what was wrong but I wouldn't tell him. I didn't want him to know I'd been thinking of killing Mr Crepsley.

Evra told me he'd met Sam and R.V. after the show. "Sam loved it," Evra said, "especially Cormac Limbs. You should have stayed to see Cormac in action. When he sawed his legs off ..."

"I'll see him next time," I said. "How did R.V. take it?"

Evra frowned. "He wasn't happy."

"Upset about the goat?" I asked.

"Yes," Evra said, "but not just that. I said we bought the goat from a butcher, so it would have been killed anyway. It was the Wolf Man, the snake and Mr Crepsley's spider which bothered him the most."

"What was wrong with *them*?" I asked.

"He was afraid they weren't being treated right. He didn't like the idea of them being locked in cages. I told him they weren't, except for the spider. I said the Wolf Man was quiet as a lamb off-stage. And I showed him my snake and how she slept with me."

"Did he believe you about the Wolf Man?" I asked.

"I think so," Evra said, "though he still seemed suspicious

when leaving. And he was *very* interested in their eating habits. He wanted to know what we fed them, how often, and where we got the food. We'll have to be careful with R.V. He could cause problems. Luckily, he should be leaving in a day or two, but until then: caution!"

We passed the day quietly. Sam didn't turn up until late in the afternoon and none of us was in much of a mood for playing. It was a cloudy day and we were all a bit out of sorts. Sam only stayed for half an hour, then trotted off home again.

Mr Crepsley summoned me to his tent shortly after sunset. I wasn't going to go, but decided it was best not to annoy him too much. He was my guardian, after all, and could probably have me booted out of the Cirque Du Freak.

"What do you want?" I snapped when I arrived.

"Stand over here, where I can see you better," the vampire said.

He tilted my head backwards with his bony fingers and rolled up my eyelids to check the whites of my eyes. He told me to open my mouth and peered down my throat. Then he checked my pulse and reflexes.

"How do you feel?" he asked.

"Tired," I said.

"Weak?" he asked. "Sick?"

"A bit."

He grunted. "Have you been drinking much blood lately?" he asked.

"As much as I'm meant to," I said.

"But no human blood?"

"No," I said softly.

"OK," he said. "Get ready. We are going out."

"Hunting?" I asked.

He shook his head. "To see a friend."

I got up on his back outside the tent and he began running.

When we were clear of the camp he flitted and the world blurred around us.

I didn't take much notice of where we were going. I was more concerned with my suit. I'd forgotten to get new clothes, and now, the more I examined it, the worse it seemed.

There were dozens of small holes and rips, and the colour was a shade greyer than it was supposed to be, because of the dirt and dust. Many strands of thread and fibres had come loose, and every time I shook an arm or a leg, I appeared to be shedding hairs.

I'd never been very worried about clothes, but I didn't want to look like a *tramp*. Tomorrow I would definitely find something new to wear.

After a while we reached a city and Mr Crepsley slowed. He stopped outside the back of a tall building. I wanted to ask where we were, but he put a finger to his lips and made the sign for silence.

The back door was locked but Mr Crepsley laid a hand over it and clicked the fingers of his other hand. It opened instantly. He led the way through a long, dark corridor, then up a set of stairs and on to a brightly-lit hallway.

After a few minutes, we came to a white desk. Mr Crepsley glanced around to make sure we were alone, then rang the bell that hung from one of the walls.

A figure appeared behind the glass wall on the other side of the desk. The door in the glass wall opened and a ginger-haired man in a white uniform and green mask stepped through. He looked like a doctor.

"How may I—" he began, then stopped. "Larten Crepsley! What the hell are you doing here, you old devil?"

The man pulled down his mask and I saw he was grinning.

"Hello, Jimmy," Mr Crepsley said. The two shook hands and smiled at each other. "Long time no see."

"Not as long as I thought it would be," the man called Jimmy said. "I heard you'd been killed. An old foe had finally rammed a stake through your rotten heart, or so the story went."

"You should not believe everything you hear," Mr Crepsley said. He placed a hand on my shoulder and nudged me forward. "Jimmy, this is Darren Shan, a travelling companion of mine. Darren, this is Jimmy Ovo, an old friend and the world's finest pathologist."

"Hello," I said.

"Pleased to meet you," Jimmy said, shaking my hand. "You aren't a ... I mean, do you belong to *the club*?"

"He is a vampire," Mr Crepsley said.

"Only half of me," I snapped. "I'm not a full vampire."

"Please," Jimmy winced. "Don't use that word. I know what you guys are, and I'm fine about it, but that 'V' word never fails to freak me out." He shivered playfully. "I think it's because of all the horror movies I watched when I was a kid. I know you're not like those cinema monsters, but it's hard to get the image out of my mind."

"What's a pathologist do?" I asked.

"I cut corpses open to see how they died," Jimmy explained. "I don't do it with many bodies – just those who died in suspicious circumstances."

"This is a city morgue," Mr Crepsley said. "They store bodies that arrive dead at the hospital, or die whilst there."

"Is that where you keep them?" I asked Jimmy, pointing at the room behind the glass wall.

"Yup," he said cheerfully. He swung up a section of the desk and invited us through.

I was nervous. I expected to see dozens of tables, heaped high with sliced-open bodies. But it wasn't like that. There was one dead body, covered from head to toe with a long sheet, but that was the only one I could spot. Otherwise it was a huge, well-lit room, with large filing cabinets set in the walls and lots of medical equipment scattered around the place.

"How is business?" Mr Crepsley asked as we sat on three chairs near the corpse on the table. Jimmy and Mr Crepsley took no notice of the dead person and, as I didn't want to look out of place, neither did I.

"Slow enough," Jimmy answered. "The weather's been good and there haven't been many road accidents. No strange diseases, no food epidemics, no collapsing buildings. By the way," he added, "I had an old friend of yours in here a few years back."

"Oh?" Mr Crepsley responded politely. "Who was that?"

Jimmy sniffed heavily through his nose, then cleared his throat.

"*Gavner Purl?*" Mr Crepsley hooted with delight. "How is the old dog – as clumsy as ever?"

They started talking about their friend, Gavner Purl. I glanced around curiously while they were speaking, wondering where the bodies were kept. Finally, when they paused for breath, I asked Jimmy. He got to his feet and told me to follow. He led the way to the large filing cabinets and pulled one of the drawers out.

There was a hissing sound and a cloud of cold air rose from inside the drawer. When it cleared, I saw a sheet-covered form and realized the filing cabinets weren't filing cabinets at all. They were refrigerated coffins!

"We store the bodies here until we're ready," Jimmy said, "or until their next of kin come to collect them."

I looked around the room, quickly counting the many rows of drawer doors. "Is there a body behind all of these?" I asked.

Jimmy shook his head. "We've only got six guests at the moment, not counting the one on the table. Like I said, it's quiet. Mind you, even during our busiest times, most of our storage space goes unused. It's rare for us to be half full. We just like to be prepared for the worst."

"Any fresh bodies in stock?" Mr Crepsley asked.

"Wait a minute and I'll check," Jimmy said. He consulted a large pad and flicked through a few pages. "There's a man in his thirties," Jimmy said. "Died in a car crash just over eight hours ago."

"Nothing fresher?" Mr Crepsley asked.

"Afraid not," Jimmy replied.

Mr Crepsley sighed. "It will have to do."

"Wait a minute," I said. "You're not going to drink from a dead person, are you?"

"No," Mr Crepsley said. He reached inside his cloak and produced several of the small bottles in which he stored his supply of human blood. "I have come for a refill."

"You can't!" I gasped.

"Why not?" he asked.

"It isn't right. It's not fair to drink from the dead. Besides, the blood will have turned sour."

"It will not be at its best," Mr Crepsley agreed, "but it will do for bottling. And I disagree: a corpse is the ideal person to drain, since it has no use for the blood. It will take a lot to fill these bottles. Too much to take from a living person."

"Not if you took a bit from several," I protested.

"True," he said. "But that would require time, effort and risk. It is easier this way."

"Darren doesn't speak like a vampire," Jimmy remarked.

"He is still learning," Mr Crepsley grunted. "Now, lead the way to the body, please. We have not got all night."

I knew it would be pointless to argue further, so I shut my mouth and followed silently behind them.

Jimmy slid out the body of a tall, blonde-haired man and whipped back the sheet. There was a nasty bruise on the dead man's head and his body was very white, but otherwise he looked like he might be sleeping.

Mr Crepsley made a long, deep cut across the man's chest, baring his heart. He arranged the bottles beside the corpse, then got out a tube and stuck one end into the first of the bottles. He stuck the other end into the dead man's heart, then wrapped his fist around the organ and squeezed it like a pump.

Slowly, blood crept along the tube and into the bottle. When it was nearly full, Mr Crepsley pulled the tube out and jammed a cork into the neck of the bottle. He stuck the mouth of the tube into the second bottle and started filling that one.

Raising the first bottle, he swallowed a mouthful and rolled it around his gums, as though tasting wine. "Good," he grunted, licking his lips. "It is pure. We can use it."

He filled eight bottles, then turned to me with a serious look on his face.

"Darren," he said, "I know you are reluctant to drink human blood, but it is time you got over your fear."

"No," I said immediately.

"Come now, Darren," he growled. "This person is dead. His blood is no good to him any more."

"I can't," I said. "Not from a corpse."

"But you will not drink from a live person!" Mr Crepsley exploded. "You will have to drink human blood eventually. This is the best way to start."

"Um, listen, guys," Jimmy said. "If you're going to feed, I think I should get out of—"

"Quiet!" Mr Crepsley snapped. His eyes were burning into me. "You have to drink," he said firmly. "You are a vampire's assistant. It is time you behaved like one."

"Not tonight," I begged. "Another time. When we go hunting. From a living person. I can't drink from a corpse. It's disgusting."

Mr Crepsley sighed and shook his head. "One night you will realize how silly you are being," he said. "I just hope, by that time, you are not beyond being saved."

Mr Crepsley thanked Jimmy Ovo for his help and the two got to talking about the past and their friends. I sat by myself while they chatted, feeling miserable, wondering how long I could go without human blood.

When they were finished, we walked downstairs. Jimmy came with us and waved goodbye. He was a nice man and I was sorry we'd had to meet under such dark circumstances.

Mr Crepsley didn't say anything the whole way home and, when we arrived back at the Cirque Du Freak, he angrily tossed me to one side and pointed a finger at me.

"If you die," he said, "it is not my fault."

"OK," I replied.

"Stupid boy," he grumbled, then stormed off to his coffin.

I stayed up a while longer and watched the sun rising. I thought a lot about my situation and what would happen when my strength faded and I began to die. A half-vampire who wouldn't drink blood; it would have been funny if it wasn't so deadly.

What should I do? That was the question which kept me awake long after the sun had risen. What should I do? Abandon my principles and drink human blood? Or stay true to my humanity and ... *die*?

CHAPTER TWENTY

I STAYED inside my tent most of the day and didn't even go out to say hello to Sam when he came round. My spirits were at their lowest ever. I didn't feel like I belonged anywhere any longer. I couldn't be a human and wouldn't be a vampire. I was torn between the two.

I got a lot of sleep that night and the next day felt better. The sun was shining and, although I knew my problems hadn't gone away, I was able to overlook them for the time being.

Evra's snake was poorly. She'd picked up a virus and Evra had to stay in to look after her.

When Sam turned up, we decided to visit that old deserted railway station of his. Evra didn't mind being left behind. He'd come with us another time.

The railway station was cool. There was a huge circular yard, paved with cracked stones; a three-storey house which had served as the guard's house, a couple of old sheds, and several abandoned train carriages. There were also railway tracks running everywhere you looked, overgrown with weeds and grass.

Sam and I walked along some of the tracks and pretended we were on tightropes high above the ground. Every time one of us slipped, he had to scream and pretend to fall heavily to earth. I was much better at the game than Sam, because my vampire powers meant my sense of balance was better than any human's.

We explored a few of the old carriages. A couple were in a sorry state, but most were OK. Very dusty and dirty, but otherwise in good condition. I couldn't understand why they'd been left here to rot.

We climbed on top of the roof of one of the carriages and stretched out to enjoy the sun.

"You know what we should do?" Sam said after a while.

"What?" I asked.

"Become blood-brothers."

I propped myself up on an elbow and stared. "Blood-brothers?" I asked. "What for? And how's it done?"

"It'd be fun," he said. "We each make a small cut in one of our hands, then join them together and swear an oath to be best friends for ever."

"That sounds all right," I agreed. "Do you have a knife?"

"We can use some glass," Sam said. He slid over to the edge of the roof, reached down and snapped a piece of glass out of one of the carriage windows. When he returned, he made a small cut in the fleshy part of his palm, then handed me the glass.

I was about to cut my palm when I remembered the vampire blood in my veins. I didn't think a small amount could do Sam any harm, but then again ...

I lowered the glass and shook my head.

"No," I said. "I don't want to do it."

"Come on," Sam urged. "There's no need to be afraid. You only have to make a small cut."

"No," I said again.

"Coward!" he snorted. "You're afraid! Chicken! Coward!" He

began to sing: "Cowardly, cowardly custard, buy yourself some mustard."

"OK, I'm a coward," I laughed. It was easier to lie than tell the truth. "Everybody's afraid of something. I didn't see you rushing to wash the Wolf Man the other day."

Sam pulled a face. "That's different."

"Horses for courses," I said smugly.

"What does that mean?" he asked.

"I'm not sure," I admitted. "It's something my dad used to say."

We joked about some more, then hopped down and crossed the yard to the guard's house. The doors had rotted off years ago and most of the glass in the windows had fallen out. We walked through a couple of small rooms, into a larger one, which had been the living room.

There was a huge hole in the middle of the floor, which we carefully avoided.

"Look up," Sam told me.

I did and discovered I was gazing directly at the roof. The floors between had fallen in some time over the years, and all that was left of them were jagged edges around the sides. I could see sunlight shining through several holes in the roof.

"Follow me," Sam said and led me to a staircase at the side of the room. He started up. I followed slowly, not sure if this was wise – the steps were creaky and looked as if they might collapse – but not wishing to be called a chicken twice in the same day.

We stopped at the third floor, where the stairs ran out. You could touch the roof from here, and we did.

"Can we get out on the roof?" I asked.

"Yes," Sam said, "but it's too dangerous. The slates are loose. You could slide off. Anyway, there's something better up here than the roof."

He set off along the side of the uppermost room of the house. The ledge was about half a metre wide most of the way, but I kept my back to the wall, not wanting to take any chances.

"This bit of floor won't collapse, will it?" I asked nervously.

"It never has before," Sam replied. "But there's a first time for everything."

"Thanks for setting my mind at ease," I grumbled.

Sam stopped a bit further on. I craned my neck so I could see past him, and realized we had come to a set of rafters. There were six or seven of them, long pieces of wood stretching from one side of the room to the other.

"This used to be the attic," Sam explained.

"I guessed that," I told him.

He looked back at me and grinned. "But can you guess what we're going to do next?" he asked.

I stared at him, then down at the rafters. "You can't mean ... You aren't going to ... You're going to walk across, right?"

"Right," he said, and set his left foot on the rafter.

"Sam, this isn't a good idea," I said. "You looked unsteady on the railway tracks. If you stumble up here ..."

"I won't," he said. "I was only fooling down below."

He set his other foot on the wooden rafter and began walking. He went slowly, his arms stretched out on either side. My heart was in my mouth. I was certain he'd fall. I glanced down and knew he wouldn't survive if he fell. There were four storeys if you included the basement. It was a long drop. A deadly one.

But Sam made it across safely to the other side, where he turned and took a bow.

"You're crazy!" I yelled.

"No," he said, "just brave. How about *you*? Care to chance it? It'd be easier for you than it was for me."

"What do you mean?" I asked.

"Chickens have wings!" he shouted.

That did it! I'd show him!

Taking a deep breath, I set across, moving quicker than Sam had, making full use of my vampire abilities. I didn't look down and tried not to think about what I was doing, and in a couple of seconds I was across and standing beside Sam.

"Wow!" He was impressed. "I didn't think you'd do it. Certainly not so quickly?"

"You don't travel with the Cirque without picking up a few tricks," I said, pleased with myself.

"Do you think *I* could go that fast?" Sam asked.

"I wouldn't try it," I advised him.

"I bet you can't do it again," he dared me.

"Just watch," I said, and darted back across, even faster.

We spent a fun few minutes crossing over and back, taking each of the rafters in turn. Then we crossed at the same time, on different rafters, yelling and laughing at one another.

Sam stopped in the middle of his rafter and turned to face me.

"Hey!" he shouted. "Let's play mirrors."

"What's that?" I asked.

"I do something and you have to copy me." He shook his left hand above his head. "Like this."

"Oh," I said, and shook my hand. "OK. As long as you don't jump to your death. That's the one thing I *won't* copy."

He laughed, then pulled a face. I pulled one too. Then he slowly stood on one leg. I did likewise. Next he bent and touched his toes. I followed his example. I couldn't wait until it was my turn. I'd do a few things – like jump from one rafter to the next – that he couldn't possibly copy. For once, I was glad of my vampire blood.

Naturally, that was the moment when it went and let me down.

There was no warning. One second I was beginning to stand, having bent to touch my toes. The next my head was spinning, my arms were flapping and my legs were shaking.

This wasn't my first dizzy spell — I'd had several recently — but I hadn't taken much notice before: just sat down and waited for the dizziness to pass. This time was different. I was four storeys up. There was nowhere to sit.

I tried lowering myself, thinking I could cling to the rafter and crawl to safety. But before I could get low enough, my feet slipped from beneath me ... and I fell!

CHAPTER TWENTY-ONE

ALTHOUGH MY vampire blood was responsible for getting me into the mess on the rafters, it also saved my life.

As I fell, I stuck out an arm — more in hope than anything else — and my hand caught the rafter. If I'd been an ordinary human boy I wouldn't have had the strength to hold on. But I wasn't ordinary. I was a half-vampire. And even though I was dizzy, I was able to grab tight and cling on.

I swung above the four-storey drop, eyes shut, hanging on by those four slim fingers and my thumb.

"Darren! Hang on!" Sam shouted. He didn't need to tell me that — I was hardly going to let go!

"I'm coming over," Sam said. "I'll be there as fast as I can. Don't let go. And don't panic."

He went on talking as he made his way across, calming me down, telling me it would be all right, he'd rescue me, I had to relax, everything was fine.

His words helped. They gave me something apart from the drop to think about. If not for Sam, I'd have been a goner.

I felt him start out along my rafter. The wood creaked, and for one terrible moment I thought the weight would cause it to break and send both of us plummeting to our deaths. But it held and he closed the gap, crawling along on his stomach, quickly but carefully.

Sam paused when he reached me.

"Now," he said, "I'm going to grab your wrist with my right hand. I'll do it slowly. Don't move while I'm doing it, and don't snatch at me with your free hand. OK?"

"OK," I said.

I felt his hand close over my wrist.

"Don't let go of the rafter," he said.

"I won't," I promised.

"I don't have the strength to pull you up," he told me, "so I'm going to swing you from one side to the other. Stretch your free arm out. When you're able, make a grab for the rafter. If you miss, don't panic, I'll still be holding on. If you get a grip, stay still for a few seconds and give your body a chance to relax. Then we can haul you up. Got that?"

"Got it, captain," I said, grinning nervously.

"OK. Here goes. And remember: everything will be all right. It's going to work. You will survive."

He began swinging me, lightly at first, then a bit harder. I was tempted to snatch at the rafter after a few swings but forced myself to wait. When I felt I was swinging high enough, I stretched out my fingers, concentrated on the thin plank of wood, and grabbed.

I caught it!

I was able to relax a little then and rest the muscles of my right arm.

"Do you feel ready to pull yourself up?" Sam asked.

"Yes," I said.

"I'll help you get your upper body up," he said. "When your belly is safe across the rafter, I'll get out of the way and give you room to draw your legs up."

Sam put his right hand on the collar of my shirt and jacket —
to catch me if I slipped — and helped yank me upwards.

I scraped my chest and belly on the rafter but the pain didn't
bother me. In fact, I welcomed it: it meant I was alive.

When I was safe, Sam backed off and I got my legs up. I
crawled after him, moving slower than necessary. When I reached
the ledge, I stayed crouched low and didn't stand until we got to
the stairs. Then I leant against the wall and let out a long,
shuddering sigh of relief.

"Wow," Sam said to the left of me. "That was *fun*! Do you
want to do it again?"

I *think* he was joking.

CHAPTER TWENTY-TWO

LATER, AFTER I'd stumbled down the stairs — my sense of balance was still dodgy, but getting better — we walked back to the carriages and rested in the shadow of one.

"You saved my life," I said softly.

"It was nothing," Sam said. "You'd have done the same for me."

"Probably," I said. "But I wasn't called upon to help. I wasn't the one who had to use his head and act coolly. You saved me, Sam. I owe you my life."

"Keep it," he laughed. "What would *I* do with it?"

"I'm serious, Sam. I owe you big-time. Anything you ever want or need, just ask, and I'll move heaven and earth to get it for you."

"You mean that?"

"Cross my heart," I swore.

"There is *one* thing," he said.

"Name it."

"I want to join the Cirque Du Freak."

"Saaaammmm ..." I groaned.

"You asked what I wanted, so I'm telling you," he replied.

"It's not that easy," I protested.

"Yes it is," he said. "You can talk to the owner and put in a good word for me. Come on, Darren, did you mean what you said or not?"

"All right," I sighed. "I'll ask Mr Tall."

"When?"

"Today," I promised. "As soon as I get back."

"All right!" Sam punched the air happily.

"But if he says no," I warned him, "that's the end of it, OK? I'll do what I can, but if Mr Tall says no, that *means* no."

"Sure," Sam said. "That's fine by me."

"Maybe there's a job for me, too," somebody said behind my back.

I spun around quickly, and there was R.V., smiling strangely.

"You shouldn't creep up on people like that," I snapped. "You gave me a fright."

"Sorry, man," R.V. said, but he didn't look very sorry.

"What are you doing out here?" Sam asked.

"I wanted to find Darren," R.V. said. "I never got a chance to thank him for my ticket."

"That's OK," I said. "I'm sorry I wasn't around to see you when it finished but I had business elsewhere."

"Sure," R.V. said, sitting down on the track beside me. "I can understand that. A show that size, there must be lots to do, huh? I bet they keep you real busy, right, man?"

"Right," I said.

R.V. beamed at the two of us. There was something about the way he was smiling that made me uneasy. It wasn't a nice smile.

"Tell me," R.V. said, "how's the Wolf Man doing?"

"He's fine," I said.

"He's chained up all the time, isn't he?" R.V. asked.

"No," I said, remembering Evra's warning.

"Isn't he?" R.V. acted surprised. "A wild beast like him, savage and dangerous, and he isn't locked up?"

"He's not really dangerous," I said. "That's an act. He's pretty tame actually." I could see Sam staring at me. He knew how wild the Wolf Man was and couldn't understand why I was lying.

"Tell me, man, what does a thing like that eat?" R.V. asked.

"Steak. Pork chops. Sausages." I forced a smile. "The usual stuff. All store-bought."

"Really? What about the goat that spider bit? Who eats that?"

"I don't know."

"Evra said the two of you bought the goat from a local farmer. Did it cost much?"

"Not really," I said. "It was quite sick, so it—"

I stopped. Evra had told R.V. we bought the goat from a *butcher*, not a farmer.

"I've been doing a spot of investigating, man," R.V. said softly. "Everybody else in my camp has been busy getting ready to move on but I've been walking around, counting sheep and cows, asking questions, digging for bones.

"Animals have been vanishing," R.V. continued. "The farmers aren't taking much notice – they don't mind the odd one or two going missing – but it fascinates me. Who do you think could be taking them, man?"

I didn't answer.

"Another thing," he said. "I was strolling along the river you're camped by, and do you know what I found downstream? Lots of small bones and scraps of skin and meat. Where do you think they could have come from, Darren?"

"I don't know," I said. Then I stood up. "I have to be going now. I'm expected back at the Cirque. Jobs to do."

"Don't let me keep you," R.V. smiled.

"When are you breaking camp?" I asked. "I might pop over to say goodbye before you leave."

"That's nice of you," R.V. said. "But don't worry, man. I won't be going anywhere soon."

I frowned. "I thought you said you were moving on."

"NOP are moving on," he said. "In fact they've already moved. They pulled out yesterday evening." He smiled icily. "But *I'm* staying a while longer. There are a few things I want to check out."

"Oh." Inside my head I cursed loudly, but outside I pretended to be happy. "That's good news. Well, see you around."

"Oh yes," R.V. said. "You'll see me around, man. You can bet on that. You'll be seeing *plenty* of me."

I grinned awkwardly.

"So long for now," I said.

"So long," R.V. replied.

"Wait up," Sam called. "I'll come with you."

"No," I said. "Come tomorrow. I'll have an answer from Mr Tall for you by then. Bye."

I took off before either of them could say anything else.

R.V.'s interest in the disappearance of the animals worried me at first, but as I walked back to camp I began to relax. When all was said and done, he was only a hairy harmless human, while those of us in the Cirque Du Freak were strange, powerful beings. What could he possibly do to hurt us?

CHAPTER TWENTY-THREE

I MEANT to report straight to Mr Tall when I got back, to tell him about R.V., but as I was heading for his van, Truska – the lady who was able to grow an incredible beard – grabbed my arm and made signs that she wanted me to follow her.

She led me to her tent. It was decorated more fancifully than most of the other tents and vans. The walls were covered with mirrors and paintings. There were huge wardrobes and dressing tables, and an enormous four-poster bed.

Truska said something in her strange seal-like voice, then stood me in the centre of the room and made a sign that I wasn't to move. She fetched a measuring tape and measured my body.

When she'd finished, she pursed her lips and thought for a few seconds, then clicked her fingers and hurried to one of the wardrobes. She rooted through it, emerging with a pair of trousers. She found a shirt in another wardrobe, a jacket in another, and a pair of shoes in a large chest. She let me pick my own vest, underpants and socks from one of the dressing-table drawers.

I stepped behind a silk screen to dress. Evra must have told her about my wish to find new clothes. It was a good job he had, as I probably would have kept on forgetting.

Truska clapped her hands when I came out and quickly pushed me in front of a mirror. The clothes fitted perfectly and, much to my surprise, I looked super-cool! The shirt was a light green colour, the trousers were dark purple, while the jacket was gold and blue. Truska found a long length of red satin cloth and wrapped it round my middle and that completed the picture: I looked just like a pirate!

"This is great!" I told her. "The only thing is," I said, pointing at my feet, "the shoes are a bit tight."

Truska took back the shoes and found a new pair. These were softer than the first and the toes curled up like Sinbad the Sailor's. I took an immediate shine to them.

"Thanks, Truska," I said, and started to leave. She raised a hand and I stopped. She pulled a chair over to one of the taller wardrobes and stood on it, reached up and brought down a huge round box. She plopped it on the floor, opened it, and pulled out a small brown hat with a feather in it, the sort that Robin Hood might have worn.

Before I could put the hat on, she made me sit down, got a pair of scissors and gave me a haircut, which I badly needed.

The haircut and hat were the icing on the cake. I almost didn't recognize myself in the mirror when I looked this time.

"Oh, Truska," I said. "I … I …" I couldn't find the words, so instead I threw my arms around her and gave her a big, sloppy kiss. I felt embarrassed when I let go, and was glad none of my friends had been around to see, but Truska was beaming.

I rushed off to show Evra my new look. He thought the clothes were great but swore he'd never asked Truska to help me. He said she must have either got sick of seeing me look so scruffy, or Mr Crepsley had asked her to fix me up, or she'd done it because she fancied me.

"She does not fancy me!" I shouted.

"Truska loves Darren," he sang. "Truska loves Darren."

"Oh, shut up, you slimy excuse for a reptile," I growled.

He laughed, not offended in the slightest.

"Darren and Truska sitting in a tree," he sang, "k-i-s-s-i-n-g. First comes love, then comes marriage, then comes Darren with the vampire carriage."

I gave a roar, jumped on him, wrestled him to the ground and wouldn't let go until he cried for mercy.

When we were finished, Evra went back to looking after his snake, while I went outside and got on with the day's jobs. I was on the go non-stop because I had to cover for Evra and do the work of two. With all that coming and going, and the excitement of having new clothes, I plain forgot about R.V. and telling Mr Tall about the eco warrior's threat to investigate the disappearing animals.

If I hadn't been so absent-minded, maybe things would have turned out differently, and perhaps our stay wouldn't have ended in bloodshed and tears.

CHAPTER TWENTY-FOUR

I WAS ready to drop by the time night came. The activity had worn me out. Evra had warned me not to sleep in his tent tonight; his snake was in a foul mood because of the virus and might bite. So I headed for Mr Crepsley's tent and made a bed on the floor beside Madam Octa's cage.

I fell asleep within a couple of minutes of lying down.

Some time later, as I was dreaming, something caught in my throat and made me gag. I coughed and awoke.

There was a figure above me, holding a small bottle to my mouth, trying to force a liquid down me. My first strange terrified thought was: "It's Mr Tiny!"

I bit the top off the bottle, cutting my lips, spilling most of the liquid. The man cursed, grabbed my chin and prised my gums apart. He tried pouring the last of the liquid into my open mouth, but I spat it out.

The man cursed again, then let go and slumped back. As my heartbeat slowed, I saw that it wasn't Mr Tiny.

It was Mr Crepsley.

"What the hell were you trying to do?" I screamed angrily. I was too mad to feel the pain in my cut lips.

He showed me the remains of the small bottle ... one of the containers he used to store human blood.

"You were trying to get me to drink!" I gasped.

"You have to," Mr Crepsley said. "You are wasting away, Darren. If you go on like this, you will be dead within a week. If you do not have the courage to drink, it must be forced into you."

I stared at him savagely. He looked uncomfortable and turned his eyes away from mine.

"I was trying to help," he said.

"If you ever try that again," I said slowly, "I'll kill you. I'll wait until day, then creep in and chop your head off."

He could tell I was serious, because he nodded glumly.

"Never again," he agreed. "I knew it would not work, but I had to try. If you had swallowed even a little, it would have kept you going a while longer, and once you had the taste, you might not be so afraid to drink again."

"I'll never have the taste!" I roared. "I won't drink human blood. I don't care if I *do* die. I won't drink it."

"Very well," he sighed. "I have done my best. If you insist on being stupid, on your own head be it."

"I'm not being stupid ... I'm being *human*," I growled.

"But you are not human," he said softly.

"I know," I replied. "But I want to be. I want to be like Sam. I want a family and ordinary friends. I want to grow old at the usual rate. I don't want to spend my life drinking blood and feeding off humans, worrying about sunlight and vampire hunters."

"Too bad," Mr Crepsley said. "It is the hand you have been dealt."

"I hate you," I snarled.

"Too bad," he said again. "You are stuck with me. If it is any compensation," he added, "I am none too fond of you either.

Turning you into a half-vampire was the worst mistake I ever made."

"So why not free me?" I wailed.

"I cannot," he said. "I would if I could. Of course, you are free to leave any time you like."

I stared at him suspiciously. "Really?" I asked.

"Really," he said. "I do not mind. In fact, I would prefer it if you did. That way, you would no longer be my responsibility. I would not have to watch you die."

I shook my head slowly. "I don't understand you at all," I said.

He smiled, almost tenderly. "Nor I you," he said.

We laughed a little then and things returned to normal. I didn't like what Mr Crepsley had tried, but understood why he'd tried it. You can't really hate someone who has your best interests at heart.

I told him what I'd done that day, about going to the railway yard with Sam and how he saved my life. I also told him about almost becoming Sam's blood-brother.

"It is a good job you stopped when you did," Mr Crepsley said.

"What would have happened if I hadn't?" I asked.

"Your blood would have tainted his. He would have developed a taste for raw meat. He would have hung around butcher shops, staring in the windows. He would have aged at a slightly slower rate than normal. It would not have been much of a difference, but it would have been enough."

"Enough to do what?" I asked.

"Drive him mad," Mr Crepsley said. "He would not have understood what was happening. He would have thought he was evil. He would not have known why his life had changed. Within ten years he would have been a screaming wreck."

I shivered at the thought of how close I'd come to destroying

Sam's life. This sort of thing was precisely why I had to stay with Mr Crepsley, until I'd learned everything about being a half-vampire.

"What do you think of Sam?" I asked.

"I have not seen much of him," Mr Crepsley said. "He comes mostly by day. But he seems nice. Very bright."

"He's been helping Evra and me with our chores," I said.

"I know."

"He's a good worker."

"So I have heard."

I licked my lips nervously. "He wants to join the Cirque," I said. Mr Crepsley's face darkened. "I was going to ask Mr Tall, but I forgot. I'll ask tomorrow. What do you think he'll say?"

"He will say you have to ask *me*. Children cannot join the Cirque Du Freak unless an independent member agrees to be their guardian."

"*I* could be his guardian," I said.

"You are not old enough. It would have to be me. I would have to give my permission. But I will not."

"Why?" I asked.

"Because it is a crazy idea," he said. "One child is bad enough. There is no way I would take on a second. Besides, he is human. I am stuck with you because of the vampire blood in your veins. Why should I put my neck on the line for a human?"

"He's my friend," I said. "He'd be company for me."

Mr Crepsley snorted. "Madam Octa is company enough."

"That's not the same," I whined.

"Tell me this," Mr Crepsley mused. "What happens when he finds out you are a vampire? You think he will understand? You think he will sleep easily, knowing his best friend would like nothing better than to slit his throat open and drink him dry?"

"I wouldn't do that!" I yelled.

"I know," Mr Crepsley agreed. "But I am a vampire. I know what you are really like. So does Mr Tall, Evra and the others. But how do you think an ordinary human would see you?"

I sighed unhappily. "You won't let him join?"

Mr Crepsley began to shake his head, then stopped and nodded slowly. "Very well," he said. "He can join."

"He *can*?" I stared at him, shocked. Even though I'd been arguing on Sam's behalf, I'd never really thought they would let him join.

"Yes," Mr Crepsley said. "He can join and travel with us and help you and Evra with your jobs. But on one condition." Mr Crepsley leant in close to me and treated me to his wickedest grin. "*He has to become a half-vampire too!*" he hissed.

CHAPTER TWENTY-FIVE

MY HEART was heavy when I saw Sam trot into camp early the next morning. I hated having to disappoint him, but knew I had to. There was no way I could let Mr Crepsley turn Sam into a half-vampire.

I'd thought about it a lot during the night, and the frightening thing was, I believed Sam would agree to become a half-vampire if I gave him the option. Smart as he was, I don't think he'd have stopped to consider the loneliness and awfulness of being a vampire.

He rushed over when he saw me, too excited to take any notice of my change of costume and hair cut.

"Did you ask him? Did you?" His face was bright, filled with hope.

"Yes," I said, smiling sadly.

"And?"

I shook my head. "Sorry, Sam. He said no."

Sam's face fell about a thousand kilometres.

"*Why?*" he shouted.

"You're too young," I said.

"You're not much older!" he snapped.

313

"But I have no parents," I lied. "I had no home to call my own when I joined the Cirque."

"I don't care about my parents," he sniffed.

"That's not true," I said. "You'd miss them."

"I could go home for holidays."

"It wouldn't work. You're not cut out for life in the Cirque Du Freak. Maybe later, when you're older."

"I don't care about 'later'!" he yelled. "I want to join *now*. I've worked hard. I've proved myself. I kept quiet when you were lying to R.V. about the Wolf Man yesterday. Did you tell that to Mr Tall?"

"I told him everything," I sighed.

"I don't believe you," Sam said. "I don't think you spoke to him at all. I want to see him myself."

I shrugged and pointed towards Mr Tall's van. "That's where you'll find him," I said.

Sam set off in a huff but slowed after a few steps, then came to a halt. He stubbed the ground miserably with his toes, then returned and sat down beside me.

"It's not fair," he grumbled. I could see tears trickling down his cheeks. "I'd made up my mind to join. It was going to be great. I had it all planned."

"There'll be other chances," I said.

"When?" he asked. "I've never heard of a freak-show playing round here before. When will I run into one again?"

I didn't answer.

"You wouldn't have liked it anyway," I said. "It's not as much fun as you think. Imagine what it's like in the middle of winter, when you have to get up at five in the morning and wash in ice-cold water and work outside in freezing blizzards."

"That doesn't bother me," Sam insisted. Then his tears stopped and he got a crafty look in his eyes. "Maybe I'll come along anyway," he said. "Maybe I'll sneak into one of the vans and stow away with you. Mr Tall would have to take me then."

"You can't do that!" I snapped. "You mustn't!"

"I will if I want," he grinned. "You can't stop me."

"I can," I growled.

"How?" he sneered.

I took a deep breath. The time had come to frighten Sam Grest away for ever. I couldn't tell him the truth about me, but I could invent a story almost as frightening, one guaranteed to send him running.

"I never told you what happened to my parents, did I, Sam? Or how I came to join the freak-show?" I kept my voice low and steady.

"No," Sam said quietly. "I often wondered but didn't want to ask."

"I killed them, Sam," I said.

"*What?*" His face went white.

"I go crazy sometimes. Like the Wolf Man. Nobody knows when it's going to happen, or why. I was in a hospital when I was younger but I seemed to be getting better. My parents brought me home for Christmas. After dinner, while I was pulling a cracker with Dad, I flipped.

"I tore him to pieces. Mum tried to drag me off but I killed her too. My little sister ran for help but I caught her. I ripped her apart the same way I'd ripped the cracker in two.

"Then, after I'd killed them ..." I locked eyes with Sam. It had to be a good act to make him believe. "*I ate them.*"

He stared at me, stunned.

"That's not true," he whispered. "It can't be."

"I killed and ate them, then ran away," I lied. "I was discovered by Mr Tall, who agreed to hide me. They have a special cage built to keep me in when I go mad. The problem is, nobody knows when it's going to happen. That's why most people avoid me.

Evra's OK because he's strong. So are some of the other performers. But ordinary humans ... I could kill them in the blink of an eye."

"You're lying," Sam said.

I picked up a large stick which was lying nearby, turned it round in my hands, then put it in my mouth and bit through it as if it was a big carrot.

"I'd chew your bones and spit you out as gristle," I told Sam. I'd cut my lips on the stick and the blood made me look a fright. "You wouldn't be able to stop me. You'd be sleeping in my tent if you joined the show and would be the one I'd go for first.

"You can't join the Cirque Du Freak," I said. "I wish you could – I'd love to have a friend – but it's not possible. I'd end up killing you if you joined."

Sam tried responding but couldn't get his mouth to work. He believed my far-fetched tale. He'd seen enough of the show to know that such things *could* happen here.

"Go away, Sam," I said sadly. "Go away and don't ever come back. It's safer this way. It's better. For both of us."

"Darren, I ... I ..." His head shook uncertainly.

"*Go!*" I roared, and pounded the ground with my hands. I bared my teeth and growled. I was able to make my voice much deeper than a human's, so it sounded like a wild animal.

Sam yelped, scrambled to his feet and sprinted for the cover of the trees, never once looking back.

I watched him go, heavy-hearted, certain my ploy had worked. He would never be back. I would see him no more. Our paths had separated and we would never meet again.

If I'd known how wrong I was – if I'd had any idea of the dreadful night which lay ahead – I'd have sped off after him and never returned to that foul circus of blood, that dreadful circus of *death*.

CHAPTER TWENTY-SIX

I WAS moping around when one of the Little People tapped me on the back. It was the one with the limp.

"What do you want?" I asked.

The tiny man – if it was a man – in the blue-hooded robes rubbed his belly with his hands. This was the sign that he and his brothers were hungry.

"You just had breakfast," I said.

He rubbed his belly again.

"It's too early for dinner."

He rubbed his belly again.

I knew that this would go on for hours if I let it. He would patiently follow me around, rubbing his belly, until I agreed to go and hunt for him.

"All right," I snapped. "I'll see what I can find. But I'm on my own today, so if I don't come back with a full bag: tough."

He rubbed his belly again.

I snorted and set off.

I shouldn't have gone hunting. I was very weak. I could still run quicker than a human and I was stronger than most kids my age, but I wasn't super-fit or extra-strong any longer. Mr Crepsley had said I would be dead within a week if I didn't drink human blood, and I knew he'd spoken the truth. I could feel myself wasting away. A few more days and I wouldn't be able to pull myself out of bed.

I tried catching a rabbit but wasn't fast enough. I worked up a sweat chasing it and had to sit down for a few minutes. Next, I went looking for road-kill, but couldn't find any dead animals. Finally, because I was tired and half-afraid of what would happen if I returned to camp empty-handed (the Little People might decide to eat *me!*), I headed for a field full of sheep.

They were grazing peacefully when I arrived. They were used to humans and barely lifted their heads when I entered the field and walked among them.

I was looking for an old sheep, or one that looked sick. That way I needn't feel so lousy about killing it. I eventually found one with skinny, trembling legs and a dazed expression, and decided she'd do. She looked as though she hadn't long to live anyway.

If I'd had my full powers, I'd have snapped her neck and she would have been dead in an instant, without any pain. But I was weak and clumsy, and didn't twist hard enough the first time.

The sheep began to bleat with agony.

She tried running away but her legs wouldn't carry her. She fell to the ground, where she lay, bleating unhappily.

I tried breaking her neck again but couldn't. In the end I fetched a stone and finished the job. It was a messy, horrible way to kill an animal and I felt ashamed of myself as I grabbed its back legs and hauled it away from the flock.

I'd almost reached the fence before I realized somebody was sitting on top of it, waiting for me. I dropped the sheep and looked up, expecting an angry farmer.

But it wasn't a farmer.

It was R.V.

And he was mad as hell.

"How could you?" he shouted. "How could you kill a poor, innocent animal in so cruel a manner?"

"I tried killing her quickly," I said. "I tried snapping her neck, but I couldn't. I'd have left her when I failed, but she was in pain. I thought it was better to finish her off than leave her to suffer."

"That's real big of you, man," he said sarcastically. "Do you think you'll get the Nobel Peace Prize for that?"

"Please, R.V.," I said. "Don't be angry. She was sick. The farmer would have killed her anyway. Even if she'd lived she would have been sent to a butcher's in the end."

"That don't make it right," he said angrily. "Just because other people are nasty, it don't mean you should be nasty too."

"Killing animals isn't nasty," I said. "Not when it's for food."

"What's wrong with vegetables?" he asked. "We don't need to eat meat, man. We don't need to kill."

"*Some* people need meat," I disagreed. "Some can't live without it."

"Then they should be left to die!" R.V. roared. "That sheep never did any harm to anyone. As far as I'm concerned, killing her is worse than killing a human. You're a murderer, Darren Shan."

I shook my head sadly. There was no point arguing with somebody this stubborn. R.V. had his way of looking at the world, while I had mine.

"Look, R.V.," I said, "I don't enjoy killing. I'd be over the moon if everyone in the world was a vegetarian. But they're not. People eat meat and that's a fact of life. I'm only doing what I have to."

"Well, we'll see what the police have to say about it," R.V. said.

"The police?" I frowned. "What do they have to do with it?"

"You've killed somebody else's sheep," he laughed cruelly. "Do you think they'll let you get away with that? They won't arrest you for murdering rabbits and foxes — more's the pity — but they'll charge you for killing a sheep. I'll have the police and health inspectors down on you like a tonne of bricks," he grinned.

"You won't!" I gasped. "You don't like the police. You're always fighting against them."

"When I have to," he agreed. "But when I can get them on my side ..." He laughed again. "They'll arrest you first, then turn your camp upside-down. I've been studying the goings-on there. I've seen the way you treat that poor hairy man."

"The Wolf Man?"

"Yes. You keep him locked away like an animal."

"He *is* an animal," I said.

"No," R.V. disagreed. "*You* are the animal, man."

"R.V., listen," I said. "We don't have to be enemies. Come back to camp with me. Talk to Mr Tall and the others. See how we live. Get to know and understand us. There's no need to—"

"Save it," he snapped. "I'm going for the police. Nothing you can say will stop me."

I took a deep breath. I liked R.V. but knew I couldn't allow him to destroy the Cirque Du Freak.

"Very well," I said. "If nothing I *say* can stop you, maybe you'll respond to something I *do*."

Summoning all my remaining strength, I threw the dead body of the sheep at R.V. It struck him in the chest and knocked him flying from the fence. He yelled with surprise, then with pain as he landed heavily on the ground.

I leapt over the fence and was on him before he could move.

"How did you do that, man?" he gasped.

"Never mind," I snapped.

"Kids can't throw sheep," he said. "How did—"

"Shut up!" I shouted and slapped his bearded face. He stared up at me, shocked. "Listen, Reggie Veggie," I growled, using the name he hated, "and listen well. You *won't* go to the police or the health people. Because, if you do, the sheep won't be the only dead body I drag back to the Cirque Du Freak today."

"What are you?" he asked. His voice was trembling and his eyes were filled with terror.

"I'm the end of you if you cross me," I swore, then dug my fingernails into the soil at either side of his face and squeezed his head between my hands, just enough to let him know how strong I was.

"Get out of here, Reggie," I said. "Go and find your friends in NOP. Stick to protesting against new roads and bridges. You're in over your head here. Me and my friends in the Cirque are freaks, and freaks don't obey the same laws as other people. Understand?"

"You're crazy," he said softly.

"Yes," I sighed. "But not as crazy as you'll be if you stay and interfere."

I stood and draped the sheep over my shoulders.

"Going to the police would be useless anyway," I said. "By the time they reach the camp, this sheep would be long gone, bones and all.

"You can do what you like, R.V. Stay or go. Report me to the police or keep your mouth shut. It's up to you. All I've left to say is this: to me and my kind, you're no different than this sheep." I gave it a shake. "We'd think no more of killing you than we would any dumb animal of the fields."

"You're a monster!" R.V. gasped.

"Yes," I agreed. "But I'm only a *baby* monster. You should see what some of the others are like." I smiled nastily at him, hating myself for acting so meanly, but knowing this was the way it had to be. "So long, Reggie Veggie," I said, and walked away.

I didn't look back. I didn't need to. I could hear the chattering of his terrified teeth practically all the way back to camp.

CHAPTER TWENTY-SEVEN

THIS TIME I went straight to Mr Tall and told him about R.V. He listened carefully, then said, "You handled him well."

"I did what I had to," I replied. "I'm not proud of it. I don't like bullying or scaring people, but there was no other way."

"By rights, you should have killed him," Mr Tall said. "That way, he could do us no harm whatsoever."

"I'm not a murderer," I told him.

"I know," he sighed. "Nor am I. It's a pity one of the Little People wasn't with you. They'd have chopped his head off without a second's hesitation."

"What do you think we should do?" I asked.

"I don't think he can cause many problems," Mr Tall mused. "He'll probably be too scared to go to the police straightaway. Even if he does, there's no evidence against you. It would be an unwanted complication, but we've had plenty of dealings with officers of the law in the past. We could cope.

"The health authorities worry me more. We could hit the road and lose them, but people in the health department tend to trail you around like hound-dogs once they've got your scent.

"We'll leave tomorrow," he decided. "There's a show

scheduled for tonight and I hate cancelling on short notice. Dawn is the earliest any health inspector could be here, so we'll break camp before then."

"You're not angry with me?" I asked.

"No," he said. "This isn't the first time we've clashed with the public. You're not to blame."

I helped Mr Tall spread the word of our departure among the camp. Everybody took it in their stride. Most seemed happy to be getting this much notice; they often had to move on with only an hour or two of warning.

It was another busy day for me. As well as preparing for the show, I had to help people get ready for leaving. I offered to help Truska pack her belongings, but her tent was already bare when I got there. She only winked when I asked how she'd packed so quickly.

I told Mr Crepsley about our morning departure when he awoke. He didn't seem surprised.

"We have been here long enough," he said.

I asked to be left out of that night's show because I wasn't feeling very well.

"I'll get to bed early," I said, "and have a long sleep."

"It will not do any good," Mr Crepsley warned. "There is only one thing that will make you feel better, and you know what it is."

Night rolled on, and soon it was time for the show to begin. There was another big crowd. The roads were blocked with cars in both directions. Everybody in the Cirque was busy, either preparing to go on stage, or getting people seated, or selling stuff.

The only two who seemed to have nothing to do were me and Evra, who wasn't performing because of his ill snake. He left her for a few minutes to watch the start of the show. We stood to one side of the stage as Mr Tall got the ball rolling and introduced the Wolf Man.

We stuck around until the first break, then strolled outside and studied the stars.

"I'll miss this place when we move on," Evra said. "I like the countryside. You can't see stars so well in a city."

"I didn't know you were interested in astronomy," I said.

"I'm not," he replied. "But I enjoy looking up at the stars."

I got dizzy after a while and had to sit down.

"You're not feeling too good, are you?" Evra asked.

I smiled weakly. "I've been better."

"Still not drinking human blood?" I shook my head. He sat beside me. "You've never told me *exactly* why you won't drink it," he said. "Surely it can't be so different to animal blood?"

"I don't know," I said. "And I don't want to find out." I paused. "I'm afraid that if I drink human blood, I'll be *evil*. Mr Crepsley says vampires aren't evil but I think they are. I think anyone who looks at humans as if they're animals *must* be evil."

"But if it's to keep you alive ..." Evra said.

"That's how it would start," I said. "I'd tell myself I was doing it to keep going. I'd swear never to drink more than I needed. But what if I couldn't stop myself? I'll need more as I grow older and larger. What if I can't control my thirst? What if I kill someone?"

"I don't think you could," Evra said. "You're *not* evil, Darren. I don't think a good person can do evil things. As long as you treat human blood like medicine, you'll be all right."

"Maybe," I said, though I didn't believe it. "Anyway, I'm OK for the time being. I don't have to make a final decision for a couple more days."

"Would you really let yourself die rather than drink?" Evra asked.

"I don't know," I answered honestly.

"I'd miss you if you died," Evra said sadly.

"Well," I said uncomfortably, "maybe it won't come to that. Maybe there's some other way I can survive, a way that Mr Crepsley doesn't want to tell me about until he has no other choice."

Evra grunted. He knew as well as me that there was no other way.

"I'm going to check on my snake," he said. "Do you want to come and sit with us a while?"

"No," I said. "I'd better get some sleep. We'll have to rise early and I'm exhausted."

We said our goodnights and parted. I didn't head straight for Mr Crepsley's tent, but wandered through the camp-site, thinking about my conversation with Evra, wondering what it would feel like to die. I'd "died" once before, and been buried, but that wasn't the same thing. If I died for real, I'd be dead for good. Life would be over, my body would decay, and then ...

I glanced up at the stars. Was *that* where I'd be heading? To the other side of the universe? Vampire Paradise?

It was a troubling time. When I was living at home I'd hardly ever thought about death; it was something that only happened to old people. Now here I was, almost face to face with it.

If only somebody else could decide for me. I should be worrying about school and making the local football team, not about whether I should drink human blood or let myself die. It wasn't fair. I was too young. I shouldn't have to—

I saw a shadow passing the front of a nearby tent but took little notice of it. It wasn't until I heard a sharp snapping sound that I wondered who it might have been. Nobody should be out here. Everyone involved with the show was in the big tent. Was it somebody from the audience?

I decided to investigate.

I headed in the direction that the shadow had taken. It was a dark night and after a few turns I couldn't figure out which way the person had gone. I was on the verge of abandoning the search when I heard another sharp snapping sound, closer this time.

A quick look around convinced me of my location, and I knew immediately where the sounds must have come from: *the Wolf Man's cage!*

Taking a deep breath to steady my nerves, I put my best foot forward and hurried to check it out.

CHAPTER TWENTY-EIGHT

THE GRASS was damp, so it bent beneath my feet and made no sound. When I reached the last caravan before the Wolf Man's cage, I paused and listened.

There was a soft jangling sound, as though heavy chains were being lightly shaken.

I stepped out from under cover.

There were dim lights at either side of the Wolf Man's cage, so I was able to see everything in perfect detail. He'd been wheeled back here after his act, as he was every night. There was a slab of meat in his cage, which normally he'd be feasting on. But not tonight. Tonight he was focused on something different.

There was a large man in front of the Wolf Man's cage. He had a huge pair of pliers with him and had cut some of the chains which were holding the door shut.

The man was trying to unwrap the chains but wasn't enjoying much success. He cursed softly to himself and lifted the pliers to cut through another link.

"What are you doing?" I shouted.

The man jumped with shock, dropped the pliers and spun around.

It was, as I had guessed, R.V.

He looked guilty and scared at first, but when he saw I was alone he grew in confidence.

"Stay back!" he warned.

"What are you doing?" I asked again.

"Freeing this poor abused creature," he said. "I wouldn't keep the wildest of animals in a cage like this. It's inhuman. I'm letting him go. I rang the police – they'll be out here in the morning – but I decided to do a bit of work of my own beforehand."

"You can't do that!" I gasped. "Are you crazy? That guy's savage. He'd kill everything within a five-kilometre radius if you let him out!"

"So *you* say," R.V. sneered. "I don't believe that. It's been my experience that animals react according to how they're treated. If you treat them like mad monsters, they'll act that way. If, on the other hand, you treat them with respect, love and humanity ..."

"You don't know what you're doing," I told him. "The Wolf Man isn't like other animals. Come away from there before you do any real damage. We can talk this over. We can—"

"No!" he screamed. "I'm through talking!"

He spun back to the chains and began struggling with them again. He reached into the cage and tugged the thickest chains through the bars. The Wolf Man watched him silently.

"R.V., stop!" I shouted and raced over to prevent him opening the door. I grabbed his shoulders and tried pulling him away but I wasn't strong enough. I punched him in the ribs a few times but he only grunted and doubled his efforts.

I grabbed for his hands, to prise them off the chains, but the bars were in the way.

"Leave me alone!" R.V. yelled. He turned his head to address me directly. His eyes were wild. "You won't stop me!" he screeched. "You won't prevent me from doing my duty. I'll free this victim. I'll see justice done. I'll—"

He stopped ranting all of a sudden. His face turned deathly white and his body shuddered, then went stiff.

There was a crunching, munching, ripping sound, and when I looked inside the cage, I realized the Wolf Man had made his move.

He'd sprung across the cage while we were arguing, grabbed both of R.V.'s arms, jammed them in his mouth and *bitten them off beneath the elbows!*

R.V. fell away from the cage, shocked. He lifted his shortened arms and watched as blood pumped from the holes at the ends of his elbows.

I tried snatching his lower arms back from the mouth of the Wolf Man – if I could retrieve them, they could be stuck back on – but he moved too quickly for me, leapt back out of reach and began chewing. Within seconds the arms were a mess and I knew they'd be no good ever again.

"Where are my hands?" R.V. asked.

I switched my attention back to the bearded man. He was staring at the stumps that were his arms, a funny look on his face, not yet feeling the pain that must surely come.

"Where are my hands?" he asked again. "They're gone. They were there a minute ago. Where did all this blood come from? Why can I see the bone inside my skin?

"Where are my hands?" He screamed this last question at the top of his voice.

"You have to come with me," I said, drawing near. "We have to get your arms seen to, before you bleed to death."

"Stay away from me!" R.V. yelled. He tried raising a hand to shove me back, then remembered he didn't have hands any more.

"You're responsible for this!" he shouted. "You did this to me!"

"No, R.V., it was the Wolf Man," I said, but he wasn't listening.

"This is your fault," he insisted. "You took my hands. You're an evil little monster and you stole my hands. My hands! My hands!"

He began screaming again. I reached for him but this time he brushed me aside, turned and ran. He tore screaming through the camp, his blood-drenched half-arms raised high above his head, yelling as loudly as he could, until he vanished into the night.

"My hands! My hands! My hands!"

I wanted to run after him, but was afraid he might attack me. I set off to find Mr Crepsley and Mr Tall – they'd know what to do – but was stopped dead in my tracks by a worrying growl behind me.

I turned slowly. The Wolf Man was at the door of the cage, which was swinging wide open! He'd somehow removed the last of the chains and freed himself.

I remained perfectly still as he stood and grinned viciously, his long, sharp teeth glinting in the dim light. He looked to the left and right, stretched out his hands and grabbed the bars to either side. Then he crouched down low and tensed his legs.

He sprang, propelling himself towards me.

I shut my eyes and waited for the end to come.

I heard and felt him land about a metre in front of me. I began to say my final prayers.

But then I heard him flying overhead and realized he'd bounced over me. For a couple of terrifying seconds I waited for his teeth to bite through the back of my neck and gnaw my head off.

But they didn't.

Confused, I turned, blinking. He was racing away from me! I glimpsed a figure ahead of him, running quickly between the caravans, and understood he was after somebody else. He'd passed me up in favour of a tastier meal.

I took several stumbling steps after the departing Wolf Man. I was smiling and silently thanking the gods. I couldn't believe how close I'd come to death. When he'd leapt through the air, I was sure—

My feet struck something and I stopped.

I looked down and saw a bag. The person the Wolf Man was chasing must have dropped it, and for the first time I wondered who it was that the wild Wolf Man was after.

I picked up the bag. It was the sort you carry over one shoulder. It was full of clothes, which I could feel through the covers. A small jar fell out as I turned the bag around. Retrieving it, I thumbed up the lid and caught the bitter aroma of ... *pickled onions!*

My heart almost stopped. Furiously, I began searching for a name tag, praying the pickled onions didn't mean what I feared.

My prayers went unanswered.

The hand writing, when I found it, was neat, but unjoined. The writing of a child.

"This bag is the property of Sam Grest," it said, and his address was just beneath. "Hands off!!" it warned at the end, which was quite ironic given what had happened a minute or so earlier with R.V.

But I hadn't time to laugh at the dark joke.

Sam! For some reason he'd sneaked out here tonight – probably to stow away with the Cirque – and must have seen and followed me. It was Sam the Wolf Man's beady eyes had spotted, standing behind me. It was Sam running for his life through the camp.

The Wolf Man was after Sam!

CHAPTER TWENTY-NINE

I SHOULDN'T have pursued them on my own. I should have gone for help. It was madness, rushing off into the darkness by myself.

But he was after Sam. Sam, who wanted to join the Cirque. Sam, who asked to be my blood-brother. Harmless, friendly, long-winded Sam. The boy who'd saved my life.

I didn't think about my own safety. Sam was in trouble and there wasn't time to seek the help of others. It might prove the death of me but I had to go after them, to try and save Sam. I owed him.

I cleared the camp quickly. The clouds had parted overhead and I spotted the Wolf Man disappearing into the trees. I hurried after him, running as fast as I could.

I heard the Wolf Man howl a while later, which was a good sign. It meant he was still chasing Sam. If he'd caught him, he'd be too busy eating to howl.

I wondered why he hadn't caught him yet. He should have. Though I had never seen him running in the open, I was sure he must be fast. Perhaps he was playing with Sam, toying with him before he moved in for the kill.

Their footprints were clear in the damp night earth, but I

would have been able to follow from their sounds in any case. It's hard to run silently through a forest, especially at night.

We ran in that fashion for several minutes, Sam and the Wolf Man far in front and out of sight, me trailing behind. My legs were beginning to tire but I forced myself on.

I thought about what I would do when I caught up. There was no way I could beat the Wolf Man in a fair fight. Perhaps I could slam him over the head with a stick or something, but it was unlikely. He was strong and fast, and had the taste of human blood. He would be pretty much unstoppable.

The most I could hope to do was throw myself in his path and take Sam's place. If I offered myself instead of Sam, maybe he'd take me and Sam could escape.

I wouldn't mind dying for Sam. I'd given up my humanity for one friend; it wasn't asking so much more to give up my life for another.

Besides, this way, if I died, it would be for a good cause. I'd no longer have to worry about drinking human blood or starving to death. I could go down fighting.

After a few more minutes, I burst into a clearing and realized where Sam had led us: the old deserted railway station.

It showed he was still thinking clearly. This was the best place to come, with plenty of hiding spots and lots of stuff – chunks of metal and glass – to use in a fight. Maybe neither of us would have to die. Maybe there was a chance we could win this battle.

I saw the Wolf Man pause in the middle of the station yard and sniff the air. He howled again, a loud spine-shivering howl, then set off towards one of the rusty carriages.

I ran around the back of the carriage, moving as quietly as I could. I listened for sounds when I got there but couldn't hear anything. I lifted myself up and looked in one of the carriage windows: nothing.

I lowered myself and slid along to the third window over. Again, I could see nothing when I looked inside.

I was lifting myself to peep in the next window, when I glimpsed a metal bar moving towards my face at high speed.

I twisted aside just in time to avoid it. It whistled by the side of my face, scratching me but not doing any serious damage.

"Sam, stop, it's *me*!" I hissed, dropping to the ground. There was silence for a moment, then Sam's face appeared in the round window.

"Darren?" he asked. "What are you doing here?"

"I followed you," I said.

"I thought you were the Wolf Man. I was trying to kill you."

"You nearly did."

"I'm sorry."

"For God's sake, Sam, don't waste time apologizing," I snapped. "We're in big trouble. We have to put our thinking caps on. Get out here quick."

He retreated from the window. There were soft shuffling sounds, then he appeared out of the carriage door. He checked to make sure the Wolf Man wasn't around, jumped down and crept over to meet me.

"Where is he?" Sam asked.

"I don't know," I whispered. "He's around somewhere, though. I saw him coming in this direction."

"Maybe he found something else to attack," Sam suggested hopefully. "A sheep or a cow."

"I wouldn't bet on it," I grunted. "He wouldn't have run all this way, just to abandon the chase at the very end."

We huddled close together, Sam covering the right with his eyes, me the left. I could feel his body trembling and I'm sure he could feel mine shaking too.

"What are we going to do?" Sam asked.

"I don't know," I replied. "Any ideas?"

"A few," he said. "We could lead him into the guard's house. He might fall through the rotten floorboards. We could trap him down there."

"Maybe," I said. "But what if *we* fall through as well? We'd be trapped for sure. He could jump down and eat us whenever he liked."

"How about the rafters?" Sam asked. "We could climb out into the middle of a rafter and hang on, back to back. We could take clubs or sticks with us and beat him off if he attacked. There'd only be one way for him to come at us up there."

"And somebody's sure to arrive from the Cirque Du Freak sooner or later," I said, thinking it over. "But what if he decides to snap the rafter at one end?"

"They're set fairly deeply into brick," Sam said. "I don't think he could break them with his bare hands."

"Would a rafter hold the weight of three of us?" I asked.

"I'm not sure," Sam admitted. "But at least if we fell from that height it'd be over quickly. Who knows: we might get lucky and fall on the Wolf Man. He could cushion our fall and get killed in the process."

I laughed sickly. "You've been watching too many cartoons. But it's a good idea. Better than any I can think of. It won't be easy to fend him off, even on a rafter, but it will make it harder for him to get at us."

"How long do you think it'll be before the people from the Cirque get here?" Sam asked.

"Depends on when they realize what's happening," I said. "If we're lucky, they'll have heard him howling and might be here in a couple of minutes. Otherwise we might have to wait until the end of the show, which could be another hour, maybe longer."

"Do you have a weapon?" Sam asked.

"No," I said. "I didn't have time to pick anything up."

He handed me a short iron bar. "Here," he said. "I had this for back-up. It's not very good, but it's better than nothing."

"Any sign of the Wolf Man?" I asked.

"No," he said. "Not yet."

"We'd better get going before he arrives," I said, then paused. "How are we going to get to the station house? It's a long run and the Wolf Man could be hiding anywhere along the way."

"We'll have to race for it and hope for the best," Sam said.

"Will we split up?" I asked.

"I'd rather not," he said. "I think we're better off together."

"I agree. Are you ready to start?"

"Give me a few seconds," he said.

I turned and watched him breathing. His face was white and his clothes were torn and dirty from running through the woods, but he looked ready for business. He was a tough little character.

"Why did you come back tonight, Sam?" I asked softly.

"To join the Cirque Du Freak," he answered.

"Even after everything I told you about me?"

"I decided to risk it," he said. "I mean, you're a friend. We have to stick by our friends, don't we? Your story made me more determined to join, once I'd recovered from my initial fright. I might have been able to help you. I've read books about personality disorders. Maybe I could have cured you."

I couldn't help grinning. "You're a moron, Sam Grest," I said.

"I know," he smiled. "So are you. That's why we make a good pair."

"If we get out of this," I told him, "feel free to join up. And you don't have to worry about me eating you: that was just a story to frighten you off."

"Really?" he asked.

"Really," I said.

"Phew." He wiped his brow. "I can rest easy now."

"You can if the Wolf Man doesn't get us," I agreed. "Ready yet?"

"I'm ready." He hitched up his trousers and prepared to run. "On the count of three," he said.

"OK," I replied.

"One," he began.

We faced in the direction of the guard's house.

"Two."

We got into sprint-start positions.

"Thr—"

Before he could finish, a pair of hairy hands darted out from underneath the carriage, where – I realized too late – the Wolf Man was hiding. The fingers wrapped around Sam's lower legs, grabbed him by the ankles and dragged him down to the ground!

CHAPTER THIRTY

SAM STARTED to scream as soon as the hands tightened on his ankles. The fall knocked the breath out of him, silencing him momentarily, but after a second or two he was back screaming again.

I fell to my knees, grabbed Sam's arms and pulled.

I could see the Wolf Man underneath the carriage, spread out on his hairy belly, grinning wildly. Drool was dripping from his jaws.

I tugged hard and Sam slid towards me, but the Wolf Man came with him, wriggling out from under the carriage, not loosening his grip.

I stopped pulling and let go of Sam. I grabbed the long iron bar which he'd dropped, jumped to my feet and began pounding the outstretched arms of the Wolf Man, who howled angrily.

The Wolf Man released one of his hairy paws and swatted at me. I ducked out of the way and struck at the hand still holding Sam. The Wolf Man yelped with pain and the fingers came free.

"Run!" I screamed to Sam as I yanked him to his feet.

We set off towards the guard's house, side by side. I could hear the Wolf Man scrabbling out from beneath the carriage. He'd been playing with us before but now he was furious. I knew he'd come at us with everything he had. The games were over. There was no way we'd make the shelter of the guard's house. He'd have us before we were halfway across the yard.

"Keep ... running," I gasped to Sam, then stopped and turned to meet the charge of the oncoming Wolf Man.

My actions took him by surprise and he ran into me. His body was hairy and sweaty and heavy. The collision sent both of us flying to the floor. Our arms and legs were all tangled up but I quickly freed myself and whacked him with the bar.

The Wolf Man roared angrily and swiped at my arm. This time he connected, just below where it joined with my shoulder. The force of the blow deadened my arm, which became a useless lump of flesh and bone. I dropped the bar, then reached for it with my good left hand.

But the Wolf Man was quicker. He snatched up the bar and tossed it far away, where it fell with a clang, lost to the darkness.

He stood slowly, grinning nastily. I could read the expression in his eyes and knew, if he could speak, he would be saying something like: "Now, Darren Shan, you're mine! You had your fun and games but now it's killing time!"

He grabbed my body by the sides, opened his mouth wide, and leant forward to bite my face off. I could smell the stench of his breath and see bits of meat and shirt from R.V.'s arms stuck between his yellowish teeth.

Before he could snap his jaws shut, something hit the side of his head and knocked him off-balance.

I glimpsed Sam behind him, a heavy chunk of wood in his hands. He hit the Wolf Man again, this time causing his hands to loosen.

"One good turn deserves another!" Sam yelled, slamming the wood into the Wolf Man for a third time. "Come on! We have to—"

I never heard Sam's next words. Because as I started towards him, the Wolf Man lashed out blindly with one of his fists. It was a wild shot but he got lucky and it slammed into my face, knocking me backwards.

My head almost exploded. I saw bright lights and huge stars, then slumped to the ground in a faint.

When I recovered a few seconds or minutes later — I'm not sure how much time had passed — the railway station was eerily quiet. I could hear nobody running or screaming or fighting. All I could hear was a steady munching sound, a little way ahead of me.

Munch. Munch. Munch.

I sat up slowly, ignoring the hammering pain in my head.

It took my eyes a few seconds to re-adjust to the darkness. When I could see again, I realized I was gazing at the back of the Wolf Man. He was crouched on all fours, head bent over something. *He* was the one making the munching sounds.

The dizziness from the punch meant it took me a while to realize it wasn't a some*thing* he was eating ... it was a some*one*.

SAM!!!

I scrambled to my feet, pain forgotten, and rushed forward, but one look at the bloody mess beneath the Wolf Man and I knew I was too late.

"*NO!*" I screamed and punched the Wolf Man with my one good hand, attacking senselessly.

He grunted and shoved me away. I sprang back and this time kicked as well as punched. He growled and tried shoving again, but I held on and pulled his hair and ears.

He howled then and finally lifted his mouth. It was red, a dark, dreadful red, full of guts and blood and bits of flesh and bone.

He rolled on top of me, forcing me down, and pinned me

with one long hairy arm. His head shot back and he howled up at the night sky. Then, with a demonic snarl, he drove his teeth towards my throat, meaning to finish me off with one quick bite.

CHAPTER THIRTY-ONE

AT ALMOST the last possible moment, a pair of hands appeared out of the darkness and grabbed the Wolf Man's jaw, halting his plunge.

The hands twisted the head to one side, causing the Wolf Man to shriek and fall off me.

His attacker climbed on to his back and held him down. I saw fists flying faster than my eyes could follow and then the Wolf Man was lying unconscious on the ground.

His attacker stood and pulled me to my feet. I found myself gazing up into the flushed, scarred face of Mr Crepsley.

"I came as soon as I could," the vampire gasped, turning my head gently to the left and right, examining the damage. "Evra heard the howls of the Wolf Man. He did not know about you and the boy. He just thought the creature had burst free.

"Evra told Mr Tall, who cancelled the rest of the show and organized a search party. Then I thought of *you*. When I saw your bed was empty, I scouted around and found your trail."

"I thought ... I was going to ... die," I moaned, finding it hard to speak. I was bruised all over and suffering from shock. "I was certain. I thought ... nobody would come. I ..."

I threw my good arm around Mr Crepsley and hugged him hard.

"Thank you," I sobbed. "Thank you. Thank you. Thank—"

I stopped, remembering my fallen friend.

"Sam!" I screamed. I let go of Mr Crepsley and rushed to where the boy was lying.

The Wolf Man had torn Sam's belly open and eaten a lot of his insides. Amazingly, Sam was still alive when I got to him. His eyelids were fluttering and he was breathing lightly.

"Sam, are you OK?" I asked. It was a stupid question, but the only one my battered lips could form. "Sam?" I brushed his forehead with my fingers but he showed no signs of hearing or feeling me. He looked quite peaceful, from the chest up at least.

Mr Crepsley knelt down beside me and checked the body.

"Can you save him?" I asked. He shook his head slowly. "You must!" I shouted. "You can close the wounds. We can call a doctor. You can give him a potion. There must be some way to—"

"Darren," he said softly, "there is nothing we can do. He is dying. The damage is too great. Another couple of minutes and ..." He sighed. "At least he is beyond feeling. There will be no pain."

"No!" I screamed and threw myself on to Sam. I was crying bitterly, sobbing so hard it hurt.

"Sam! You can't die! Sam! Stay alive! You can join the Cirque and travel with us all over the world. You can ... you ..."

I could say no more, only lower my head, cling to Sam, and weep.

In the deserted old railway yard, the Wolf Man lay unconscious to my rear. Mr Crepsley sat silently by my side. Beneath me, Sam Grest – who'd been my friend and saved my life – remained perfectly still and slipped further and further into the final sleep of an untimely, horrible death.

CHAPTER THIRTY-TWO

AFTER A while, I felt a slight tugging at the sleeve of my left arm. I looked around. Mr Crepsley was standing over me, looking miserable.

"Darren," he said, "it will not seem like the right time but there is something you must do. For Sam's sake. And your own."

"What are you talking about?" I wiped some of the tears from my face and stared up at him. "Can we save him? Tell me if we can. I'll do anything."

"There is nothing we can do to save his *body*," Mr Crepsley told me. "He is dying and nothing can change that. But there is something we can do for his *spirit*.

"Darren," he said, "*you must drink Sam's blood.*"

I went on staring at him, but now it was a stare of disbelief, not hope.

"How could you?" I asked softly. "One of my best friends is dying, and all you can think about ... You're sick! You're a sick, twisted monster. You should be dying, not Sam. I hate you. Get out of here."

"You do not understand," he said.

"Yes I do!" I screamed. "Sam's dying, but all you're worried

345

about is blooding me. Do you know what you are? You're a no-good—"

"Do you remember our discussion about vampires being able to absorb part of a person's spirit?" he asked.

I'd been about to call him something awful but his question confused me.

"What's that got to do with this?" I asked.

"Darren, this is important. Do you remember?"

"Yes," I said softly. "What about it?"

"Sam is dying," Mr Crepsley said. "A few more minutes and he will be gone. For ever. But you can keep part of him alive within you if you drink from him now and take his life before the wounds of the Wolf Man can."

I couldn't believe what I was hearing.

"You want *me* to kill Sam?" I screamed.

"No," he sighed. "Sam has already been killed. But if you finish him off before he dies from the bites of the Wolf Man, you will save some of his memories and feelings. In you he can live on."

I shook my head. "I can't drink his blood," I whispered. "Not Sam's." I glanced down at the small, savaged body. "I can't."

Mr Crepsley sighed. "I will not force you to," he said. "But think carefully about it. What happened tonight is a tragedy which will haunt you for a very long time, but if you drink from Sam and absorb part of his essence, dealing with his death will be easier. Losing a loved one is hard. This way, you need not lose all of him."

"I can't drink from him," I sobbed. "He was my friend."

"It is *because* he was your friend that you must," Mr Crepsley said, then turned away and left me to decide.

I stared down at Sam. He looked so lifeless, as though he'd already lost that which made him human, alive, unique. I thought of his jokes and long words and hopes and dreams, and how awful it would be if all of that simply vanished with his passing.

Kneeling, I placed the fingers of my left hand on Sam's red neck. "I'm sorry, Sam," I moaned, then dug my sharp nails into his soft flesh, leant forward and stuck my mouth over the holes they'd made.

Blood gushed in and made me gag. I nearly fell away, but with an effort I held my place and gulped it down. His blood was hot and salty and ran down my throat like thick creamy butter.

Sam's pulse slowed as I drank, then stopped. But I went on drinking, swallowing every last drop, absorbing.

When I'd finally sucked him dry, I turned away and howled at the sky like the Wolf Man had. For a long time that's all I could do, howl and scream and cry like the wild animal of the night which I'd become.

CHAPTER THIRTY-THREE

MR TALL and a handful of others from the Cirque Du Freak — including four Little People — arrived a bit later. I was sitting by Sam's side, too tired to howl any more, staring blankly into space, feeling his blood settle in my stomach.

"What's the story?" Mr Tall asked Mr Crepsley. "How did the Wolf Man get free?"

"I do not know, Hibernius," Mr Crepsley replied. "I have not asked and do not intend to, not for a night or two at least. Darren is in no fit shape for an interrogation."

"Is the Wolf Man dead?" Mr Tall asked.

"No," Mr Crepsley said. "I merely knocked him out."

"Thank heaven for small mercies," Mr Tall sighed. He clicked his fingers and the Little People chained up the unconscious Wolf Man. A van from the show pulled up and they bundled him into the back.

I thought about demanding the Wolf Man's death but what good would it have been? He wasn't evil, just naturally mad. Killing him would have been pointless and cruel.

When they'd finished with the Wolf Man, the Little People's attention turned to Sam's shredded remains.

"Hold on," I said, as they bent to pick him up and cart him away. "What are they going to do with Sam?"

Mr Tall coughed uncomfortably. "I, ah, rather imagine they intend to *dispose* of him," he said.

It took me a moment to realize what that meant. "They're going to *eat* him?" I shrieked.

"We can't just leave him here," Mr Tall reasoned, "and we don't have time to bury him. This is the easiest—"

"No," I said firmly.

"Darren," Mr Crepsley said, "we should not interfere with—"

"No!" I shouted, striding over to shove the Little People backwards. "If they want to eat Sam, they'll have to eat me first!"

The Little People stared at me wordlessly, with hungry green eyes.

"I think they'd be quite happy to accommodate you," Mr Tall said drily.

"I mean it," I growled. "I won't let them eat Sam. He deserves a proper burial."

"So that worms can devour him?" Mr Tall asked, then sighed when I glared at him, and shook his head irritably.

"Let the boy have his way, Hibernius," Mr Crepsley said softly. "You may return to the Cirque with the others. I will stay and help dig the grave."

"Very well," Mr Tall shrugged. He whistled and cocked a finger at the Little People. They hesitated, then backed away and grouped around the owner of the Cirque Du Freak, leaving me alone with the dead Sam Grest.

Mr Tall and his assistants left. Mr Crepsley sat down beside me.

"How are you?" he asked.

I shook my head. There was no simple answer to that.

"Do you feel stronger?"

"Yes," I said softly. Even though it hadn't been long since I'd drank Sam's blood, already I noticed a difference. My eyesight had improved, as had my hearing, and my battered body didn't hurt nearly as much as it should.

"You will not have to drink again for a long time," he said.

"I don't care. I didn't do it for me. I did it for Sam."

"Are you angry with me?" he asked.

"No," I sighed.

"Darren," he said, "I hope—"

"I don't want to talk about it!" I snapped. "I'm cold, sore, miserable and lonely. I want to think about Sam, not waste words on you."

"As you wish," he said, and began digging in the soil with his fingers. I dug beside him in silence for a few minutes, then paused and looked over.

"I'm a real vampire's assistant now, aren't I?" I asked.

He nodded sadly. "Yes. You are."

"Does that make you glad?"

"No," he said. "It makes me feel ashamed."

As I stared at him, confused, a figure appeared above us. It was the Little Person with the limp. "If you think you're taking Sam ..." I warned him, raising a dirt-encrusted hand. Before I got any further, he jumped into the shallow hole, stuck his wide, grey-skinned fingers into the soil, and clawed up large clumps.

"He's helping us?" I asked, puzzled.

"It seems like it," Mr Crepsley said, and laid a hand on my back. "Rest," he advised. "We can dig faster by ourselves. I will call you when it is time to bury your friend."

I saw sense in that, nodded, crawled out and lay down on the bank beside the quickly forming grave. After a while I shuffled out of the way and sat, waiting, in the shadows of the old railway station. Just me and my thoughts. And Sam's dark red blood on my lips and between my teeth.

CHAPTER THIRTY-FOUR

WE BURIED Sam without much ado — I couldn't think of anything fitting to say — and filled in the grave. We didn't camouflage it, so he'd be discovered by the police and given a real burial soon. I wanted his parents to be able to give him a proper send-off, but this would keep him safe from scavenging animals (and Little People) in the meantime.

We broke camp before dawn. Mr Tall told everybody there was a long trek ahead. Sam's disappearance would create a fuss, so we had to get as far away from here as possible.

I wondered, as we set off, what had become of R.V. Had he bled to death in the forest? Had he made it to a doctor in time? Or was he still running and screaming: "My hands! My hands!"?

I didn't care. Although he'd been trying to do the right thing, this was R.V.'s fault. If he hadn't gone messing with the locks on the Wolf Man's cage, Sam would be alive. I didn't hope R.V. was dead, but I didn't say a prayer for him either. I'd leave him to fate and whatever it had in store.

Evra sat beside me at the rear of a van as the Cirque pulled out. He started to say something. Stopped. Cleared his throat. Then he placed a bag on my lap. "I found that," he muttered.

"Thought you might want it."

Through stinging eyes I read the name — "Sam Grest" — then burst into tears and wept bitterly over it. Evra put his arms around me and held me tight and cried along with me.

"Mr Crepsley told me what happened," Evra mumbled eventually, recovering slightly and wiping his face clean. "He said you drank Sam's blood to keep his spirit alive."

"Apparently," I replied weakly, unconvinced.

"Look," Evra said, "I know how much you didn't want to drink human blood, but you did this for Sam. It was an act of goodness, not evil. You shouldn't feel bad for drinking from him."

"I guess," I said, then moaned at the memory and wept some more.

The day grew old, the Cirque Du Freak rolled on, but thoughts of Sam couldn't be left behind. As night closed upon us, we pulled over to the side of the road for a short break. Evra went to look for food and refreshments.

"Can I get you anything?" he asked.

"No," I said, my face pressed against the window pane. "I'm not hungry."

He started to leave.

"Wait a sec," I called him back.

There was a strange taste in my mouth. Sam's blood was still hot on my lips, salty and terrible, but that wasn't what had set the buds at the back of my tongue tingling. There was something I wanted which I'd never wanted before. For a handful of confusing moments I didn't know what it was. Then I placed the strange craving and managed the thinnest of smiles. I searched Sam's bag, but the jar must have been left behind when we broke camp.

Looking up at Evra, I wiped tears from my eyes, licked my lips, and asked in a voice which sounded a lot like that of a curious, smartass kid I once knew, "Do we have any pickled onions?"

DARREN SHAN

TUNNELS OF BLOOD

THE SAGA OF DARREN SHAN
BOOK 3

For:

Declan – the original "mr happy"

OBEs (Order of the Bloody Entrails) to:
Jo "the jaguar" Williamson
Zoë "ze zombie" Clarke

The usual monsters:
Liam "Frankenstein" and Biddy "The Bride"
Gillie "rip yer guts out" Russell
the hungry HarperCollins cannibals
and
Emma & Chris – "who ya gonna call?"

PROLOGUE

THE SMELL of blood is sickening. Hundreds of carcasses hang from silver hooks, stiff, shiny with frosty blood. I know they're just animals — cows, pigs, sheep — but I keep thinking they're human.

I take a careful step forward. Powerful overhead lights mean it's bright as day. I have to tread easily. Hide behind the dead animals. Move slowly. The floor's slippery with water and blood, which makes progress even trickier.

Ahead, I spot him ... the vampire ... Mr Crepsley. He's moving as quietly as I am, eyes focused on the fat man a little way ahead.

The fat man. He's why I'm here in this ice-cold abattoir. He's the human Mr Crepsley intends to kill. He's the man I have to save.

The fat man pauses and checks one of the hanging slabs of meat. His cheeks are chubby and red. He's wearing clear plastic gloves. He pats the dead animal — the squeaky noise of the hook as the carcass swings sets my teeth on edge — then begins whistling. He starts to walk again. Mr Crepsley follows. So do I.

Evra is somewhere far behind. I left him outside. No point

the two of us risking our lives.

I pick up speed, moving slowly closer. Neither knows I'm here. If everything works out as planned, they won't know, not until Mr Crepsley makes his move. Not until I'm forced to act.

The fat man stops again. Bends to examine something. I take a quick step back, afraid he'll spot me but then I see Mr Crepsley closing in. Damn! No time to hide. If this is the moment he's chosen to attack, I have to get nearer.

I sprint forward several metres, risking being heard. Luckily Mr Crepsley is entirely focused on the fat man.

I'm only three or four metres behind the vampire now. I bring up the long butcher's knife which I've been holding down by my side. My eyes are glued to Mr Crepsley. I won't act until he does – I'll give him every chance to prove my terrible suspicions wrong – but the second I see him tensing to spring...

I take a firmer grip on the knife. I've been practising my swipe all day. I know the exact point I want to hit. One quick cut across Mr Crepsley's throat and that'll be that. No more vampire. One more carcass to add to the pile.

Long seconds slip by. I don't dare look to see what the fat man is studying. Is he never going to rise?

Then it happens. The fat man struggles to his feet. Mr Crepsley hisses. He gets ready to lunge. I position the knife and steady my nerves. The fat man's on his feet now. He hears something. Looks up at the ceiling – wrong way, fool! – as Mr Crepsley leaps. As the vampire jumps, so do I, screeching loudly, slashing at him with the knife, determined to kill...

CHAPTER ONE

One month earlier...

MY NAME'S Darren Shan. I'm a half-vampire.

I used to be human, until I stole a vampire's spider. After that, my life changed for ever. Mr Crepsley – the vampire – forced me to become his assistant, and I joined a circus full of weird performers, called the Cirque Du Freak.

Adapting was hard. Drinking blood was harder, and for a long time I wouldn't do it. Eventually I did, to save the memories of a dying friend (vampires can store a person's memories if they drain all their blood). I didn't enjoy it – the following few weeks were horrible, and I was plagued by nightmares – but after that first blood-red drink there could be no going back. I accepted my role as a vampire's assistant and learnt to make the best of it.

Over the course of the next year Mr Crepsley taught me how to hunt and drink without being caught; how to take just enough blood to survive; how to hide my vampire identity when mixing with others. And in time I put my human fears behind me and became a true creature of the night.

*

A couple of girls stood watching Cormac Limbs with serious expressions. He was stretching his arms and legs, rolling his neck around, loosening his muscles. Then, winking at the girls, he put the middle three fingers of his right hand between his teeth and bit them off.

The girls screamed and fled. Cormac chuckled and wriggled the new fingers which were growing out of his hand.

I laughed. You got used to stuff like that when you worked in the Cirque Du Freak. The travelling show was full of remarkable people, freaks of nature with wonderful and sometimes frightening powers.

Apart from Cormac Limbs, the performers included Rhamus Twobellies, capable of eating a full-grown elephant or a tank; Gertha Teeth, who could bite through steel; the Wolf Man, half-man half-wolf, who'd killed my friend Sam Grest; Truska, a beautiful and mysterious woman, who could grow a beard at will; and Mr Tall, who could move as fast as lightning and seemed to be able to read people's minds. Mr Tall owned and managed the Cirque Du Freak.

We were performing in a small town, camped behind an old mill, inside which the show was staged every night. It was a run-down tip, but I was used to such venues. We could have played the grandest theatres in the world and slept in luxurious hotel rooms – the Cirque made a load of money – but it was safer to keep a low profile and stick to places where the police and other officials rarely wandered.

I hadn't changed much since leaving home with Mr Crepsley nearly a year and a half before. Because I was a half-vampire I aged at only a fifth the rate of humans, which meant that though eighteen months had passed, my body was only three or four months older.

Although I wasn't very different on the outside, inside I was an entirely new person. I was stronger than any boy my age, able to run faster, leap further, and dig my extra-strong nails into brick walls. My hearing, eyesight and sense of smell had improved vastly.

Since I wasn't a full-vampire, there was lots of stuff I couldn't do yet. For instance, Mr Crepsley could run at a super-quick speed, which he called flitting. He could breathe out a gas which knocked people unconscious. And he could communicate telepathically with vampires and a few others, such as Mr Tall.

I wouldn't be able to do those things until I became a full-vampire. I didn't lose any sleep over it, because being a half-vampire had its bonuses: I didn't have to drink much human blood and – better yet – I could move about during the day.

It was day when I was exploring a rubbish tip with Evra, the snake-boy, looking for food for the Little People – weird small creatures who wore blue hooded cloaks and never spoke. Nobody – except maybe Mr Tall – knew who or what they were, where they came from, or why they travelled with the Cirque. Their master was a disturbing man called Mr Tiny (he liked to eat *children!*), but we didn't see much of him at the Cirque.

"Found a dead dog," Evra shouted, holding it above his head. "It smells a bit. Do you think they'll mind?"

I sniffed the air – Evra was a long way off, but I could smell the dog from here as well as a human could up close – and shook my head. "It'll be fine," I said. The Little People ate just about anything we brought.

I had a fox and a few rats in my bag. I felt bad about killing the rats – rats are friendly with vampires and usually come up to us like tame pets if we call them – but work is work. We've all got to do things we don't like in life.

There were lots of Little People with the Cirque – twenty of them – and one was hunting with Evra and me. He'd been with the Cirque since soon after me and Mr Crepsley joined. I could tell him apart from the others because he had a limp in his left leg. Evra and me had taken to calling him Lefty.

"Hey, Lefty!" I shouted. "How's it going?" The small figure in the blue hooded cloak didn't answer – he never did – but patted his stomach, which was the sign we needed more food.

"Lefty says to keep going," I told Evra.

"I figured as much," he sighed.

As I prowled for another rat, I spotted a small silver cross in the rubbish. I picked it up and brushed off the dirt. Studying the cross, I smiled. To think I used to believe vampires were terrified of crosses! Most of that stuff in old films and books is hokum. Crosses, holy water, garlic: none of those matter to vampires. We can cross running water. We don't have to be invited into a house before entering. We cast shadows and reflections (though a full-vampire can't be photographed: something to do with bouncing atoms). We can't change shape or fly.

A stake through the heart will kill a vampire. But so will a well-placed bullet, or fire, or a falling heavy object. We're harder to kill than humans but we aren't immortal. Far from it.

I placed the cross on the ground and stood back. Focusing my will, I tried making it jump into my left hand. I stared hard for all of a minute, then clicked the fingers of my right hand.

Nothing happened.

I tried again but still couldn't do it. I'd been trying for months, with no success. Mr Crepsley made it look simple – one click of his fingers and an object would be in his hand, even if it was several metres away – but I hadn't been able to copy him.

I was getting on quite well with Mr Crepsley. He wasn't a

bad old sort. We weren't friends, but I'd accepted him as a teacher and no longer hated him as I had when he first turned me into a half-vampire.

I pocketed the cross, and proceeded with the hunt. After a while I found a half-starved cat in the remains of an old microwave oven. It was after rats as well.

The cat hissed at me and raised its hackles. I pretended to turn my back on it, then spun quickly, grabbed it by the neck and twisted. It gave a strangled little cry and then went limp. I stuck it in the bag and went to see how Evra was doing.

I didn't enjoy killing animals, but hunting was part of my nature. Anyway, I had no sympathy for cats. The blood of cats is poisonous to vampires. Drinking from one wouldn't have killed me but it would have made me sick. And cats are hunters too. The way I saw it, the less cats there were, the more rats there'd be.

That night, back in camp, I tried moving the cross with my mind again. I'd completed my jobs for the day, and the show wouldn't be starting for another few hours, so I'd plenty of time to kill.

It was a cold, late-November night. There hadn't been any snow yet, but it was threatening. I was dressed in my colourful pirate costume: a light green shirt, dark purple trousers, a gold and blue jacket, a red satin cloth round my belly, a brown hat with a feather in it, and soft shoes with toes that curled in on themselves.

I strolled away from the vans and tents and found a secluded spot around the side of the old mill. I stuck the cross on a piece of wood in front of me, took a deep breath, concentrated on the cross and willed it into the palm of my outstretched hand.

No good.

I shuffled closer, so my hand was only centimetres away from the cross.

"I command you to move," I said, clicking my fingers. "I order you to move." Click. "Move." Click. "*Move!*"

I shouted this last word louder than intended and stamped my foot in anger.

"What are you doing?" a familiar voice asked behind me.

Looking up, I saw Mr Crepsley emerging out of the shadows.

"Nothing," I said, trying to hide the cross.

"What is that?" he asked. His eyes missed nothing.

"Just a cross I found while hunting," I said, holding it out.

"What were you doing with it?" Mr Crepsley asked suspiciously.

"Trying to make it move," I said, deciding it was time to ask the vampire about his magic secrets. "How do you do it?"

A smile spread across his face, causing the long scar that ran down the left side to crinkle. "So that is what has been bothering you," he chuckled. He stretched out a hand and clicked his fingers, causing me to blink. Next thing I knew, the cross was in *his* hand.

"How's it done?" I asked. "Can only full-vampires do it?"

"I will demonstrate again. Watch closely this time."

Replacing the cross on the piece of wood, he stood back and clicked his fingers. Once again it disappeared and turned up in his hand. "Did you see?"

"See what?" I was confused.

"One final time," he said. "Try not to blink."

I focused on the small silver piece. I heard his fingers clicking and — keeping my eyes wide open — thought I spotted the slightest blur darting between me and the cross.

When I turned to look at him he was tossing the cross

from hand to hand and smiling. "Rumbled me yet?" he asked.

I frowned. "I thought I saw ... It looked like ..." My face lit up. "You didn't move the cross!" I yelled excitedly. "*You* moved!"

He beamed. "Not as dull as you appear," he complimented me in his usual sarcastic manner.

"Do it again," I said. This time I didn't look at the cross: I watched the vampire. I wasn't able to track his movements – he was too fast – but I caught brief snaps of him as he darted forward, snatched up the cross and leapt back.

"So you're not able to move things with your mind?" I asked.

"Of course not," he laughed.

"Then why the click of the fingers?"

"To distract the eye," he explained.

"Then it's a trick," I said. "It's got nothing to do with being a vampire."

He shrugged. "I could not move so fast if I were human, but yes, it is a trick. I dabbled with illusions before I became a vampire and I like to keep my hand in."

"Could I learn to do it?" I asked.

"Maybe," he said. "You cannot move as fast as I can, but you could get away with it if the object was close to hand. You would have to practise hard – but if you wish, I can teach you."

"I always wanted to be a magician," I said. "But ... hold on..." I remembered a couple of occasions when Mr Crepsley had opened locks with a click of his fingers. "What about locks?" I asked.

"Those are different. You understand what static energy is?" My face was a blank. "Have you ever brushed a comb through your hair and held it up to a thin sheet of paper?"

"Yeah!" I said. "The paper sticks to it."

"That is static energy," he explained. "When a vampire flits, a very strong static charge builds up. I have learned to harness that charge. Thus I am able to force open any lock you care to mention."

I thought about that. "And the click of your fingers?" I asked.

"Old habits die hard," he smiled.

"But old vampires die easy!" a voice growled behind us, and before I knew what was happening, someone had reached around the two of us and pressed a pair of razor-sharp knives to the soft flesh of our throats!

CHAPTER TWO

I FROZE at the touch of the blade and the threatening voice, but Mr Crepsley didn't even blink. He gently pushed the knife away from his throat, then tossed the silver cross to me.

"Gavner, Gavner, Gavner," Mr Crepsley sighed. "I always could hear you coming from half a mile away."

"Not true!" the voice said peevishly, as the blade drew back from my throat. "You couldn't have heard."

"Why not?" Mr Crepsley said. "Nobody in the world breathes as heavily as you. I could pick you out blindfolded in a crowd of thousands."

"One night, Larten," the stranger muttered. "One night I'll catch you out. We'll see how smart you are then."

"Upon that night I shall retire disgracefully," Mr Crepsley chuckled.

Mr Crepsley cocked an eyebrow at me, amused to see I was still stiff and half-afraid, even though I'd figured out our lives weren't in danger.

"Shame on you, Gavner Purl," Mr Crepsley said. "You have frightened the boy."

"Seems all I'm good for," the stranger grunted. "Scaring

children and little old ladies."

Turning slowly, I came face to face with the man called Gavner Purl. He wasn't very tall but he was wide, built like a wrestler. His face was a mass of scars and dark patches, and the rims around his eyes were extremely black. His brown hair was cut short and he was dressed in an ordinary pair of jeans and a baggy white jumper. He had a broad smile and glittering yellow teeth.

It was only when I glanced down at his fingertips and spotted ten scars that I realized he was a vampire. That's how most vampires are created: vampire blood is pumped into them through the soft flesh at the ends of their fingers.

"Darren, this is Gavner Purl," Mr Crepsley introduced us. "An old, trusted, rather clumsy friend. Gavner, this is Darren Shan."

"Pleased to meet you," the vampire said, shaking my hand. "*You* didn't hear me coming, did you?"

"No," I answered honestly.

"There!" he boomed proudly. "See?"

"Congratulations," Mr Crepsley said dryly. "If you are ever called upon to sneak into a nursery, you should have no problems."

Gavner grimaced. "I see time hasn't sweetened you," he noted. "As cutting as ever. How long *has* it been? Fourteen years? Fifteen?"

"Seventeen next February," Mr Crepsley answered promptly.

"Seventeen!" Gavner whistled. "Longer than I thought. Seventeen years and as sour as ever." He nudged me in the ribs. "Does he still complain like a grumpy old woman when he wakes up?" he asked.

"Yes," I giggled.

"I could never get a positive word out of him until midnight. I had to share a coffin with him once for four whole months." He shivered at the memory. "Longest four months of my life."

"You *shared* a coffin?" I asked incredulously.

"Had to," he said. "We were being hunted. We had to stick together. I wouldn't do it again though. I'd rather face the sun and burn."

"You were not the only one with cause for complaint," Mr Crepsley grunted. "Your snoring nearly drove me to face the sun myself." His lips were twitching and I could tell he was having a hard time not smiling.

"Why were you being hunted?" I asked curiously.

"Never mind," Mr Crepsley snapped before Gavner could answer, then glared at his ex-partner.

Gavner pulled a face. "It was nearly sixty years ago, Larten," he said. "I didn't realize it was classified information."

"The boy is not interested in the past," Mr Crepsley said firmly. (I most certainly was!) "You are on *my* soil, Gavner Purl. I would ask you to respect my wishes."

"Stuffy old bat," Gavner grumbled, but gave in with a nod of his head. "So, Darren," he said, "what do you do at the Cirque Du Freak?"

"Odd jobs," I told him. "I fetch food for the Little People and help the performers get ready for—"

"The Little People still travel with the Cirque?" Gavner interrupted.

"More of them than ever," Mr Crepsley answered. "There are twenty with us at the moment."

The vampires shared a knowing glance but said no more about it. I could tell Gavner was troubled by the way his scars knit together into a fierce-looking frown.

"How goes it with the Generals?" Mr Crepsley enquired.

"Usual old routine," Gavner said.

"Gavner is a Vampire General," Mr Crepsley told me. *That* sparked my interest. I'd heard of the Vampire Generals, but nobody had told me exactly who or what they were.

"Excuse me," I said, "but what's a Vampire General? What do they *do*?"

"We keep an eye on rogues like this," Gavner laughed, nudging Mr Crepsley. "We make sure they don't get up to mischief."

"The Vampire Generals monitor the behaviour of the vampire clan," Mr Crepsley added. "They make sure none of us kill innocents or use our powers for evil."

"How do they do that?" I asked.

"If they discover a vampire who has turned bad," Mr Crepsley said, "they kill him."

"Oh." I stared at Gavner Purl. He didn't look like a killer, but then again, there were all those scars...

"It's a boring job most of the time," Gavner said. "I'm more like a village policeman than a soldier. I never did like the term 'Vampire Generals'. Far too pompous."

"It is not just evil vampires that Generals clamp down on," Mr Crepsley said. "It is also their business to crack down on foolish or weak vampires." He sighed. "I have been expecting this visit. Shall we retire to my tent, Gavner, to discuss the matter?"

"You've been *expecting* me?" Gavner looked startled.

"Word was bound to leak out sooner or later," Mr Crepsley said. "I have made no attempt to hide the boy or suppress the truth. Note that please: I will use it during my trial, when I am called upon to defend myself."

"Trial? Truth? The boy?" Gavner was bewildered.

Glancing down at my hands, he spotted the vampire marks on my fingertips and his jaw dropped. "The boy's a *vampire*?" he shrieked.

"Of course." Mr Crepsley frowned. "But surely you knew."

"I knew nothing of the sort!" Gavner protested. He looked into my eyes and concentrated hard. "The blood is weak in him," he mused aloud. "He is only a half-vampire."

"Naturally," Mr Crepsley said. "It is not our custom to make full-vampires of our assistants."

"Nor to make assistants of children!" Gavner Purl snapped, sounding more authoritative than he had before. "What were you thinking?" he asked Mr Crepsley. "A *boy!* When did this happen? Why haven't you informed anybody?"

"It has been nearly a year and a half since I blooded Darren," Mr Crepsley said. "Why I did it is a long story. As for why I have not yet told anyone, that is simpler to answer: you are the first of our kind we have encountered. I would have taken him to the next Council if I had not run into a General beforehand. Now that will not be necessary."

"It bloody well will be!" Gavner snorted.

"Why?" Mr Crepsley asked. "You can judge my actions and pass verdict."

"*Me?* Judge *you?*" Gavner laughed. "No thanks. I'll leave you to the Council. The last thing I need is to get involved in something like this."

"Excuse me," I said again, "but what's this all about? Why are you talking about being judged? And who or what are the Council?"

"I shall tell you later," Mr Crepsley said, waving my questions aside. He studied Gavner curiously. "If you are not here about the boy, why have you come? I thought I made it clear when last we met that I wanted no more to do with the Generals."

"You made it crystal clear," Gavner agreed. "Maybe I'm just here to discuss old times."

Mr Crepsley smiled cynically. "After seventeen years of leaving me to my own devices? I think not, Gavner."

The Vampire General coughed discreetly. "There is trouble brewing. Nothing to do with the Generals," he added quickly. "This is personal. I've come because I feel there's something you should know." He paused.

"Go on," Mr Crepsley urged him.

Gavner looked at me and cleared his throat. "I have no objections to speaking in front of Darren," he said, "but you seemed anxious to steer him clear of certain areas when we were discussing our past a while ago. What I have to tell you may not be for his ears."

"Darren," Mr Crepsley said immediately, "Gavner and I shall continue our discussion in my quarters, alone. Please find Mr Tall and tell him I shall be unable to perform tonight."

I wasn't happy – I wanted to hear what Gavner had to say: he was the first vampire I'd met apart from Mr Crepsley – but from his stern expression, I knew his mind was made up. I turned to leave.

"And Darren," Mr Crepsley called me back. "I know you are curious by nature, but I warn you: do not attempt to eavesdrop. I shall take a dim view of it if you do."

"What do you think I am?" I said. "You treat me like—"

"Darren!" he snapped. "No eavesdropping!"

I nodded glumly. "All right."

"Cheer up," Gavner Purl said as I walked away dejectedly.

"I'll tell you all about it, as soon as Larten's back is turned."

As Mr Crepsley spun round, with fire in his eyes, the Vampire General quickly raised his hands and laughed. "Only joking!"

CHAPTER THREE

I DECIDED to do the act with Madam Octa — Mr Crepsley's spider — by myself. I was well able to handle her. Besides, it was fun to take over from Mr Crepsley. I'd been on stage with him loads of times, but always as his sidekick.

I went on after Hans Hands — a man who could run a hundred metres on his hands in less than eight seconds — and had great fun. The audience cheered me off, and later I sold loads of candy spiders to clamouring customers.

I hung out with Evra after the show. I told him about Gavner Purl and asked what he knew about Vampire Generals.

"Not much," he said. "I know they exist but I've never met one."

"What about the Council?" I asked.

"I think that's a huge meeting they have every ten or fifteen years," he said. "A big conference where they gather and discuss things."

That was all he could tell me.

A few hours before dawn, while Evra was tending to his snake, Gavner Purl appeared from Mr Crepsley's van — the vampire preferred to sleep in the basements of buildings, but there had been no suitable rooms in the old mill — and asked me to walk with him a while.

The Vampire General walked slowly, rubbing the scars on his face, much as Mr Crepsley often did when thinking.

"Do you enjoy being a half-vampire, Darren?" he asked.

"Not really," I answered honestly. "I've got used to it, but I was happier as a human."

He nodded. "You know that you will age at only a fifth of the human rate? You've resigned yourself to a long childhood? It doesn't bother you?"

"It bothers me," I said. "I used to look forward to growing up. It bugs me that it's going to take so long. But there's nothing I can do about it. I'm stuck, amn't I?"

"Yes," he sighed. "That's the problem with blooding a person: there's no way to take the vampire blood back. It's why we don't blood children: we only want people who know what they're getting into, who wish to abandon their humanity. Larten shouldn't have blooded you. It was a mistake."

"Is that why he was talking about being judged?" I asked.

Gavner nodded. "He'll have to account for his error," he said. "He'll have to convince the Generals and Princes that what he did won't harm them. If he can't..." Gavner looked grim.

"Will he be killed?" I asked softly.

Gavner smiled. "I doubt it. Larten is widely respected. His wrists will be slapped but I don't think anybody will look for his head."

"Why didn't you judge him?" I asked.

"All Generals have the right to pass judgement on non-ranked vampires," he said. "But Larten's an old friend. It's best for a judge to be unbiased. Even if he'd committed a real crime, I would have found it hard to punish him. Besides, Larten's no ordinary vampire. He used to be a General."

"Really?" I stared at Gavner Purl, stunned by the news.

"An important one too," Gavner said. "He was on the verge of being voted a Vampire Prince when he stood down."

"A *prince?*" I asked sceptically. It was hard to imagine Mr Crepsley with a crown and royal cloak.

"That's what we call our leaders," Gavner said. "There are very few of them. Only the noblest and most respected vampires are elected."

"And Mr Crepsley almost became one?" I said. Gavner nodded. "What happened?" I asked. "How did he end up travelling with the Cirque Du Freak?"

"He resigned," Gavner said. "He was a couple of years shy of being invested – we call the process of Prince-making an investiture – when one night he declared he was sick of the business and wanted nothing more to do with the Generals."

"Why?" I asked.

Gavner shrugged. "Nobody knows. Larten never gave much away. Maybe he just got tired of the fighting and killing."

I wanted to ask who it was the Vampire Generals had to fight, but at that moment we cleared the last of the town houses and Gavner Purl smiled and stretched his arms.

"A clear run," he grunted happily.

"You're leaving?" I asked.

"Have to," he said. "A General's schedule is a busy one. I only dropped by because it was on my way. I'd like to stay and chat over old times with Larten, but I can't. Anyway, I think Larten will be on the move soon himself."

My ears perked up. "Where's he going?" I asked.

Gavner shook his head and grinned. "Sorry. He'd scalp me alive if I told. I've already said more than I should. You won't tell him I told you about his being a General, will you?"

"Not if you don't want me to," I said.

"Thanks." Gavner crouched down and faced me. "Larten's a pain in the butt sometimes. He plays his cards too close to his chest, and getting information out of him can be like prying teeth from a shark. But he's a good vampire, one of the best. You couldn't hope for a better teacher. Trust him, Darren, and you won't go wrong."

"I'll try," I smiled.

"This can be a dangerous world for vampires," Gavner said softly. "More dangerous than you know. Stick with Larten and you'll be in a better position to survive than many of our kind. You don't live as long as he has without learning more than your fair share of tricks."

"How old *is* he?" I asked.

"I'm not sure," Gavner said. "I think about a hundred and eighty or two hundred."

"How old are *you*?" I asked.

"I'm a whippersnapper," he said. "Barely past the hundred mark."

"A hundred years old!" I whistled softly.

"That's nothing for a vampire," Gavner said. "I was barely nineteen when first blooded and only twenty-two when I became a full-vampire. I could live to be a good five hundred years old, the gods of the vampires permitting."

"Five hundred...!" I couldn't imagine being so old.

"Picture trying to blow out the candles on *that* cake!" Gavner chuckled. Then he stood. "I must be off. I've fifty kilometres to make before dawn. I'll have to slip into overdrive." He grimaced. "I hate flitting. I always feel sick afterwards."

"Will I see you again?" I asked.

"Probably," he replied. "The world's a small place. I'm sure our paths will cross again one fine gloomy night." He shook my hand. "So long, Darren Shan."

"Until next time, Gavner Purl," I said.

"Next time," he agreed, and then he was off. He took several deep breaths and started to jog. After a while he broke into a sprint. I stood where I was, watching him run, until he hit flitting speed and disappeared in the snapping of an eyelid, at which point I turned and headed back to camp.

I found Mr Crepsley in his van. He was sitting by the window (it was completely covered with strips of dark sticky tape, to block out the sun during the day), staring moodily off into space.

"Gavner's gone," I said.

"Yes," he sighed.

"He didn't stay long," I remarked.

"He is a Vampire General," Mr Crepsley said. "His time is not his own."

"I liked him."

"He is a fine vampire and a good friend," Mr Crepsley agreed.

I cleared my throat. "He said *you* might be leaving too."

Mr Crepsley regarded me suspiciously. "What else did he say?"

"Nothing," I lied quickly. "I asked why he couldn't stay longer and he said there was no point, as you'd probably be moving on soon."

Mr Crepsley nodded. "Gavner brought unpleasant news," he said carefully. "I will have to leave the Cirque for a while."

"Where are you going?" I asked.

"To a city," he responded vaguely.

"What about me?" I asked.

Mr Crepsley scratched his scar thoughtfully. "That is what I have been contemplating," he said. "I would prefer not to take you with me but I think I must. I may have need of you."

"But I like it here," I complained. "I don't want to leave."

"Nor do I," Mr Crepsley snapped. "But I must. And you have to come with me. Remember: we are vampires, not circus performers. The Cirque Du Freak is a means of cover, not our home."

"How long will we be away?" I asked unhappily.

"Days. Weeks. Months. I cannot say for sure."

"What if I refuse to come?"

He studied me ominously. "An assistant who does not obey orders has no purpose," he said quietly. "If I cannot rely on your cooperation, I will have to take steps to remove you from my employ."

"You mean you'd sack me?" I smiled bitterly.

"There is only one way to deal with a rebellious half-vampire," he answered, and I knew what that way was – a stake through the heart!

"It's not fair," I grumbled. "What am I going to do by myself all day in a strange city while you're asleep?"

"What did you do when you were a human?" he asked.

"Things were different," I said. "I had friends and a family. I'm going to be alone again if we leave, like when I first joined up with you."

"It will be hard," Mr Crepsley said compassionately, "but we have no choice. I must be away with the coming of dusk – I would leave now, were we not so near to dawn – and you must come with me. There is no other..."

He stopped as a thought struck him. "Of course," he said slowly, "we could bring another along."

"What do you mean?" I asked.

"We could take Evra with us."

I frowned as I considered it.

"The two of you are good friends, yes?" Mr Crepsley asked.

"Yes," I said, "but I don't know how he'd feel about leaving. And there's his snake: what would we do with that?"

"I am sure somebody could look after the snake," Mr Crepsley said, warming to the idea. "Evra would be good company for you. And he is wiser: he could keep you out of mischief when I am not around."

"I don't need a babysitter!" I huffed.

"No," Mr Crepsley agreed, "but a guardian would not go amiss. You have a habit of getting into trouble when left to your own devices. Remember when you stole Madam Octa? And the mess we had with that human boy, Sam whatever his name was?"

"That wasn't my fault!" I yelled.

"Indeed not," Mr Crepsley said. "But it happened when you were by yourself."

I pulled a face but didn't say anything.

"Will I ask him or not?" Mr Crepsley pressed.

"*I'll* ask him," I said. "You'd probably bully him into going."

"Have it your own way." Mr Crepsley rose. "I will go and clear it with Hibernius." That was Mr Tall's first name. "Be back here before dawn so I can brief you – I want to make sure we are prepared to travel as soon as night falls."

Evra took a lot of time deciding. He didn't like the idea of parting company with his friends in the Cirque Du Freak – or with his snake.

"It won't be for ever," I told him.

"I know," he said uncertainly.

"Look on it as a holiday," I suggested.

"I like the idea of a holiday," he admitted. "But it would be nice to know where I was going."

"Sometimes surprises are more fun," I said.

"And sometimes they aren't," Evra muttered.

"Mr Crepsley will be asleep all day," I reminded him. "We'll be free to do as we like. We can go sightseeing, to cinemas, swimming, whatever we want."

"I've never been swimming," Evra said, and I could tell by the way he grinned that he'd decided to come.

"I'll tell Mr Tall you're coming?" I asked. "And get him to arrange for your snake to be looked after?"

Evra nodded. "She doesn't like the cold weather in any case," he said. "She'll be asleep most of the winter."

"Great!" I beamed. "We'll have a wonderful time."

"We'd better," he said, "or it'll be the last time I come on 'holiday' with you."

I spent the rest of the day packing and unpacking. I only had two small bags to bring, one for me and one for Mr Crepsley, but – apart from my diary, which went everywhere with me – I kept changing my mind about what to put in.

Then I remembered Madam Octa – I wasn't bringing *her* along – and hurried off to find somebody to look after her. Hans Hands agreed to mind her, though he said there was no way he'd let her out of her cage.

Finally, after hours of rushing about – Mr Crepsley had it easy, the wily old goat! – night fell and it was time to leave.

Mr Crepsley checked the bags and nodded curtly. I told him about leaving Madam Octa with Hans Hands and again he nodded. We picked up Evra, said goodbye to Mr Tall and some of the others, then faced away from the camp and began walking.

"Will you be able to carry both of us when you flit?" I asked Mr Crepsley.

"I have no intention of flitting," he said.

"Then how are we going to travel?" I asked.

"Buses and trains," he replied. He laughed when I looked

surprised. "Vampires can use public transport as well as humans. There are no laws against it."

"I suppose not," I said, grinning, wondering what other passengers would think if they knew they were travelling with a vampire, a half-vampire and a snake-boy. "Shall we go, then?" I asked.

"Yes," Mr Crepsley answered simply, and the three of us headed into town to catch the first train out.

CHAPTER FOUR

IT FELT strange being in a city. The noise and smell nearly drove me mad the first couple of days: with my heightened senses it was like being in the middle of a whirring food blender. I lay in bed during the daytime, covering my head with the thickest pillow I could find. But by the end of the week I'd grown used to the super-sharp sounds and scents and learned to ignore them.

We stayed at a hotel situated in the corner of a quiet city square. In the evenings, when traffic was slow, neighbourhood kids gathered outside for a game of football. I'd have loved to join in but dared not — with my extra strength, I might accidentally end up breaking somebody's bones, or worse.

By the start of our second week we'd fallen into a comfortable routine. Evra and me rose every morning — Mr Crepsley went off by himself at night without telling us where — and ate a big breakfast. After that we'd head out and explore the city, which was big and old and full of interesting stuff. We'd get back to the hotel for nightfall, in case Mr Crepsley wanted us, then watch some TV or play computer games. We usually got to bed between eleven and twelve.

After a year with the Cirque Du Freak, it was a thrill to live like a normal human again. I loved being able to sleep late in the morning, not having to worry about finding food for the Little People; it was great not to be rushing about, running errands for the performers; and sitting back at night, stuffing my face with sweets and pickled onions, watching TV shows – that was heaven!

Evra was enjoying himself too. He'd *never* known a life like this. He'd been part of the circus world for as long as he could remember, first with a nasty side-show owner, then with Mr Tall. He liked the Cirque – I did too – and was looking forward to returning, but he had to admit it was nice to have a break.

"I never realized TV could be so addictive," he said one night, after we'd watched five soap operas in a row.

"My mum and dad never let me watch too much," I told him, "but I knew guys in school who watched five or six hours of it every night of the week!"

"I wouldn't take it that far," Evra mused, "but it's fun in small doses. Perhaps I'll buy a portable set when we return to the Cirque Du Freak."

"I never thought of getting a TV since I joined," I said. "So much else was going on, it was the last thing on my mind. But you're right – it would be nice to have a set, even if only for reruns of *The Simpsons*." That was our favourite show.

I wondered sometimes what Mr Crepsley was up to – he'd always been mysterious, but never *this* secretive – but in truth I wasn't overly bothered: it was nice to have him out of my hair.

Evra had to wrap up in layers of clothes whenever we went out. Not because of the cold – though it *was* chilly: the first snow had fallen a couple of days after our arrival – but because of how he looked. Though he didn't mind people gawping at him – he was used to it – it was easier to get around if he was able to pass for a normal human. That way he didn't have to stop every five or ten minutes to explain to a curious stranger who and what he was.

Covering his body, legs and arms was easy — trousers, a jumper and gloves — but his face was tricky: it wasn't as strongly scaled or coloured as the rest of him, but it wasn't the face of an ordinary human. A thick cap took care of his long yellow-green hair, and dark glasses shaded much of the upper half of his face. But as for the lower half...

We experimented with bandages and flesh-coloured paints before hitting on the answer: a fake beard! We bought it in a joke shop and though it looked silly — nobody could mistake it for a real one — it did the job.

"We must look a right pair," Evra giggled one day as we strolled around a zoo. "You in your pirate costume, me in this get-up. People probably think we're a couple of escaped crazies."

"The folks at the hotel definitely do," I giggled. "I've heard the bellboys and maids talking about us and they reckon Mr Crepsley is a mad doctor and we're two of his patients."

"Yeah?" Evra laughed. "Imagine if they knew the truth — that you're a couple of vampires and I'm a snake-boy!"

"I don't think it would matter," I said. "Mr Crepsley tips well and that's the important thing. 'Money buys privacy', as I heard one of the managers say when a maid was complaining about a guy who'd been walking about naked in the corridors."

"I saw him!" Evra exclaimed. "I thought he'd locked himself out of his room."

"Nope," I smiled. "Apparently he's been walking about starkers for four or five days. According to the manager, he comes every year for a couple of weeks and spends the entire time roaming around, naked as a baby."

"They let him?" Evra asked incredulously.

"'Money buys privacy,'" I repeated.

"And I thought the Cirque Du Freak was a strange place to live," Evra muttered wryly. "Humans are even weirder than us!"

As the days passed the city became more and more Christmassy as people geared themselves up for the twenty-fifth of December. Christmas trees appeared; lights and decorations lit up the streets and windows at night; Father Christmas touched down and took orders; toys of every shape and size filled shop shelves from floor to ceiling.

I was looking forward to Christmas: last year's had passed unnoticed, since Christmas was something hardly anyone associated with the Cirque Du Freak bothered celebrating.

Evra couldn't understand what the fuss was about.

"What's the *point* of it?" he kept asking. "People spend loads of money buying each other presents they don't really need; they drive themselves half-crazy getting a fancy dinner ready; trees and turkeys are bred and slaughtered in frightening numbers. It's ridiculous!"

I tried telling him that it was a day of peace and goodwill, for families to come together and rejoice, but he was having none of it. As far as he was concerned, it was a mad, money-spinning racket.

Mr Crepsley, of course, only snorted whenever the subject was mentioned. "A silly human custom," was how he put it. He wanted nothing to do with the festival.

It would be a lonely Christmas without my family – I missed them more at this time of the year than ever, especially Annie – but I was looking forward to it all the same. The hotel staff were throwing a big party for the guests. There'd be turkey and ham and Christmas pudding and crackers. I was determined to drag Evra into the spirit of the day: I was sure he'd change his opinion when he experienced Christmas first-hand.

"Want to come shopping?" I asked one frosty afternoon, wrapping a scarf around my neck (I didn't need it – my vampire blood kept me warm – nor the thick coat or woolly jumper, but I'd draw attention if I went out without them).

Evra glanced out of the window. It had been snowing earlier and the world outside was frosty-white.

"I can't be bothered," he said. "I don't feel like getting into heavy clothes again." We'd been out that morning, throwing snowballs at each other.

"OK," I said, glad he wasn't coming: I wanted to look over a few presents for him. "I won't be more than an hour or two."

"Will you be back before dark?" Evra asked.

"Maybe," I said.

"You'd better be." He nodded towards the room where Mr Crepsley lay sleeping. "You know how it goes: the one night you aren't here when he wakes will be the one night he wants you."

I laughed. "I'll risk it. Want me to bring you back anything?" Evra shook his head. "OK. See you soon."

I walked through the snow, whistling to myself. I liked snow: it covered up most of the smells and muffled a lot of the noise. Some of the kids who lived in the Square were out building a snowman. I stopped to watch them but moved on before they could ask me to join in: it was easier not to get involved with humans.

As I stood outside a large department store, studying the window display, wondering what to buy Evra, a girl walked over and stood beside me. She was dark-skinned, with long black hair, about my age, and a little shorter than me.

"Ahoy, cap'n," she said, saluting.

"Excuse me?" I replied, startled.

"The costume," she grinned, tugging my coat open. "I think it's cool, you look like a pirate. You going in or just looking?"

"I don't know," I said. "I'm looking for a present for my brother, but I'm not sure what to get him." That was our cover story — that Evra and me were brothers, and Mr Crepsley was our father.

"Right," she nodded. "How old is he?"

"A year older than me," I said.

"Aftershave," she said firmly.

I shook my head. "He hasn't started shaving yet." And never would: hairs wouldn't grow on Evra's scales.

"OK," she said. "How about a CD?"

"He doesn't listen to much music," I said. "Although if I got him a CD player, he might start."

"Those are expensive," the girl said.

"He's my only brother," I said. "He's worth it."

"Then go for it." She held out a hand. She wasn't wearing gloves, despite the cold. "My name's Debbie."

I shook her hand – mine looked very white compared with her dark skin – and told her my name.

"Darren and Debbie." She smiled. "That sounds good, like Bonnie and Clyde."

"Do you always talk like this to strangers?" I asked.

"No," she said. "But we're not strangers."

"We're not?" I frowned.

"I've seen you around," she said. "I live in the Square, a few doors up from the hotel. That's how I knew about the pirate costume. You hang out with that funny guy in glasses and a fake beard."

"Evra. He's the one I'm buying the present for." I tried placing her face but couldn't remember seeing her with the other kids. "I haven't noticed you around," I said.

"I haven't been out much," she replied. "I've been in bed with a cold. That's why I spotted you — I've been spending my days staring out the window, studying the Square. Life gets really boring when you're stuck in bed."

Debbie blew into her hands and rubbed them together.

"You should be wearing gloves," I told her.

"Look who's talking," she sniffed. I'd forgotten to pull on a pair before leaving. "Anyway, that's what I'm here for — I lost my gloves earlier and I've been stomping about from shop to shop trying to find an identical pair. I don't want my parents to find out I lost them on only my second day out of bed."

"What were they like?" I asked.

"Red, with fake fur round the wrists," she said. "My uncle gave them to me a few months ago but didn't say where he got them."

"Have you tried this place yet?" I asked.

"Uh-uh," she said. "I was on my way in when I spotted you."

"Want to come in with me?" I asked.

"Sure," she said. "I hate shopping by myself. I'll help you choose a CD player if you want, I know a lot about them."

"OK," I said, then pushed the door open and held it for her.

"Why, Darren," she laughed, "people will think you fancy me."

I felt myself blushing and tried to think of a suitable response — but couldn't. Debbie giggled, walked in, and left me to trail along behind her.

CHAPTER FIVE

DEBBIE'S SURNAME was Hemlock and she hated it.

"Imagine being named after a poisonous plant!" she fumed.

"It's not that bad," I said. "I quite like it."

"Shows what sort of taste *you* have," she sniffed.

Debbie had only moved here recently with her parents. She had no brothers or sisters. Her Dad was a computer whiz, who regularly flew around the world on business. They'd swapped homes five times since she was born.

She was interested to learn that I was also used to moving around. I didn't tell her about the Cirque Du Freak but said I was on the road a lot with my dad, who was a travelling salesman.

Debbie wanted to know why she hadn't seen my father in the Square. "I've seen you and your brother loads of times, but never your dad."

"He's an early riser," I lied. "He gets up before dawn and doesn't come back till after dark most days."

"He leaves the two of you alone in the hotel?" She pursed her lips as she considered it. "What about school?" she asked.

"Are these like the gloves you want?" I side stepped the question, picking a pair of red gloves off a rack.

"Nearly," she said, studying them. "Mine were a shade darker."

We went on to another store and looked at loads of CD players. I didn't have much money on me, so I didn't buy anything.

"Of course, after Christmas they'll be reduced in the sales," Debbie sighed, "but what can you do? If you wait, you'll look mean."

"I'm not worried about the money," I said. I could always get some from Mr Crepsley.

After failing to find the right sort of gloves in another couple of shops, we strolled about for a while, watching the lights come on above the streets and in the windows.

"I love this time of evening," Debbie said. "It's as if one city goes to sleep and a new one wakes up."

"A city of night-walkers," I said, thinking of Mr Crepsley.

"Hmmm," she said, looking at me oddly. "Where are you from? I can't place your accent."

"Here and there," I answered vaguely. "Around and about."

"You're not going to tell me, are you?" she asked directly.

"My dad doesn't like me telling people," I said.

"Why not?" she challenged me.

"Can't tell you." I grinned weakly.

"Hmmm," she grunted, but let the matter drop. "What's your hotel like?" she asked. "It looks kind of stuffy. Is it?"

"No," I said. "It's better than most places I've been. The staff don't hassle you if you play in the corridors. And some of the customers..." I told her about the guy who walked about nude.

"No!" she squealed. "You're kidding!"

"Honest," I swore.

"They don't kick him out?"

"He's paying. As far as they're concerned he has the right to walk about however he pleases."

"I'll have to come over sometime," she grinned.

"Whenever you like," I said, smiling. "Except during the day," I added quickly, remembering the slumbering Mr Crepsley. The last thing I wanted was for Debbie to walk in on a vampire while he was sleeping.

We headed back for the Square, taking our time. I liked being with Debbie. I knew I shouldn't be making friends with humans – it was too dangerous – but it was hard to reject her. I hadn't been around anyone my own age, except Evra, since becoming a half-vampire.

"What will you tell your parents about the gloves?" I asked as we stood on the front step of her house.

She shrugged. "The truth. I'll start coughing when I tell them. Hopefully they'll feel sorry for me and won't get too mad."

"Devious," I laughed.

"With a name like Hemlock, are you surprised?" She smiled, then asked, "Do you want to come in for a while?"

I checked my watch. Mr Crepsley would be up and about by now and had probably already left the hotel. I didn't like the idea of leaving Evra alone too long: he might get annoyed if he thought I was neglecting him, and decide to return to the Cirque Du Freak. "Better not," I said. "It's late. I'm expected back."

"Suit yourself," Debbie said. "Feel free to pop over tomorrow if you want. Any time. I'll be in."

"Won't you be at school?" I asked.

She shook her head. "With the holidays so close, Mum said I needn't bother going back until the New Year."

"But she let you out to look for gloves?"

Debbie bit her lip with embarrassment. "She doesn't know I've been out walking," she admitted. "I left in a taxi, telling her I was off to see a friend. I was supposed to come back in a taxi too."

"Ah-ha!" I smiled. "I see the chance for a spot of blackmail."

"Just try it!" she snorted. "I'll cook up a witch's brew and turn you into a frog." She fished a key out of her purse and paused. "You *will* come round, won't you? It gets pretty dull by myself. I haven't made many friends here yet."

"I don't mind coming," I said, "but how will you explain my presence to your mother? You can hardly tell her we met in a taxi."

"You're right." Her eyes narrowed. "I didn't think of that."

"I'm not just a pretty face," I said.

"Not *even* a pretty face!" she laughed. "How about I come over to the hotel?" she suggested. "We can go on to the cinema from there, and I can tell Mum that's where we met."

"OK," I said, and told her my room number. "But not too early," I warned. "Wait until five or six, when it's good and dark."

"OK." She tapped her foot on the doorstep. "*Well?*" she said.

"Well what?" I replied.

"Aren't you going to ask?"

"Ask what?"

"Ask me to go to the cinema," she said.

"But you just—"

"Darren," she sighed. "Girls *never* ask boys out."

"They don't?" I was confused.

"You haven't a clue, have you?" she chuckled. "Just ask me if I want to go to the cinema, OK?"

"OK," I groaned. "Debbie — will you come to the cinema with me?"

"I'll think about it," she said, then unlocked the door and disappeared inside.

Girls!

CHAPTER SIX

EVRA WAS watching TV when I got in. "Any news?" I asked.

"No," he replied.

"Mr Crepsley didn't miss me?"

"He barely noticed you were gone. He's been acting weirdly lately."

"I know," I said. "I'm due a feed of human blood, but he hasn't mentioned it. Normally he's very fussy about making sure I feed on time."

"Are you going to feed without him?" Evra asked.

"Probably. I'll slip into one of the rooms late tonight and take some blood from a sleeping guest. I'll use a syringe." I wasn't able to close cuts with spit like full-vampires could.

I'd come a long way in a year. Not so long ago I'd have jumped at the chance to skip a feed; now I was feeding because I wanted to, not because I'd been told.

"You'd better be careful," Evra warned me. "If you get caught, Mr Crepsley will raise a stink."

"Caught? Me? Impossible! I'll breeze in and out like a ghost."

I did, too, about two in the morning. It was easy for one

with my talents: by sticking an ear to a door and listening for sounds within, I could tell how many people were in a room and whether they were light sleepers or deep sleepers. When I found an unlocked room with a single man snoring like a bear, I let myself in and took the required amount of blood. Back in my own room, I squeezed the blood into a glass and drank.

"That'll keep me going," I said as I finished. "It'll get me through tomorrow anyway, and that's the important thing."

"What's so special about tomorrow?" Evra asked.

I told him about meeting Debbie and arranging to go to the cinema.

"You've got a date!" Evra laughed with delight.

"It's not a date!" I snorted. "We're just going to the cinema."

"*Just?*" Evra grinned. "There's no such thing as *just* with girls. It's a date."

"OK," I said, "it's *kind* of a date. I'm not stupid. I know I can't get involved."

"Why not?" Evra asked.

"Because she's a normal girl and I'm only half-human," I said.

"That needn't stop you going out together. She won't be able to tell you're a vampire, not unless you start biting her neck."

"Ha ha," I laughed dryly. "It's not that. In five years she'll be a grown woman, while I'll still be like this."

Evra shook his head. "Worry about the next five *days*," he advised, "not the next five *years*. You've been hanging around Mr Crepsley too much – you're getting as gloomy as he is. There's no reason for you not to date girls."

"I suppose you're right," I sighed.

"Of course I am."

I chewed my lip nervously. "Assuming it *is* a date," I said, "what do I *do*? I've never been on a date before."

Evra shrugged. "Neither have I. But I guess you just act normal. Chat to her. Tell her a few jokes. Treat her like a friend. Then..."

"*Then...?*" I asked when he stopped.

He puckered up his lips. "Give her a snog!" he chortled.

I threw a pillow at him. "I'm sorry I told you," I grumbled.

"I'm only kidding. But I'll tell you what." He turned serious. "*Don't* tell Mr Crepsley. He'd probably move us on to a new city straightaway, or at least a new hotel."

"You're right," I agreed. "I'll keep quiet about Debbie when he's around. It shouldn't be hard: I barely see him. And when I do, he hardly says anything. He seems to be in a world of his own."

Though I couldn't have known it then, it was a world me and Evra would soon be part of ... and Debbie too.

The next day passed slowly. My belly was a jumble of nerves. I had to drink warm milk to calm it down. Evra didn't help matters. He kept reading the time out loud and commenting: "Five hours to go!" "Four hours to go!" "Three and a half..."

Luckily I didn't have clothes to worry about: I only had the one kind of suit, so there was no problem choosing what to wear. That said, I did spend a couple of hours in the bathroom, checking that I was spotlessly clean.

"Calm down," Evra said eventually. "You look great. I'm half tempted to go out with you myself."

"Shut up, stupid," I snorted, but couldn't help grinning.

"Well, anyway," Evra said, "do you want me to disappear before Debbie arrives?"

"Why?" I asked.

"You might not want me here," he muttered.

"I want to introduce you to her. She thinks you're my brother. It'd look strange if you weren't here when she turns up."

"It's just – well – how will you explain?" Evra asked.

"Explain *what*?"

"My looks," he said, rubbing a few of the scales along his arm.

"Oh," I said, as it finally dawned on me. Debbie didn't know Evra was a snake-boy. She was expecting an ordinary boy.

"I might frighten her," Evra said. "Lots of people get scared when they find themselves face to face with a guy like me. Maybe it would be for the best if—"

"Listen," I said firmly. "You're my best friend, right?"

"Right," Evra smiled weakly. "But—"

"No!" I snapped. "No 'buts'. I like Debbie a lot, but if she can't handle the way you look, too bad."

"Thanks," Evra said quietly.

Night fell and Mr Crepsley arose. The vampire looked haggard. I'd fixed a meal for him – bacon, sausages, pork chops – so he'd eat quickly and leave before Debbie arrived.

"Are you feeling all right?" I asked as he wolfed down the food.

"Fine," he mumbled.

"You look terrible," I told him bluntly. "Have you fed recently?"

He shook his head. "I have not had time. I may tonight."

"I took blood from a guest last night," I said. "It'll keep me going for another week or so."

"Good," he said absentmindedly. It was the first time I'd fed by myself and I'd been expecting some sort of a compliment, but he didn't seem to care. It was like he'd lost interest in me.

I tidied up once he'd left, then sat down to watch TV with Evra and wait for Debbie.

"She's not going to come," I said after what felt like a couple of hours. "She's stood me up."

"Relax," Evra laughed. "You've only been sitting here ten minutes. It's early yet."

I checked my watch – he was right. "I can't go through with this," I groaned. "I've never been out with a girl before. I'll mess it up. She'll think I'm dull."

"Don't get so wound up," Evra said. "You *want* to go out with her and you *are* going out with her, so why worry?"

I started to reply, but was interrupted by Debbie knocking on the door. Forgetting my nerves in an instant, I leapt up to let her in.

CHAPTER SEVEN

I'D EXPECTED Debbie to dress up, but she was in a pair of jeans and a baggy jumper, wrapped in a long thick coat.

I noticed she was wearing a pair of red gloves.

"You found the gloves?" I asked.

She pulled a face. "They were in my room all along," she groaned. "They'd fallen behind the radiator. Of course, I only found them *after* I'd told Mum about walking about outside without them.

"Are your father and brother here?" she asked.

"Mr Cre— I mean, *Dad's* out. Evra's in." I paused. "There's something you should know about Evra," I said.

"What?"

"He's not like other people."

"Who is?" Debbie laughed.

"You see," I began to explain, "Evra's a—"

"Look," Debbie interrupted, "I don't care what sort of an odd bod he is. Just take me in and make the introductions."

"OK." I grinned shakily and gestured for her to enter. Debbie swished on confidently ahead of me. A couple of steps into the room, she spotted Evra and stopped.

"Wow!" she exclaimed. "Is that a costume?"

Evra smiled nervously. He was standing in front of the telly, arms crossed stiffly.

"Debbie," I said, "this is Evra, my brother. He's—"

"Are those *scales*?" Debbie asked, surging forward.

"Uh-huh," Evra said.

"Can I touch them?" Debbie asked.

"Sure," Evra told her.

She ran her fingers up his left arm — he was wearing a T-shirt — and down his right.

"Wow!" Debbie gasped. "Have you always been like this?"

"Yes," Evra said.

"He's a snake-boy," I explained.

Debbie whirled fiercely on me. "That's a horrible thing to say!" she snapped. "You shouldn't call him names just because he looks different."

"I wasn't calling him—" I began, but she interrupted.

"How would *you* like it if somebody made fun of that stupid costume you wear?" she fumed. I looked down at my suit. "Oh yes!" she snorted. "I could have said plenty about that crazy get-up, but didn't. I figured, if you wanted to look like something out of *The Pirates of Penzance*, that was your choice."

"It's OK," Evra said softly, "I *am* a snake-boy." Debbie stared at Evra uncertainly. "I am, really," he vowed. "I have many serpentine qualities: I shed my skin, I'm cold-blooded, I have snake-like eyes."

"Still," Debbie said, "it's not nice to be compared to a snake."

"It is if you *like* snakes," Evra laughed.

"Oh." Debbie looked back at me, half-ashamed. "Sorry," she said.

"It's OK," I said, secretly pleased that she'd reacted like she had – it proved she wasn't prejudiced.

Debbie was fascinated by Evra and kept asking him questions. What did he eat? How often? Was he able to talk to snakes? After a while I told him to show her his tongue – he had an incredibly long tongue and was able to stick it up his nose.

"That's the grossest, greatest thing I've ever seen!" Debbie howled when Evra demonstrated his nostril-licking abilities. "I wish *I* could do that. It'd freak the life out of everybody at school."

Eventually it was time to leave for the cinema.

"I won't be late back," I told Evra.

"Don't rush on my account," he said, and winked.

It was a short walk to the cinema and we arrived in plenty of time for the start of the film. We bought popcorn and drinks and headed in. We chatted away to one another during the ads and trailers.

"I like your brother," Debbie said. "He seems a little shy, but I guess that's to do with the way he looks."

"Yes," I agreed. "Life hasn't been easy for him."

"Is anybody else in your family snake-like?" she asked.

"No," I said. "Evra's one of a kind."

"Your mum isn't unusual?" I'd told Debbie my mum and dad were divorced and that Evra and me spent half the year with each. "Or your dad?"

I smiled. "Dad's strange too," I said, "but not like Evra."

"When can I meet him?" she asked.

"Soon," I lied. Debbie had warmed immediately to the snake-boy, but how would she react to a vampire? I'd a feeling she wouldn't take so kindly to Mr Crepsley, not if she knew what he was.

The film was a silly romantic comedy. Debbie laughed more than me.

We discussed the movie afterwards as we walked back to

the Square. I pretended to like it more than I did. As we walked down a dark alley, Debbie took my hand in hers and held on to me for comfort, which made me feel great.

"Aren't you afraid of the dark?" she asked.

"No," I said. The alley seemed quite bright to my vampire-enhanced eyes. "What's to be afraid of?" I asked.

She shivered. "I know it's silly," she said, "but I'm always half-afraid a vampire or werewolf's going to jump out and attack me." She laughed. "Stupid, huh?"

"Yeah," I said, laughing weakly. "Stupid."

If only she knew...

"Your nails are really long," she commented.

"Sorry," I said. My nails were incredibly tough. Scissors couldn't cut them. I had to chew on them with my teeth to keep them down.

"No need to apologize," she said.

As we emerged from the alley, I felt her studying me by the light of the street lamps. "What are you looking at?" I asked.

"There's something different about you, Darren," she mused. "It's not something I can put my finger on."

I shrugged, trying to make light of it. "It's because I'm so good-looking," I joked.

"No," she said seriously. "It's something inside you. I see it in your eyes sometimes."

I looked away. "You're embarrassing me," I grumbled.

She gave my hand a squeeze. "My dad often gives out about that. He says I'm too inquisitive. My mind's always ticking over and I'm forever saying what's on it. I should learn to keep quiet."

We arrived at the Square and I walked Debbie to her door. I stood awkwardly on the front step, wondering what to do next.

Debbie solved the problem for me.

"Want to come in?" she asked.

"Aren't your parents home?" I responded.

"That's OK – they won't mind. I'll tell them you're a friend of a friend."

"Well ... OK," I said. "If you're sure."

"I am," she said, smiling, then took my hand and opened the door.

I was almost as nervous going in as I had been the night I crept down the cellar in the old theatre in my home town, and stole Madam Octa from the sleeping Mr Crepsley!

CHAPTER EIGHT

As it turned out, I had nothing to worry about. Debbie's parents were as nice as she was. Their names were Jesse and Donna – they wouldn't let me call them Mr and Mrs Hemlock – and they made me feel welcome as soon as I walked in.

"Hello!" Jesse said, spotting me first as we entered the living room. "Who's this?"

"Mum, Dad, this is Darren," Debbie said. "He's a friend of Anne's. I ran into him at the cinema and invited him back. Is that OK?"

"Sure," Jesse said.

"Of course," Donna agreed. "We were about to have supper. Would you like some, Darren?"

"If it's no trouble," I said.

"No trouble at all," she beamed. "Do you like scrambled egg?"

"It's my favourite," I told her. It wasn't really, but I guessed it would pay to be polite.

I told Jesse and Donna a bit about myself as we ate.

"What about school?" Jesse asked, as Debbie had before him.

"My dad used to be a teacher," I lied, having given some

thought to the matter since yesterday. "He teaches Evra and me."

"More egg, Darren?" Donna asked.

"Yes please," I said. "It's lovely." It was too. Much nicer than any scrambled egg I'd had before. "What's in it?"

"A few extra spices," Donna said, smiling proudly. "I used to be a chef."

"I wish they had someone like you in the hotel," I sighed. "Their food isn't very good."

I offered to wash the dishes when we were finished but Jesse said he'd do them. "It's my way of unwinding at the end of a hard day," he explained. "Nothing I like better than scrubbing a few dirty dishes, polishing the banisters and Hoovering the carpets."

"Is he kidding?" I asked Debbie.

"Actually, no," she said. "OK if we go up to my room?" she asked.

"Go ahead," Donna told her. "But don't stay nattering too long: we've got a couple of chapters of *The Three Musketeers* to finish, remember?"

Debbie pulled a face. "All for one and one for all," she groaned. "How exciting – I don't think!"

"You don't like *The Three Musketeers*?" I asked.

"Do *you*?"

"Sure. I've seen the movie at least eight times."

"But did you ever read the book?" she asked.

"No, but I read a comic about them once."

Debbie shared a scornful glance with her mother and the two burst out laughing.

"I have to read a bit of a so-called classic every night," Debbie grumbled. "I hope you never learn just how boring those books can be."

"Be down soon," she told her mum, then showed me the way upstairs.

Her room was on the third floor. A big, fairly empty room, with large built-in wardrobes and hardly any posters or ornaments.

"I don't like feeling cluttered," Debbie explained when she saw me looking around.

There was a bare artificial Christmas tree in one corner of the room. There'd been one in the living room too, and I'd noticed a couple more in other rooms on my way up the stairs.

"Why all the trees?" I asked.

"Dad's idea," Debbie said. "He loves Christmas trees, so we get one for every room in the house. The ornaments are in little boxes underneath" – she pointed to a box under the tree – "and we open them on Christmas Eve and decorate the trees. It's a lovely way to pass the night, and it tires you out, so you fall asleep almost as soon as your head hits the pillows."

"It sounds like fun," I agreed wistfully, remembering what it had been like to decorate the Christmas tree at home with my family.

Debbie studied me silently. "You could come over on Christmas Eve," she said. "You and Evra. Your dad too. You could help us with the trees."

I stared at her. "You mean that?"

"Sure. I'd have to check with Mum and Dad first, but I doubt if they'd object. We've had friends over to help before. It's nicer with more people."

I was pleased that she'd asked me, but hesitated before accepting.

"Shall I ask them?" she said.

"I'm not sure if I'll still be here at Christmas. Mr Cre— Dad is unpredictable. He goes wherever the job takes him, whenever."

"Well, the offer's there," she said. "If you're here, great. If not"— she shrugged — "we'll manage by ourselves."

We got talking about Christmas presents. "Are you going to get the CD player for Evra?" Debbie asked.

"Yeah. And a few CDs too."

"That just leaves your dad," she said. "What are you getting him?"

I thought about Mr Crepsley and what he might like. I wasn't going to buy him anything — he'd only turn up his nose at presents — but it was interesting to consider what I *could* buy him. What was there that a vampire could possibly be interested in?

I started to smile. "I know," I said. "I'll get him a sun lamp."

"A sun lamp?" Debbie frowned.

"So he can work up a tan." I began to laugh. "He's rather pale. He doesn't get much sun."

Debbie couldn't understand why I was laughing so hard. I'd have liked to let her in on the joke — it would be worth buying the sun lamp just to see the disgusted expression on the vampire's face — but didn't dare.

"You've a weird sense of humour," she muttered, bewildered.

"Trust me," I said, "if you knew my dad, you'd know why I was laughing." I'd tell Evra about my idea when I got home: he'd be able to appreciate it.

We chatted for another hour or so. Then it was time for me to go.

"Well?" Debbie said, as I stood up. "Don't I get a goodnight kiss?"

I thought I was going to collapse.

"I ... um ... I mean ... that is ..." I became a stuttering wreck.

"Don't you want to kiss me?" Debbie asked.

"Yes!" I gasped quickly. "It's just ... I ... um..."

"Hey, forget it," Debbie said, shrugging. "I'm not bothered one way or the other." She got up. "I'll show you out."

We walked quickly down the stairs. I wanted to say goodbye to Jesse and Donna, but Debbie didn't give me the chance. She went straight to the front door and opened it. I was still trying to get back into my coat.

"Can I come round tomorrow?" I asked, struggling to find the left arm of the coat.

"Sure, if you want to," she said.

"Look, Debbie," I said, "I'm sorry I didn't kiss you. I'm just—"

"Scared?" she asked, smiling.

"Yeah," I admitted.

She laughed. "OK," she said. "You can come round tomorrow. I *want* you to. Only next time, be a little braver, OK?" And she closed the door behind me.

CHAPTER NINE

I LINGERED on the step for ages, feeling stupid. I started back for the hotel but found I was reluctant to return – I didn't want to admit to Evra how dumb I'd been. So I walked around the Square a couple of times, letting the cold night air fill my lungs and clear my head.

I was due to meet Debbie tomorrow, but suddenly felt I couldn't wait that long. My mind made up, I stopped in front of her house and glanced about to make sure I wasn't being watched. I couldn't see anybody, and with my superior eyesight I was sure no one could see me.

I slipped off my shoes and climbed the drainpipe that ran down the front of the house. The window to Debbie's room was three or four metres from the pipe, so when I came level with it, I dug my tough nails into the brick of the building and clawed my way across.

I hung just beneath the window and waited for Debbie to appear.

About twenty minutes later, the light in Debbie's room snapped on. I rapped softly on the glass with my bare knuckles, then rapped again, a little harder. Footsteps approached.

Debbie opened the curtains a notch and stared out, confused. It took her a few seconds to look down and notice me. When she did, she almost collapsed with surprise.

"Open the window," I said, mouthing the words clearly in case she couldn't hear me. Nodding, she dropped to her knees and shoved up the lower pane of glass.

"What are you *doing*?" she hissed. "What are you holding on to?"

"I'm floating on air," I joked.

"You're crazy," Debbie said. "You'll slip and fall."

"I'm perfectly safe," I assured her. "I'm a good climber."

"You must be freezing," she said, spotting my feet. "Where are your shoes? Come in, quick, before you—"

"I don't want to come in," I interrupted. "I climbed up because ... well ... I..." I took a deep breath. "Is the offer still on?"

"What offer?" Debbie asked.

"The offer of a kiss," I said.

Debbie blinked, then smiled. "You *are* mad," she chuckled.

"One hundred per cent crazy," I agreed.

"You went to all this trouble just for that?" she asked.

I nodded.

"You could have knocked on the door," she said.

"I didn't think of that," I smiled. "So – how about it?"

"I suppose you deserve one," she said, "but quickly, OK?"

"All right," I agreed.

Debbie stuck her head out. I leaned forward, heart beating, and pecked her lips.

She smiled. "Worth coming up for?" she asked.

"Yes," I said. I was shaking, and it wasn't from the cold.

"Here," she said. "Here's another one."

She kissed me sweetly and I almost lost my grip on the wall.

When she moved away, she was smiling mysteriously. I could feel myself grinning like an idiot.

"See you tomorrow, Romeo," she said.

"Tomorrow," I sighed happily.

As the window shut and the curtains closed, I climbed down, delighted with myself. I practically bounced back to the hotel. I was almost at the door before I remembered my shoes. Dashing back, I retrieved them, shook the snow off and stuck them on.

By the time I got to the hotel, I'd regained my composure. I opened the door of my room and entered. Evra was watching TV. He was focused on the screen and barely noticed me coming in.

"I'm back," I said, taking off my coat. He didn't reply. "I'm back!" I repeated, louder.

"Um," he grunted, waving distractedly at me.

"That's a fine attitude," I sniffed. "I thought you'd be interested in how the evening went. I'll know better next time. In future, I'll just—"

"Have you seen the news?" Evra asked quietly.

"It may surprise you to learn, young Evra Von," I said sarcastically, "that they don't show news reels in cinemas any longer. Now, do you want to hear about my date or not?"

"You should watch this," Evra said.

"Watch *what*?" I asked, irritated. I walked around behind him and saw it was a news programme. "The *news*?" I laughed. "Turn it off, Evra, and I'll tell you about—"

"Darren!" Evra snapped in a most unusual tone. He looked up at me and his face was a mask of worry. "You should watch this," he said again, slowly this time, and I realized he wasn't fooling.

Sitting down, I studied the screen. There was a picture of the outside of a building on it, then the camera dissolved to an interior shot and scanned round the walls. A caption informed viewers that the photographs were from stock footage, which meant they'd been filmed sometime in the past. A reporter was waffling on about the building.

"What's the big deal?" I asked.

"This is where they found the bodies," Evra said softly.

"What bodies?"

"Watch," he said.

The camera came to rest in a dark room that looked the same as all the others, held on the scene for a few seconds, then dissolved back to a view of the building's exterior. The caption informed us that these new pictures had been shot earlier today. As I watched, several policemen and doctors emerged from the building, pushing mobile stretchers, each of which held a motionless object covered by a body bag.

"Are those what I think they are?" I asked quietly.

"Corpses," Evra confirmed. "Six so far. The police are still searching the building."

"What does it have to do with *us*?" I asked uneasily.

"Listen." He turned up the sound.

A reporter was talking into the camera now, live, explaining how the police found the bodies – a couple of teenagers had stumbled over them while exploring the deserted building as a dare – and when, and how the search was progressing. The reporter looked rather stunned.

The newsreader in the studio asked the reporter a question about the bodies, to which she shook her head.

"No," she said, "the police aren't issuing names, and won't until the relatives of the deceased have been notified."

"Have you learned any more about the nature of their

deaths?" the newsreader asked.

"No," the reporter replied. "The police have blocked the flow of information. We've only the early reports to go on. The six people – we don't know if they're men or women – appear to be victims of a serial killer or some sort of sacrificial cult. We don't know about the last two bodies brought up, but the initial four all shared the same bizarre wounds and conditions."

"Could you explain once again what those conditions were?" the newsreader asked.

The reporter nodded. "The victims – at least the first four – have slit throats, which seem to be the means by which they were killed. In addition, the bodies appear – and I must stress that this is an early, unverified report – to have been drained of all their blood."

"Possibly sucked out or pumped dry?" the newsreader suggested.

The reporter shrugged. "As of the moment, nobody can answer that, except the police." She paused. "And, of course, the murderer."

Evra switched the sound off but left the picture on.

"See?" he said softly.

"Oh no," I gasped. I thought of Mr Crepsley, who'd been out alone every night since we arrived, prowling the city for reasons he wouldn't reveal. I thought of the six bodies and the reporter's and newsreader's comments: "...drained of all their blood." "Possibly sucked out or pumped dry."

"Mr Crepsley," I said. And for a long time I gazed in silence at the screen, unable to say anything more.

CHAPTER TEN

I PACED furiously around the hotel room, hands clenched into fists, cursing angrily, Evra watching mutely.

"I'm going to kill him," I finally muttered. "I'll wait for day, pull back the curtains, drive a stake through his heart, chop his head off, and set him on fire."

"You don't believe in taking chances, do you?" Evra remarked wryly. "I suppose you'll scoop his brains out too and stuff the space inside his head with garlic."

"How can you make jokes at a time like this?" I howled.

Evra hesitated. "It mightn't have been him."

"Come off it!" I barked. "Who else could it have been?"

"I don't know."

"The blood was sucked out of them!" I shouted.

"That's what the reporters *think*," Evra said. "They weren't certain."

"Maybe we should wait," I huffed. "Wait for him to kill another five or six, huh?"

Evra sighed. "I don't know what we should do," he said. "But I think we should have proof before we go after him. Chopping a person's head off is kind of final. If we find out later we were mistaken, there's no going back. We can't glue his head back on and say, 'Sorry, all a big mistake, no hard feelings'."

He was right. Killing Mr Crepsley without proof would be wrong. But it had to be him! Those nights out, acting so strangely, not telling us what he was doing – it all added up.

"There's something else," Evra said. I glanced down at him. "Let's say Mr Crepsley *is* the killer."

"I've no problem accepting that," I grunted.

"Why would he do it?" Evra asked. "It's not his style. I've known him longer than you have, and I've never seen or heard of him doing anything like this. He's not a killer."

"He probably killed when he was a Vampire General," I said. I'd told Evra about my conversation with Gavner Purl.

"Yes," Evra agreed. "He killed evil vampires, who deserved to be killed. What I'm saying is, if he did kill these six people, maybe *they* had to be killed too. Maybe they were vampires."

I shook my head. "He gave up being a Vampire General years ago."

"Gavner Purl could have persuaded him to join again," Evra said. "We don't know anything about the Vampire Generals or how they work. Perhaps that's why Mr Crepsley came here."

It sounded halfway reasonable, but I didn't believe it.

"Six evil vampires on the loose in one city?" I asked. "What are the odds against that?"

"Who knows?" Evra said. "Do *you* know how an evil vampire behaves? *I* don't. Maybe they form gangs."

"And Mr Crepsley wiped them out by himself?" I said. "Vampires are tough to kill. He'd have no problem killing six humans, but six vampires? No way."

"Who says he was alone?" Evra asked. "Maybe Gavner

Purl was with him. Maybe there's a load of Vampire Generals in town."

"Your argument's getting weaker by the second," I commented.

"Possibly," Evra said, "but that doesn't mean I'm wrong. *We don't know*, Darren. You can't kill Mr Crepsley on a hunch. We have to wait. Think about it and you'll see I'm right."

I calmed down and thought it over. "OK," I sighed. "He's innocent till proven guilty. But what should we do? Sit back and pretend nothing's happened? Report him to the police? Ask him straight to his face?"

"If we were at the Cirque Du Freak," Evra mused, "we could tell Mr Tall and leave it in his hands."

"But we're not at the Cirque," I reminded him.

"No," he said. "We're on our own." His narrow eyes narrowed even further as he mulled it over. "How about this? We track him every night when he leaves, see where he goes and what he gets up to. If we find out he's the killer, and that these are ordinary humans, then we kill him."

"You'd do that?" I asked.

Evra nodded. "I've never killed before," he said quietly, "and I hate the thought of it. But if Mr Crepsley is murdering without good cause, I'll help you kill him. I'd rather leave it to someone else, but since there isn't anybody..."

His face was set and I knew I could rely on him.

"But we have to be *sure*," Evra warned me. "If there's even a glimmer of doubt, we mustn't do it."

"Agreed," I said.

"And it has to be a joint decision," Evra added. "You have to promise you won't kill him without my approval."

"OK."

"I'm serious," he told me. "If I think Mr Crepsley is

innocent, and you go after him, I'll do everything I can to stop you. Even if it means..." He left the threat unfinished.

"Don't worry," I said. "This isn't something I'm looking forward to. I've grown used to Mr Crepsley. The last thing I want to do is kill him."

I was telling the truth. I'd love it if my suspicions turned out to be unwarranted. But I had an awful feeling they wouldn't.

"I hope we're wrong about this," Evra said. "Saying we'll kill him is easy, but doing it would be a lot harder. He's not the sort to lie there and do nothing while under attack."

"We'll worry about that later," I said. "For the moment, let's turn the sound back up. If we're lucky, the police will solve the case and it'll be nothing more than a crazy human who's seen one too many Dracula films."

I sat down beside Evra and we spent the rest of night watching the news, rarely speaking, waiting for the vampire — the *killer*? — to return.

CHAPTER ELEVEN

SHADOWING MR Crepsley wasn't easy. The first night we lost him after a couple of minutes: he shot up a fire escape and by the time we got to the top he was nowhere to be seen. We wandered around the city for a few hours, hoping to chance upon him, but saw neither hide nor hair of him for the rest of the night.

We learned from that experience. While Mr Crepsley slept the next day, I went and bought a pair of mobile phones. Evra and me tested them out before dusk and they worked pretty well.

That night, when Mr Crepsley took to the rooftops, Evra stuck to the ground. He couldn't move as fast as me. By myself, I was able to keep track of the vampire and pass the information on to Evra, who followed on the ground.

Even alone, it was difficult to keep up. Mr Crepsley could move a lot quicker than me. Fortunately, he had no idea I was after him, so he didn't go as fast as he could, since he didn't think he'd any need to.

I kept him in sight for three hours that night, before losing him when he slipped down to street level and took a couple of turns that I missed. The next night I stuck with him until dawn. It varied after that: some nights I'd lose him within an hour; others I'd be on his tail till morning.

He didn't do much while I was following him. Sometimes he'd stop in one place for ages, above crowds of people, and observe them silently (picking out his next victim?). Other times he roamed without pause. His routes were unpredictable: he might go the same way two or three nights in a row, or try entirely new directions every night. It was impossible to second-guess him.

Evra was exhausted at the end of each night – I kept forgetting he wasn't as powerful as me – but he never complained. I said he could stay in a few nights if he wanted, but he shook his head and insisted on coming with me.

Maybe he thought I'd kill Mr Crepsley if he wasn't around.

Maybe he was *right*.

No fresh bodies had been discovered since news of the six in the building broke. It had been confirmed that all the bodies had been drained of their blood, and that they were ordinary humans: two men and four women. All were young – the oldest was twenty-seven – and from different parts of the city.

Evra's disappointment was evident when he heard the victims were normal people – it would have made life much easier if they'd been vampires.

"Would doctors be able to tell the difference between a human and a vampire?" he asked.

"Of course," I replied.

"How?"

"Different sort of blood," I said.

"But they were drained of blood," he reminded me.

"Their cells wouldn't be the same. Atoms act strangely in vampires – that's why they can't be photographed. And they'd have extra tough nails and teeth. The doctors would know, Evra."

I was trying to keep an open mind. Mr Crepsley hadn't killed anyone while we'd been following him, which was a hopeful sign. On the other hand, maybe he was waiting for the fuss to die down before striking again – at the moment, if somebody was late home from school or work, alarm bells rang immediately.

Or perhaps he *had* killed. Maybe he knew we were following him and was only killing when he was certain he'd lost us. That was unlikely, but I didn't rule it out completely. Mr Crepsley could be cunning when he wanted. I wouldn't have put anything past him.

Though I was sleeping through most of the days – in order to stay awake at night – I made a point of waking a couple of hours before sunset to spend some time with Debbie. Usually I went over to her house and we sat upstairs in her bedroom and played music and talked – I was always looking to conserve energy for the night chase ahead – but sometimes we'd go for a walk or hit the shops.

I was determined not to let Mr Crepsley ruin my friendship with Debbie. I loved being with her. She was my first girlfriend. I knew we'd have to part sooner rather than later – I hadn't forgotten what I was – but I wouldn't do anything to shorten our time together. I'd given up my nights to pursue Mr Crepsley. I wasn't going to give up my days too.

"How come you don't come round after dark any more?" she asked one Saturday as we emerged from a cinema matinée. I'd risen earlier than usual, in order to spend the day with her.

"I'm afraid of the dark," I whimpered.

"Seriously," she said, pinching my arm.

"My dad doesn't like me going out at night," I lied. "He feels a bit guilty, not being around during the day. He likes Evra and me to sit with him at night and tell him what we've been up to."

"Surely he wouldn't mind if you went out now and then," Debbie protested. "He let you out the night of our first date, didn't he?"

I shook my head. "I sneaked out," I said. "He went mad when he found out. Wouldn't talk to me for a week. That's why I haven't taken you round to meet him — he's still fuming."

"He sounds like a right old misery-guts," Debbie said.

"He is," I sighed. "But what can I do? He's my dad. I have to stick by him."

I felt bad lying to her, but I could hardly tell her the truth. I smiled to myself when I imagined breaking the news: "That guy I say is my father? He's not. He's a vampire. Oh, and I think he's the one who killed those six people."

"What are you smiling at?" Debbie asked.

"Nothing," I said quickly, wiping the smile from my face.

It was a strange double life — normal boy by day, deadly vampire-tracker by night — but I was enjoying it. If it had been a year or so earlier, I'd have been confused; I'd have tossed and turned in my sleep, worrying about what the next night would bring; my eating habits might have been affected and I'd have become depressed; I'd probably have chosen to focus on one thing at a time, and stopped meeting Debbie.

Not now. My experiences with Mr Crepsley and the Cirque Du Freak had changed me. I was able to handle two different roles. In fact, I liked the variation: tracking the vampire at night made me feel big and important — Darren

Shan, protector of the sleeping city! – and seeing Debbie in the afternoons let me feel like a normal human boy. I had the best of both worlds.

That stopped when Mr Crepsley zoomed in on the next victim – the fat man.

CHAPTER TWELVE

I DIDN'T realize at first that Mr Crepsley was following someone. He was hovering above a busy shopping street, where he'd been for the better part of an hour, studying the shoppers. Then, without warning, he climbed to the top of the building he'd been clinging to and started across the roof.

I rang Evra. He never rang me, for fear the vampire would hear my phone. "He's on the move again," I said quietly.

"About time," Evra grumbled. "I hate it when he stops. You don't know how cold it gets, standing still down here."

"Go get something to eat," I told him. "He's moving pretty slowly. I think you can take five or ten minutes off."

"Are you sure?" Evra asked.

"Yes," I said. "I'll ring you if anything happens."

"OK," Evra said. "I fancy a hot dog and a cup of coffee. You want me to pick something up for you?"

"No thanks," I said. "I'll keep in touch. See you soon." I hit the off switch and started after the vampire.

I didn't like eating stuff like hot dogs, burgers or French fries while tracking Mr Crepsley: his nose could easily detect such strong scents. I ate dry slices of bread – which produced almost no smell – to keep hunger at bay. I had ordinary tap water in a bottle to drink.

After several minutes I grew curious. The other nights, he'd either kept to one spot or wandered about without direction. He was moving with purpose this time.

I decided to get closer. It was dangerous, especially since he wasn't rushing – he was more likely to spot me – but I had to see what he was up to.

Closing the gap by a third – as near to him as I dared get – I saw that he was sticking his head out over the edge of the roof, keeping a watch on the street below.

Glancing down at the well-lit street, I couldn't spot who he was after. It was only when he paused above a lamp that I noticed the fat man at the base, adjusting his laces.

That was it! Mr Crepsley was after the fat man! I knew by the way the vampire stared, waiting for him to tie his laces and move on. When the fat man did eventually stand and start walking again, sure enough, Mr Crepsley followed.

Taking a few steps back, I rang Evra.

"What's up?" he asked. I could hear him munching on his hot dog. There were voices in the background.

"Action," I said simply.

"Oh hell!" Evra gasped. I heard him dropping the hot dog and shuffling away from the people behind him, to a quieter spot. "Are you sure?" he asked.

"Positive," I said. "Quarry has been sighted."

"OK," Evra sighed. He sounded nervous. I didn't blame him – I was nervous too. "OK," he said again. "Give me your position."

I read out the name of the street. "But don't rush," I told him. "They're moving slowly. Stay a couple of streets back. I don't want Mr Crepsley spotting you."

"*I* don't want him spotting me either!" Evra snorted. "Keep me up to date."

"Will do," I promised. Switching off, I started after the pursuing vampire.

He trailed the fat man to a large building, which the human disappeared into. Mr Crepsley waited half an hour, then slowly circled the building, checking on windows and doors. I trudged along behind, keeping my distance, ready to race after him if he entered.

He didn't. Instead, when he was through examining the place, he retired to a nearby rooftop, from where he had a perfect view of all the entrances, and sat down to wait.

I told Evra what was happening.

"He's just sitting there?" Evra asked.

"Sitting and watching," I confirmed.

"What sort of a place is it?"

I'd read the name on the walls while I was passing, and seen in a couple of the windows, but I could have told Evra what went on in the building simply by the foul smell of animal blood in the air.

"It's an abattoir," I whispered.

There was a long pause. Then: "Maybe he's just here for the animal blood," Evra suggested.

"No. He would have entered by now if that was the case. He didn't come for the animals. He came here for the human."

"We don't *know* that," Evra said. "Maybe he's waiting for it to close before going in."

"He'd have a long wait," I laughed. "It stays open all night."

"I'm coming up," Evra said. "Don't move until I get there."

"I'll move when Mr Crepsley moves, whether you're here or not," I said, but Evra had switched off and didn't hear me.

He arrived a few minutes later, his breath stinking of

mustard and onions. "Dry bread for you from now on," I muttered.

"Do you think Mr Crepsley will smell me?" Evra asked. "Maybe I should go back down and—"

I shook my head. "He's too close to the abattoir," I said. "The smell of blood will block everything else out."

"Where is he?" Evra asked. I pointed the vampire out. Evra had to squint, but eventually spotted him.

"We have to be extra quiet," I said. "Even a slight noise could have him swooping down on us."

Evra shivered — whether because of the cold, or the thought of being attacked, I don't know — and settled down. We said little to each other after that.

We had to breathe into our cupped fists to stop our breath from showing. We'd have been all right if it had been snowing — the snow would have hidden the smoke-like tendrils — but it was a clear and frosty night.

We sat there until three in the morning. Evra's teeth were chattering, and I was on the point of sending him home before he froze to death, when the fat man emerged. Mr Crepsley started after him immediately.

Too late, I realized the vampire was going to pass by us on his way back. There was no time to hide. He'd see us!

"Keep perfectly still," I whispered to Evra. "Don't even breathe."

The vampire came towards us, walking steadily across the icy roofs in his bare feet. I was certain he'd spot us, but his eyes were trained on the human. He passed within five metres of us — his shadow crept over me like some awful ghost — and then he was gone.

"I think my heart's stopped," Evra said shakily.

I heard the familiar thump-thump sounds of the snake-boy's heart (it beat slightly slower than a normal human's) and smiled. "You're OK," I told him.

"I thought we were done for," Evra hissed.

"Me too." I stood and checked which way the vampire was going. "You'd better slip back down to the street," I told Evra.

"He's not going fast," Evra said. "I can keep up."

I shook my head. "There's no telling when he'll speed up: the man might get in a cab or have a lift waiting. Besides, after our narrow escape, it's better we split: that way, if one of us gets caught, the other can sneak back to the hotel and pretend he wasn't involved."

Evra saw the sense in that and clambered down the nearest fire escape. I began dogging the tracks of the vampire and the fat man.

He walked back the way he'd come, past the deserted street where we'd first picked him up, on to a block of flats.

He lived in one of the central flats on the sixth floor. Mr Crepsley waited for the lights to go off inside, then went up in the lift. I ran up the stairs and watched from the far end of the landing.

I expected him to open the door and enter – locks were no problem for the vampire – but all he did was check the door and windows. Then he turned around and went back to the lift.

I hurried down the stairs and tagged the vampire as he strolled away from the flats. I told Evra what had happened and where the vampire was heading. A few minutes later he joined up with me and we followed Mr Crepsley as he jogged through the streets.

"Why didn't he go in?" Evra asked.

"I don't know," I said. "Maybe there was somebody else there. Or maybe he plans to come back later. One thing's for sure: he didn't go up there to post a letter!"

After a while, we rounded a corner into an alley and spotted Mr Crepsley bent over a motionless woman. Evra gasped and started forward. I caught his arm and yanked him back.

"*What are you doing?*" he hissed. "Didn't you see? He's attacking! We have to stop him before—"

"It's OK," I said. "He isn't attacking. He's feeding."

Evra's struggles ceased. "You're sure?" he asked suspiciously.

I nodded. "He's drinking from the woman's arm. The corpses in the building had their throats cut, remember?"

Evra nodded uncertainly. "If you're wrong..."

"I'm not," I assured him.

Minutes later, the vampire moved on, leaving the woman behind. We hurried down the alley to check. As I'd guessed, she was unconscious but alive, a small fresh scar on her left arm the only sign that she had been feasted upon.

"Let's go," I said, standing. "She'll wake in a few minutes. We'd better not be here when she does."

"What about Mr Crepsley?" Evra asked.

I looked up at the sky, gauging how long was left until dawn. "He won't kill anyone tonight," I said. "It's too late. He's probably heading back for the hotel. Come on – if we don't get back before him, we'll have a hell of a time trying to explain where we were."

CHAPTER THIRTEEN

BEFORE DUSK descended the next night, Evra went round to the block of flats to keep watch on the fat man. I stayed home, in order to follow Mr Crepsley. If the vampire headed for the flats, I'd join Evra. If he went elsewhere, we'd discuss the situation and decide whether Evra should desert his post or stay.

The vampire rose promptly as the sun went down. He was looking more cheerful tonight, though he still wouldn't have appeared out of place in a funeral parlour.

"Where is Evra?" he asked, tucking into the meal I'd prepared.

"Shopping," I said.

"By himself?" Mr Crepsley paused. For a moment I thought he was suspicious, but he was just looking for the salt.

"I think he's buying Christmas presents," I said.

"I thought Evra was above such absurdities. What is the date, anyway?"

"The twentieth of December," I answered.

"And Christmas is the twenty-fifth?"

"Yes," I said.

Mr Crepsley rubbed his scar thoughtfully. "My business here may have come to an end by then," he said.

"Oh?" I tried not to sound curious or excited.

"I had planned to move on as soon as possible, but if you wish to remain here for Christmas, we can. I understand the staff are hosting some kind of celebration?"

"Yes," I said.

"You would like to attend?"

"Yes." I forced a smile. "Evra and me are buying presents for each other. We're going to eat dinner with the rest of the guests and pull crackers and stuff ourselves with turkey. You can take part too, if you want." I tried to make it sound like I wanted him there.

He smiled and shook his head. "Such follies do not appeal to me," he said.

"Suit yourself," I replied.

As soon as he left, I started after him. He led me straight to the abattoir, which surprised me. Maybe it wasn't the fat man he was interested in: perhaps there was something – or somebody – else here that he had his eye on.

I discussed it with Evra over the phone.

"It's curious," he agreed. "Maybe he wants to catch him when he's entering or leaving work."

"Maybe," I said uncertainly. Something seemed odd about it. The vampire wasn't behaving as I'd expected him to.

Evra stayed where he was, to follow the fat man. I chose a safe spot to hide, next to a warm pipe that kept some of the cold out. My view of the abattoir wasn't as good as it had been last night, but I had a clear sight of Mr Crepsley, which was what mattered.

The fat man arrived at the scheduled time, Evra soon after him. I moved to the edge of the roof when I saw them, ready to leap down and intervene if Mr Crepsley made his move. But the vampire remained stationary.

And that was it for the night. Mr Crepsley sat on his ledge; Evra and me crouched on ours; the workers kept the abattoir ticking over. At three in the morning, the fat man re-appeared and went home. Once again Mr Crepsley followed and once again we followed Mr Crepsley. This time the vampire didn't go up to the landing, but that was the only variation in the routine.

The next night, the exact same thing happened.

"What's he up to?" Evra asked. The cold was getting to him and he was complaining about cramps in his legs. I'd told him he could leave but he was determined to stick it out.

"I don't know," I said. "Perhaps he's waiting for a special time to act. Maybe the moon has to be in a certain position or something."

"I thought werewolves were the only monsters affected by the moon," Evra said, half-jokingly.

"I thought so too," I said. "But I'm not sure. There's so much Mr Crepsley hasn't told me about being a full-vampire. You could fill a book with all the stuff I know nothing about."

"What are we going to do if he attacks?" Evra asked. "Do you think we stand a chance against him in a fight?"

"Not a fair fight," I said. "But in a dirty one..." I pulled out a long rusty butcher's knife, let Evra's eyes focus on it, then slipped it back beneath my shirt.

"Where did you get that?" Evra gasped.

"I came sniffing round the abattoir today, to familiarize myself with the layout, and found this knife lying in a bin out back. I guess it was too rusty to be of any use."

"That's what you're going to use?" Evra asked quietly.

I nodded. "I'll slit his throat," I whispered. "I'll wait for him to make his move, then..." I clenched my jaw shut.

"You reckon you can do it? He's really fast. If you miss your first chance, you're unlikely to get a second."

"He won't be expecting me," I said. "I can do it." I faced Evra. "I know we agreed to do this together, but I want to go after him by myself when the time comes."

"No way!" Evra hissed.

"I have to," I said. "You can't move as quietly or as quickly as me. If you come, you'll be in the way. Besides," I added, "if things go badly and I fail, you'll still be around to take another shot at him. Wait for day and get him while he's sleeping."

"Maybe that's the best solution," Evra said. "Maybe we should *both* wait. The main reason we're here is to confirm he's the killer. If he is, and we get proof, why don't we wait and—"

"No," I said softly. "I won't let him murder that man."

"You know nothing about him," Evra said. "Remember what I suggested: that the six dead people may have been killed because they were evil? Perhaps this guy's rotten."

"I don't care," I said stubbornly. "I only agreed to go along with Mr Crepsley because he convinced me he wasn't bad, that he didn't kill people. If he is a killer, I'm guilty too, for believing him and helping him all this time. I could do nothing to stop the first six murders – but if I can prevent number seven, I will."

"OK," Evra sighed. "Have it your own way."

"You won't interfere?"

"No," he promised.

"Even if I run into trouble and look like I need help?"

He hesitated before nodding. "All right. Not even then."

"You're a good friend, Evra," I said, clasping his hands.

"Think so?" He smiled bitterly. "Wait until you run foul of Mr Crepsley and end up trapped, screaming for help, only for me to ignore you. We'll see what sort of a friend you think I am then!"

CHAPTER FOURTEEN

ON THE night of the twenty-second of December, Mr Crepsley made his move.

Evra spotted him. I was taking a short break, resting my eyes — even a half-vampire's eyes get sore after hours of concentration — when Evra gave a sudden alarmed jump and grabbed my ankle.

"He's moving!"

I sprang forward, just in time to see the vampire leaping on to the roof of the abattoir. He wrestled open a window and quickly slipped inside.

"This is it!" I moaned, leaping to my feet and setting off.

"Wait a sec," Evra said. "I'm coming with you."

"No!" I snapped. "We discussed this. You promised—"

"I won't come all the way in," Evra said. "But I'm not going to sit over here, worrying myself mad. I'll wait for you inside the abattoir."

There was no time to argue. Nodding curtly, I ran. Evra hurried after me as fast as he could.

I paused at the open window and listened carefully for sounds of the vampire. There were none. Evra pulled up beside me, gasping from the exertion of the run. I climbed in and Evra followed.

We found ourselves in a long room filled with pipes. The floor was covered in dust, in which Mr Crepsley's footprints were clearly visible. We traced the prints to a door, which opened on to a tiled corridor. The dust that Mr Crepsley's feet had picked up crossing the room now marked his path across the tiles.

We followed the dusty trail along the corridor and down a flight of stairs. We were in a quiet part of the abattoir – the workers were grouped near the other end – but we moved cautiously nevertheless: it wouldn't do to be caught at this delicate stage of the game.

As the dust grew fainter by the step, I worried about losing the vampire. I didn't want to have to cast blindly about the abattoir for him, so I quickened my pace. Evra matched me.

As we turned a corner, I glimpsed a familiar red cloak and promptly stopped. I stepped back out of sight, dragging Evra with me.

I mouthed the words, "Say nothing," then cautiously peered around the corner, to see what Mr Crepsley was up to.

The vampire was tucked behind cardboard boxes which were stacked against one of the walls. I saw nobody else, but I could hear footsteps approaching.

The fat man appeared through a door. He was whistling and looking through some papers attached to a clipboard which he was carrying. He stopped at a large automated door and pressed a button in the wall. With a sharp, grinding noise, it opened.

The fat man hung the clipboard on a hook on the wall, then entered. I heard him press a button on the other side. The door stopped, creaked and came down at the same slow pace with which it had gone up.

Mr Crepsley darted forward as the door was closing and slid underneath.

"Go back up to the room with the pipes and hide," I told Evra. He began to complain. "Just do it!" I snapped. "He'd spot you here on his way back if you stayed. Go up and wait. I'll track you down if I succeed in stopping him. If not..." I found his hands and squeezed hard. "It's been nice knowing you, Evra Von."

"Be careful, Darren," Evra said, and I could see the fear in his eyes. Not fear for himself. Fear for *me*. "Good luck."

"I don't need luck," I said bravely and pulled out my knife. "I've got this." Giving his hands another squeeze, I fled down the corridor and threw myself under the closing door, which soon shut behind me, locking me in with the fat man and the vampire.

The room was full of animal carcasses, which hung on steel hooks from the ceiling. It was refrigerated, to keep the animals fresh.

The stench of blood was ghastly. I knew the bodies were only those of animals, but I kept imagining they were humans.

The lights overhead were incredibly bright, so I had to move very carefully: a stray shadow could mean the end of me. The floor was slippery — water? blood? — so I had to watch where I put my feet.

There was a strange rosy glow around the carcasses, a result of the bright light and blood. You wouldn't want to be a vegetarian in a place like this!

After a few seconds of seeing nothing but dead animals, I spotted Mr Crepsley and the fat man. I fell in behind the pair and kept pace with them.

The fat man stopped and checked one of the carcasses. He

must have been feeling cold, because he blew into his hands to warm them up, even though he was wearing gloves. He gave the dead animal a slap when he finished examining it – the hook creaked creepily as the carcass swung to and fro – and began to whistle the same tune he'd been whistling outside.

He started walking again.

I was closing the gap between myself and Mr Crepsley – I didn't want to get left too far behind – when all of a sudden the fat man stooped to examine something on the ground. I stopped and began to slip back, afraid he'd spot my feet, then noticed Mr Crepsley creeping up on the crouching human.

I cursed beneath my breath and raced forward. If Mr Crepsley had been paying attention, he would have heard me, but he was concentrating on the man ahead.

I stopped a few metres behind the vampire and drew out my rusty knife. That would have been the perfect time to attack – the vampire was standing still, focused on the human, unaware of my presence, an ideal target – but I couldn't. Mr Crepsley had to make the first move. I'd refuse to believe the worst about him until he actually attacked. As Evra had said, if I killed him, there could be no bringing him back to life. This was no time to make a mistake.

The seconds seemed like hours as the fat man crouched, studying whatever it was that had grabbed his attention. Finally he shrugged and got back on his feet. I heard Mr Crepsley hiss and saw his body tense. I raised my knife.

The fat man must have heard something, because he looked up – the wrong way; he should have been looking backwards – an instant before Mr Crepsley leapt.

I'd been anticipating the move, but even so, I was wrong-footed. If I'd lunged at the same time as the vampire, I would have been able to lash out with the knife and hit where I was aiming: his throat. As it was, I hesitated a split second, which meant I was off target.

I yelled as I bounded after him, screaming loudly, partly to shock him out of his attack, partly because I was so horrified by what I was doing.

The scream caused Mr Crepsley to whip around. His eyes widened incredulously. Since he wasn't looking ahead any longer, he crashed awkwardly into the fat man and the two went sprawling to the ground.

I fell on Mr Crepsley and struck with the knife. The blade cut into the top of the vampire's left arm and bit deeply into his flesh. He roared with pain and tried shoving me off. I pushed him down – he was in a difficult position, his extra weight and strength no use to him – and drew back my arm, meaning to bring the knife down with all my force in a long, lethal strike.

I never made the killer cut. Because, as my arm flew back, it connected with somebody. Somebody floating downwards. Somebody who'd jumped from above. Somebody who screeched as my arm struck him, and rolled away from me as fast as he could.

Forgetting the vampire for a moment, I looked over my shoulder at the rolling figure. I could tell it was a man, but that was all I could tell until he stopped moving and got to his feet.

When he stood and looked at me, I found myself wishing he'd kept on rolling right out of the room.

He was a fearsome sight. A tall man. Broad and bloated. Dressed in white from head to ankle, an immaculate white suit, spoiled only by smudges of dirt and blood he'd picked up while rolling.

In total contrast to his white suit was his skin, hair, eyes, lips and nails. The skin was a blotchy purple colour. The rest were a dark, vibrant red, as though they'd been soaked in blood.

I didn't know who or what this creature was, but I could tell immediately that he was an agent of evil. It was written all over him, the way he stood, the way he sneered, the way madness danced in his unnatural red eyes, the way his ruby-red lips pulled back over his sharp, snarling teeth.

I heard Mr Crepsley curse and clamber to his feet. Before he got up, the white-suited man bellowed and ran towards me at a speed no human could have managed. He lowered his head and butted me, almost rupturing the walls of my stomach, driving the wind out of me.

I flew backwards, into Mr Crepsley, unwillingly driving him back to the floor.

The creature in white shrieked, hesitated a moment, as though contemplating an attack, then grabbed hold of a carcass and dragged himself up. He leapt up high and grabbed hold of a windowsill – for the first time, I realized windows ran around the entire top of the room – smashed the glass and slithered out.

Mr Crepsley cursed again and shoved me out of the way. He mounted a carcass and jumped up to the windowsill after the purple-skinned man, wincing from the pain in his injured left arm. He hung there a moment, listening intently. Then his head dropped and his shoulders sagged.

The fat human – who'd been blubbering like a baby – got to his knees and began crawling away. Mr Crepsley noticed him and, after one last desperate look through the window, dropped to the ground and hurried over to the man, who was trying to rise.

I watched helplessly as Mr Crepsley pulled the human up and glared into his face: if he was set on killing the man, there was nothing I could do to stop him. My ribs felt as though they'd been battered by a ram. Breathing was painful. Moving was out of the question.

But Mr Crepsley didn't have murder on his mind. All he did was breathe gas into the fat man's face, who stiffened, then slumped to the floor, unconscious.

Then Mr Crepsley whirled and advanced on me, rage in his eyes, the like of which I'd never seen before. I began to worry about my own life. He picked me up and shook me like a doll. "You idiot!" he roared. "You interfering, mindless fool! Do you realize what you have done? Do you?"

"I was ... trying to ... stop..." I wheezed. "I thought..."

Mr Crepsley pressed his face against mine and growled: "He has escaped! Because of your damned meddling, an insane killer has waltzed off scot-free! This was my chance to stop him and you ... you..."

He couldn't say any more: rage had seized his tongue. Dumping me to the ground, he spun away and sank to his haunches, cursing and groaning — at times he seemed to be almost crying — with undisguised disgust.

I looked from the vampire to the sleeping human to the broken window, and realized (it hardly took a genius to figure it out) that I'd made a dreadful — perhaps fatal — mistake.

CHAPTER FIFTEEN

THERE WAS a long, edgy period of silence, minutes passing slowly. I felt around my ribs – none was broken. I stood and gritted my teeth as my insides flared with pain. I'd be tender for days to come.

Making my way over to Mr Crepsley, I cleared my throat. "Who *was* that?" I asked.

He glared at me and shook his head. "Idiot!" he growled. "What were you doing here?"

"Trying to stop you killing him," I said, pointing to the fat man. Mr Crepsley stared at me. "I heard about those six dead people on the news," I explained. "I thought you were the killer. I trailed—"

"You thought *I* was a murderer?" Mr Crepsley roared. I nodded glumly. "You are even dumber than I thought! Do you have so little faith in me that you—"

"What else was I to think?" I cried. "You never tell me anything. You disappeared into the city each night, not saying a thing about where you were going or what you were doing. What was I supposed to think when I heard six people had been found drained of their blood?"

Mr Crepsley looked startled, then thoughtful. Finally he nodded wearily. "You are right," he sighed. "One must show trust in order to be trusted. I wished to spare you the gory details. I should not have. This is my fault."

"That's OK," I said, taken aback by his gentle manner. "I guess I shouldn't have come after you like I did."

Mr Crepsley glanced at the knife. "You meant to kill me?" he asked.

"Yes," I said, embarrassed.

To my surprise, he chuckled dryly. "You are a reckless young man, Master Shan. But I knew that when I took you on as my assistant." He stood and examined the cut to his arm. "I suppose I should be grateful that I did not come out of this even worse."

"Will you be OK?" I asked.

"I will live," he said, rubbing spit into the cut, to heal it.

I looked up at the broken window. "Who *was* that?" I asked again.

"The question is not 'who'," Mr Crepsley said. "The question is 'what'. He is a *vampaneze*. His name is Murlough."

"What's a vampaneze?"

"It is a long story. We do not have time. Later, I will——"

"No," I said firmly. "I almost killed you tonight because I didn't know what was going on. Tell me about it *now*, so there can be no further mix-ups."

Mr Crepsley hesitated, then nodded. "Very well," he said. "I suppose here is as good a place as any. I do not think we will be disturbed. But we dare not delay. I must give this unwelcome turn of events much thought and begin planning anew. I will be brief. Try not to ask unnecessary questions."

"I'll try," I promised.

"The vampaneze are..." he searched for words. "In olden

nights, humans were looked down upon by many vampires, who fed on them as people feed on animals. It was not unusual for vampires to drink dry a couple of people a week. Over time, we decided this was not acceptable, so laws were established which forbade needless killing.

"Most vampires were content to obey the laws — it is easier for us to pass unnoticed amongst humans if we do not kill them — but some felt our cause had been betrayed. Certain vampires believed humans were put on this planet for us to feed upon."

"That's crazy!" I shouted. "Vampires start off as humans. What sort of—"

"Please," Mr Crepsley interrupted. "I am only trying to explain how these vampires thought. I am not condoning their actions.

"Seven hundred years ago, events came to a head. Seventy vampires broke away from the rest and declared themselves a separate race. They called themselves the vampaneze and established their own rules and governing bodies.

"Basically, the vampaneze believe it is wrong to feed from a human without killing. They believe there is nobility in draining a person and absorbing their spirit — as you absorbed part of Sam Grest's when you drank from him — and that there is shame in taking small amounts, feeding like a leech."

"So they always kill those they drink from?" I asked. Mr Crepsley nodded. "That's terrible!"

"I agree," the vampire said. "So did most of the vampires when the vampaneze broke away. There was a huge war. Many vampaneze were killed. Many vampires were too, but we were winning. We would have hunted them out of existence, except..." He smiled bitterly. "The humans we were trying to protect got in the way."

"What do you mean?" I asked.

"Many humans knew about vampires. But, as long as we did not kill them, they let us be – they were afraid of us. But when the vampaneze started slaughtering people, the humans panicked and fought back. Unfortunately they could not tell the difference between vampires and vampaneze, so both were tracked down and killed.

"We could have handled the vampaneze," Mr Crepsley said, "but not the humans. They were on the verge of wiping us out. In the end, our Princes met with the vampaneze and a truce was agreed. We would leave them alone if they stopped murdering so freely. They would only kill when they needed to feed, and would do all they could to keep their murders secret from humanity.

"The truce worked. When the humans realized they were safe, they stopped hunting us. The vampaneze travelled far away to avoid us – part of the agreement – and we have had virtually nothing to do with them for the last several centuries, apart from occasional clashes and challenges."

"*Challenges?*" I asked.

"Vampires and vampaneze live roughly," Mr Crepsley said. "We are forever testing ourselves in fights and competitions. Humans and animals are interesting opponents, but if a vampire really wants to test himself, he fights a vampaneze. It is common for vampires and vampaneze to seek each other out and fight to the death."

"That's stupid," I said.

Mr Crepsley shrugged. "It is our way. Time has changed the vampaneze," he went on. "You noticed the red hair and nails and eyes?"

"And lips," I added. "And he had purple skin."

"These changes have come about because they drink more

blood than vampires. Most vampaneze are not as colourful as Murlough – he has been drinking dangerously large amounts of blood – but they all have similar markings. Except for young vampaneze – it takes a couple of decades for the colours to set in."

I thought over what I'd been told. "So the vampaneze are evil? They're why vampires have such a bad reputation?"

Mr Crepsley rubbed his scar thoughtfully. "To say they are *evil* is not entirely true. To humans, they are, but to vampires they are more misdirected cousins than out-and-out ghouls."

"*What?*" I couldn't believe he was defending them.

"It depends on how one looks at it," he said. "You have learned to take no notice of drinking from humans, yes?"

"Yes," I said, "but—"

"Do you remember how against it you were in the beginning?"

"Yes," I said again, "but—"

"To many humans, *you* are evil," he said. "A young half-vampire who drinks human blood ... how long do you think it would be before somebody tried to kill you if your true identity was known?"

I chewed my lower lip and considered his words.

"Do not get me wrong," Mr Crepsley said. "I do not approve of the vampaneze and their ways. But nor do I think they are evil."

"You're saying it's OK to kill humans?" I asked warily.

"No," he disagreed. "I am saying I can see their point. Vampaneze kill because of their beliefs, not because they enjoy it. A human soldier who kills in war is not evil, is he?"

"This isn't the same thing," I said.

"But it falls along similarly murky lines. To humans, vampaneze are evil, plain and simple. But for vampires – and you belong to the vampire clan now — it is not so easy to judge. They are kin.

"Also," he added, "the vampaneze have their noble points. They are loyal and brave. And they never break their word — when a vampaneze makes a promise, he sticks by it. If a vampaneze lies, and his kinsmen find out, they will execute him, no questions asked. They have their faults, and I have no personal liking for them, but *evil?*" He sighed. "That is hard to say."

I frowned. "But you were going to kill this one," I reminded him.

Mr Crepsley nodded. "Murlough is not ordinary. Madness has invaded his mind. He has lost control and kills indiscriminately, feeding his lunatic lust. Were he a vampire, he would have been judged by the Generals and executed. The vampaneze, however, look more kindly upon their less fortunate members. They are loath to kill one of their own.

"If a vampaneze loses his mind, he is ejected from the ranks and set loose. If he keeps clear of his kind, they make no move to hinder or harm him. He is—"

A groan made us jump. Looking behind, we saw the fat man stirring.

"Come," Mr Crepsley said. "We will continue our discussion on the way to the roof."

We let ourselves out of the refrigerated room and started back.

"Murlough has been roaming the world for several years," Mr Crepsley said. "Normally, mad vampaneze do not last that long. They make silly mistakes and are soon caught and killed by humans. But Murlough is more cunning than most. He still has sense enough to kill quietly, and to hide the bodies. You know the myth about vampires not being able to enter a house unless they are invited inside?"

"Sure," I said. "I never believed it."

"Nor should you. But, like most myths, it has its roots in fact. The vampaneze almost never kill humans at home. They catch their prey outside, kill and feed, then hide the bodies, or disguise the wounds to make their death look accidental. Mad vampaneze normally forget these fundamental rules, but Murlough has remembered. That is how I knew he would not attack the man at home."

"How did you know he was going to attack him at all?" I asked.

"The vampaneze are traditionalists," Mr Crepsley explained. "They select their victims in advance. They sneak into their houses while the humans are sleeping and mark them – three small scratches on the left cheek. Did you notice such marks on the fat man?"

I shook my head. "I wasn't looking."

"They are there," Mr Crepsley assured me. "They are negligible – he probably thought he scratched himself while sleeping – but unmistakable once one knows what to look for: always in the same spot and always the same length.

"That is how I latched on to this man. Until that night I had been searching blindly, scouring the city, hoping to stumble across Murlough's trail. I spotted the fat man by chance and followed him. I knew the attack would come either here or on his way home from work, so it was just a matter of sitting back and waiting for Murlough to make his move." The vampire's face darkened. "Then *you* arrived on the scene." He was unable to keep the bitterness out of his voice.

"Will you be able to find Murlough again?" I asked.

He shook his head. "Discovering the marked human was

a stroke of incredible good fortune. It will not happen twice. Besides, though Murlough is mad, he is no fool. He will abandon any humans he has already marked and flee this city." Mr Crepsley sighed unhappily. "I suppose I will have to settle for that."

"*Settle* for it?" I asked. "Aren't you going to follow him?" Mr Crepsley shook his head. I stopped on the landing — we were almost at the door of the room with the pipes — and stared at him, aghast. "Why not?" I barked. "He's crazy! He's killing people! You've got to——"

"It is not my business," the vampire said gently. "It is not my place to worry about creatures such as Murlough."

"Then why get involved?" I cried, thinking of all the people the mad vampaneze was going to kill.

"The hands of the Vampire Generals are tied in matters such as these," Mr Crepsley said. "They dare not take steps to eliminate mad vampaneze, for fear of sparking an all-out war. As I said, vampaneze are loyal. They would seek revenge for the murder of one of their own. We can kill vampaneze in a fair fight, but if a General killed a mad vampaneze, his allies would feel compelled to strike back.

"I got involved because this is the city where I was born. I lived here as a human. Though everyone I knew then has long since died, I feel attached — this city, more than any place, is where I consider home.

"Gavner Purl knew this. When he realized Murlough was here, he set about tracking me down. He guessed — correctly — that I would not be able to sit back and let the mad vampaneze wreak havoc. It was a sly move on his part, but I do not blame him — in his position, I would have done the same."

"I don't get it," I said. "I thought the Vampire Generals wanted to avert a war."

"They do."

"But if you'd killed Murlough, wouldn't—"

"No," he interrupted. "I am not a General. I am a mere vampire, with no connection to any others. The vampaneze would have come after me if they learned I had killed him, but the Generals would not have been implicated. It would have been personal. It would not have led to war."

"I see. So, now that your city is safe, you don't care about him any more?"

"Yes," Mr Crepsley said simply.

I couldn't agree with the vampire's position — I'd have hunted Murlough down to the ends of the Earth — but I could understand it. He'd been protecting "his" people. Now that the threat against them had been removed, he no longer considered the vampaneze his problem. It was a typical piece of vampire logic.

"What happens now?" I asked. "We go back to the Cirque Du Freak and forget about this?"

"Yes," he said. "Murlough will avoid this city in future. He will slope away into the night and that will be that. We can return to our lives and get on with them."

"Until next time," I said.

"I have only one home," the vampire responded. "In all likelihood, there will be no next time. Come," he said. "If you have further questions, I will answer them later."

"OK." I paused. "What we said earlier — about no more holding important stuff back — is that still on? Will you trust me now and tell me things?"

The vampire smiled. "We will trust each other," he said.

I returned his smile and followed him, into the room with the pipes.

"How come I didn't spot Murlough's footsteps earlier?" I

asked, retracing the marks we'd made on our way into the building.

"He entered via a different route," Mr Crepsley said. "I did not want to get close to him until he made his move, in case he saw me."

I was on my way out of the window when I remembered Evra.

"Hold on!" I called Mr Crepsley back. "We've got to collect Evra."

"The snake-boy knew about this too?" Mr Crepsley laughed. "Hurry and get him. But do not expect me to tell the story again on his behalf. I will leave such details to you."

I cast around for my friend.

"Evra," I called quietly. When there was no response I shouted a little louder. "Evra!" Where was he hiding? I glanced down and found a lone pair of footprints in the dust, leading away under a mass of pipes.

"Evra!" I shouted again, starting after his trail. He'd probably seen me talking with the vampire and wasn't sure what was going on. "It's OK," I yelled. "Mr Crepsley isn't the killer. It's another—"

There was a sharp crunching noise as my foot came down on something and crushed it. Taking a step back, I bent and picked up the object for a closer examination. With a sinking feeling in my gut, I realized what it was – the broken remains of a mobile phone.

"Evra!" I screamed, dashing forward. I encountered signs of a scuffle further on – the dust in this area had been severely disturbed, as though somebody had been thrashing about in it. Thousands of dust motes were drifting in unsettled clouds through the air.

"What is it?" Mr Crepsley asked, approaching warily. I

showed him the crushed phone. "Evra's?" he guessed.

I nodded. "The vampaneze must have got him," I said, horrified.

Mr Crepsley sighed and hung his head. "Then Evra is dead," he said bluntly, and kept his gaze lowered as I started to cry.

CHAPTER SIXTEEN

MR CREPSLEY booked us out of the hotel as soon as we got back, in case the staff noticed Evra's disappearance, or the vampaneze forced him to reveal our location.

"What if he escapes?" I asked. "How will he know where to find us?"

"I do not believe he will escape," Mr Crepsley said regretfully.

We checked into a new hotel not far from the old one. If the man behind the desk was surprised to find a solemn-looking man with a scar and a distraught young boy in a pirate costume booking in at such a strange hour, he kept his suspicions to himself.

I begged Mr Crepsley to tell me more about the vampaneze. He said they never drank from vampires – our blood was poisonous to other vampires and vampaneze. They lived slightly longer than vampires, though the difference was minimal. They ate very little food, preferring to keep going on blood. They only drank from animals as a last resort.

I listened closely. It was easier not to think about Evra if I had something else to focus on. But, when dawn came and Mr Crepsley headed for bed, I was left alone to dwell on what had happened.

I watched the sun rise. I was tired but unable to sleep. How could I face the nightmares that were surely lying in wait? I fixed a large breakfast, but my appetite fled after one small mouthful and I ended up tossing it in the bin. I switched on the TV and flicked between channels, barely noticing what was on.

Every so often I'd think it must have been a dream. Evra couldn't be dead. I'd fallen asleep on the roof while watching Mr Crepsley and dreamt it all. Any minute now, Evra would shake me awake. I'd tell him about my dream and we'd both laugh. "You won't get rid of me that easily," he'd chuckle.

But it wasn't a dream. I *had* come face to face with the mad vampaneze. He *had* abducted Evra. He *had* either killed him or was preparing to. These were facts and had to be faced.

The trouble was, I didn't dare face them. I was afraid I might go mad if I did. So, rather than accept the truth and deal with it, I buried it deep, where it couldn't bother me — then went to see Debbie. Maybe she could cheer me up.

Debbie was playing in the Square when I arrived. It had snowed heavily during the night and she was building a snowman with some of the local kids. She was surprised but happy to see me so early. She introduced me to her friends, who regarded me curiously.

"Want to come for a walk?" I asked.

"Can it wait till I finish the snowman?" she replied.

"No," I said. "I'm restless. I need to walk. I can come back later if you want."

"That's all right. I'll come." She looked at me oddly. "Are you OK? Your face is white as a sheet, and your eyes ... have you been crying?"

"I was peeling onions earlier," I lied.

Debbie turned to her friends. "See you later," she said, and took my arm. "Anywhere special you want to go?"

"Not really," I said. "You lead. I'll tag along."

We didn't say much while we were walking, until Debbie tugged my arm and said, "I've got some good news. I asked Mum and Dad if you could come over on Christmas Eve to help put up the decorations and they said you could."

"Great," I said, forcing a smile.

"They've invited you for dinner too," she said. "They were going to ask you over for Christmas Day, but I know you've made plans to spend it in the hotel. Besides, I don't think your dad would want to come, would he?"

"No," I said softly.

"But Christmas Eve's OK, isn't it?" she asked. "Evra can come as well. We'll be eating early, about two or three in the afternoon, so there'll be plenty of time for decorating the trees. You can—"

"Evra won't be able to come," I said shortly.

"Why not?"

I found myself struggling to think up a suitable lie. Finally, I said, "He's got flu. He's in bed and can't move."

"He seemed fine yesterday," Debbie frowned. "I saw the two of you going out in the evening. He looked—"

"How did you see us?" I asked.

"Through the window," she said. "It's not the first time I've noticed you going out after dark. I never said anything about it before, because I thought you'd have told me what you were up to if you'd wanted me to know."

"It's not nice to spy on people," I snapped.

"I wasn't spying!" Debbie looked hurt by my accusation and tone. "I just happened to see you. And if that's going to be your attitude, you can forget Christmas Eve." She turned to leave.

"Wait," I said, catching her arm (careful not to grab too hard). "I'm sorry. I'm in a really bad mood. I don't feel so good. Maybe I've picked up something from Evra."

"You *do* look under the weather," she agreed, her face softening.

"As for where we go at night, it's just to meet our dad," I said. "We join him after work and go out for something to eat, or to see a movie. I'd have invited you along, but you know how things stand with my dad."

"You should introduce us," Debbie said. "I bet I'd be able to get him to like me, if I only had the chance."

We started walking again.

"So, how about Christmas Eve?" she asked.

I shook my head. Sitting down to dinner with Debbie and her parents was the last thing I wanted to think about. "I'll have to get back to you on that one," I said. "I'm not sure if we'll be here. We might be moving on."

"But Christmas Eve is tomorrow!" Debbie exclaimed. "Surely your dad's told you his plans by now."

"He's strange," I said. "He likes to leave things till the very last minute. I could arrive back after this walk and find him packed and ready to go."

"He can't leave if Evra's sick," she said.

"He can and will, if he wants," I told her.

Debbie frowned and stopped walking. There was a street grille a metre or so over, out of which warm air was blowing. She moved closer to it and stood on the bars. "You won't leave without telling me, will you?" she asked.

"Of course not," I said.

"I'd hate it if you disappeared into thin air without a word," she said, and I could see tears gathering in the corners of her eyes.

"I promise," I said. "When *I* know I'm leaving, *you'll* know too. Word of honour." I crossed my heart.

"Come here," she said, and pulled close and gave me a big hug.

"What was that for?" I asked.

"Does there have to be a reason?" she smiled, then pointed ahead. "Let's turn at the next corner. That'll lead us back to the Square."

I took Debbie's arm, meaning to walk her back, then remembered I'd changed hotels. If I returned to the Square, she'd expect me to enter the hotel. She might grow suspicious if she spotted me skulking away.

"I'll carry on walking," I said. "I'll ring tonight or in the morning to let you know whether I can come round tomorrow or not."

"If your Dad wants to leave, try twisting his arm to get him to stay," she suggested. "I'd really love to have you over."

"I'll try," I vowed, and watched through sad eyes as she strolled to the corner and turned out of sight.

It was then that I heard a soft chuckling noise beneath my feet. Glancing down through the bars of the grille, I saw nobody, and thought I must have been hearing things. But then a voice came up out of the shadows.

"I like your girlfriend, Darren Shan," it giggled, and I knew instantly who was down there. "A very tasty dish. Good enough to eat, wouldn't you say? Much tastier-looking than your other friend. Much tastier than Evra."

It was Murlough — the mad vampaneze!

CHAPTER SEVENTEEN

I DROPPED to my knees and peered through the bars of the grille. It was dark down there, but after a few seconds I was able to make out the rough figure of the fat vampaneze.

"What's your girlfriend's name, hmmm?" Murlough asked. "Anne? Beatrice? Catherine? Diane? Elsa? Franny? Geraldine? Henrietta? Eileen? Josie—" He stopped and I could sense him frowning. "No. Wait. Eileen begins with an 'E', not an 'I'. Are there any women's names beginning with 'I'? I can't think of any off-hand. How about you, Darren Shan? Any ideas, hmmm? Any notions?" He pronounced my first name oddly, so that it rhymed with Jarwren.

"How did you find me?" I gasped.

"That was easy." He leaned forward, carefully avoiding the rays of sunlight, and tapped the side of his head. "Used my brains," he said. "Young Murlough's got plenty of brains, yes he does. I played a tune on your friend – Snakey Von. He told me where the hotel was. I set up camp outside. Watched carefully. Saw you passing with your girlfriend, so I followed."

"What do you mean, 'Played a tune'?" I asked.

The vampaneze laughed out loud. "With my knife," he explained. "My knife and a few sets of scales. Get it? *Scales*. Scales on Snakey, scales on a piano. Ha! Brains, I told you, brains! A stupid man couldn't make jokes so cunning, jokes so shrewd. Young Murlough has brains the size of—"

"Where's Evra?" I interrupted, pounding the bars of the grille to shut him up. I gave them a yank, to see if I could get down to him, but they were set firm in the path.

"Evra? Evra Von?" Murlough did a strange little half-dance in the darkness beneath the grille. "Evra's strapped up," he told me. "Hanging by his ankles. Blood rushing to his head. Squealing like a piggie. Begging to be let free."

"Where is he?" I asked desperately. "Is he alive?"

"Tell me," he said, ignoring my questions, "where are you and the vampire staying? You've moved hotels, haven't you? That's why I didn't see you coming out. What were you doing in the Square anyway? No!" he shouted as I opened my mouth to speak. "Don't tell me, don't tell me! Give the brains a chance to work. Young Murlough's got plenty of brains. Brains oozing out his ears, some would say."

He paused, his little eyes darting to and fro, then clicked his fingers and hooted. "The girl! Darren Shan's little friend! She lives in the Square, hmmm? You wanted to see her. Which house is hers? Don't tell me, don't tell me! I'll figure it out. I'll track her down. Juicy-looking girl. Plenty of blood, hmmm? Lovely salty blood. I can taste her already."

"Stay away from her!" I screamed. "If you go near her, I'll—"

"Shut up!" the vampaneze barked. "Don't threaten me! I won't take lip from a runtish half-vampire like you. Any more like that and I'm off, and that'll be the end of Snakey."

I brought myself under control. "Does that mean he's

still alive?" I asked shakily.

Murlough grinned and tapped his nose. "Maybe he is, maybe he isn't. No way for you to know for sure, is there?"

"Mr Crepsley said vampaneze have to keep their word," I said. "If you give me your word that he's alive, then I'll know."

Murlough nodded slowly. "He's alive."

"You give me your word?"

"I give you my word," he said. "Snakey's alive. Trussed up and strung up. Squealing like a piggie. I'm keeping him for Christmas. He'll be my Christmas dinner. Snakey instead of turkey. Do you think that's foul of me, hmmm?" He laughed. "Get it? *Foul*. Not one of my subtler jokes, but it'll do. Snakey laughed. Snakey does everything I tell him to. You would too, in his position. Dangling by his ankles. Squealing like a piggie."

Murlough had an irritating way of repeating himself.

"Look," I said, "let Evra go. Please, he's done you no harm."

"He interfered with my schedule!" the vampaneze shrieked. "I was ready to feed. It was going to be glorious. I would have drained the fat man, then skinned him alive and stuck his corpse up with the rest in the cold room. Made cannibals of some poor unsuspecting humans. It would have been great sport, hmmm?"

"Evra didn't get in your way," I said. "That was me and Mr Crepsley. Evra was outside."

"*In*side, *out*side – he wasn't on *my* side. But he soon will be." Murlough licked his blood-red lips. "On my side and in my tummy. I never had snake-boy before. I'm looking forward to it. Maybe I'll stuff him before feeding. Make it more Christmassy."

"I'll kill you!" I screamed, tugging at the grille again, losing my self-control. "I'll track you down and tear you apart, limb from limb!"

"Oh my!" Murlough laughed, pretending to be scared. "Oh

heavens! Please don't hurt me, nasty little half-vampire. Young Murlough's a good chap. Say you'll leave me be."

"Where's Evra?" I roared. "Bring him up here now, or I'll—"

"All right," Murlough snapped, "that's enough! I didn't come here to be shouted at, no I didn't. There's plenty of other places I can go if I want people shouting at me, hmmm? Now shut up and listen."

It took a lot of effort, but I finally managed to calm down.

"Good," Murlough grunted. "That's better. You're not as stupid as most vampires. A bit of brains in Darren Shan, hmmm? Not as smart as me, of course, but who is? Young Murlough's got more brains than..."

"Enough." He dug his nails into the wall beneath the grille and climbed up a couple of metres. "Listen carefully." He sounded sane now. "I don't know how you found me – Snakey couldn't tell me, no matter how many scales I played – and I don't care. That's your secret. Keep it. We all need secrets, don't we, hmmm?

"And I don't care about the human," he went on. "He was just a meal. Plenty more where he came from. Plenty more blood in the fleshy human sea.

"I don't even care about *you*," he snorted. "Half-vampires don't interest me. You were only following your master. You don't worry me. I'm prepared to let you live. You and Snakey and the human.

"But the vampire – Larten Crepsley." The vampaneze's red eyes filled with hate. "*Him* I care about. He should have known better than to get in my way. Vampires and vampaneze don't mix!" he roared at the top of his voice. "Even the fools of the world know that! It's been agreed upon. We don't interfere with one another's ways. He broke the laws. He must be made to pay."

"He broke no law," I said defiantly. "You're mad. You were killing people all over the city. You had to be stopped."

"*Mad?*" I'd expected Murlough to react furiously to the insult, but he only chuckled. "Is that what he told you? *Mad?* Young Murlough isn't mad! I'm as sane a vampaneze as ever walked. Would I be here if I was mad? Would I have had sense enough to keep Snakey alive? Do you see me foaming at the mouth? Do you hear me gabbling like an idiot? Hmmm?"

I decided to humour him. "Maybe not," I said. "You seem pretty smart now that I think about it."

"Of course I'm smart! Young Murlough's got brains. Can't be mad if you've got brains, not unless you get rabies. See any rabid animals?"

"No," I said.

"There you are!" he declared triumphantly. "No crazy animals, so no crazy Murlough. You follow, hmmm?"

"I follow," I said quietly.

"Why did he interfere?" Murlough asked. He sounded confused and petulant. "I was doing nothing to him. I wouldn't have got in his way. What did he have to go and mess things up for?"

"This used to be his city," I explained. "He lived here when he was a human. He felt it was his duty to protect the people."

Murlough stared at me incredulously. "You mean he did it for *them?*" he screeched. "The *blood-carriers?*" He laughed crazily. "He must be a loony! I thought maybe he wanted them for himself. Or else I'd killed somebody close to him. I never for a second thought he did it because of ... of..."

Murlough started laughing. "That clinches it," he said. "I can't let a lunatic like that run around. No telling what he'll get up to next. Listen to me, Darren Shan. You look like a smart boy. Let's you and me do a deal. Sort this mess out, hmmm?"

"What sort of a deal?" I asked suspiciously.

"A swap," Murlough said. "I know where Snakey is. You know where the vampire is. One for the other. What do you say?"

"Give up Mr Crepsley for Evra?" I sneered. "What sort of a deal is that? Exchange one friend for another? You can't believe I'd—"

"Why not?" Murlough asked. "The snake-boy is innocent, hmmm? Your best friend, he told me. The vampire's the one who took you away from your family, from your home. Evra told me you hated him."

"That was a long time ago," I said.

"Even so," the vampaneze went on, "if you had to choose between the two, who would you pick? If their lives hung in the balance and you could only save one, who would it be?"

I didn't have to consider that very long. "Evra," I said evenly.

"There you are!" Murlough boomed.

"But Mr Crepsley's life *isn't* in danger," I said. "You want me to use him to get Evra off the hook." I shook my head sadly. "I won't do that. I won't betray him or lead him into a trap."

"You don't have to," Murlough said. "Just tell me where he is. The name of the hotel and his room number. I'll do the rest. I'll sneak in while he's sleeping, do the business, then take you to get Evra. I give you my word that I'll let both of you go. Think about it, hmmm? Weigh up the options. The vampire or Snakey. Your choice."

Again I shook my head. "No. There's nothing to think about. I'll swap places with Evra myself, if that—"

"I don't care about *you!*" Murlough screamed. "It's the vampire I want. What would I do with a stupid little half-vampire? Can't drink from you. Nothing to gain by killing you. It's Crepsley or no deal."

"Then it's no deal," I said, sobs rising in my throat as I considered what my words meant for Evra.

Murlough spat at me in disgust. His spit bounced back off the grille. "You're a fool," he snarled. "I thought you were smart, but you're not. So be it. I'll find the vampire myself. Your girlfriend, too. I'll kill them both. Then I'll kill you. Wait and see if I don't."

The vampaneze let go of the wall and dropped into the darkness. "Think of me, Darren Shan," he shouted as he slipped away down a tunnel. "Think of me when Christmas comes round, as you're biting into your turkey and ham. Do you know what *I'll* be biting into? Do you?" His laugh echoed eerily as he waltzed away down the tunnel.

"Yes," I said softly. I knew exactly what he'd be biting into.

Getting to my feet, I wiped the tears from my face, then set off to wake Mr Crepsley and tell him about my meeting with Murlough. After a couple of minutes, I climbed up a fire escape and travelled over the rooftops, just in case the vampaneze had stuck around in the hope of following me back.

CHAPTER EIGHTEEN

MR CREPSLEY wasn't surprised that Murlough had been watching the hotel – he'd half-expected it – but *was* stunned that I'd gone back to the Square.

"What were you thinking of?" he snapped.

"You didn't warn me to stay away," I replied.

"I did not think I needed to," he groaned. "What could have possessed you to return?"

I decided it was time to tell him about Debbie. He listened wordlessly as I explained.

"A girlfriend," he said at the end, shaking his head wonderingly. "Why did you think I would disapprove? There is no reason you should not befriend a girl. Even full-vampires sometimes fall in love with humans. It is complicated, and not to be recommended, but there is nothing wrong with it."

"You're not angry?" I asked.

"Why should I be? Matters of your heart are no concern of mine. You acted properly: you made no promises you could not keep, and you remained aware of the fact that it could only be temporary. All that worries me about your friendship with this girl is how it ties in with the vampaneze."

"You think Murlough will go after her?"

"I doubt it," he said. "I think he will stay clear of the Square. Now that we know he has been there, he will expect us to check on the area in future. However, you should be careful. Do not go to see her when it is dark. Enter by the back door. Keep away from the windows."

"It's OK for me to go on meeting her?" I asked.

"Yes," he smiled. "I know you consider me something of a killjoy, but I would never intentionally make you feel miserable."

I smiled back gratefully.

"And Evra?" I asked. "What will happen to him?"

Mr Crepsley's smile faded. "I am not sure." He thought about it for a couple of minutes. "You truly refused to swap my life for his?" He sounded as if he thought I might be making it up to impress him.

"Honestly," I said.

"But *why*?"

I shrugged. "We said we'd trust each other, remember?"

Mr Crepsley turned aside and coughed into his fist. When he faced me again, he looked ashamed of himself. "I have gravely underestimated you, Darren," he said. "I will not do so again. I made a wiser choice than I realized when I chose you to serve as my assistant. I feel honoured to have you by my side."

The compliment made me feel awkward – I wasn't used to the vampire saying nice things – so I grimaced and tried to make little of it.

"What about Evra?" I asked again.

"We shall do what we can to rescue him," Mr Crepsley said. "It is unfortunate that you refused to swap me for him: had we known Murlough would make the offer, we could have laid a trap. Now that you have shown loyalty towards me, he will not offer again. Our best chance to beat him has slipped away.

"But there is hope yet," he said. "Today is the twenty-third. We know that Evra will not be killed before the twenty-fifth."

"Unless Murlough changes his mind," I said.

"Unlikely. The vampaneze are not renowned for being indecisive. If he said he would not kill Evra until Christmas Day, that is when he will kill him. We have all tonight and tomorrow night to search for his lair."

"But he could be anywhere in the city!" I cried.

"I disagree," Mr Crepsley said. "He is not *in* the city – he is *under* it. Holed up in the tunnels. The drainpipes. The sewers. Hiding from the sun, free to move about as he wishes."

"You can't know that for sure," I said. "He might have only been down there today in order to follow me."

"If he was," Mr Crepsley said, "we are sunk. But if he *has* made his base down there, we stand a chance. Space is not so plentiful beneath the ground. Noises are easier to detect. It will not be easy, but there is hope. Last night, we did not even have that.

"If all else fails," he added, "and we end up empty-handed..." His face hardened. "I will call to our murderous cousin and offer him the deal which you yourself put to him earlier."

"You mean...?"

"Yes," he said darkly. "If we do not find Evra in time, I will trade *my* life for his."

There was more space beneath the ground than Mr Crepsley had predicted. It was an endless twisting maze down there. The pipes seemed to go every which way, as though thrown down at random. Some were big enough to stand in, others barely large enough to crawl through. Many were in use, half-full of streams of water and waste. Others were old and dried-up and cracked.

The stench was terrible. One thing was certain: we might happen to hear or glimpse Murlough or Evra, but we'd certainly never be able to sniff them out!

The place was awash with rats and spiders and insects. But I soon discovered that if you ignored them, they generally ignored you back.

"I do not understand why they need so many tunnels," Mr Crepsley said grimly, after several hours of fruitless searching. We seemed to have walked halfway across the city, but when he stuck his head above ground to check our position, he found we'd come less than three-quarters of a kilometre.

"I guess different tunnels were made at different times," I said. My dad used to work for a building firm and had explained a bit about underground systems to me. "They wear out in places, eventually, and it's usually easier to dig new shafts than go back and patch up the old ones."

"What a waste," Mr Crepsley grumbled, disdainfully. "You could fit a small town into the space these damned pipes are taking up." He looked around. "There seem to be more holes than concrete," he said. "I am surprised the city has not fallen in upon itself."

After a while, Mr Crepsley stopped and cursed.

"Do you want to stop?" I asked.

"No," he sighed. "We shall continue. It is better to search than sit back and wait. At least this way we are exerting some sort of control over our destiny."

We used torches in the tunnels. We needed some sort of light: even vampires can't see in total darkness. The beams increased the chances of Murlough's spotting us before we spotted him, but that was a risk we had to take.

"There's no way of hunting him down telepathically, is there?" I asked as we paused for a break. All this crawling and stooping was exhausting. "Couldn't you search for his thoughts?"

The vampire shook his head. "I have no connection with Murlough," he said. "Tuning into a person's mental signals requires radar-like emissions on both sides." He held up his two index fingers about half a metre apart. "Say this is me." He wiggled his right finger. "This is Mr Tall." He wiggled the left. "Many years ago, we learnt to recognize each other's mental waves. Now, if I want to find Mr Tall, I emit a radar-like series of waves." He bent his right finger up and down. "When these signals connect with Hibernius, part of his mind automatically signals back, even if his conscious mind remains unaware of it."

"You mean you could find him even if he didn't want to be found?"

Mr Crepsley nodded. "That is why most people refuse to share their wave identity. You should only reveal it to one you truly trust. Less than ten people on Earth can find me that way, or I them." He smiled thinly. "Needless to say, none of those ten is a vampaneze."

I wasn't sure I understood entirely about mental waves, but I'd gathered enough to know Mr Crepsley couldn't use it to find Evra.

One more hope struck from the list.

But the conversation had set me thinking. I was sure there must be some way of bettering the odds. Mr Crepsley's plan – to roam the tunnels and pray we fell upon the vampaneze – was weak. Was there nothing else we could do? No way to prepare a trap and lure Murlough into it?

I focused my immediate thoughts on the search – if we stumbled upon the mad vampaneze, I didn't want to be caught with my head in the clouds – but devoted the rest to serious thinking.

Something the vampaneze had said was niggling away at the back of my brain, but I couldn't put my finger on it. I went back over everything he'd said. We'd talked about Evra and Mr Crepsley and Debbie and doing a deal and...

Debbie.

He'd teased me about her, said he was going to kill and drink from her. At the time I'd dismissed it as an idle threat, but the more I thought about it, the more I began to wonder how much he really was interested in her.

He would be hungry, down here in the depths. He was used to feeding regularly. We'd ruined his schedule. He'd said he was looking forward to drinking Evra's blood, but *was* he? Vampires couldn't drink from snakes and I was willing to bet vampaneze couldn't either. Maybe Evra's blood would prove undrinkable. Perhaps Murlough would only be able to kill the snake-boy on Christmas Day, not drink from him as planned. He'd commented a couple of times on how tasty Debbie looked. Was that a clue that Evra *didn't* look tasty?

As the time ticked by, thoughts turned over in my head. I said nothing when Mr Crepsley told me we should return to the surface (he had a natural in-built clock), in case Murlough was shadowing us and listening to our every word. I kept quiet as we climbed out of the tunnel and trudged through the streets, then took to the roofs again. I held my tongue as we sneaked through our hotel window and sank into chairs, tired, miserable and gloomy.

But then, hesitantly, I coughed to attract the vampire's attention. "I think I have a plan," I said, and slowly spelt it out for him.

CHAPTER NINETEEN

JESSE ANSWERED the phone when I rang Debbie's house. I asked if I could speak to her.* "You could if she was up," he laughed. "Do you know what time it is?"

I checked my watch: a few minutes before seven a.m. "Oh," I said, crestfallen. "Sorry. I didn't realize. Did I wake you?"

"No," he said. "I have to pop into the office, so it's business as usual for me. You just caught me, in fact – I was on my way out the door when the phone rang."

"You're working on Christmas Eve?"

"No rest for the wicked," he laughed. "But I'll only be there a couple of hours. Tying up some loose ends before the Christmas break. I'll be back in plenty of time for dinner. Speaking of which, are we to expect you or not?"

"Yes please," I said. "That's why I was ringing, to say I could come."

"Great!" He sounded genuinely pleased. "How about Evra?"

"Can't make it," I said. "He's still not well."

"Too bad. Listen, do you want me to wake Debbie? I can—"

"That's OK," I said quickly. "Just let her know I'll be there. Two o'clock?"

"Two's fine," Jesse said. "See you later, Darren."

"Bye, Jesse."

I hung up and went straight to bed. My head was still buzzing from all the talking me and Mr Crepsley had been doing, but I forced my eyes shut and concentrated on sweet thoughts. Moments later, my tired body drifted off to sleep and I slept soundly until one in the afternoon, when the alarm clock went off.

My ribs were aching as I got up and my belly was purple and blue with bruises, where Murlough had head-butted me. It wasn't too bad after a few minutes of walking about, but I was careful not to make any sudden movements, and bent down as little as possible.

I had a good shower, and sprayed deodorant all over myself when I was dry – the smell of the sewers was hard to get rid of. I dressed, and picked up a bottle of wine Mr Crepsley had bought for me to take to Debbie's.

I knocked on Debbie's back door as Mr Crepsley had advised. Donna opened it. "Darren!" she said, kissing me on both cheeks. "Merry Christmas!"

"Merry Christmas," I replied in return.

"Why didn't you use the front door?" she asked.

"I didn't want to dirty your carpets," I said, scraping my shoes on the mat inside the door. "My shoes are wet from the dirty slush."

"Silly," she smiled. "As if anyone cares about carpets at Christmas. Debbie!" she called upstairs. "There's a handsome pirate here to see you."

"Hi," Debbie said, coming down the stairs. She kissed me on both cheeks as well. "Dad told me you rang. What's in the bag?"

I produced the bottle of wine. "For dinner," I said. "My dad gave it to me to bring over."

"Oh, Darren, that's kind," said Donna. She took the wine and called to Jesse, "Look what Darren brought."

"Ah! Vino!" Jesse's eyes lit up. "Better than the wine we'd got in. We invited the right man over. We should have him round more often. Where's the corkscrew?"

"Wait a while," Donna laughed. "Dinner isn't ready yet. I'll stick it in the fridge. You lot head for the living room. I'll yell when it's time."

We pulled some crackers while we were waiting, and Debbie asked me if my dad had decided about moving on yet. I said he had, and that we were leaving tonight.

"*Tonight?*" She looked dismayed. "Nobody travels anywhere except home on Christmas Eve. I've a good mind to go over to that hotel, drag him out and—"

"That's where we're going," I interrupted. "Home. Mum and Dad are getting together again, just for Christmas Day, to give Evra and me a treat. It's supposed to be a surprise, but I heard him on the phone this morning. That's why I rang so early – I was excited."

"Oh." I could tell Debbie was upset by the news, but she put on a brave face. "That's wonderful. I bet it's the best present you could have hoped for. Maybe they'll patch things up and get back together for good."

"Maybe," I said.

"So this is your last afternoon together," Jesse remarked. "Fate has driven the young romantics apart."

"*Da-a-a-ad!*" Debbie moaned, punching him. "Don't say things like that! It's embarrassing!"

"That's what fathers are for," Jesse grinned. "It's our job to embarrass our daughters in front of boyfriends."

Debbie scowled at him, but I could see she was enjoying the attention.

The meal was magnificent. Donna had put all her years of expertise to great use. The turkey and ham practically melted in my mouth. The roast potatoes were crisp and the veg was sweet as candyfloss. Everything looked wonderful and tasted even better.

Jesse told a few jokes which had us all in stitches, and Donna did her party trick: balancing a roll on her nose. Debbie took a mouthful of water and gargled her way through *Silent Night*. Then it was my turn to do a bit of entertaining.

"This meal is so good," I sighed, "I could even eat the cutlery." While everybody laughed, I picked up a spoon, bit off the head, chewed it into tiny pieces, and swallowed.

Three pairs of eyes practically popped out of their sockets.

"How did you do that?" Debbie squealed.

"You pick up more than dust when you're on the road," I said, winking at her.

"It was a fake spoon!" Jesse roared. "He's having us on."

"Hand me yours," I told him. He hesitated, tested his spoon to make sure it was real, then passed it over. It didn't take long to gulp it down, my tough vampire teeth making short work of it.

"That's incredible!" Jesse gasped, clapping wildly. "Let's try him with a ladle."

"Hold it!" Donna yelled as Jesse reached across the table. "These are part of a set and hard to replace. You'll be letting him loose on my grandmother's good china next."

"Why not?" Jesse said. "I never did like those old plates."

"Watch it," Donna warned, tweaking his nose, "or I'll make *you* eat the plates."

Debbie was smiling, and leant over to squeeze my hand.

"I feel thirsty after those spoons," I joked, getting to my feet. "I think it's time for my wine now."

"Hear, hear!" Jesse cheered.

"I can get it," Donna said, rising.

"Not at all," I said, gently pushing her back down. "You've been serving all afternoon. It's time someone waited on you for a change."

"Hear that?" Donna beamed at the other two. "I think I'll exchange Debbie for Darren. He'd be much more useful to have around."

"That's it!" Debbie snorted. "No presents for *you* tomorrow!"

I was smiling to myself as I fetched the wine from the fridge and peeled back the tin-foil from the top. The corkscrew was in the sink. I rinsed it, then opened the bottle. I sniffed – I didn't know much about wine, but it certainly smelt nice – and found four clean glasses. I rooted through my pockets for a couple of seconds, then fiddled with three of the glasses. Next I poured the wine and returned to the table.

"Hurrah!" Jesse shouted when he saw me coming.

"What took you so long?" Debbie asked. "We were about to send a search party to look for you."

"Took me a while to get the cork out," I said. "I'm not used to it."

"You should have just bitten the top off," Jesse joked.

"I didn't think of that," I said seriously. "I'll do it next time. Thanks for the advice."

Jesse stared at me uncertainly. "Nearly had me going!" he laughed suddenly, shaking a finger, "Nearly had me going!"

His brief bit of repetition reminded me momentarily of Murlough, but I swiftly put all thoughts of the vampaneze from my mind and raised my glass.

"A toast," I declared. "To the Hemlocks. Their name might be poison, but their hospitality is first class. Cheers!" I'd rehearsed the toast earlier, and it went down as well as I'd hoped. They groaned, then laughed and raised their glasses, clinking them against mine.

"Cheers," Debbie said.

"Cheers," Donna added.

"Bottoms up!" Jesse chuckled.

And we drank.

CHAPTER TWENTY

Late Christmas Eve. Down in the tunnels.

WE'D BEEN searching for a couple of hours, but it felt longer. We were sweating and covered with dirt, our feet and trousers soaked through with filthy water. We were moving as fast as we could, making a lot of noise in the process. My ribs hurt me to begin with, but I was over the worst of it now and barely noticed the stabbing pain as I bent and stooped and twisted.

"Slow down!" Mr Crepsley hissed several times. "He will hear us if you keep this up. We must be more careful."

"To hell with being careful!" I yelled back. "This is our last chance to find him. We've got to cover as much ground as possible. I don't care how much noise we make."

"But if Murlough hears us—" Mr Crepsley began.

"—We'll chop off his head and stuff it with garlic!" I snarled, and moved ahead even faster, making still more noise.

Soon we reached a particularly large tunnel. The water level was higher in most of the tunnels than it had been last night, because of the melting snow on the ground, but this one was dry. Perhaps it was an emergency pipe, in case the others overflowed.

"We will rest here," Mr Crepsley said, collapsing. The search was harder for him than for me, since he was taller and had to bend more.

"We don't have time for a rest," I snapped. "Do you think Murlough is resting?"

"Darren, you must calm down," Mr Crepsley said. "I understand your agitation, but we cannot help Evra by panicking. You are tired, as am I. A few minutes will make no difference, one way or the other."

"You don't care, do you?" I sulked. "Evra's down here somewhere, being tormented or cooked, and all you're worried about are your tired old legs."

"They *are* old," Mr Crepsley growled, "and they *are* tired, and so, I am sure, are yours. Sit down and stop acting like a child. If we are destined to find Evra, we shall. If not..."

I snarled hatefully at the vampire and stepped in front of him. "Give me that torch," I said, trying to prise it from his hands. I'd dropped mine earlier and broken it. "I'll go on ahead by myself. You sit here and *rest*. I'll find Evra on my own."

"Stop it," Mr Crepsley said, pushing me away. "You are behaving intolerably. Calm down and—"

I gave a ferocious tug and the torch flew out of Mr Crepsley's hands. It also spun out of mine, and shattered to pieces against the tunnel wall. We were thrust into complete darkness.

"You idiot!" Mr Crepsley roared. "Now we will have to go back up and find a replacement. You have cost us time. I told you something like this would happen."

"Shut up!" I shouted, shoving the vampire in the chest. He fell down hard and I backed away blindly.

"Darren!" Mr Crepsley shouted. "What are you doing?"

"Going to find Evra," I said.

"You cannot! Not by yourself! Come back and help me up: I have twisted my ankle. We will return with stronger torches and work faster. You cannot search without a light."

"I can hear," I replied. "And I can feel. And I can shout. Evra!" I yelled, to prove my point. "Evra! Where are you? It's me!"

"Stop! Murlough will hear. Come back and keep quiet!"

I heard the vampire scrabbling to his feet. Taking a deep breath, I ran. I fled far into the tunnel, then slowed and found a small pipe leading out of the large one. I slipped into it and crawled. Mr Crepsley's shouts grew dimmer and dimmer. Then I came to another pipe, and scurried down it. Then another. And another. Within five minutes I'd lost the vampire.

I was alone. In the dark. Underground.

I shivered, then reminded myself why I was there and what was at stake. I scouted about for a larger tunnel, feeling my way with my fingers.

"Evra," I called softly. I cleared my throat and this time yelled. "Evra! It's me! Darren! Can you hear? I'm coming to find you. Yell if you can hear me. Evra. Evra? Evra!"

Shouting and calling, I advanced, hands outstretched, ears straining for any sound, eyes useless – a perfect target for all the demons of the dark.

I'm not sure how long I was down there. There was no way of telling time in the tunnels. I had no sense of direction either. I might have been going in circles. I just moved forward, calling Evra's name, scraping my hands on the walls, feeling my feet and lower legs turn numb from the damp and cold.

Sometimes a draught of air tickled my nostrils, a reminder

of the world above. I moved fast whenever I felt the air, afraid of losing my nerve if I stopped to breathe it in.

I was moving downwards, getting deeper into the system of pipes and tunnels. I wondered how many people had been down here over the years. Not many. In some of the older pipes, I might be the first human (*half*-human) to pass in decades. If I'd had time, I would have stopped to scrawl my initials on the walls.

"Evra! Can you hear me? Evra!" I repeated.

There'd been no response so far. I wasn't really expecting one. If I did chance upon Murlough's lair, it was a pretty sure thing he would have taped over Evra's mouth. The vampaneze wasn't the sort to overlook a minor detail like that.

"*Evra!*" I croaked, my voice beginning to crack from the strain. "Are you there? Can you—"

All of a sudden, with no warning, a hand jammed hard into my back and sent me crashing to the floor. I gave a yell of pain and rolled over, gazing blindly into the pitch-black depths.

"Who's there?" I asked shakily. A dry chuckle answered me. "Who is that?" I gasped. "Mr Crepsley? Is that you? Did you follow me down? Is it—"

"No," Murlough whispered in my ear. "It's not." He flicked on a torch, directly in front of my eyes.

The light was blinding. I gasped and shut my eyes, thoughts of defending myself forgotten. It was what the vampaneze had been waiting for. Before I could react, he ducked forward, opened his mouth and breathed on me ... the breath of the undead ... the gas which knocks people out.

I tried drawing back, but it was too late. The gas was in me. It raced up my nostrils and down my throat, flooding my lungs, forcing me to double over, coughing fitfully.

The last thing I remember was falling forwards, Murlough's bare purple feet growing larger as I dropped towards them.

And then ... nothing. Just black.

CHAPTER TWENTY-ONE

WHEN I came to, I found myself face to face with a skull. Not any old skull, either — this still had flesh on it, and one of the eyeballs was floating in its socket.

I screamed and tried pulling away, but couldn't. Looking up (*up?* Why wasn't I looking *down?*) at my body, I realized I was bound tightly with ropes. After a few seconds of puzzled panic, I noticed another rope around my ankles, and it dawned on me that I was hanging upside down.

"I bet the world looks different from there, hmmm?" Murlough said. Twisting around — I couldn't move my limbs, but I could swing about — I saw him sitting a little way from the skull, chewing on a fingernail. He stuck out a foot and began rocking the skull. "Say hello to Evra," he chuckled.

"*No!*" I screamed, swinging forward, baring my teeth, trying to bite deep into his leg. Unfortunately, the rope wouldn't stretch that far. "You promised you wouldn't kill him before Christmas!" I cried.

"You mean it *isn't* Christmas?" Murlough asked innocently. "Whoops! Sorry. Bit of a boo-boo, hmmm?"

"I'll kill you," I swore. "I'm going to—"

A groan stopped me short. Turning, I noticed I wasn't alone. Somebody else was strung upside down, a couple of metres away.

"Who's that?" I asked, certain it was Mr Crepsley. "Who's there?"

"D-D-D-Darren?" a tiny voice said.

"*Evra?*" I gasped with disbelief.

Murlough laughed and flicked on a strong torch. It took my eyes a few seconds to adjust to the light. When they did, I was able to make out the familiar shape and features of the snake-boy. He looked hungry, exhausted and scared – but he was alive.

Evra was alive!

"Fooled you, didn't I?" Murlough giggled, shuffling closer.

"What are you doing here, Darren?" Evra moaned. His face was badly cut and bruised, and I could see a pinkish patch on his right arm and shoulder where scales had been brutally hacked off. "How did he—"

"That's enough out of you, reptile!" Murlough growled, kicking out at Evra, sending him snapping back on his rope.

"Stop that!" I roared.

"Make me," Murlough laughed. "Be quiet," he warned Evra. "If you speak again without permission, they'll be your last words. Understand?" Evra nodded feebly. All the fight had been hammered out of him. He was a pitiful sight. But at least he was alive. That was the main thing.

I began to take in my surroundings. We were in a large cavern. It was too dark to tell if it was natural or man-made. Evra and me were hanging from a steel bar. Skeletons littered the floor. I could hear water dripping somewhere, and spotted a rough bed in one corner.

"Why have you brought me here?" I asked.

"Snakey was lonely," Murlough answered. "I thought you'd be good company for him, hmmm?"

"How did you find me?"

"Wasn't hard," Murlough said. "Wasn't hard. Heard you and the vampire coming from miles away. Followed you. Murlough knows these pipes like the back of his teeth, yes he does. Young Murlough's smart. Been down here long enough. Wasn't just twiddling my thumbs."

"Why didn't you attack?" I asked. "I thought you wanted to kill Mr Crepsley."

"I *will*," Murlough said. "Biding my time. Waiting for the right moment. Then you stormed off and made things easy. Young Murlough couldn't pass up a gift. I'll get the vampire later. You'll do for now. You and Snakey."

"Mr Crepsley was alone," I baited him. "He had no torch. He was in the dark. But you decided to come after *me*. You're a coward. You were too scared to attack someone your own size. You're no better than—"

Murlough's fist connected with my jaw and I saw stars.

"Say that again," he hissed, "and I'll slice off an ear."

I stared at the vampaneze with loathing, but held my tongue.

"Murlough's afraid of nothing!" he told me. "Especially not a weak old vampire like Crepsley. What sort of a vampire is it that consorts with children, hmmm? He isn't worth bothering with. I'll pick him off later. You have more guts. You're more hot-blooded." Murlough bent and tweaked my cheeks. "I like hot blood," he said softly.

"You can't drink from me," I said. "I'm a half-vampire. I'm off limits."

"Perhaps I'm finished with limits. I'm a free agent. I answer to no one. The laws of the vampaneze don't trouble me down here. I'll do what I like."

"It's poison," I gasped. "Vampire blood is poison to vampaneze."

"Is it?"

"Yes. So's snake blood. You can't drink from either of us."

Murlough pulled a face. "You're right about the snake blood," he grumbled. "I took a bit from him — just testing, you understand, just testing — and threw up for hours after."

"I told you!" I said triumphantly. "We're no good to you. Our blood's worthless. It can't be drunk."

"You're right," Murlough murmured, "but it can be *shed*. I can kill and eat the two of you, even if I can't drink from you." He began pushing us, so that we were soon swinging about wildly. I felt sick.

Then Murlough went to fetch something. When he returned, he was carrying two huge knives. Evra began whimpering quietly when he saw the blades.

"Ah! Snakey remembers what these are for," Murlough laughed evilly. He sliced the knives together, producing a sharp, grating sound that made me shiver. "We had some fun with these, didn't we, reptile?"

"I'm sorry, Darren," Evra sobbed. "He made me tell him where you were. I couldn't help it. He cut my scales off and ... and..."

"It's all right," I said calmly. "It's not your fault. I would have talked too. Besides, that wasn't how he caught me. We left the hotel before he found it."

"You must have left your brains behind, too," Murlough said. "Did you really think you could waltz down here into my lair, rescue the snake-boy and trot along like a merry little lamb? Did it never occur to you that I am master of this domain, and would do all in my power to stop you?"

"It occurred to me," I said softly.

"But you came anyway?"

"Evra's my friend," I said simply. "I'd do anything to help him."

Murlough shook his head and snorted. "That's the human in you. If you were a full-vampire, you'd have known better. I'm surprised Crepsley came so far with you before bottling out."

"He didn't bottle out!" I shouted.

"Yes he did, yes he did," Murlough laughed. "I followed him to the top. That's why I didn't come after you sooner, hmmm? He ran as if the sun itself was at his back."

"You're lying," I said. "He wouldn't run. He wouldn't leave me."

"No?" The vampaneze grinned. "You don't know him as well as you think, boy. He's gone. He's out of the game. He's probably halfway back to wherever it was he came from by now, fleeing with his tail between his legs."

Murlough leapt forward without warning and swung the two knives at my face, one from either side. I screamed and shut my eyes, expecting him to draw blood. But he stopped just millimetres short of my flesh, tapped my ears with them, then drew back.

"Just testing," he said. "Wanted to see how much moral fibre you have. Not much, hmmm? Not much. Snakey didn't scream until the fourth or fifth lunge. You're going to be less fun than I thought. Maybe I won't bother torturing you. Perhaps I'll kill you outright. Would you like that, half-vampire? It would be for the best: no pain, no suffering, no nightmares. Snakey has nightmares. Tell him about your nightmares, reptile. Tell him how you jerk awake, screaming and sobbing like a baby."

Evra pulled his lips in tight and said nothing.

"Oh-ho!" Murlough smirked. "Getting brave again in front of your friend, are you? Rediscovering your courage, hmmm? Well, don't worry — we won't be long knocking it out of you."

He scraped the knives together again and circled around behind us, where we couldn't see him. "Which one shall I start with?" he mused, hopping about behind us. "I think ... I'll choose..." He went very quiet. I could feel the hairs on the back of my neck standing upright.

"*You!*" he suddenly roared, and threw himself on ... *me*.

CHAPTER TWENTY-TWO

MURLOUGH PULLED my head back. I felt the blade of a knife poking into the soft flesh of my throat. I stiffened in anticipation of the cut. I wanted to scream, but the blade stopped me. "This is it," I thought. "This is the end. What a lousy, useless way to die."

But the vampaneze was only teasing me. He slowly removed the knife and laughed nastily. He had all the time in the world. There was no reason for him to rush. He wanted to play with us a while.

"You shouldn't have come," Evra muttered. "It was stupid." He paused. "But thanks anyway," he added.

"Would *you* have left *me*?" I asked.

"Yes," he said, but I knew he was lying.

"Don't worry," I told him. "We'll figure a way out of this yet."

"*A way out?*" Murlough boomed. "Don't talk rubbish. How are you going to escape? Chew through the ropes? You could if you could reach them with your teeth, but you can't. Snap them with your super vampire strength? No good. They're too strong. I tested them myself in advance, hmmm?

"Face it, Darren Shan – you're doomed! Nobody's going to ride to the rescue. Nobody can find you down here. I'm going to take my time, cut you up into iddy-biddy pieces, drop you all over the city – like confetti – and there isn't a thing you can do about it, so *wise up!*"

"At least let Evra go," I begged. "You've got me. You don't need him. Think how horrible it'd be for him if you let him go: he'd have to live with the knowledge that I'd died in his place. That would be a terrible burden. It would be even worse than killing him."

"Maybe," Murlough grunted. "But I'm a simple man. I like simple pleasures. It's a nice idea, but I'd rather slice him up slowly and painfully, if it's all the same to you. Fewer complications."

"Please," I sobbed. "Let him go. I'll do anything you want. I ... I ... I'll give you Mr Crepsley!"

Murlough laughed. "No go. You had the chance to do that earlier. You blew it. Besides, you couldn't lead me to him now. He's bound to have changed hotels again. Might even have fled the city."

"There must be something I can give you!" I yelled desperately. "There must be some way I can..." I stopped.

I could practically hear Murlough's ears stiffening.

"What is it?" he asked curiously after several seconds of silence. "What were you going to say?"

"Wait a minute!" I snapped. "I have to think something through." I could feel Evra's eyes on me, half-hopeful, half-resigned to the fate he felt neither of us could escape.

"Hurry up," Murlough prompted me, coming round in front of me. His purple face didn't show up well in the dim light of the cavern, so his eyes and lips appeared to be three, free-floating globs of red, while his discoloured hair looked like a strange sort of bat. "I haven't got all night," he said. "Speak while you're able."

"I was just thinking," I said quickly. "You're going to have to leave town after this, aren't you?"

"*Leave?*" Murlough bellowed. "Leave my beautiful tunnels? Never! I love it here. You know what being down here makes me feel like? As if I'm inside the body of the city. These tunnels are like veins. This cavern is the heart, where the blood of the city flows in and out." He smiled, and for once it wasn't an evil leer. "Can you imagine?" he said softly. "Living in a body, roaming the veins – the tunnels of blood – freely, as you please."

"Nevertheless," I said bluntly, "you *will* have to leave."

"What's this talk of leaving?" he snapped, jabbing me with the knife. "You're beginning to annoy me."

"I'm just being practical," I said. "You can't stay here. Mr Crepsley knows where you are. He'll return."

"That coward? I doubt it. He'll be too—"

"He'll return with *help*," I interrupted. "With other vampires."

Murlough laughed. "The Vampire Generals, do you mean?"

"Yes," I said.

"Nonsense! They can't come after me. There's an agreement between them and us. They don't interfere. Crepsley isn't a General, is he?"

"No," I said. "He's not."

"There you are!" Murlough yelled triumphantly. "He couldn't have come after me if he was. Rules and laws and ways of living. They mean as much to the vampires as they do to the vampaneze."

"All the same, the Generals *will* come," I insisted quietly. "They couldn't before, but now they can. Maybe tonight. Tomorrow for sure. Perhaps this is what Mr Crepsley intended all along."

"What are you blabbering about?" Murlough looked uneasy.

"You said something interesting a while ago," I said. "You were surprised Mr Crepsley came down here with me. I didn't think anything of it at the time, but now that I've considered it, I agree: it *was* odd of him. I thought it was because he wanted to help me find Evra, but now..."

"*What?*" Murlough screeched when I didn't go on. "Say what you're thinking. Out with it, or..." He raised the knives threateningly.

"The pact between the vampires and vampaneze," I said quickly. "It says one side can't interfere with the other, right?"

"Right," Murlough agreed.

"*Unless* it's to defend or avenge themselves."

Murlough nodded. "This is so."

I smiled weakly. "Don't you see? *I'm* a half-vampire. If you kill *me*, the Generals will have an excuse to come after you. Mr Crepsley must have planned this all along." I took a deep breath and looked Murlough straight in the eye. "He *let* you find me. He *wanted* you to grab me. He *meant* for you to kill me."

Murlough's eyes widened. "No," he wheezed. "He wouldn't."

"He's a vampire," I said. "Of course he would. This is his city. I'm just his apprentice. Which would *you* choose to sacrifice?"

"But ... but..." The vampaneze scratched his face nervously. "I didn't make the first move!" he shouted. "*You* came after *me*."

I shook my head. "*Mr Crepsley* came after you. I'm innocent. I pose no threat. If you kill me, you'll be held accountable. The Generals will descend on you, and no vampaneze will step in to defend you."

Murlough let my words sink in, in silence, then he started

jumping up and down on the spot, cursing furiously. I let him rage for a while, then I said, "It's not too late. Let me go. Let Evra go, too. Flee the city. They can't touch you then."

"But I love these tunnels," Murlough groaned.

"Do you love them enough to die for them?" I asked.

His eyes narrowed. "You're very smart, aren't you?" he snarled.

"Not really," I said. "I wouldn't have come down here if I was. But I *am* able to see the truth when it's staring me in the face. Kill me, Murlough, and you sign your own death warrant."

His shoulders sagged and I knew I was safe. Now there was only Evra to worry about...

"Snakey," Murlough said menacingly. "*He* isn't a vampire. There's nothing to stop me killing *him*, hmmm?"

"No!" I shouted. "If you harm Evra, I'll go to the Generals myself and tell them—"

"Tell them *what?*" Murlough interrupted. "Do you think they'd care? Do you think they'd risk war for the sake of a reptile?" He laughed. "Young Murlough's in a killing mood. I mightn't be able to have the little half-vampire, but I won't be cheated out of Snakey too. Watch, Darren Shan. Watch as I carve the snake-boy a new mouth – *in his belly!*"

He grabbed the ropes around Evra and tugged him forward with his left hand. With his right, he positioned one of the knives and prepared to make the first cut.

"Wait!" I screamed. "Don't do it! Don't do it!"

"Why shouldn't I?" Murlough sneered.

"I'll swap places!" I yelled. "Me for Evra."

"No good," Murlough said. "You're a half-vampire. No deal."

"I'll give you somebody else! Somebody even better!"

"Who?" Murlough laughed. "Who could you give me, Darren Shan?"

"I'll give you..." I gulped deeply, shut my eyes, and whispered the terrible words.

"What was that?" Murlough asked, pausing suspiciously. "Speak up. I didn't hear you."

"I said..." I licked my lips and forced the words out again, louder this time. "I said I'll give you my girlfriend. If you spare Evra, I'll give you ... *Debbie.*"

CHAPTER TWENTY-THREE

A STUNNED silence greeted my obscene offer. Evra was the first to break it.

"No!" he screamed. "Don't do it! You can't!"

"Debbie for Evra," I said, ignoring Evra's pleas. "How about it?"

"Debbie?" Murlough scratched his cheeks slowly. It took him a few seconds to work out who I was referring to. Then he remembered and smiled. "Ah! *Debbie!* Darren Shan's tasty girlfriend." His eyes twinkled as he thought about her.

"She'd be more use to you than Evra," I said. "You could drink from her. You said you'd like to. You said she'd have nice blood."

"Yes," Murlough agreed. "Salty. Juicy." He took a step back from Evra. "But why choose?" he mused aloud. "Why not have both? Kill the snake-boy now, drink from Debbie later. She won't be hard to find. I can watch the Square tomorrow, find out where she lives, and as soon as night comes..." He grinned.

"You don't have time," I said. "You must leave the city tonight. You can't wait."

"Still yapping on about leaving?" Murlough snorted. "If I

let you go — as you've convinced me I should — I won't have to leave."

"Yes you will," I contradicted him. "It'll take a while for the vampires to discover I'm alive. The Generals will come straight down these tunnels when they arrive. They'll find out about me eventually, but if they kill you beforehand..."

"They wouldn't dare!" Murlough shrieked. "It would mean war!"

"But they wouldn't know that. They'd think they were in the right. They'd pay dearly for their mistake, but that would be no consolation as far as you're concerned. You must leave, as soon as possible. You can return in a couple of weeks, but if you stick around now, it'll be a recipe for disaster."

"Young Murlough doesn't want to leave," the vampaneze pouted. "I like it here. I don't want to go. But you're right," he sighed. "For a few nights, at least, I must get out. Find a dark abandoned cellar. Hole up. Lay low."

"That's why Debbie would be better than Evra," I pressed on. "You must be hungry. You'll want to feed before leaving, yes?"

"Oh yes," Murlough agreed, rubbing his bloated belly.

"But feeding without planning is dangerous. Vampires are used to it, but vampaneze aren't, are they?"

"No," Murlough said. "We're smarter than vampires. We think ahead. Plan it out. Mark our meals in advance."

"But you can't do that now," I reminded him. "You need a quick snack to keep you ticking over while you're away. *I* can provide that. Agree to my terms and I'll take you to Debbie. I can get you in and out without anybody knowing."

"Darren! Stop!" Evra roared. "I don't want this! You can't—"

Murlough punched Evra hard in the belly, shutting him up.

"How can I trust you?" the vampaneze hissed. "How do I know you won't trick me?"

"How could I?" I retorted. "Keep my hands bound behind my back. Keep a knife close to my throat. Leave Evra where he is – I'll come back for him later, once you've fed and left. If I try anything, I'll be dooming us both. I'm not stupid. I know what's at stake."

Murlough hummed tunelessly as he thought it over.

"You mustn't do this," Evra moaned.

"It's the only way," I said softly.

"I don't want to trade Debbie's life for mine," he said. "I'd rather die myself."

"See if you think that way tomorrow," I grunted.

"How can you do it?" he asked. "How can you give her up as if she was just a ... a..."

"A *human*," I said shortly.

"I was going to say *animal*."

I smiled thinly. "To a vampire it's the same thing. You're my best friend, Evra. Debbie's just a human I was soft on."

Evra shook his head. "I don't recognize you any longer," he said sadly, and turned away from me.

"All right," Murlough reached a decision. He drew back his knives, then thrust them forward. I winced, but he only cut the rope around my ankles. I fell heavily to the floor. "We'll do it your way," the vampaneze declared. "But if you put one foot out of place..."

"I won't," I said, getting up. "Now – how about your word?"

"What?"

"You haven't given it to me yet. I'm not leaving without it."

The vampaneze grinned. "Clever boy," he gurgled. "All right. I give you my word – the girl for Snakey. Debbie for Evra.

Is that good enough for you?"

I shook my head. "Say you'll let me go when you're finished with Debbie. Say you won't stop me coming back to free Evra. Say you'll do nothing to harm either of us afterwards."

Murlough laughed. "Oh, you're clever all right. Almost as clever as young Murlough. Very well. I'll let you go. I'll do nothing to stop you coming back, or hurt you once you're free." He raised a finger. "But if you ever return to this city, or if our paths cross in the future, it'll be death. This is a temporary reprieve, not a long-term guarantee. Agreed?"

"Agreed."

"Very well. Shall we make a start?"

"Aren't you going to undo a few of these ropes?" I asked. "I can barely walk like this."

"*Barely* is good enough," Murlough laughed. "I'm not going to take any chances with you. I've got a feeling you wouldn't miss a trick." He shoved me hard in the back. I stumbled, then found my feet and began to walk.

I glanced over my shoulder at Evra. "I won't be long," I said. "I'll be back before dawn and we'll both go home to the Cirque Du Freak, OK?"

He didn't answer. He refused to even look at me.

Sighing, I turned around and started out of the lair, Murlough guiding me through the tunnels, singing gruesome little songs as he skipped along after me, telling me what he was going to do once he got his foul hands on Debbie.

CHAPTER TWENTY-FOUR

WE PASSED quickly through the tunnels. Murlough marked the walls as he went, scratching them with his nails. He didn't want to, but I told him the deal was off if he didn't. This way, I would only have to follow the marks when I returned. Much simpler than trying to remember every twist and turn.

Murlough had to carry me whenever crawling or climbing was required. I hated being so close to him – his breath stank of human blood – but had to put up with it. He wasn't going to loosen the ropes around my arms, no matter what the circumstances.

We left the tunnels by a drain close to the Square. Murlough hauled me up, only to yank me down sharply when a car passed nearby.

"Have to be careful," he hissed. "Police have been over the city like flies since they found the bodies. Most annoying. In future I'll bury bones more carefully."

He brushed some dirt off his white suit when he stood, but made no effort to clean mine. He tutted, annoyed. "Have to get new clothes when I come back," he said. "Very awkward. Can never visit the same tailor twice, hmmm?"

"Why not?" I asked.

He cocked an eyebrow at me. "Is this a face you would forget in a hurry?" he asked, pointing to his purplish skin and red features. "Nobody would. That's why I have to kill any tailor once he's measured and fitted me. I'd steal clothes from shops if I could, but I am of uncommon build." He patted his gross belly and giggled.

"Come," he said. "Lead on. Take the back route. Less chance of being seen."

The streets were virtually deserted – it was late on Christmas Eve, and the melting snow meant walking was a slippy business – and we met no one. We trudged through the slush, Murlough shoving me to the floor whenever a car drove by. I was getting sick of it – unable to break my fall with my hands, my face was taking the worst of the punishment – but he only laughed when I complained.

"Toughen you up, hmmm?" he said. "Build muscles."

Eventually we reached Debbie's. Murlough paused at the darkened back door and glanced around nervously. The surrounding houses were in darkness, but still he hesitated. For a moment I thought he was going to back out of our deal.

"Scared?" I asked softly.

"Young Murlough's scared of nothing!" he snapped immediately.

"Then what are you waiting for?"

"You seem very keen to lead me to your girlfriend," he said suspiciously.

I shrugged as best I could beneath the ropes. "The longer I have to wait, the worse I'm going to feel," I said. "I know what has to be done. I don't like it, and I'll feel awful afterwards, but all I want right now is to have it over and done with, so I can fetch Evra and find someplace warm to lie down and relax. My feet are like blocks of ice."

"Poor little half-vampire," Murlough giggled, then used one of his sharp vampaneze nails to cut a circle in the glass of the back door window. Reaching in, he opened the door and shoved me through.

He listened quietly to the noises of the house.

"How many people live here?" he asked.

"Three," I said. "Debbie and her parents."

"No brothers or sisters?" I shook my head. "No lodgers?"

"Just the three of them," I repeated.

"I might nibble one of the parents when I'm finished with the girl," he muttered.

"That wasn't part of the deal!" I hissed.

"So what? I never said I'd spare them. I doubt if I'll be hungry after, but maybe I'll come back another night, pick them off one by one. They'll think it's a family curse." He giggled.

"You're disgusting," I growled.

"You're only saying that because you like me," he chuckled. "Go on," he said, snapping back to serious business. "Up the stairs. The parents' bedroom first. I want to make sure they're asleep."

"Of course they're asleep," I said. "It's the middle of the night. You'd hear them if they were awake."

"I don't want them walking in on me," he said.

"Look," I sighed, "if you want to check on Jesse and Donna, fine, I'll take you to them. But you're wasting time. Wouldn't it be better if we got in and out as quickly as possible?"

The vampaneze thought it over. "Very well," he said. "But if they pop up unexpected, young Murlough will kill them, yes he will, and it'll be *your* fault."

"Fair enough," I said, and started up the stairs.

It was a long, tense walk. Being bound by ropes, I wasn't able to move as quietly as usual. Every time a step creaked, I winced and paused. Murlough was tense too: his hands were twitching and he drew in a sharp breath whenever I made a noise and stopped.

When I got to Debbie's door, I leant my head against it and sighed morosely. "This is it," I said.

"Out of the way," Murlough snapped, and shoved me to one side. He stood there, sniffing, then smiled. "Yes," he gurgled. "I can smell her blood. You can smell it too, I bet, hmmm?"

"Yes," I said.

He turned the handle and eased the door open. It was dark inside, but our eyes were used to the greater darkness of the tunnels, so they adjusted quickly.

Murlough glanced around the room, noting the wardrobes and chests of drawers, the few posters and pieces of furniture, the bare Christmas tree near the window.

Debbie's outline could just be seen beneath the covers of her bed, moving about slightly, as a person does when they're having a bad dream. The smell of her blood was thick in the air.

Murlough started forward, then remembered me. He tied me to the door handle, tugged at it hard to make sure the knot was secure, then jammed his face up to mine and sneered.

"Have you ever seen death before, Darren Shan?" he asked.

"Yes," I said.

"It's wonderful, isn't it?"

"No," I said bluntly. "It's horrible."

The vampaneze sighed. "You cannot see the beauty. Never mind. You are young. You will learn as you grow." He pinched my chin between a couple of purple fingers and a thumb. "I want you to watch," he said. "Watch as I rip her throat open. Watch as I suck her blood out. Watch as I steal her soul and make it mine."

I tried turning my eyes away but he pinched harder and forced them back. "If you don't watch," he said, "I go straight to the parents' room after this and kill the two of them too. Understand?"

"You're a monster," I gasped.

"*Understand?*" he repeated menacingly.

"Yes," I said, jerking my chin free. "I'll watch."

"Good boy," he chuckled. "Clever boy. You never know – you might like it. This could be the making of you. Perhaps you'll come with me when I leave. How about it, Darren Shan? Fancy abandoning that boring old vampire and becoming young Murlough's assistant, hmmm?"

"Just get on with it," I said, not bothering to hide my disgust.

Murlough crossed the room slowly, making no sound. He drew his two knives as he walked and twirled them about like a pair of batons. He began whistling, but softly, too softly for any but the most advanced ears to hear.

The slight movements continued beneath the covers.

I watched, stomach churning, as he closed in on his prey. Even if I hadn't been under orders to watch, I couldn't have torn my eyes away. It was a dreadful sight but fascinating. Like watching a spider zoom in on a fly. Only *this* spider carried knives, ate humans and had an entire city for a web.

He approached the bed from the side nearest the door, stopping half a metre away. Then he produced something from one of his pockets. Straining my eyes, I realized it was a bag. Opening it, he took out some kind of salt-like substance and sprinkled it on the floor. I wanted to ask what it was for, but didn't dare speak. I guessed it was some ritual that vampaneze performed when they killed somebody at home. Mr Crepsley had told me they were big on rituals.

Murlough walked around the bed, sprinkling the "salt", muttering words I could make no sense of. When he was finished, he strolled back to the foot of the bed, glanced over to make sure I was watching, and then, in one swift move — almost too quick for me to follow — leapt on the bed, landed with a foot on either side of the sleeping form, jerked back the covers and lashed out with both knives, killer cuts which would slash open Debbie's throat and end her life in an instant.

CHAPTER TWENTY-FIVE

MURLOUGH'S KNIVES swished through air, through the space where Debbie's neck should have been, and through the soft fabric of the pillows and the mattress.

But not through Debbie.

Because Debbie wasn't there.

Murlough stared down at the creature tied to the bed, its hooves and snout bound as tightly as I was.

"It's ... a..." His jaws quivered. He couldn't bring himself to say the word.

"It's a *goat*," I finished for him, smiling grimly.

Murlough turned slowly, his face a mask of confusion. "But ... but ... but..."

While he was spluttering, trying to figure out what was happening, the door of one of the wardrobes opened and Mr Crepsley stepped out.

The vampire looked even more sinister than the vampaneze, with his blood-red clothes and cloak, his orange crop of hair and ugly scar.

Murlough froze when he saw Mr Crepsley. His red eyes bulged out of his head and his purple skin lightened a couple of shades as blood rushed from his face.

From the movies I'd seen, I was expecting a long, exciting fight. I thought the two would trade insults first, then Mr Crepsley would draw a knife or a sword and they'd lunge and parry at one another, battling their way around the room, nicking each other in the early stages, gradually working up to the more serious wounds.

But it wasn't like that. This was a fight between super-fast predators of the night who were only interested in killing, not impressing action-hungry audiences. There were just four moves in the conflict, and it was over in the space of two blurred and furious seconds.

Mr Crepsley made the first move. His right hand zipped out and sent a short knife flying through the air. It struck Murlough in the upper left of his chest, a few centimetres higher than its target — his heart. The vampaneze recoiled and drew in air to scream.

While Murlough's mouth was opening, Mr Crepsley sprang forward. One huge leap was all it took, then he was at the side of the bed, in position to go hand-to-hand with the vampaneze.

That was the second move of the fight.

The third move was Murlough's — his only one. In a panic, he lashed out at Mr Crepsley with his left-handed knife. The blade glittered through the air at a frightening speed and would have made an end of the vampire had it been on target. But it wasn't. It soared a good six centimetres above the vampire's head.

As Murlough's left arm followed through on the swing, it left a gap which Mr Crepsley exploited. Using only his bare right hand, he delivered the killer blow. Keeping the hand flat, rough nails jutting out like five sharp blades, he drove it into Murlough's belly.

And when I say into, I *mean* into!

Murlough gasped and went deathly still. The knife dropped from his hand and he gazed down. Mr Crepsley's hand had disappeared into the flesh of the vampaneze's belly, all the way up to his forearm.

He left the hand there a moment, then yanked back sharply, bringing guts and a torrent of dark blood with it.

Murlough groaned and collapsed to his knees, almost squashing the goat in the process, then toppled to the floor, where he rolled over on to his back and tried closing the hole in his belly with spit he'd quickly licked on to the palms of his hands.

But the hole was too wide. The vampaneze's healing spit was useless. There was nothing he could do to seal the flesh or stop his precious blood from pumping out. He was finished.

Mr Crepsley stepped back from the dying vampaneze, picked up one of the bedsheets and wiped his hand on it. His face was expressionless. He appeared neither pleased nor saddened by what he had done.

After a couple of seconds, Murlough realized his situation was hopeless. Flopping over on to his belly, his eyes settled on me, and he began crawling towards me, gritting his teeth against the pain.

"Mr Crepsley?" I said shakily.

Mr Crepsley studied the crawling vampaneze, then shook his head. "Do not worry. He can do you no harm." But, taking no chances, he walked over, freed me, and stood by my side, ready to strike again if needed.

It was a long, agonized crawl for the vampaneze. I almost felt sorry for him, but had only to think of Evra strung up, and what he'd planned to do to Debbie, to remind myself that he deserved everything he'd got.

He paused more than once, and I thought he was going to

die midway, but he was determined to have his final say, and fought on, even though he must have known he was hastening the moment of his death.

He collapsed on his face at my feet and breathed heavily into the carpet. Blood was gushing out of his mouth and I knew the end was almost upon him. He raised a trembling finger and crooked it, beckoning me to lean down.

I glanced questioningly at Mr Crepsley.

The vampire shrugged. "He is harmless now. It is up to you."

I decided to see what the dying vampaneze had to say. I bent down and leant close to his mouth. He had only seconds left.

His red eyes rolled directionlessly in their sockets. Then, with an immense effort, they fixed on me and his lips split into one last leer. He raised his head as high as he could and whispered something that I couldn't hear.

"I didn't catch that," I told him. "You'll have to speak up." I jammed my ear closer to his mouth.

Murlough licked his lips, clearing some blood and making space for air. Then, with his final breath, he got out the words that seemed so important to him.

"Cluh-cluh-clever buh-buh-buh-boy, hmmm?" he gurgled, then smiled blankly and fell forward.

He was dead.

CHAPTER TWENTY-SIX

WE BUNDLED Murlough's body into a large black plastic bag. We'd drop him off later in the tunnels of blood he'd loved so much. As fitting a burial place as any for him.

We stuck the goat in a bag too, but made a couple of air holes in it. We'd expected Murlough to kill the goat, which I'd stolen earlier from the children's section of the city zoo. Mr Crepsley wanted to take it back to the Cirque Du Freak — it would provide a nice snack for Evra's snake or the Little People — but I persuaded him to set it free.

Next we cleaned up the mess. Murlough had shed a lot of blood, all of which had to be mopped up. We didn't want the Hemlocks to find it and start asking questions. We worked quickly but it took a couple of hours.

With the cleaning finished, we climbed up to the attic and brought down the sleeping bodies of Jesse, Donna and Debbie, and laid them in their respective beds.

The entire night had been planned. The wine I brought for dinner? I drugged it when I was in the kitchen. I added one of Mr Crepsley's potions to the wine, a tasteless little concoction that knocked everybody out within ten minutes.

They'd be asleep for several more hours yet, and wake with sore heads, but otherwise no ill-effects.

I smiled as I wondered what they'd think when they woke in bed, fully dressed, with no memories of the previous night. It would be a mystery, one they'd never solve.

It hadn't been a perfect plan. Lots of things could have gone wrong. For starters, there was no guarantee that Murlough would find me when I had my "fight" with Mr Crepsley and stormed off on my own, and no guarantee that he wouldn't kill me straightaway if he did.

He could have gagged me when he caught me, in which case I would have been unable to convince him that he ought to let me live. Or he might have disregarded my warning about the Vampire Generals — what I said was true, but the trouble was, Murlough was mad. There was no telling how a mad vampaneze would act. He might have laughed at the threat of the Generals and sliced me up anyway.

Convincing him to swap Evra for Debbie was always going to be the trickiest bit. For it to work, I'd had to deliver a perfect performance. If I'd come straight out and made the offer, Murlough might have been suspicious and not walked into the trap. If he'd been in full control of his senses, I don't think he *would* have fallen for it, regardless of my performance, so on that score his madness worked in our favour.

And, of course, there was the killing of him to account for. Murlough *could* have beaten Mr Crepsley. If he had, all six of us would have died: Mr Crepsley, me and Evra, Debbie, Donna and Jesse.

It had been a dangerous gamble — and unfair to the Hemlocks, who knew nothing of their role in the deadly game — but sometimes you've got to take chances. Was it wise to risk five lives for the sake of one? Probably not. But it was *human*. If I'd learned nothing else from my encounter with the mad vampaneze it was that even the undead could be human. We *had* to be — without a touch of humanity, we'd be like Murlough, nothing more than bloodthirsty monsters of the night.

I tucked Debbie in under the fresh covers. There was a tiny scar near her left ankle, where Mr Crepsley had drawn blood earlier. He'd needed the blood to smear on the goat, in order to mislead Murlough's sense of smell.

I looked up at the vampire. "You did well tonight," I said quietly. "Thanks."

He smiled. "I did what had to be done. It was *your* plan. I should be the one offering the thanks, were it not for the fact that you got in the way when I first had him in my sights. In my eyes, that makes us even, so neither need thank the other."

"What will happen when the vampaneze find out we killed him?" I asked. "Will they come after us?"

Mr Crepsley sighed. "With luck, they will not find the body. If they do, they will hopefully be unable to trace him to us."

"But if they do?" I pressed him for an answer.

"Then they will hunt us to the ends of the Earth," he said. "And they will kill us. We would not stand a chance. They would come in their dozens and the Generals would not assist us."

"Oh," I said. "I wish I hadn't asked."

"Would you rather I'd lied?"

I shook my head. "No. No more lies." I smiled. "But I think it'll be for the best if we don't tell Evra. What he doesn't know can't worry him. Besides, he's mad enough at me as it is. He thought I was really going to trade Debbie's life for his. He's furious."

"He will calm down when the facts are explained," Mr

Crepsley said confidently. "Now – shall we go and collect him?"

I hesitated and glanced down at Debbie. "Can I have a couple of minutes to myself?" I asked.

"Of course," Mr Crepsley said. "But do not delay: dawn approaches and I do not wish to spend tomorrow trapped in those godforsaken tunnels. I will be downstairs." He departed.

I checked my watch. Nearly four in the morning. That meant this was the twenty-fifth of December. Christmas Day.

I worked quickly. I placed the bare Christmas tree to one side of Debbie's bed, opened the box of decorations and covered the tree with glittering balls, tiny figures, streams of tinsel and twinkling lights. When I had finished, I turned Debbie so that she was facing towards the tree. It would be the first thing she'd see when she opened her eyes in the morning.

I felt bad about leaving without saying goodbye. This way, I hoped to make it up to her. When she woke and saw the tree, she'd know I hadn't slipped away thoughtlessly. She'd know I'd been thinking of her, and hopefully wouldn't hold my sudden disappearance against me.

I stood over her a few seconds, studying her face. This would almost certainly be the last time I'd ever see her. She looked so sweet, lying there asleep. I was tempted to find a camera and take a photo, but I didn't need to – this was one picture I'd always be able to remember in perfect detail. It would join those of my parents, my sister, Sam – cherished faces which would never fade in the mental galleries of my memory.

Leaning forward, I kissed her forehead and brushed a stray lock of hair out of her eyes. "Merry Christmas, Debbie," I said softly, then turned and left, and went to rescue Evra.